Praise for W
Kathlee

MW00830226

"...it is the vibrant and perceptive panorama on the Anasazi culture that makes this novel stand out amidst the crowd of archaeological who-done-its."

— *The Midwest Book Review* on *Bone Walker*

"Both *The Visitant* and *The Summoning God* are so steeped in southwestern archaeology and lore of the Anasazi culture that one can smell the dust and see the brightly painted katsinas on the side of the cliff dwellings."

— *The Amarillo Sunday News*

"The Gears have done it again...This crafty weaving of past and present is a wonderful journey of learning and adventure."

— *Romantic Times* on *The Visitant*

"An exciting, skillfully crafted, and fast-paced story that also serves as an engrossing look at ancient culture."

— *Publishers Weekly* on *People of the Silence*

Hunting Shadows

Also by W. Michael Gear and Kathleen O'Neal Gear

Hunting Shadows
The Anasazi Mysteries Part Six

W. Michael Gear

Kathleen O'Neal Gear

WOLFPACK
PUBLISHING
— EST 2013 —

Hunting Shadows
Paperback Edition
Copyright © 2023 (As Revised) W. Michael Gear and
Kathleen O'Neal Gear

Wolfpack Publishing
9850 S. Maryland Parkway, Suite A-5 #323
Las Vegas, Nevada 89183

wolfpackpublishing.com

Cover Image *A Hopi Man* provided by the Amon Carter Museum of
American Art, in Fort Worth, Texas.
Chapter Illustration by Ellisa Mitchel.

Paperback ISBN 978-1-63977-392-3
eBook ISBN 978-1-63977-393-0

Hunting Shadows

to Longtail Village

Farmer Arroyo

Farmer Group

Aztec North

Great North Road

North House

West Group

Kiva of Worlds

Sunrise House

Dusk House

Estes Arroyo

Aztec Ruins

Animas River

NORTH

Pottery House

Spindle
Whorl

War Club
Village

The Great
Kiva

Talking
Stitch
Tseh

Casa
Rinconada

Scorpion
Village

Owl House
Bc 60

NORTH

1

SUN CYCLE OF THE GREAT HORNED OWL
THE FALLING RIVER MOON
STRAIGHT PATH CANYON

Browser, War Chief of the Katsina's People, split his small force of warriors into four parties. Night was falling on the ruins of Kettle Town where he, his deputy Catkin, and an odd collection of Katsina's and Mogollon warriors hid. Theirs was a desperate mission: to hunt, find, and destroy the legendary First People's witch, Two Hearts, and his insidiously twisted daughter, Shadow Woman. They were hidden here. Somewhere among the abandoned great and small houses that were strewn the length of the sandstone rimmed canyon.

But who hunted whom?

That very day, a party of Flute Player warriors, under the command of Matron Blue Corn, had searched Kettle Town in an attempt to find and kill Browser's little band. Fortunately, the decrepit ruin was filled with hiding places.

The other threat were the White Moccasins, the secretive cult of assassins who waged war on the Made People in retribution for the long-ago murder of the First People. White Moccasins, too, hid somewhere in the canyon, or just beyond in the wreckage of High Sun House.

Hunters hunting hunters.

That knowledge had Browser's stomach twisted and queasy as he gave the signal and watched his parties of warriors slip away into the night. Each took a different path south across Straight Path Wash. Their mission was to scout Corner Canyon Town where the collection of multiroom buildings, kivas, and pithouses clustered under the southern sandstone wall. If everything went according to plan, they would all converge by moonrise. In the absolute worst case, should anyone be discovered and unable to flee, others could cover their retreat.

If Two Hearts were hiding anywhere in the canyon, it should be in Corner Canyon Town.

Browser took one last look around the huge Kettle Town plaza. The faded images of the katsinas that had once painted the front of the town had cracked and flaked off. He could discern patches of huge eyes, black beaks, and fanged muzzles, but little else.

He raised his hand, motioning Catkin and his few Bow warriors forward in a trot.

"This must have been a remarkable place one hundred sun cycles ago," Clay Frog, one of the Mogollon Bow warriors, remarked as she followed Browser's gaze. She wore a gray knee-length war shirt.

"Yes," he replied softly. "It must have been."

"Do you think we'll ever build anything like it again?" the woman asked wistfully.

Browser shook his head uncertainly and, from behind

him, heard Catkin respond, "How can we? When we killed the First People, we killed their knowledge. Do you know a mason today who can construct a five-story building? I don't."

Sadness added to Browser's unease. The glory was draining out of his people, like water down one of the washes. To stand here, before Kettle Town, and imagine it as it had been, was to feel a hole open in his heart. His people had once raised stunning towns like this, now they spent their lives running in fear, desperately searching for their next meal, and thinking up ways to kill each other.

Were the old gods so bad, Browser? Is Two Hearts right when he says our troubles were brought by the katsinas?

The question possessed him as he and Catkin trotted away from Kettle Town and onto the broad thoroughfare that had long ago linked Kettle Town and Talon Town, just to the west, to the smaller towns across Straight Path Wash. Now rain-washed and windswept, the road was yet another reminder of his ancestors' greatness.

He could feel Catkin's eyes boring into his back. She had been looking at him strangely, and he knew she must have seen Obsidian enter his chamber.

Obsidian. Another complication in his life. She'd insisted on coming on the hunt. Beautiful, sensual, and magnetic, she hid the terrible secret that she was one of Two Hearts' daughters. Sister to Shadow Woman, and born of First People's blood. But worse, the old witch wanted her. Blood of his blood, he could cut Obsidian's heart from her body, and through witchery, use it to prolong his own life.

He would tell Catkin about Obsidian's visit. But not now.

Earlier that day, when Obsidian had slipped into his quarters, she'd begged him to take her. When he'd looked into Obsidian's eyes, he'd seen desperation. He had never had a beautiful woman throw herself on his mercy that way—and he was certain she had an ulterior motive. Was she working with Two Hearts? Trying to get him to abandon the Katsinas' People? Or did she truly wish to marry him? As a descendent of the First People himself, should he?

Before you decide anything, you must kill Two Hearts.

He led the way down into the wash. Inky darkness made the descent tricky, and he had to feel for each foothold.

At the bottom, he reached out and took Catkin's hand, guiding her. She tightened her grip in his, and for the moment he maintained the contact, led her across the gravel bottom of the wash.

He had to release her in order to climb up the other side, and there, stepping up onto the canyon floor again, she resumed her position behind him.

He knew this road; he'd taken it many times when the Katsinas' People had lived in Straight Path Canyon. It led to the great kiva in Corner Canyon. Had anyone used the kiva since the Katsinas' People had held their last cere-monies there? Or had the huge subterranean ceremonial center been left to the pack rats, mice, and bats?

Fearing ambush, Browser left the rutted road and followed a meandering route that wound through tawny patches of grass. When the Katsina's People had lived in Hillside village, an extended family had eked out an exis-tence in Pottery House. Browser remembered one of the little girls, a whip-thin urchin with a curious brown discol-oration on her face.

Catkin made a faint click with her tongue, and Browser immediately sank to his haunches, listening to the darkness, sniffing the air. True to their training, the Bow warriors dropped and did the same. The faint hint of smoke rode the cold breeze that drifted down the canyon. Perhaps someone still lived in Pottery House?

Browser reached back, tapped Catkin's knee twice to indicate an advance, and rose. He could feel Catkin walking close behind him; the Bow Society warriors followed.

Browser circled downwind of Pottery House, approaching slowly. It wouldn't do for them to be discovered by either turkeys or dogs. But only the musty scent of decay came to his nostrils. Humans left traces of boiling food, of cloth and baking corn, and of course their excrement, on the wind.

He eased up to the western side of the house and placing an ear to the stone, heard nothing. He moved slowly along the dressed-stone wall. Midway down the room block, a weathered pole ladder sagged against the wall. Browser bent down and touched the soil at the base of the ladder. Bristly weeds met his fingers, not packed earth from the passage of moccasins or sandals.

Catkin tapped his shoulder and pointed up the ladder. He nodded, and she started up.

He and the Fire Dogs waited in silence. He might have passed fifty breaths before Catkin's body darkened the top of the ladder, and she carefully descended.

"Gone," she whispered. "They're long gone. Each of the roof entrances is open. It's blacker than the First World inside. Nothing to smell but mold."

"Then let's move on. Spindle Whorl House is a bow shot to the south."

At Spindle Whorl, the results were the same. The seven irregular rooms, and the solitary kiva on the east side of the structure, had been abandoned for at least a sun cycle. The place lay in disrepair.

Browser led his team past the villages that clustered around the great kiva. Talking Stitch Town stood silent and ghostly in the slanted glow of the rising moon. No evidence of violence could be seen, but two corpses sat outside the northern kiva. They had been there so long that only white bones, many scattered about, were left.

"So many left unburied," Browser whispered as he looked down on the nameless dead.

"It is the times," Catkin answered.

"Let it not be so for us," Clay Frog added. "Death does not frighten me. But being left alone, to wander forever in search of one's ancestors, that is frightening."

Browser toed one of the gleaming bones from the path and led the way to War Club village, a bow shot to the east.

They ran in silence until they saw it. Long and hooked at one end, the masonry village was a sprawling collection of roomblocks.

A sun cycle ago, six families had lived in War Club village. True, they hadn't kept the place like it had been in the First People's days, but it had been a community. The people had grown enough in the nearby fields to feed their families and to trade for trinkets.

Browser led the way as he scuttled into the shadows of the northern wall and looked for a ladder. When they couldn't find one, Catkin and Red Dog boosted Browser to the roof. He had made two steps when he came upon a ladder that had been pulled up and stowed on the roof. He glanced back at the new moon; its white light silhouetted him. Taking a chance, he placed each foot with care, pausing by one smoke hole after another and sniffing.

At the third, he caught the dissipated odor of a warming fire, and could hear the faint burr of a sleeping man inside.

Browser crouched and searched the rooftops for the humped shape of a sentry huddled under a blanket. For thirty heartbeats he waited, seeing nothing. Were Two

Hearts here, he would be heavily guarded. Browser checked the other rooms but found no one else.

He lowered himself over the wall and dropped lightly to the ground.

"One room occupied," he whispered after leading them into the shadows. "I could hear someone sleeping, smell his fire. But he was alone."

"A traveler," Catkin guessed. "Someone passing through. We've checked, the weeds have grown up here, too. The lower kivas haven't been used recently."

"I agree. There was no sentry posted." He leaned back against the wall and studied the moonlit canyon rim.

"There's been no sign of movement." Catkin exhaled and her breath rose in the pale light. "Are you sure he's not up there at High Sun? That's where the White Moccasins are."

Browser frowned, aware of the way Clay Frog and Red Dog watched him. Expected him to know where Two Hearts was hiding, as though he were some sort of oracle.

"He might be there," Browser agreed. "But that's for tomorrow night. I want to be sure that we're not missing something here." He pointed at the staircase, a dark slit in the rock where it hid in the shadows. "It wouldn't do to be caught halfway from the top with warriors above you and more below."

"I agree," Red Dog said with his heavily accented voice. "Like Clay Frog, I want to lose my soul at home, where it can be cared for. Not here, where so many enemy ghosts prowl."

"Let's all stay alive." Catkin playfully tapped his shoulder with her war club. "You have my promise that I will guard your back."

"And I will guard yours," Red Dog responded and grinned.

Catkin had always had a way with the other warriors;

they instinctively liked and respected her, whereas he had to earn every warrior's confidence.

"Let's check Scorpion village next." Browser pointed to the blocky buildings four bow shots to the southwest. They gleamed in the moonlight, standing near a pillar of rimrock that had defied the ages.

"Keep low," Catkin reminded. "Move slowly. We don't know how many scouts they have up on the rim."

Browser's leg muscles flexed as he skirted the talus that had tumbled from the rim. The boulders helped to screen them from above.

He knew Scorpion village well. He and the Katsinas' People had lived there before moving across the canyon to repair and reconsecrate the great kiva at Talon Town. When they had lived in Scorpion village, the town consisted of a block of fourteen rooms and five kivas. While the Katsinas' People hadn't built onto the place, they had replastered it and fixed the leaky roofs.

Browser scrambled the last distance into the shadow of the west wall. A small drainage that ran from the rimrock to the southwest cut down close to the town. In his day, it had watered the corn, bean, and squash fields. From the looks of the place, no one had planted the fields since.

Browser took the ladder to the roof, moving cautiously as he crossed the second story. He paused, listening as he reached his old room. Here, he had lived with Ash Girl and his son, Grass Moon. A spear of pain made him catch his breath. He closed his eyes, remembering his sick son. How was he to know that bubbling laughter would soon give way to frothy blood, that the flesh would melt from those strong bones and leave nothing but a weak shell?

Praise the gods that we cannot see too far into the future.

How would he have borne the knowledge that his

little boy would soon be dead? That his wife would betray him for her witch father, and that he would kill her to save Catkin's life?

An owl hooted, high above and to the west. Browser looked up at the rimrock. He could see the bird against the dark sky, its feathers outlined by the ghostly thin light of the moon. On silent wings it flew to the top of the small ridgetop house, screeched, then soared away like a black arrow, heading toward the Corner Canyon kiva.

Browser felt as if an invisible hand had just reached through his chest and stroked his heart.

Yes. There. That's where Springbank had lived. Up on the gray shale ridge in a five-room building, attached to a single kiva. He had insisted on living separately, saying he needed time alone to communicate with the katsinas.

Browser stepped around and stared up at the square-roofed building. Owl House, Springbank had called it, in what most people thought was jest.

Was that Two Hearts's evil lair? Is that where he'd lain with Ash Girl, heedless of the fact that she was his daughter as well as Browser's wife? Is that where he'd broken her so thoroughly that a monster soul had slipped inside her?

"Browser?"

He jumped at the hand that settled on his shoulder and instinctively raised his war club, ready to strike.

"Sorry," Catkin whispered. "You were taking too long. We've checked the rest of the town. No one is here tonight, but people camp here with some regularity."

He took a breath, stilling his frantic heart. "Yes," he answered. "I was just..."

"Lost in the past," she answered, knowing him too well.

He pointed with his war club. "Did you hear the owl screech? It went to perch up there."

"I heard no owl."

He felt cold, as though a mantle of snow had settled on his shoulders. The chase was coming to its conclusion. His gaze lifted to the rimrock. "Two Hearts is here, somewhere, Catkin. I know he is."

ROBERTSON AND STEWART ARCHAEOLOGICAL
CONSULTANTS OFFICE
ALBUQUERQUE, NEW MEXICO

William "Dusty" Stewart used the jack to lower the old Holiday Rambler camp trailer onto the hitch of Dale's big red Dodge 2500 four-wheel drive. He'd always think of it that way: Dale's Dodge, the truck he'd finally splurged to buy after years and nearly three hundred thousand miles in the old IH Scout. Would this truck last so long, or go so far? Dale would never have the chance to find out. Dusty blinked and his dry eyes burned, as though longing for tears he could not allow himself to shed.

Instead he concentrated on the hitch. Anything to keep from thinking about the fact that Dale had been murdered out at Chaco Canyon. Buried upside down in a kiva, a hole drilled in his head. The soles of the old archaeologist's feet had been skinned, and a piece of rotten human flesh had been left in his mouth. All signs of ancient Southwestern witchcraft.

God, what a terrible way to die.

The hitch thunked onto the ball and Dusty snapped the latch home. He was hooking up the safety chains as a pickup pulled into the office parking lot. Plugging in the lights, Dusty smacked the dust from his hands and straightened.

Rupert Brown, Park Superintendent out at Chaco Canyon, stepped out of the green Park Service truck. On the other side, Maggie Walking Hawk Taylor, also in a pale green park uniform, opened the passenger-side door. She clutched a brown paper bag in her right hand.

"Hey, Dusty," Rupert greeted and extended a hand. "Hoped I'd catch you here."

"Hi, Rupert. Welcome to the big city."

"Hello, Dusty." Maggie walked up and hugged Dusty fiercely. Then she stepped back and handed him the bag. "Aunt Sage sent you this."

Dusty opened it and looked in to find fry bread.

"It's her traditional gift to a grieving family. She makes it a little different," Maggie told him. "She uses cinnamon and sugar."

"Tell her how much I appreciate it." He smiled his thanks. "I'll see if I can't get out to see her sometime soon to thank her personally."

"She's not...well, she's not receiving visitors these days, Dusty. So don't worry about it. I'll tell her you said thanks."

"The cancer?" Dusty asked, another wound lancing his heart.

Maggie nodded. "She won't go to hospice or even take anything for the pain." Maggie avoided his eyes. "I've been staying out there. We've been discussing things. Things she said I was going to have to know."

Dusty looked down at the sack of fry bread, wondering how long it would be before he would have to reciprocate, sending a gift of food to Maggie. He'd forgotten that Pueblo tradition after Aunt Hail had died. With the tenderness of Dale's death eating into his soul, he promised he'd do better next time.

"You about ready?" Rupert propped his hands on his slim hips, looking over the trailer.

"I'm pretty well packed." Dusty indicated the stack of screens in the pickup bed. Shovels and pickaxes were laid out on the bed along with two big army-green footlockers that contained the dig kits: level forms, Ziploc bags, artifact bags, soil sample containers, a camera in an ammo box, a chalkboard for photo notes, north arrows and metric scales, line levels, a collection of pointing and square trowels, string, and the other minutiae of good excavation.

Rupert arched an eyebrow. "Didn't you hear agent whatshisname? You're not digging."

"I know, but Nichols told me I could watch from the sidelines." Dusty opened the passenger door and set the fry bread inside. "Michall Jefferson talked to me this morning. She's the principal investigator for the dig. We're renting her the equipment for her crew. It's a business deal. All above board. She's paying for it with real coin of the realm. Good old US cash, legal tender for all debts public and private. We've even got a contract, signed and sealed."

"Uh-huh." Rupert pulled sunglasses from his pocket, slipped them onto his thin face, and studied Dusty. "She used to work for Dale, back before she started her own company, didn't she?"

"Half the archaeologists in the Southwest worked for Dale. And the other half just wished they could have."

Rupert's lips twitched. "How much is she paying?"

"A dollar."

Rupert chuckled. "You don't mention that around the FBI, all right?"

"Right." Dusty nodded.

Rupert's smile faded. "We just came from a meeting with the feds. We're working with them hand in glove. Their ERT team has some pretty strict rules for handling evidence if we find anything. At a moment's notice the archaeologists may have to bail out while the scene is sealed."

Dusty glanced up at the bright midday sun. "What do they think we're going to find down there? A drug lab? It's going to be subtle, Rupert. Something your standard run-of-the-mill FBI white guy would walk right past."

Rupert sighed. "You and I think a lot alike. That's why I insisted that Maggie handle this."

Magpie looked away. "I didn't want to. I mean, God, Dusty, it's Dale. The place they left him." Her expression pinched. "You didn't see him. Not when they brought him out of the ground."

Dusty's hands clenched of their own will. "Did you?"

"Yes, and I swear the very air smelled of evil." She let out a breath. "But I've been talking to Aunt Sage. I'm prepared. I can do this." Her determined eyes met his. "Aunt Sage says I can, and I must."

"You're sure?"

Maggie nodded. "If Michall cuts anything, I'll recognize it. Not only that, if it's as bad as we all think, I'll find someone to handle it."

Dusty said, "I'll help you," but wondered how the FBI ERT guys were going to take having a couple of Keres tribal elders showing up on-site to conduct the kind of rituals necessary to capture and destroy ancient witchery.

"You want to follow us up?" Rupert asked, jerking a thumb at the truck.

"No, I have to get back to Santa Fe. Maureen took the Bronco to my place. We have to buy groceries, lantern fuel, get propane, all that."

"You and Maureen?" Maggie lifted an eyebrow suggestively. "You know, Dale always had hopes for the two of you."

Dusty smiled sadly. "It's not like that. We're friends. That's all. It's just that we were together, you know, when it happened. It's as hard on her as it is on me."

"I doubt that," Maggie said. "But I'm glad she's here, so you don't have to do this alone."

Dusty jammed his hands farther into his pockets. "Yeah, well, I haven't had much of a chance to be alone. It seems I'm very popular these days. I even had a visit from my mother last night."

Rupert straightened, a keenness in his expression. Dusty wished like hell he could have seen the man's eyes, hidden now by the sunglasses. "Ruth's here? In Albuquerque?"

"No. Santa Fe. She was staying at La Fonda. That is, unless Agent Nichols snapped her up as a witness. We called him immediately. Figured it would do her good to sit in for an FBI grilling."

"You think she had something to do with this?" Maggie asked, incredulous.

"Yeah, something," Dusty admitted. "But not directly. This whole thing goes into the past, something between her, Dale, my dad, and Hawsworth."

Rupert tilted his head and examined Dusty. "I'm surprised. After what she did to you, I never thought she'd have the guts to come back and face you."

Dusty tried to shrug it off. "I think she's terrified, Rupert. She had to talk to me to find out what I knew about Dale's death."

Rupert straightened to his full six feet six inches, and softly asked, "Are you okay?"

Dusty nodded. "Yeah. I'm okay."

They stood in companionable silence for a few seconds; then Rupert looked at his watch.

"Maggie, we've got a hard three hours back to the barn. That, or we'll have to file the paperwork for overtime."

"That's the life of a federal drudge, sir."

Rupert made a face. "I get no respect."

He started toward the truck but stopped and turned back. He had a strange look on his face. "When you get to the canyon, find me. Dale always told me to keep my mouth shut about the past. Especially with you, Dusty. He didn't want me stirring the ashes in fires long dead. I don't know everything, but I know some things."

"*What* things?" Dusty started.

"When you get to the canyon, we'll talk," Rupert called over his shoulder as he opened the pickup door and slid into the driver's seat. "And if you see your mother, tell her I've got beer on ice. See what kind of reaction that gets out of her."

"Beer on ice?"

"Yeah." Rupert backed out of the parking lot. Just before putting the truck into drive, he called, "I didn't think much of her back then, Dusty. Maybe she's changed, huh?"

Dusty watched him drive away, remembering her from last night. "Then again, maybe she hasn't."

I n his room, deep in the recesses of Kettle Town,
Browser's uncle, Stone Ghost, pulled a brown fabric
bag from his pack, tugged the laces open, and
poured the dried onions into the boiling pot that hung on
the tripod over his warming bowl. The old pot bore a thick
coating of soot, which almost obscured the gray clay
beneath.

The strange little girl who called herself Bone Walker
crouched across the fire with her arms folded atop her
knees, and her cornhusk doll in her right hand. The heavy
turquoise necklace Stone Ghost had given her still draped
her neck. She might have been nine, or maybe an emaciated ten years old? Stick thin, with large and haunted dark
eyes.

That morning he'd heard her running through the
hallways, running like a scared rabbit, making soft pained
sounds. He'd called her name, and she'd climbed the
ladder to get to his chamber, then run into his arms—the
first time she'd let him touch her. Stone Ghost had held
her in silence until she'd fallen asleep. Often throughout
the afternoon, she'd awakened from nightmares, shaking.

"This is not much of a supper," he said. "Onion soup thickened with a little blue cornmeal. Are you hungry?"

Bone Walker stared at the far wall through wide empty eyes. The eyes of the old Bone Walker, days ago, before they'd started talking. Dirt streaked her pretty face and faded blue dress. She must have slid her hand through the grime on the floor while she slept, then rubbed her nose.

Stone Ghost wondered what terrible thing or things had happened to her.

He added three more twigs to the low fire in the warming bowl and watched the flames lick up around the base of his soup pot. The spicy scent of onions mixed with the sweetness of the blue corn to create a mouthwatering aroma.

Yesterday, he'd thought he might be making headway with Bone Walker, getting her to trust him a little, but for most of today she'd been quiet, hiding in corners, sleeping with her blanket pulled over her head.

"I have some juniper berry tea made. Would you like some, Bone Walker?"

She didn't seem to hear him, but the cornhusk doll was turned as if to peer at the teapot resting beside the warming bowl.

Stone Ghost dipped a cupful from the pot and handed it to her. When she didn't take it, he set the cup on the floor beneath the doll.

Stone Ghost picked up his own teacup. Juniper berry tea had a tangy pungent flavor. He took a long drink before lowering his cup to his lap.

In a tender voice, Stone Ghost asked, "Where do you go, Bone Walker, when you aren't speaking? Do you go to a place deep inside you or a place far outside?"

Bone Walker's head tilted toward him, but she didn't look at him. She looked past him.

"I'm curious because once, when I was a boy, the village bully struck me in the head with a big rock."

Stone Ghost used his fingers to part the white hair on the right side of his head so that she could see the scar. "I fell flat on my face, and I think my breath-heart soul slipped from my body. I found myself looking down at this bloody-headed boy, but I was floating like a milkweed seed, going higher and higher. My mother told me that she had tried to wake me for two days, but I just lay on my hides staring at nothing. So, I went somewhere outside my body. I..."

Bone Walker shuddered and clutched her doll more tightly.

"Bone Walker?"

"Are you going to m-make me go away?"

Stone Ghost's bushy white brows lowered. "Why would I do that? You've been a good girl."

The soup pot bubbled and spat.

"But if my parents were bad, would you make me go away?"

Stone Ghost smoothed his fingers down the warm side of his cup. "No, child. I wouldn't blame you for things your parents did."

Bone Walker blinked and her eyes had a human inside them again. A small shaky breath escaped her mouth. She rose, trotted around the fire, and crawled into his lap. With her free hand, she reached up and grabbed hold of the leather ties of his cape where they knotted beneath his chin. As though this would keep them together, no matter what.

Stone Ghost patted her back gently.

After a short interval, he asked, "Are your parents bad people, Bone Walker?"

She tucked her head inside his cape, hiding her face, but he heard her whisper, *"I hate them."*

Stone Ghost looked down. The desperate love in those words lanced his heart. Tan dust and old juniper needles filled her tangled hair. He patted her again. "Who are they? What are their names?"

Bone Walker leaned against his chest. It took some time before she said, *"Daybreak beasts."*

Stone Ghost's hand hovered over her back. Where had she heard that? Almost no one these days knew about the daybreak beast. It was very, very old.

"Yes," he said and stroked her tangled hair. "I understand."

Grandfather Snowbird told Stone Ghost the story when he'd seen five or six summers. When Wolf finally led the First People up through the last underworld into the light, he told them: *"For you it will always be daybreak on the second day of the world, my children. You will forever live suspended between Father Sun's first and second coming. Remember the daybreak beast. You cannot kill him, but you can tame him and use his Power."*

It was on the second day of the world that Father Sun decided the First People needed company, and he'd turned buffalo, ants, coyotes, and other animals into humans: created the Made People.

Stone Ghost had always wondered about the final moments of glory when there were just First People walking like gods on a shining new world.

Before there was an "us" and a "them."

Before they realized paradise was gone forever, and the daybreak beast was born in their hearts.

Catkin, Clay Frog, Red Dog, and Browser crouched in the shadows of Scorpion Town. Browser kept running his hands up and down the shaft of his war club. Catkin had seen him like this before. When battle was close, he couldn't seem to stay still.

She glanced up at the block of rooms two bow shots above them. Owl House was poorly lit by the fingernail moon. Did Springbank lie up there? She could imagine him, age-wasted, pale, his lungs mottled black with old blood. His skin would be tight, eyes sunken into his skull. Those withered brown lips would be drawn back to expose his peg like incisors. Did the old witch really believe that by taking Obsidian's heart he would be able to prolong his foul life?

Catkin hefted her war club. "How do you wish to do this?"

"The main party of White Moccasins are camped at High Sun, one half-hand's run from here, but there will be guards above us somewhere. We can assume that they haven't seen us yet. Had they, an alarm would have been raised."

"A half-hand isn't much time," Clay Frog reminded. "It is even less when you are involved in a fight for your life. That main party could be here before we know it."

Browser gripped his club as if testing its weight. "Let's split into two parties and work up the slope from different directions."

"Or come back tomorrow night with more people," Catkin suggested. Her belly squirmed. Something told her they should not do this tonight. "By the time Sister Moon rises tomorrow, we could have the job done."

"And it's possible we'd have cloud cover, like we did at sunset tonight," Clay Frog added, sensing Catkin's hesitance.

Browser's eyes slitted as he studied the ridgetop structure above them. She could feel his need to storm up there, to rush the place, and end it once and for all.

"Tonight," Browser said. "Too much could go wrong between now and then."

Catkin took a deep breath. "All right. Perhaps we should take the rest of the night to slowly get into position, then spring on them as dawn approaches. Men are the most tired then."

Browser's eyes remained fixed on the dark ruins of Owl House. "Clay Frog, take Red Dog and circle, stick to the shadows next to the cliff and move from boulder to boulder. It will give you a little more protection. Catkin and I will work our way to the toe of the ridge. From there we will crawl from bush to bush as we make our way up."

"Yes, War Chief."

But no one moved. Red Dog and Clay Frog exchanged worried glances.

"Let's do this," Catkin said and rose to her feet.

Clay Frog and Red Dog cautiously slipped off to the

right; then Browser started up the hill. They had made less than four paces when a cry carried on the still night.

From long practice, Catkin dropped to a crouch, her eyes searching the darkness. Where he walked ahead of her, Browser was already down, frozen in place in the trail. Clay Frog and Red Dog had followed their lead, their figures hunched ten paces away.

"Who was that?" Browser's voice was barely above a whisper. "One of ours?"

Catkin swallowed hard, whispering, "I thought for a moment we were discovered, but I think it came from over by the staircase."

"Agreed," Clay Frog hissed. "That was not a warning cry."

"Follow me," Browser ordered. "No matter who it was, they are alert up there now. We won't be able to get to them."

In a low bobbing line they duck-walked back to the protective shadows of the village walls. No sooner had Catkin reached the shadows than a piping whistle, the sound like a night bird's, carried on the still air. Moments later, another responded from the ridge where Owl House looked ever more impregnable.

"Gods," Browser whispered. "Something has alerted them. Let us hope it is not our other scouting party." He hesitated and shook his head. "Back. Let's go back."

Catkin prayed that Jackrabbit, Straighthorn, Carved Splinter, and Fire Lark were being equally smart.

As they turned to go, Catkin cast one last glance over her shoulder, and there, faintly visible atop the roof at Owl House, she could see a person staring off toward the staircase to the south. A glittering haze of windblown hair swam around the person. Was it a trick of the distance, or was it a woman?

5

CANYON ROAD, SANTA FE, NEW MEXICO

Maureen saw the man as she drove the Bronco into Dusty's driveway. Sunset cast slanting shadows through the winter-bare cottonwoods and across his tall thin body. He leaned against a white Chevrolet with his arms crossed nonchalantly. In his sixties, he looked lean to the point of being bony. Despite a receding hairline, he wore his white hair long, pulled back in a ponytail. That coupled with the tweed coat, brown Dockers, and snazzy black turtleneck gave him an upscale cachet. She would have immediately placed him as trendy Santa Fe, even without the big silver belt buckle with the large chunk of turquoise. The car sported New Mexico plates, traces of road grime around the wheel wells, and a scattering of small dents.

No expression crossed his face as he watched her drive in.

When she looked into his cold blue eyes, Maureen knew him. She'd seen him at Dale's memorial ceremony, and again on the photo Agent Nichols had shown her: *Carter Hawsworth.*

Maureen cut the ignition, gathered her purse, and slipped a hand inside to push the 911 buttons on her cellular phone. If necessary, all she'd have to do was thumb the SEND button and scream out "Upper Canyon Road."

She kept one hand inside her buffalo purse, a finger on the button, as she stepped out of the Bronco and slammed the door. "Hello. May I help you?"

The man straightened, the move oddly graceful. "I was looking for William Stewart. I understood that this was his address." He pointed to the pathetic aluminum trailer hunkering on the creek bank.

"Thought you'd try it in the daylight this time, Dr. Hawsworth?"

He gave her a speculative look. "Do I know you?"

"No. I'm Dr. Maureen Cole."

He considered her, lips pursed. "I don't remember having heard of you. You are a colleague of Dale's?"

"I was. Though recently I've been working with the FBI. In fact, I was just discussing you with FBI Special Agent Sam Nichols. He's very interested in talking to you."

To her surprise, Hawsworth sighed and chuckled. "Yes, I know. My sister has been leaving that message on my answering machine. I rather suppose that I should give the agent a call."

"Why did you leave Dale's memorial without introducing yourself?"

He stared down at the ground. "It was one of those things I just had to do. You see, in the beginning, I thought it was Dale."

"What was?"

He stepped away from his car. "About a month ago I

started receiving messages. The first was a sand painting. An image of me that had been done in the middle of the night on my doorstep. A yucca leaf, like a spear, was thrust through the image's chest."

"You thought Dale had done that?"

"No. But some of the other things...well, suffice it to say that Dale was among the few people on earth who would have known the significance a yucca hoop has for me."

He looked suddenly frightened. Maureen took her hand off the cell phone and reached for the key to Dusty's trailer. "I don't suppose you still have this yucca hoop?"

Evidence. Everything always came down to evidence.

"Bloody hell, do you think I'd have kept such a thing? God no, I immediately burned it. The same with the messages that came in on the fax. As soon as I detected Dale's subtle hand, I called him. Told him to stop it, that I knew it was him."

"Is that why you went to his memorial service?"

"No, no." Hawsworth waved it away irritably. "When I heard he'd been found in Chaco, and how he'd died, I knew it was something else."

"Something else? Not someone?"

He studied her, his pale blue eyes prying away as if to determine what she really knew. "If I told you that witch-craft is always more than 'someone,' would you immediately consider me a lunatic? Some New Age fruitcake? Or would you allow me the courtesy of my professional identity as an anthropologist and grant me the benefit of the doubt?"

She gave him a thin smile. "I'd give you the benefit of the doubt, Dr. Hawsworth."

"Thank you, Dr. Cole." He steepled his fingers as though addressing undergraduates in the lecture hall and started pacing lithely before her. "You see, one need not believe in witchcraft itself. I mean, I don't accept that it works as its practitioners believe, but you must understand that the followers are ardent. That *they* believe is sufficient. As a result, it isn't witchcraft itself that carries power, but their belief and the extent to which they pursue their ends. Thus it is—"

Maureen interrupted, "Dr. Hawsworth, I'm more than passingly familiar with the professional literature. Get to the point."

He seemed slightly off balance as if by derailing his train of thought, she'd made him lose his place.

"You were telling me why you went to Dale's memorial and left before it was over."

"Yes, you see, I-I," he stammered, then seemed to catch himself. He squared his thin shoulders. "I'm sure the witch was there."

"The person who killed Dale?"

His cold blue eyes seemed to enlarge. "That's right. I hoped I would see him. Recognize him. And then, all of a sudden, I saw you looking at me, and I realized immediately that going there was a mistake. Because as easily as I might have picked out the witch, so might he have singled me out of the crowd. I had already received his unwelcome attention. I did not wish to solicit more."

"Didn't you keep any of the things he sent you? As evidence?"

"Of course not! Why on earth do you think I would have cared about evidence? I immediately swept the walk after I discovered the sand painting. The faxes I burned as a way of cleansing."

She impatiently jangled Dusty's keys. "Who were the faxes from?" *The Wolf Witch?*

He frowned. "When I received my phone bill, I checked. The faxes had all been sent from a hotel. The business office at the Hotel El Dorado, right here in Santa

Fe. It seems that anyone can just walk in and have the hotel send a fax. They only make a record if it is charged to a room. The faxes sent to me were paid for in cash. The sender only signed his name as someone called Kwewur. I looked it up, found the reference in Fewkes. It's the name of a Wolf Katchina."

Maureen studied him thoughtfully, wondering what Ruth Ann Sullivan had ever seen in this man. "Why haven't you told all this to the FBI?"

His lips tightened in an expression like a cartoon turtle might have made. "I'm not sure I could adequately relate the serious nature of Southwestern witchcraft to American federal agents. They don't believe in it, you see. They would be suspicious, perhaps misinterpret my motives in trying to discover the witch."

"They don't seem to misinterpret much, Dr. Hawsworth."

He looked genuinely pained. "But I doubt they have the facilities to pursue a witch. It's not in their cognitive framework. The witch could be right under their official noses, flipping them the proverbial finger, as it were, and they'd never see him."

"Would you?"

"Absolutely. You see, Dr. Cole, I've been studying witchcraft for the last forty years. It brought me here, to the Southwest. Since then, I've followed it to Australia, Polynesia, and Africa. I have over fifty publications in professional journals. If there is a modern expert on prelit-erate witchcraft, I fear I am he."

"Why did you follow Dr. Sullivan here last night?"

Hawsworth paused, his frown deepening. "I beg your pardon?"

"You followed Ruth Ann Sullivan here from her hotel at around two A.M. last night, didn't you?"

"Who? Ruth? Last night?" He looked perplexed. "She

was here?" He looked around as though the surroundings had suddenly been tainted.

"Someone followed Ruth Ann Sullivan from her hotel to this place last night. She assumed it was you."

He made a distasteful face. "Why would I do that?"

"I haven't the slightest notion. As I said, she assumed it was you. Her reasons for making that assumption are her own, but I would imagine that something must have warranted them."

He folded his arms again. "Perhaps it was the knowledge that I would love to drive a stake through her black heart. Had I known she was coming here last night, I would indeed have followed her. Did she seem frightened of me?"

Maureen nodded.

"Good!" he exclaimed with true glee and clapped his hands together. "If you see her again, tell her I'd take great pleasure in flaying her skin from her body." He smiled. "But slowly, Dr. Cole. Very slowly."

"I take it you and Dr. Sullivan aren't on the best of terms."

"In Africa I was working in the Namibian bush. I met the most fascinating reptile there. The snake is called the black mamba, *Dendroaspis polylepis,* to be precise. It's a beautiful thing, slim and graceful, and it moves through the grass with such sinuous grace. When encountered, it lifts its head up, and being more than ten feet long, it stares at a man at eye level. The only defense is to move your hand back and forth." He made a motion, as if polishing glass. "The reason is that if the snake strikes, it will hit your hand instead of your face or throat. In the intervening two minutes that you have to live, you might be able to amputate your hand or arm in time to save your life."

"Does this have a point?"

"Indeed, Dr. Cole. Mambas reminded me a lot of our dear Ruth. Unlike the snakes, however, she strikes at a man's crotch as well as his face."

Maureen clutched the keys and said, "Weren't you the man who wooed her away from her husband and son once upon a time?"

Hawsworth gave her the same condescending smile a tolerant adult would give a child. "That was more than thirty years ago. She was young, beautiful, and only beginning to develop poison sacs."

"But you were together for two years after she ditched Samuel Stewart."

"Yes." His lips thinned again. "Remarkable, isn't it?"

"What are you doing here? What do you want?"

He pulled himself up, that scholar's frown deepening in his forehead. "I was hoping to find this William Stewart. I hear that everyone calls him Dusty."

"That's right."

Carter Hawsworth scowled at her, as if trying to evaluate her character. "I should probably speak to him."

"I don't think he's anxious to talk to you, Dr. Hawsworth. He associates you with one of the more traumatic moments in his life."

Hawsworth waved it off. "Oh, you should have seen him. A squalling brat in dirty clothes. Most unruly. He was a little monster. I can understand Ruth wanting to leave him and this shabby trailer behind—though they only came here between the field seasons. Sometimes the housing was a great deal rougher than this."

Maureen narrowed her eyes. "If you want to talk to him, he's going to want to know why he should listen instead of breaking your jaw first."

"I beg your pardon?" he said as though stunned. "I'm here to help him."

"Dr. Hawsworth, you ran off with his mother. He's

hated you all of his life. Why in the world would you want to help him now?"

Hawsworth blinked, as if he truly didn't understand. "Dr. Cole, that was *thirty years ago!* What difference would it make today? But that's all right"—he pushed out with his hands, as if to ward her off—"if he doesn't want to see me, that's well and fine."

She sighed irritably. "Look, that's his decision. What do you want to tell him? I'll deliver your message. After that, it's up to him."

Hawsworth turned, flipped his white ponytail, and stalked to his car. He got in, rolled down the window, and said, "Tell him...tell him I have reason to believe that no one from those days is safe. If he wants to know more, he can contact me. Assuming he wants to discuss this matter in a mature and sensible way, we will decide what to do about Kwewur."

"Right." Maureen stepped up to the man's car door. "How does he reach you?"

"I'll call him. His number, like this address, is in the book." Hawsworth twisted the key. The Chevy roared to life.

Maureen was smiling as Hawsworth backed around, shifted the transmission into gear, and accelerated away. The little white tag hanging from his rearview mirror had said: SANTA FE HILTON PARKING. Better yet, the expiration was still three days away.

6

Browser knelt in a collapsed room high in Kettle Town and watched the morning glow change from gray to pink. Jackrabbit, the Bow warrior Fire Lark, and Straighthorn had just returned, and stood behind him, breathing hard, covered with dust.

"We got separated, War Chief," Jackrabbit said. Sweat streaked the young warrior's face, cutting dark lines across his pug nose and around his wide mouth. "We were taking our time, moving slowly, checking abandoned houses. We split up to check several old pit houses. I sent Fire Lark and Straighthorn ahead to War Club village. We were supposed to meet there. Carved Splinter was behind me when we left the last pit house. A moment later, when I looked back, he was gone. I didn't think too much about it since we were all supposed to meet at War Club village anyway." The young warrior shook his head.

"Carved Splinter wouldn't have just wandered off." He swallowed hard. "A half-hand of time later, we heard a cry, like someone being hurt. Then came whistles, and I knew that something had gone terribly wrong. We waited for a half-hand of time, just in case there was something we could do...or in case Carved Splinter showed up. Then the warriors came."

"What warriors?"

"White Moccasins, War Chief. Straighthorn saw them first. At least ten climbed down the stairway, dressed in long white capes. I made the decision to draw back. We took shelter in a drainage and waited. Just before daylight we withdrew and returned here."

Browser carefully searched the approaches to Kettle Town, hoping desperately to see Carved Splinter trotting in. He did not wish to tell old White Cone that he had already lost one of the Bow Society's best warriors.

The plain with its abandoned ditches and cornfields remained empty, but for a slight breeze that whisked a swirl of dust off to the east.

IIIIIIIIIIIIIIIIIIIIIIIIIIIIIIIIIIIIII

7

SANTA FE, LORETTO HOTEL

T he thing about Santa Fe, Maureen had discovered, was that even in early November, the weather could be incredible. With a bright sunny day, and temperatures bumping up against seventy Fahrenheit, the outdoor dining area at Nellie's proved the perfect place for lunch.

Dusty had dropped her off that morning while he ran errands to the bank, the hardware shop, and the place that did lube jobs down on Cerrillos. After promising to meet him at Nellie's at noon—the restaurant attached to the Loretto Hotel—she had drifted in and out of the shops around the plaza.

What was it about the Southwest? She could browse with passionate disinterest through the trendy shops on Queen Street in Toronto and rarely have the craving to do anything extravagant. But in the first fifteen minutes in Santa Fe, she could easily have blown her yearly salary. It wasn't just that it was Indian artwork. She'd seen that at Sainte Marie Among the Hurons in northern Ontario.

The difference was that here, in the Southwest, Native art had made the transition from being quaint relics to something beautifully relevant to the twenty-first century.

Studying the katchinas in their wealth of styles, she couldn't help but wonder why her Iroquoian contemporaries at Six Nations couldn't find a way to share the power and beauty of the Society of Faces. Iroquoian False Face dancers were every bit as delightful as katchinas, and often a great deal more colorful.

She considered that as the midmorning sun warmed the outdoor restaurant. It reflected from the cement and the bright yellow napkins on the table. The historic Loretto chapel stood immediately to the south, guarded by overarching cottonwoods. Behind her a traditional-looking ramada enclosed the server's stations and fireplace. In front of her, the plastered walls of the Hotel Loretto, with its plastic-shrouded luminarias, glowed in the clear morning.

"Excuse me?"

Maureen started from her reverie. The tall woman standing beside her table wore a gray wool suit with matching waist-length cape, opaque white nylons, and brown pumps. Her perfect silver hair was accented by the red silk scarf knotted at her neck.

"Hello, Dr. Sullivan, fancy meeting you here." Maureen felt her happy mood evaporate.

"I was sitting over there." She pointed to the far corner table beside the cement railing. "I thought perhaps you might like company?"

Subduing her first instinct to say no, Maureen moved her bison-hide purse from the other chair. "Be my guest."

Ruth Ann Sullivan seated herself, looking every inch an East Coast matron. She unhooked her cloak and spread it over the chair. Back straight, posture perfect, she crossed her arms primly and studied Maureen through hard blue eyes. "You're not the sort I would have figured my son would attract."

"You don't know anything about your son."

Maureen raised the big yellow coffee cup to signal for a refill. They had marvelous coffee here, rich and black—even better than her favorite Tim Horton's off the QEW back home.

"Just after I escaped the Gestapo treatment inflicted by Agent Nichols, I did some research." Ruth Ann smiled coldly.

"Gestapo? Like white lights, a wooden chair, black leather gloves, and rubber hoses?" Maureen asked.

"No, him, me, and my lawyer, in the Santa Fe residency." Ruth Ann arched an eyebrow. "Did you really think I killed Dale?"

"No, but I thought you might know who did." Maureen leaned back as her cup was refilled, and the waitress, a middle-aged woman, asked if they were ready to order.

"Just coffee for me," Ruth Ann said.

"I'll order later, please," Maureen replied and waited until the waitress had stepped out of earshot. "Whoever killed Dale knew enough to make it look like Southwestern witchcraft."

"Perhaps the killer read too many Tony Hillerman novels." Ruth Ann loosened the red scarf at her throat. "I wish I had known who you were the other night at the trailer." The woman smiled wearily. "I really would not have expected someone of your reputation to be with William."

"What sort would you have expected?"

"A field bimbo. The rotating sort we used to call teepee creepers. Usually young, out on their own for the first time, bursting with desire to crawl into the crew chief's bedroll and benefit from his status."

She waved a thin hand. "It's not just in archaeological field camps, of course. We train our young women to be that way. It's fascinating. I spent a year at a high school, watching the most popular girls: blond, buxom, and beautiful, from educated, upper-class households. They just couldn't wait to pair themselves off with the football heroes, the boys with expensive cars, and the track stars."

Maureen sipped her coffee and thought about all of the problems Dusty had relating to women. Even the field bimbos would have scared him. "You thought Dusty would be shacked up with a golden girl?"

"I would have imagined. What we think of as silly high school girls is really a microcosm of adult female behavior. We still teach our females to create their self-identity through their husbands' status and their husbands' possessions."

"Somewhere along the line, I missed that lecture. Must have been because of the poor schools on the Reserve." Maureen studied Ruth Ann across her coffee cup.

"Then you aren't as good a physical anthropologist as your vitae would indicate. The same behavior is exhibited in a troop of Gelada baboons. Females want to be bred by alpha males. They gravitate toward them through an attraction as magnetic now as it was in the middle of the Pleistocene."

"Much the same way you were attracted to Carter Hawsworth some thirty years ago?" Maureen asked.

Ruth Ann tipped her face to the sun. "Exactly the same way. Have you and William been lovers for long? Or is this just a field affair?"

"Dusty and I are professional colleagues and good friends," she said. "Only."

Ruth Ann's mouth pinched. "Maybe, but the way you look at him, either you've been in his bed, or will be soon."

"Would that bother you?"

She laughed. "What sort of relationship do you think I have with him? I couldn't care less who he screws."

Maureen toyed with her cup. "I've been wondering why the killer was so certain he could lure you here through those faxes. What could have happened back then to make you feel you had to come back here—"

"You're fishing," Ruth Ann responded archly.

Maureen sipped her coffee, but her eyes never left Ruth Ann's. She said, "Something brought you here. Something as innocent as curiosity or as powerful as guilt. Either way, if you'd cut the ties with the past as cleanly as you would have us believe, you wouldn't be here."

Ruth Ann exhaled, then nodded slightly. "Dr. Cole, why don't you and I just lay our cards on the table? At this stage, I'm not sure where scoring points for being clever will get us."

"Very well, did you have Dale killed?"

For a long moment Ruth Ann's hard eyes bored into Maureen's. Finally she said, "Dale and I hadn't spoken in years. Why on earth would I suddenly place myself and my career at risk to murder him?"

"You used to be lovers. Maybe you hold a grudge."

Ruth Ann laughed and slapped the table. "You're right! There is *always* a reason to kill an ex-lover. What did Dale tell you about me?"

"Not much. He told me a little about Dusty's childhood, and about how you treated him and Sam. He told me about you and Hawsworth. That's all. We didn't know that you and Dale were lovers until we began reading the journals."

"I would appreciate the opportunity to look through those journals," she said stiffly, "especially as they regard me."

Maureen took another drink and savored the rich

flavor for a time before she answered, "So would we. Someone broke into Dale's house and stole them while we were up at Chaco."

Ruth Ann leaned back and looked around the airy restaurant while she considered the information. "Rupert?"

"Rupert?" Maureen started. "The park superintendent?"

"Or Carter."

"Why Rupert?"

"Oh, come on. You don't think he's some saintly Indian, do you? He used to pick women up at bars, fuck them, and drop them off at the nearest bus station. That's how he met his wife. Sandy, for God's sake."

"Rupert Brown couldn't have taken the journals. He was at Chaco with us. It would have been impossible for him to be in two places at once. And believe me, he was still there after we left. He couldn't have beaten us home." Maureen leveled a finger, "You, however, have been sight unseen for days, eh?"

"I didn't even know about Dale's journals." The answer sounded lame to Maureen.

"He was a young field archaeologist living out of his truck. Are you telling me you didn't know he kept a journal while he was in the field?"

She made a dismissive gesture. "Oh, I might have. That was so long ago, how would I remember?"

Maureen let her have it her way. Instead she said, "Tell me about it. Your side, I mean. Just how deeply are you involved in witchcraft?"

"I'm an anthropologist, dear. You don't study human culture without running into witchcraft. The first article I published was on Southwestern witchcraft. But I am not 'involved' in it."

"But you know what it means when a man's feet are

skinned, his body is buried in a yucca hoop, and a hole is drilled in his head. Someone stuffed another human's muscle tissue into Dale's mouth, and he was buried upside down in an archaeological site."

Sullivan's face remained expressionless as she listened. "The actual methods of witchery were Carter's fascination, not mine. If you look up that article, you'll find he was the senior author. He's the one who got me involved in witchcraft stories in the first place. Him and his witch."

Maureen shifted uneasily. "Was that before you ran out on Samuel?"

Sullivan's mouth hardened. "I wouldn't try to sound so judgmental, Dr. Cole. You weren't there."

"Then inform me, please."

"I don't think so. That was in a different millennium, a different life." She toyed with the tabletop, thoughtfully running her fingers over the surface, then looked up suddenly. Her smile was as sharp as cut glass. "Oh, what the hell. They're dead...Sam...Dale. I could just wish Carter was. Now there, Dr. Cole, is someone I wouldn't mind going to jail for murdering. It would damn near be worth it."

"If Carter was that bad, how could Samuel Stewart have been worse?"

She snorted. "God! Sam was a crusader. It was the sixties. How do I explain the world then? Most of us truly believed that we would die in thermonuclear explosions. Our friends were dying in Vietnam and our government was lying to us. Samuel was one of those free spirits who thought that by knowing people in the past, we could know our future. Avoid the mistakes that kill civilizations and maybe build a better world for ourselves and the whole planet."

"That doesn't sound like justification for desertion."

She glared at Maureen from under lowered eyelids. "Have you ever lived with an idealistic fanatic? In the beginning, it's heady stuff, this charging windmills and rewriting the future of man. After a couple of years the endless abrasive enthusiasm begins to wear holes in your soul. After William was born, I was supposed to become some sort of maternal clan-elder Earth mother goddess. The pure virgin mother, symbol of fertility, but not sexuality. To hear Samuel tell it in those days, breast milk was to a child as rain was to the Shalako. Motherhood wasn't biology, it became religion."

"You still wanted your career."

"Which I wasn't about to find in a laundromat in Gallup."

"Did Dale and you...I mean, you and Dale were lovers long before you met Samuel. What happened there?"

Ruth Ann cocked her head slightly, trying to read Maureen's reaction. "Have you ever been tied up in a love triangle?"

"Once, a long, long time ago in high school. It wasn't pleasant."

"It's less so when your husband and old lover are best friends. Sam and Dale liked each other in spite of my incendiary presence. Dale might have been the biggest mistake I ever made."

"How is that?"

She smiled at something in the distant past. "He didn't write it in his journals?"

"If he did, we didn't get to it before the thief ripped them off."

She fingered the tabletop. "Dale never married. For that I'm sorry."

"Why?"

"I did that to him." She ran a manicured hand through her silver hair. "Oh, I knew it would break his heart when

I showed up with Samuel. I wanted it over with. Samuel was new, exciting, and, I thought, brave. He'd just walked out on a fortune. Told his family to go fuck off, that he was going to be a field archaeologist, and they could take their mansion and money and suck eggs."

"So you left Dale?"

"Dale was getting too close." Ruth Ann looked up. "He was a possessive kind of person. Even in his old age. You knew him. A dominant male. When you worked with Dale, there was never any doubt who was in control. Yes, he was a team leader, and always took your input and made it part of the project final report. He wanted your best effort and rewarded you appropriately to the quantity and quality of your work. But he was the boss. Period."

"I think that's what made him one of the greatest anthropologists of the twentieth century," Maureen stated bluntly.

"No doubt that's an accurate assessment. As a lover, however, an independent and self-possessed woman looks for something a bit more egalitarian." Ruth Ann tugged at her red scarf again. "You never had an affair with Dale, I take it?"

Maureen just stared at her.

"Don't look so shocked. Dale had affairs with lots of women," Ruth Ann continued thoughtfully. "He liked smart, strong, and independent women. He couldn't stand the others, the golden girls we referred to earlier. He called them 'breeding stock' for the species. Absolutely necessary but not worth his time. So he was always caught on the horns of a dilemma. He wasn't attracted to women who didn't challenge him intellectually, but he always had to have them in an inferior position."

"And as soon as they subordinated themselves," she finished, "Dale lost interest?"

"Yes. Curious, isn't it? Dale knew it, too. Hell, I told

him over and over. He just couldn't accept a woman as an equal. Or a man, either."

"Well," Maureen said, and looked down into her coffee cup, "at least in that regard, Dale was an egalitarian."

Ruth Ann shook her head. "What is it about men, always trying to make women into something they're not?"

"So you thought Samuel would be a way of shutting Dale down. Using one man to handle another? Risky. Especially when you end up married."

"And pregnant. Giving birth? That was the biggest mistake of all."

"But one you could correct, eh? You just attached yourself to a man with a plane ticket to London."

Maureen watched the angry red rising in Ruth Ann's cheeks. After several seconds, Maureen added, "It's kind of like stepping-stones to avoid getting wet in the river of responsibility, isn't it? Dale, Samuel, Carter, and Dusty, all left behind on the grander road to fame."

"You should know. You're world-renowned in your field. I wager there were a number of stepping-stones in your life as well."

Maureen picked up her coffee and drank. The sun had warmed the yellow cup, and it felt good against her chilly fingers. "What drew you back here, Dr. Sullivan? You and Carter are the only two left from those times. It's up to you to break this thing open."

"What makes you think it's just us? God, Cole, there were others, too. You don't think we just lived in a vacuum, do you?"

Maureen's fingers tightened around her cup. "What others?"

"Colleagues from that time and place. How should I know? I never kept track. I wanted to forget that part of my life." She lifted a mocking eyebrow. "It might even be my son, for all you know. How did he feel when he learned that his adopted father and mentor, the noble Dale Emerson Robertson, had fucked his mother long before his father did? Dale never told him, did he? Surprise me and tell me I'm wrong, that Dale could actually have admitted it to the boy."

"Dusty didn't kill Dale. He was with me."

"Ah, yes, your platonic relationship crops up again."

Ruth Ann reorganized the silverware with her long fingers. "Tell me, Doctor, what is it like to be so morally superior that you can't allow yourself to be a woman in the presence of the man who loves you? Or is William his father's son? Afraid to lay a finger on the woman he's in love with?"

Ruth Ann stood, retrieved her cape, and threw a couple of dollars onto the table. "If he ever tries, let me know if he's as impotent as his father was."

Ruth Ann strode purposefully to the low stairs that led down into the Loretto gardens.

Maureen turned back to her yellow coffee cup. In the back of her mind, a voice kept whispering, *"Him and his witch, him and his witch..."*

Browser tossed in his sleep, desperate to understand what his dead son was trying to tell him. Grass Moon had come to him right after he'd fallen asleep at dawn and kept waking him throughout the morning. But Browser couldn't hear the little boy. Each time Grass Moon opened his mouth to speak, he broke into violent coughs that ended with blood on his lips.

"Try again, son," Browser pleaded, seeing the fear in Grass Moon's eyes.

The little boy took a breath and tried to form words, but blood sprayed from his mouth, speckling the soil at his feet. Grass Moon reached out to touch Browser, and gasped, *"Owl..."*

Browser jerked awake and in the sunlight percolating down through the rifts in the roof, he saw Catkin lying on her belly beside him. He had his arm across her shoulders. Her attractive oval face and turned-up nose gleamed golden.

Browser inhaled and the scents of woman, moldering wood, and dust filled his lungs.

When they had crawled into their blankets, exhausted

from the night's activity, they'd been an arm's length apart. When had he curled against her?

He closed his eyes for a moment and let himself enjoy the yucca soap fragrance of her straight black hair, then dared to press closer. As the curves of her body conformed to his, she stirred, but didn't wake. A soft contented murmur came from her lips.

Browser savored the feel of her, the angles of her shoulders against his muscular chest, her round bottom pressed firmly against his groin. The hardening of his penis sent an insistent tingle through his loins. He couldn't help himself as he tightened his hold on her.

He knew the moment she woke, felt her move, but not away, no, closer, pressing against him. Browser tensed as she reached back, slid her hand under his blanket, and grasped him.

Catkin opened her eyes, and a soft smile turned her lips.

"I didn't mean to wake you," he said.

"It was a pleasant way to wake up, Browser. But why are you up? We've slept barely five hands of time."

"I had a strange dream. My son, Grass Moon, came to me. He was trying to tell me something, but I only understood one word, 'owl.'"

Catkin released him, and her smile drained away. "Owl House?"

"Maybe. I..." he started and heard the faint grating of a leather-clad foot on the floor in the next chamber.

By the time Yucca Whip ducked into their doorway, they were separated, a respectable space between them.

"Yes?" Browser asked, trying to still his rapid breathing.

"Someone is coming, War Chief. We thought you should know."

"Who?"

"One man and two dogs."

"Carved Splinter?"

"No. An old man."

Browser threw back his blanket and reached for his weapons. Thankfully his war shirt hung loosely as he rose. By the time he followed Yucca Whip through the labyrinth of passageways, his ardor had faded to a pleasant memory. Catkin followed quietly behind him, displaying no evidence of the precipice upon which they had just balanced.

Yucca Whip led them up several ladders to the third floor. There, in the doorway, Fire Lark peered out at the midday sunlight.

"Where is he?" Yucca Whip asked.

"He just vanished from view. Down there." Fire Lark pointed to the southeastern wall. "His dogs went with him. I assume he's...There."

Browser watched as a man appeared and clambered up over the southern room block that restricted access to the plaza. He was old, white-haired, and brown-skinned, but limber and active. The two dogs, one black the other brown, sniffed around at the open doorways as they jumped down from the crumbled walls. The man proceeded to the pilastered front of the building and disappeared out of Browser's sight under the wall.

"Come on," Browser said. "I know the bottom floor. We can trap him inside."

"Perhaps we should avoid him?" Catkin asked.

"II he lives here, he may have information about Two Hearts. If he's just innocently passing through, we may have to take other measures. Or perhaps he is bringing us information about Carved Splinter. Regardless, we must know who he is and why he's here."

Browser led the way back through two rooms to a ladder that poked out of a roof opening. Taking the rungs one at a time, he dropped down into the blackness of Kettle Town. He stayed close to the outside wall, where enough light filtered in to illuminate his passage.

Behind him, Catkin, Yucca Whip, and Fire Lark followed on silent feet. The dilapidated warren that was Kettle Town had survived the sun cycles better than Talon Town. Perhaps because less fighting had taken place here. Or, maybe the builders who erected the giant town had taken more care in its construction. While the upper floor had collapsed, the spectacular destruction that made travel through Talon Town a risk to life and limb didn't yet apply to Kettle Town.

Browser gestured silence as he crept across a room and hunched over a ladder leading down to the second floor. After listening a time, he climbed down and led his party through three rooms. Again, he stopped and perched over a ladder that led into the room block below.

A low growl came from beneath and Browser made a gesture of futility. He had misjudged the air currents that wafted through the huge town. This one carried the scent down.

"Who's there?" a voice called.

Browser made a quick gesture, sending Catkin and Yucca Whip back the way they had come. He waited for a moment and said calmly, "You are now surrounded. My warriors have gone to block the exits. Who are you and what do you want here?"

"Browser? Is that you?" Steps grated on sand. "It's Old Pigeontail."

Pigeontail? The Trader? What was he doing here? Browser chewed his lip, glancing at Fire Lark, who shrugged in return. Pigeontail was known to practically everyone. For sixty sun cycles he had run the roads, trading from one end of the world to the other. Most people considered him to be a scoundrel. He charged scandalous prices for his goods.

"Where are you?" Pigeontail called up. "I'm alone, but for my dogs."

"I know you're alone. I watched you come in."

"Then why didn't you hail me, War Chief?"

In the gloom Browser could see him, a thin old man with a wrinkled face, his white hair pinned in a bun. He wore what looked like a brown tunic and carried a pack on his back. Both of the dogs growled.

"Calm your dogs," Browser said. "I heard they almost ripped old Lizard Bone's leg off up in Northern House."

"He shouldn't have been teasing them. Anyone who teases a Trader's dogs gets what he deserves." Pigeontail swung his pack off his back and rested it on the floor. To the dogs, he said, "Lie down and guard."

Both dogs immediately lay down on either side of the pack. Pigeontail's bony brown hands grasped the polished ladder, and he climbed toward Browser.

Browser backed away to allow the old man to climb into the room.

With his strange light-brown eyes, Pigeontail studied Fire Lark. "So, it's true. You've taken up with the Fire Dogs."

"Circumstance and prophecy, it would seem, have made us allies," Browser said.

Pigeontail scanned the ruined chamber. "Did you know that you're surrounded here?"

Browser nodded. "Blue Corn and her Flute Player warriors are on top at Center Place, and the White Moccasins are at High Sun House. Do you know where my warrior is? The one who was taken last night?"

Pigeontail heaved a tired breath. "I imagine that he's dead by now. Maybe in a stewpot." A pause. "Shadow got him last night, oh, it must have been a hand of time after you checked my room in War Club village."

"That was you?" Browser's eyes narrowed. "The man I checked on didn't wake."

Pigeontail smiled warily. "That's because his dogs alerted him the moment you stepped out onto the roof. He told them to be quiet while he feigned deep sleep. Had you been foolish enough to come creeping down my ladder, I would have brained you from behind, and while the dogs savaged your fallen body, I'd have dealt with the second fool to come down that ladder."

"Why are you here, in the canyon?"

"I'm on my way south, War Chief." He glanced at Fire Lark and smiled. "You'd be amazed at the wealth of turquoise, jet, and shell beads I traded for in Flowing Waters Town. I even have copper bells, but you'd know a lot more about where they came from than I would." The old man went silent and looked around the room again. "War Chief, is there somewhere more pleasant for us to talk than here in this wrecked room?"

Low growls came from below.

"Your warriors?" Pigeontail asked. "The ones sent to cut me off?"

"Catkin?" Browser called. "We're up here. It's Old Pigeontail. He says he wants to talk."

"The dogs won't bother you, Deputy Catkin," Pigeontail called down. "So long as you step wide around the pack."

Within moments Catkin and Yucca Whip climbed into the chamber. Catkin shot glances up and down Pigeontail's lean body.

"I don't suppose there's a stew on?" Pigeontail asked.

"We're a little short on rations," Browser answered.

"Then you're in luck." Pigeontail fingered his chin. "I just might have a jar filled with cornmeal. Excellent stuff, milled on Matron Blue Corn's mealing bins by practiced young maidens. It's even spiced with beeweed."

"Are we to be your guests?" Catkin asked, cocking her head suspiciously.

"No, but I might be induced to trade." Pigeontail grinned. "It's the times, you see. So many of these bits and pieces of the First People's wealth are floating around. A jar of cornmeal for perhaps a couple of those turquoise frogs? No? Well then, maybe one of those jet bracelets?"

Browser replied, "We're a war party, not a trading company, but we'll see what we can come up with to barter for dinner."

"Any news of Carved Splinter?" Catkin asked Browser.

Browser's gut knotted at the anxious look in Catkin's eyes. "Pigeontail says that Shadow has him."

Her jaw hardened. She could well guess the terrors that had befallen the young warrior. "Is there a chance he's still alive?"

"If he is," Pigeontail said emphatically, "he's in the bottom of the deepest kiva in High Sun House, surrounded by White Moccasins. And you have a reputation for not leaving people behind, War Chief." He shot a meaningful look at Catkin. "So I'm sure the White Moccasins are expecting you."

Pigeontail studied the Fire Dogs again, evaluating, before he continued, "With enough brave warriors, you might fight your way in there, War Chief, but I can promise you, you won't fight your way out."

S tone Ghost eased up to the door and leaned against the plastered wall to listen. He'd seen Straighthorn enter the chamber fifty heartbeats ago. The scent of pack rat urine burned his nose. He looked up and saw sticky streaks of it flowing down the wall to his left.

"I don't know," Bone Walker said.

Straighthorn's voice had gone low and threatening. "If you know something, you'd better tell me. Right now. That was you, wasn't it? In the rock shelter with Redcrop?"

Feet shuffled and Stone Ghost heard Bone Walker sucking on her lip.

"Do you remember Redcrop?" Straighthorn asked with an ache in his voice.

Redcrop had been killed by White Moccasins right after the kiva fire in Longtail village. Straighthorn had loved her very much.

Straighthorn said, "Redcrop. She was the girl who was tied up with you in the rock shelter near Longtail village. Do you remember her?"

Bone Walker made a high-pitched sound, as though straining to get away from a hard hand.

Straighthorn heaved an angry sigh and said, "I'm sorry. Maybe you aren't the same girl. Maybe I just want you to be so that I can drive a stiletto through your heart the way the White Moccasins did Redcrop's heart."

Bone Walker's voice was a tiny tremor: *"My heart? You want my heart?"*

"No, I'm sorry. I didn't mean to frighten you. It's just that I—"

In a choking sob, Bone Walker said, "If you kill my heart, I won't be able to look inside it!"

"What do you mean, look inside it?"

"I mean first. I have to look in it first."

Stone Ghost squeezed his eyes closed and listened to the blood surge in his ears. He was growing to love this child. It would shred his souls if she—

"Do you know who Two Hearts is?" Straighthorn asked.

Bone Walker didn't answer.

"He's a very powerful witch. We are trying to find him so we can kill him."

A soft suffocating sound filled the chamber, and Stone Ghost realized that Bone Walker must be crying.

"I'm going to kill him myself," Straighthorn assured her. "With this stiletto on my belt. Do you see this?"

Bone Walker sobbed.

Stone Ghost clamped his jaw. He knew he should stop this, but he needed to hear her answers.

"What about Shadow Woman?" Straighthorn pressed. "Is she your mother? I'm going to kill her, too. She's a monster. A hideous animal disguised as a human."

The little girl stuttered, "S-sometimes she has b-bead days!"

"Bead days? What's that?"

Bone Walker said, "B-bad days."

Straighthorn's cape rustled, as though he'd stood up. "Do you know Shadow Woman? If she's your mother, why hasn't she come to look for you? Maybe she doesn't care about you."

Stone Ghost peered around the door into the room. Bone Walker stood with her head tipped far back, staring up at Straighthorn. She had her tiny fists clenched at her sides.

Straighthorn glared down at her. He'd cut his hair in mourning for Redcrop and the irregular black locks framed his thin face and hooked nose. "Just remember. If you know anything, you'd better come and tell me."

He turned to leave, and his threadbare red cape swung around him.

Stone Ghost backed out of the room.

As Straighthorn passed him, Stone Ghost gripped his arm and motioned for Straighthorn to follow him. Straighthorn's fiery brown eyes tightened, but he nodded and followed Stone Ghost down the hall to a nearby chamber.

When they stood alone in the musty darkness, Stone Ghost said, "Who told you the child might know Two Hearts and Shadow Woman?"

Straighthorn gave Stone Ghost a disgruntled look. "Obsidian. She said that you questioned her about it. That you thought the child might be related to them."

"Did Obsidian say the child was related to them?"

Straighthorn frowned. "No. She just mentioned the possibility."

Stone Ghost smiled in a grandfatherly way and put a hand on Straighthorn's shoulder. "Thank you, Straighthorn. If she tells you anything else, I would appreciate it if you would let me know."

"Of course, Elder."

Straighthorn bowed respectfully and left.

Stone Ghost braced his aching knees and listened to the youth's steps echo down the long hallway.

So, Obsidian wishes the child dead. Why?

Obsidian knew how much Straighthorn had loved Redcrop. Just planting the thought that Bone Walker might be related to Redcrop's murderers could have been enough. Fortunately, today, it wasn't. But who knew about tomorrow? Who else had Obsidian told?

Stone Ghost hobbled back down the hall and reentered the room where Bone Walker had been standing. It took him several moments to find her. She lay in the darkest corner, covered with fallen stones she must have collected from the floor. She had her back turned to Stone Ghost.

"Bone Walker?" he called softly. "Are you all right?"

The stones rattled, then one hit the wall, hard.

He walked over and sat down next to her. All he could see beneath the stones was a sliver of her blue dress and a lock of her long black hair.

"Rocks have souls, you know," he repeated her words. "Be careful who you hurt."

The stones rattled again.

Then her dirty hand snaked from beneath the stones and reached for the rock she'd thrown.

She dragged it back and petted it gently.

Stone Ghost smiled. Perhaps there was hope.

SANTA FE

Dusty watched Maureen thoughtfully poke at her lamb-stuffed poblano pepper, shoving the last bits around her plate with her fork.

The Coyote Café brimmed with patrons. The clatter of silverware and dishes melded with the background murmur of animated conversations. He had led her up the green cement stairs from Water Street and into the tan interior with its rounded fireplace, north-facing windows, and ornate wooden reception desk.

Her eyes fixed on the wooden animals who lived on the hood over the open kitchen. The howling coyotes with their kitsch neckerchiefs seemed to hold her attention.

"Something you'd like to tell me?"

She looked at him. "Actually I was just thinking that you're the luckiest man alive."

He speared his last cube of tenderloin and ate it. "I'd be curious to know how you figure that."

"The greatest stroke of luck in your life occurred when your mother abandoned you."

Dusty leaned back in his chair and wiped his mouth with his napkin. "It didn't feel that way at the time."

"No, I'm sure it didn't. Nonetheless."

Dusty wiped his hands and refolded the napkin.

Maureen had a strange, almost angry look in her eyes as she said, "I imagine that Agent Nichols is about finished wringing him out by now. I want my chance next."

"You think Hawsworth did it?"

He placed the folded napkin on the table.

"We'll know if Nichols arrests him." Maureen rested her fork on her plate, as though her hunger had vanished.

She wore a pale blue sweater, and her long braid seemed to pick up the hues, glinting azure in the dim cafe light. She leaned forward to brace her elbows on the table. "Ruth Ann could have done it, too, Dusty. Something about her just isn't right, and she's certainly not telling us everything. Something happened back in the past. Something between her, Dale, and Carter."

"You mean besides a little fornication and frolic?"

Maureen ignored his attempt at humor. "Your mother said something that's been bothering me. She said that Carter had his own witch."

"You don't *have* a witch, Maureen. They have you."

Maureen picked up her honey-coated blue corn bread, and aimed it at him. "She made it sound like the witch was Carter's private teacher."

Dusty pushed his plate across the marble tabletop. "Well, it's possible. Hawsworth is an expert on the subject. Somebody had to show him the ropes."

"Yes, but let's not forget that Ruth Ann's first article was on witchcraft in the Southwest. Did Carter's witch show her the ropes, as well?"

He thought she was beautiful when her black eyes turned cool and accusing.

"I wouldn't doubt it," he said, wanting to discuss anything but this, and added, "Let's order dessert."

All through his cactus mousse custard he pondered what a man would have to do to have his own "private" witch?

He was still thinking of that as he drove up Canyon Road.

Maureen silently watched the galleries pass, then as they neared the turn off to his trailer, said, "You're better than all of them, Dusty. I don't know how, but you came out a better human being."

"I came out fine because of Dale."

"Yes." She nodded. "But Ruth Ann made a good point. She said that Dale could never deal with a woman on an equal basis."

"That's nonsense. Dale dealt with females just fine. He thought you were the finest physical anthropologist in the world."

"But I was part of his team, Dusty. Don't you see? Did you ever know him to work for anyone else? Dale was always the boss. Ruth Ann says that's why he never married. He couldn't maintain a relationship, no matter how much he was attracted to a woman."

"Yeah, well," he said. "I've been called the 'Two-Month Wonder' by a number of women—because that's how long they could stand me."

"I've stood you for three months," she noted.

"Yes, but have you enjoyed it?"

She gave him an amused look. "Acrually...yes. Very much."

He smiled and pulled into the drive that led to his trailer. Stopping beside Dale's truck, he shut off the engine and looked at her. "That's because we're friends, Maureen. Not lovers. Something changes when you go to bed with a woman."

"I wouldn't know. I've never gone to bed with a woman."

"Well I have, and believe me, something changes. They get crazy."

"You mean you get crazy."

Dusty opened his door. "Yeah, well, maybe."

She got out of the Bronco and closed the door. "The point I was trying to make is that unlike Dale, you can work with women as equals."

Dusty watched her march toward the trailer door. "You think I treat women as equals?" He walked up behind her, searching for the key. "You're the first female to say so."

He stood behind her, close enough that he could smell her delicate scent on the evening breeze. Finally, he found the shiny new key, unlocked the door, and flicked on the lights. As he headed for the kitchen, he asked, "Coffee?"

She set her purse by the door. The way she was looking at him made his nerves begin to vibrate. The chilly air had brought color to her cheeks and her black eyes seemed to be stirring with some emotion he couldn't understand. Dear God, she was beautiful.

"Can I ask a question?" her voice had lowered, softening.

"Yeah, sure."

"Did you ever hear about your father being impotent?"

That caught him flat-footed, one hand on the refrigerator handle. "What?"

"Did you ever hear that?"

He turned and braced a hand on the kitchen counter. "No, but who would tell me?"

"Ruth Ann claimed Samuel was impotent."

Dusty hesitated, thinking about that, then turned back to the refrigerator. "She hated him, Maureen."

Maureen shrugged out of her coat and went to stand before the picture of Samuel Stewart. "Not at first. From what I can gather, your father was a kind and sensitive idealist. He probably fell head-over-heels for Ruth Ann. She was beautiful, sexy, and available. She must have seemed like a dream come true until she grew tired of him and the Southwest."

"And me," Dusty added pointedly.

Maureen seemed to be lost in the photograph of Sam beside the pickup. "She must have made his life a living hell."

"And everyone else's life who ever knew her."

Maureen walked to the table and slid onto a chair. "When she talked about his impotence this morning, Dusty, she meant it. It wasn't just spite."

Dusty pulled a bottle of stout from the refrigerator and pried off the cap. The rich scent of Guinness made him feel better. He took a long drink, then said, "I can understand how a woman like her would make a man impotent."

The lines around Maureen's mouth deepened. "Poor Sam. She broke him, and then she left him in the dust."

Dusty set his Guinness down and reached for the coffee. As he spooned grounds into the basket, he said, "It's more than that—she killed him. Maybe she wasn't in the room when Dad stuffed his finger into the light socket, but she might as well have been."

Maureen turned her level eyes on him. "Maybe she regretted that— and wanted to be there when she killed Dale."

T he fire popped, and tentative flames licked around the curved bottom of the corrugated cooking pot. Flickering light illuminated the faces of the people crouched anxiously around the walls, their eyes on the pot. The delightful smell of boiling blue corn mixed tauntingly with the antelope bone butter. Catkin's stomach twisted around itself in anticipation.

Stone Ghost sat in the rear of the chamber with the little girl's head in his lap. Half asleep, she had her corn-husk doll clutched in her hands. Stone Ghost had spread his feather cape over the girl. He must have been cold, but he seemed content.

Browser settled himself between Catkin and Old Pigeontail. She was intimately aware of his thigh pressed against hers. She had to fight the urge to reach down and touch him.

"It's an interesting problem, War Chief," Pigeontail said. "You are boxed by two larger parties." He cast his appraising glance across the room to where Obsidian hunched with her back to the wall, speaking with Stone Ghost. She had washed her hair to its usual gloss.

"Are you trying to give me advice, Elder?" Browser asked.

"If it were me, I would wait until nightfall, drop into the drainage, and follow it away. By morning I would be long gone."

Catkin asked suddenly, "Elder, why are you here? You always seem to show up at the most inappropriate times."

Pigeontail smiled. "I'm curious, that's all. I would see the people brave enough to corner Two Hearts in his own lair."

Conversation stopped as all eyes turned to Pigeontail.

Catkin said, "How do you know this is his lair?"

Pigeontail refilled his teacup from the pot at the edge of the coals and swirled the liquid, as though examining it. "The man you knew as Elder Springbank committed terrible crimes at Longtail village. You unmasked him there, but he lived here for many sun cycles before that. Isn't it an odd coincidence that you have come here, to this place, just after Gray Thunder's murder, and just after word has gone out that Two Hearts seeks the heart of the beautiful Obsidian?" He glanced meaningfully across the room.

Obsidian's dark eyes widened.

"How do you know that?" Browser asked.

Pigeontail opened his hands. "I am a Trader, War Chief. I go a great many places and hear a great many things. I have been doing this for more seasons than anyone alive. Oh, I have traded with the White Moccasins for sun cycles, just as I have traded with the Mogollon and the Hohokam. I go everywhere and speak to everyone. I am alive today because I keep people's secrets."

"But not the secret that Elder Springbank wishes Obsidian's heart," Catkin said.

Pigeontail gave her an amused look. "It is not a secret, Deputy Catkin. Besides, the White Moccasins trust me."

"And you were just there," Stone Ghost said from the rear.

Pigeontail turned to smile at him. "Yes. I was." He glanced at Obsidian again. "You will be glad to know, incidentally, that Two Hearts says if he can't get your heart he will have to find another relative to provide the heart."

Obsidian lifted her chin haughtily. "Then he should take Shadow's worm-ridden heart. It would fit him well."

The little girl jerked upright in Stone Ghost's lap. Utter terror twisted her young face. Stone Ghost said something soft to her and stroked her hair.

Catkin glared at Pigeontail. "You just visited the White Moccasins? What's the matter with you? Don't you care that they killed, beheaded, and stripped the meat from the people at Aspen village? Or that Springbank burned half of our children to death in Longtail village?"

Catkin started to rise, but Browser's hand stopped her.

"Wait," he whispered.

Pigeontail just sipped his tea, apparently unflustered. After a moment of silence he said, "Catkin, I have lived over seventy summers. In that time I have seen atrocity after atrocity."

He cocked his head, his eyes, like ambered pine, on hers. "What one might consider a vicious and evil massacre is considered by the perpetrators as a just and morally correct response to aggression. Look around you. Your people have always considered the Fire Dogs to be cowardly fiends. Yet, here you are, sharing their companionship, fighting side by side, the slights and insults of the past forgotten for the needs of the present. One person's fiend is another's hero."

"Yes, but Two Hearts is a witch, Pigeontail," Browser said. "We've always hunted down witches."

Pigeontail raised his hands. "Yes, you have. You've hunted them because you're not witches yourselves.

Listen to me, I can only tell you the rules under which I must live as a Trader. I take no one's side. I tell only what people want told. By following those rules I have stayed alive all these sun cycles. It is not pleasant to deal with friends who murder other friends, but it is how I must live."

He paused, holding Catkin's gaze. "Would you have me leave here knowing I could go to Center Place and tell Blue Corn that you are in Kettle Town? Or would you have me go to High Sun, my head full of things to tell the White Moccasins?"

"I would smack your brains out," Catkin said, "before I let you take one step from here."

"Then you understand, Deputy Catkin." Pigeontail smiled disarmingly.

Stone Ghost rose and hobbled forward unsteadily. When he lowered himself to the floor beside Pigeontail, the old Trader winced.

Stone Ghost's thin white hair blazed in the firelight. "But it brings up a good question," Stone Ghost said. "I have known you since you were a boy and have never seen you act brashly."

"Me? Brash?" Pigeontail asked.

Stone Ghost smiled, but it only reached his lips. His eyes remained keen and unamused. "Surely you know that we are in great danger, and that by coming here, you are in great danger. Why take the chance?"

Pigeontail's brows arched. "Momentous things are happening, old friend. You are in the middle of them. I would see what happens." He chuckled. "Look at me! Have you ever heard of a Trader who lived as long as I have? On rare occasions, yes, but look at me. I can still run the roads. My old bones and joints continue to carry me on my journeys. Perhaps it is the will of the gods that I have been to so many places and talked to so many people.

But I can't go on forever. I feel the stiffness and my back hurts every time I shoulder a pack. I have seen so much in my time, have watched our peoples through the coming of the coughing sickness, and watched them waste into death. I have seen the increasing warfare, the growth of the Katsinas' People, and the rise of the Flute Player warriors. I have walked through the ruins of once thriving towns, kicked the unburied bones of friends out of the way to clear my path. I have seen the rebirth of the White Moccasins, and now word that the First People still live is spreading across the land. Gray Thunder, a prophet from the Fire Dogs, has been murdered in Blue Corn's Sunrise House, and Mogollon and Straight Path warriors hunt the old witch Two Hearts in retaliation." His smile was crafty. "I may not live much longer, but what a story I will tell on my deathbed."

Stone Ghost rubbed his hands together. "Then, I take it you have forgiven me for the murder of your brother?"

Catkin started, watching Stone Ghost and Pigeontail with renewed interest.

"My brother did what he thought he had to. As did you, Stone Ghost." Pigeontail seemed to be staring into the past. "I told you, I, too, have to live by the rules. Tell me this: In the same situation, would you do it again?"

Stone Ghost stared down at his hands and nodded. "I, too, have had a long life, Trader. His death taught me a great many lessons." Stone Ghost filled his lungs. "You should know, if anything happens to me, that he hangs in the bag—the one made of Hohokam cotton with red stitching— from my roof pole at Smoking Mirror Butte. If I don't get back, find him. Take him home. And tell him I will see him in the afterlife."

Pigeontail's eyes had narrowed, and the sudden tension could be felt, straining the air.

The skull in the bag? Catkin remembered with a flash

of inspiration. Crooked Nose! She could see Stone Ghost as he had been that night, snow drifting in through the holes in his roof while he cradled a polished skull in his lap.

"Crooked Nose says you saw the Blue God." The old man's words rolled around her head.

"He knew!" Catkin looked up, aware that all eyes were on her. Had she spoken aloud?

"Knew what?" Browser asked.

"Crooked Nose," she said, and turned her attention to Stone Ghost. "How did he know?"

Pigeontail had shifted, fire in his eyes. "What are you talking about?"

"He told you, Elder. Remember? That night in your house under Smoking Mirror Butte. He told you I had seen the Blue God."

Obsidian couldn't help hissing as she drew in her breath.

"Yes, I remember. You said you didn't believe in her," Stone Ghost reminded gently.

Catkin tightened her fist. "That was a long time ago, Elder. Back when the world was much simpler."

"You only thought so, Catkin." Stone Ghost smiled. "Now it flies around you like a whirlwind."

"Why did you come here now?" Browser asked suddenly. "You could have gone any direction after you left Flowing Waters Town. You carry some of the First People's wealth that you traded for in Flowing Waters Town. Why bring it south? To trade it back to the White Moccasins?"

"That is another reason, yes, but mostly I was curious about Gray Thunder's murder." Pigeontail looked at White Cone, asking in fluent Mogollon, "Bow Elder? Did you do that to stop him from spreading heresy?"

"We had no hand in Gray Thunder's death." White

Cone lifted his right hand. "After he prophesied his death, I would have cut off this arm to have taken him alive back to my kiva. His death came from outside."

Stone Ghost said, "Given the manner of it, he was killed by Two Hearts, and most likely Shadow. Two Hearts and Ash Girl killed the warrior Whiproot in the same manner in Talon Town."

"Yes, I remember." Pigeontail nodded.

"Shadow had an ally in Flowing Waters Town," Stone Ghost said. "Someone had to pass her through the sentries."

"We were very closely watched," White Cone said. "A woman approaching Gray Thunder's room would have been seen. When this is finished here, we must go back and question the guard who watched Gray Thunder's room that night."

Pigeontail said, "Whatever he knew, he has taken it down to the Land of the Dead. That is why Blue Corn pursues you. Her guard was killed the night you left. She is rabid to find you. To avenge his death."

Stone Ghost bowed his head and stared into the fire. "Then perhaps it was not Shadow Woman who killed the prophet, but someone else."

"But she was there, Elder," Catkin said. "I *saw* her."

"Yes," he murmured. "Fortuitous, wasn't it?"

"I don't understand, Uncle." Browser looked perplexed. "Gray Thunder's body was treated exactly the way my warrior's was at Talon Town. The details were the same right down to the tracks in the blood."

"That only means that the real murderer was cunning."

"Why?" Catkin asked in frustration.

Stone Ghost looked at Pigeontail. "Tell me, when Whiproot was murdered in Talon Town, was it talked about? You were there soon afterward, did you bear the tale?"

"Every Trader in the region did. I, myself, was taken into the room later by Peavine. She showed me how he was found, how his arms and legs were. The bloodstains were all over the walls. I told as many people as I could."

The orphan girl sat up, and Stone Ghost turned to look at her. Her freshly washed face made her huge dark eyes seem even larger, like black bottomless pits.

Stone Ghost didn't take his eyes from her when he said, "I think you had best prepare, Nephew. Given the fact that Pigeontail walked in here in bright daylight, Blue Corn's scouts must know we are here."

"The White Moccasins, too," Catkin reminded and gave Pigeontail a look of sheer loathing.

"I shall say nothing," Pigeontail replied. "You have my word on that."

Catkin said, "It's already too late."

"Yes. It is." Browser nodded wearily. "Which means our quest to corner Two Hearts in his own lair will have to wait."

"Why is that?" Pigeontail asked.

Browser bent his head. "Because very soon we are going to be attacked. You like to carry stories, Trader. Well, tonight, you will either see me defeat two large parties of warriors with my handful of Fire Dogs, or you shall leave here with the story of our deaths."

Pigeontail grinned in a way that turned Catkin's stomach. He said, "Either way, I assure you, it will be heroic."

SANTA FE

Concentration had never been a big problem for Dusty. But this morning it was. He'd already overcooked the eggs. He stood over the stove, head wreathed in the aroma of eggs, green chilis, and his homemade Anasazi and black bean refritos. But his mind drifted. He used a spoon to taste, making sure that the right mixture of fresh cilantro, cumin, and chopped white onion had been achieved. With the spatula he eased the eggs onto the corn tortillas and spooned hot salsa over them. He crumbled cheddar onto the whole and dished refritos onto the side of the plate. There. Done. Even if the eggs were hard as rocks. The coffee had just begun to perk.

The sound of the shower had stopped ten minutes ago, but he'd yet to see Maureen.

He glanced at his foldout couch, his bed from last night already stowed, then turned to study the hallway that led to his bedroom. Would he ever be able to sleep there again without thinking of Maureen's body?

He sighed and poured two hot cups of coffee. He set them on the kitchen table, then glanced at his watch. Eight-thirty. They'd slept late, and it was a long drive to Chaco, especially pulling a trailer on those roads.

Dusty cupped a hand to his mouth and called, "Maureen? Breakfast is on the table."

"Be there in just a second!"

As Dusty reached for a bottle of hot sauce, he heard a car pull in. Through the louvered kitchen window, he watched Sam Nichols step out of a government Dodge.

"We've got company," he called down the hallway. "Agent Nichols is here."

By the time he opened the door, Nichols was climbing onto his rickety porch. "You're out early," he greeted. "Come on in. Had breakfast?"

Nichols gave him a thin smile and looked curiously around his trailer. The place seemed to shock him.

"Well, it's homey," Dusty defended. "And it was Dad's. And yeah, I know, it's not much."

"Upper Canyon Road," Nichols added. "Driving up here I had, well, a different idea."

Dusty smiled and stepped out of the way to let Nichols into the trailer. "Right. Most people do. So, if you ever get called in to investigate my murder, start with the lawyer next door. He's getting desperate enough to hire a hitman to get me out of here."

Nichols cocked his head, his mind chewing over something that had apparently occurred to him.

"Uh, you didn't say anything about breakfast. I can throw another egg—"

"No, no." Nichols shook his head. "Smells great though. I'd take a cup of coffee."

"You got it." Dusty walked back to the kitchen and poured another cup. As he delivered it, he said, "Have a seat," and pointed to the couch.

Nichols remained standing, but he sipped the coffee. "Have you heard from Rhone?"

"Sylvia? Not today. Why? Should I have?"

Nichols's one good eye missed nothing. "Not necessarily."

Maureen stepped out of the bathroom and made her way down the hall. Her braided hair was still damp and she looked wonderful. Dusty stopped short to enjoy her, skin damp and flushed. She wore blue jeans and a black turtleneck.

"Good morning, Agent Nichols." Maureen shook his hand and turned to the breakfast plates. "My god, that smells wonderful. I'm starving."

"Dig in," Dusty told her. "Don't let it get cold."

Nichols propped an elbow on the file cabinet and sipped. "Good coffee. Go ahead and eat."

"You're sure you don't want some?" Dusty indicated his plate as he sat. "It would just take a minute."

"I ate," Nichols said. "Thanks for the leads on both Dr. Sullivan and Dr. Hawsworth. Sullivan pretty well expected me to drop in on her. She's moved from La Fonda to the Loretto, says it's much nicer. Hawsworth is still at the Hilton. I assume that after our little talk, he's not going anywhere except back to his house in Taos."

"Any arrests?" Maureen asked, trying to be casual as she fished for information.

Nichols scowled down into his coffee. "Look, before we can make an arrest, we have to have a case. So far, we can't build a case on what we have."

Dusty balanced *huevos* on his fork. "Ruth Ann and Carter both say it has something to do with the past." Dusty had noticed that people who knew her forty years ago called her Ruth, but he would always think of her as Ruth Ann. Somehow it sounded more menacing.

"Dr. Sullivan said that Carter had his own witch."

Maureen took a drink of coffee. "Maybe he'd tell you who—"

"Way ahead of you, Dr. Cole. The guy's name was Cochiti. He died over a year ago. Kind of mysterious circumstances. Coroner's report said he fell down a canyon slope. They attributed all the bruises and the cranial trauma to the fall."

Dusty lifted his gaze to pin Nichols. "It was out on the reservation, right?"

"Yeah. Place called Tsegi Canyon."

Maureen turned suddenly. "Isn't that traditional?"

"Yes."

"What's traditional?" Nichols asked.

Dusty used a piece of tortilla to scoop up eggs and chili. "The way they take care of witches. In the old days, they stoned them to death and buried them. Western law has problems with such doings, so today, suspected witches 'fall' off the rimrock."

"I see." Nichols stared into his coffee. "Hawsworth was in Taos, with witnesses, when it happened. We couldn't find a link."

"What about his calls to Dale?" Maureen asked. "Could he explain them?"

"Hawsworth says he was getting faxes. Threatening messages from someone called Kwewur. He says he thought Dr. Robertson was sending them, and he called him to get him to stop." Nichols sipped the coffee. "We checked the phone records. Nothing conclusive."

"He told me," Maureen said, "that they were sent to his home from a hotel, the El Dorado in Santa Fe."

Nichols blinked. "What else did he tell you?" He set his coffee aside as he pulled out his notebook.

Dusty finished his breakfast and went to wash the plate as Maureen outlined her conversations with Hawsworth and Ruth Ann.

When she was done, Nichols watched Dusty dry his plate and put it in the cupboard. "So, tell me, Stewart, what do you really think they're going to find when they dig up that site out there at Chaco?"

Dusty reached out. "Maureen, if you're finished, hand me your plate."

As Dusty washed it, he said, "I think we're going to find the reason Dale was killed. But before you get your hopes up, I want you to prepare yourself."

"What for?"

"I don't think the evidence is going to make any sense to you, Agent Nichols, and I doubt it will be something you can take to a prosecuting attorney."

"Such as?" Nichols asked.

"I think we're going to find a witch." Dusty dried Maureen's plate and stacked it atop his in the cupboard. He'd been finding witches in every archaeological site he'd dug in the past two years. They seemed to be his lot in life. "Alive or dead, he's there."

"We're back to witches again." Nichols sighed. "Put there by Dr. Robertson's killer, I suppose?"

Dusty shook his head. "No, it'll be prehistoric. But he's there."

"How do you know?" Maureen asked.

Dusty gave her a solemn look. "There was an old pot hunter's hole. Do you remember?"

Maureen frowned. "Yes."

"I think the person who killed Dale dug that hole. I think he found something in there that tied him and Dale together, and I think I can—"

"Sylvia Rhone," Nichols said out of the blue. "How long has it been since you've talked to her?"

Dusty shook his head, puzzled by the abrupt shift in conversation. "Yesterday, why?"

Nichols pushed his glasses up on his nose. "How well do you know her?"

"Very well. She's a good friend."

"How long since you've seen her?"

"I saw her at Dale's wake in the office." Dusty leaned across the counter. "What is this about, Nichols?"

"We can't confirm her whereabouts on the weekend of Dr. Robertson's death."

"Well, I can." Dusty straightened up. "She was in Colorado doing a pipeline survey."

Nichols nodded. "That's what she told us. But no one saw her out there."

"Of course not, it was Saturday, and she was in the middle of nowhere."

Nichols seemed to be thinking about that. "She had a gasoline and dinner receipt from Cuba, New Mexico. Does that make sense to you?"

"Sure. It's on the way to the project area."

Nichols lifted a finger and pointed it at Dusty's heart. "It's also the closest town to where Dr. Robertson was killed out at Chaco."

Dusty folded his arms like a shield over his chest. "Coincidence, Nichols. I have a work order in the office from the pipeline company. She was supposed to be up there."

Nichols took a sip of his coffee, and his eyes drifted around the trailer as though cataloging every spiderweb that draped the windows. "To your knowledge, did Robertson ever have an affair with Rhone? You know, a field camp fling?"

Dusty's eyes turned to stone. "Dale never had an affair with a student, period. Why?"

"Just wondering. Michall Jefferson hired Rhone to help with the dig, so I did some research. She has an extensive file with the Social Services department office in Idaho."

"Yeah, so?" Over the years, Sylvia had told him a lot about her childhood. She'd spent the first eight years of her life being shunted from one foster home to another, and not all of her "parents" had been guardians.

Nichols took a few seconds to absorb Dusty's hostile tone, then said, "You think she needs your protection?"

An odd squirming sensation invaded Dusty's chest. "Well, if anyone needs my protection, it's Sylvia. If you're thinking she's a suspect, forget it."

Nichols ran his thumb over the handle of his cup. "You and Rhone seem very close, why?"

"I don't know," he responded defensively, "maybe because we both had screwed-up childhoods. Sometimes I think she knows me better than I know myself."

"Uh-huh. And do you know her better than she knows herself?"

Dusty stared angrily at Nichols. "You'd have to ask her."

"Did you know, for example, that Rhone tried to murder one of her foster fathers in his sleep? She used a pair of scissors. Rhone claimed she didn't even remember the event. The Social Services people jerked her out of the home immediately, of course, but it took a long time before they could find her another home."

"How old was she?" Dusty asked.

"Four."

Dusty nodded, remembering Sylvia telling him a story about one of her "fathers" in Idaho. The man had sneaked into her room every night for months when Sylvia had been four years old. All Sylvia remembered was the feel of his mouth over hers, and his stinking smell, like gin mixed with saltwater, but the description had been enough to turn Dusty's stomach.

Dusty said, "Maybe he deserved it."

Nichols smiled, as though he'd just confirmed one of his pet theories, and it irked Dusty. Especially since he didn't know what the theory was.

Nichols said, "Let's change the subject for a moment. Weren't you ever curious about your father's family?"

Dusty felt oddly as though he was being methodically bludgeoned. Either Nichols was very good at his job, or he was a sadist.

"Sure I was. Dale didn't want to talk about them, but I used to ask. He told me he had called Dad's folks, and they didn't want me. He'd asked if they'd fight his taking custody of me, and they said no. Dale ended up as my legal guardian. End of story."

"But you never called them? Never wrote letters?" Nichols asked.

"What for? Sure, I thought about them sometimes, but my family was Dale. They didn't want me. I didn't want them. What could I possibly have in common with a bunch of Philadelphia rich people?"

"Probably nothing," Nichols said, "but if Dr. Sullivan ever brings them up, tell me about it."

"Right." Dusty frowned. "Why should she? As I understand it, she never even met them."

Nichols glanced at the rolled sleeping bags and bags of food stacked by the door. "I take it you're headed for Chaco Canyon?"

"As soon as we lock up here." Maureen stood.

"I wanted to remind you, Dusty"—Nichols fixed him with his good eye— "that your position is a little delicate out there. You are not to compromise that dig in any way. Do you understand me? If you so much as touch anything, my team will consider it to be obstruction of an investigation. I'll file those charges and slap you in front of a judge's bench before you can whistle."

"I understand."

"See that you don't *forget* in the heat of a discovery."

Dusty turned on the hot water and let it run on his hands while he thought about Sylvia, and the demons that haunted her sleep. As steam curled up around his face, Dusty said, "Tell me something, will you, Nichols? If I can compromise the investigation so easily, why are you allowing me to go out there at all?"

Nichols walked over and stood across the counter from Dusty. The wind outside had blown wisps of his thick black hair over his horn-rimmed glasses. "That's simple, Stewart. Killers really do love to return to the scene of the crime—it gives them some perverted kick—and Hawsworth told me that he believes everyone from that time is in danger."

"Yeah, so?" Dusty asked.

Nichols put his empty coffee cup on the counter, and his eyes glinted. "So, either you're the killer, or you're bait for the killer."

Dusty felt suddenly hollow, floating. He heard his mouth say, "Okay."

"Good. One last question."

"What?"

He could see Nichols's square jaw grinding beneath his shaved cheeks. "You've been on a lot of excavations with Rhone. Does she sleepwalk?"

Dusty didn't answer. He was remembering the time they'd made camp on a mesa top, and she'd almost walked off the cliff at midnight. "Maybe. How should I know?"

Nichols nodded as though he knew Dusty was lying. He turned away and seemed to be looking absently at the door.

Dusty lifted both of his wet hands in a gesture of surrender. "Nichols, listen, I don't care what you think, Sylvia is not capable of murder. I *know* her."

Nichols tucked his notebook back in his coat pocket and shifted as though not certain he should respond to that.

"I'm not accusing her of consciously doing anything wrong, Stewart. Abused children often do things they don't remember. It's as though their young minds were shattered by unendurable pain, and to protect themselves they had to sever the neural pathways to the memories. But the memories are still there, and sometimes, late at night, they peek out. The adult does anything she has to to shove them down and get that door locked again." He opened the door. "I'll see you out at the crime scene."

Nichols left.

Dusty braced his hands on the counter and closed his eyes. In an agonized whisper, he said, "I'm starting to hate that guy."

13

Browser lay on his stomach in the collapsed remains of a fourth-floor room, watching as Pigeontail walked south across the flats toward War Club village. His two dogs trotted at his heels.

"Why did you let him go?" Catkin asked from where she crouched under the slanting roof. "He'll tell everyone where we are."

"I let him go because it doesn't matter who he tells."

Catkin frowned. "Why not?"

"Because by now the White Moccasins know exactly where we are. Carved Splinter will have told them."

Catkin's grip tightened on the hilt of her war club. They both knew the effect of torture. A man would shout out anything if his tormentor was cutting the flesh from his body and dropping it into a cooking pot before his eyes.

Catkin whispered, "Then the White Moccasins may have been watching us for some time, probably from the south rim. Pigeontail's visit here was just the final confirmation."

"Yes." Browser nodded. "They will be here just after dusk. As soon as they can approach without being seen.

They will want to make sure we don't escape under the cover of darkness."

"What about Blue Corn's warriors?"

"I think Blue Corn will be unsure. All they saw was an old Trader and his dogs walk across the canyon to Kettle Town. Then, after a couple of hands time, he walked back."

He ducked under the sagging roof and walked to the ladder. Climbing down, he led her through the labyrinth of passageways to the main room. There, in the crackling light of the fire, Stone Ghost and White Cone talked. Obsidian was tending the fire. She turned her large eyes on Browser and smiled at him as they entered. Several of the Mogollon lay wrapped in their blankets, sleeping.

"Nephew?" Stone Ghost asked.

Browser glanced around the chamber. "Where's the little girl?" He was accustomed to seeing her with Stone Ghost.

"I don't know," Stone Ghost said, and his wrinkles rearranged into sad lines. "She disappeared right after Pigeontail left. I looked for her, but I haven't found her yet."

Obsidian said, "I thought it was strange that we could be cooking and she wouldn't be hovering over the pot like a starving weasel."

Stone Ghost gave her a murderous look.

Browser said, "If she's not back by the time we have to move, she will have to take her chances."

Stone Ghost bowed his white head and nodded. "I know, Nephew."

Browser turned his attention to White Cone. "Elder? I need your warriors."

White Cone's black eyes tensed. "You've had my warriors at your disposal for days now. That is why Carved Splinter is missing."

"Yes, Elder, I'm sorry. He was a fine warrior. But since he vanished, your people are more leery of my orders. In our present situation I must take some desperate measures to save us. I was hoping you might acknowledge my authority."

"A great War Chief should be able to achieve respect without another's help. You once had a reputation as a great War Chief. Recently, people have said you lost your Power, that the gods abandoned you."

Browser felt the sting of humiliation. "Elder, I cannot always know the ways of the gods. My concern is how to defeat two different enemies at the same time. As to the belief that I have lost my abilities and Power, well, Elder, I'm counting on just that."

"How will you do this?"

Browser knotted anxious fingers around the hilt of his belted war club. "I have heard that the Society of the Bow produces warriors who can kill with the silence and swiftness of Falcon. Is it true?"

White Cone's eyes were keen and alert. "It is." The old man aimed a finger at the empty mat beside him. "Sit down and tell me *exactly* what you plan."

The Coleman lantern illuminated the interior of the battered old camp trailer with soft yellow light. Maureen slid into the booth with a steaming cup of tea, forcing Sylvia Rhone and Michall Jefferson to slide around the table. They didn't even seem to notice. Both were engrossed in discussing how they would open the excavation tomorrow.

Dusty stood in the kitchen, making a lettuce and tomato salad. His blue eyes were a million miles away, probably walking some trail with Dale. Though he'd yet to display any real grief, she could see it in his slow, careful movements, as though if he didn't concentrate, he wouldn't even be able to toss a salad.

Maureen ran her hand over the scarred tabletop and thought back to other times when she had sat with Dale in this little booth. He would always fill her memories. She could see him as he had been at the 10K3 site, and then at Pueblo Animas: his wiry gray hair matted from his fedora hat and his bushy mustache curled with his smile. He was peering at her with knowing brown eyes from the past. At this little square table, Dale had been at his imperial best.

Some of the most important artifacts in the Southwest had rested upon this vinyl surface. Now it supported a plate of baked beans and tamales: the canned variety warmed in a skillet. To her amazement, a boxed chocolate cake sat to her left—compliments of Dusty's shopping expertise and Safeway.

Sylvia shoved a lock of shoulder-length brown hair behind her ears, and her green eyes pinched as she listened to Michall line out the excavation units. "So, we're going to start digging right on the spot where Dale was killed?"

"That's what the FBI wants," Michall said. She'd pinned her red hair on top of her head with bobby pins, most of which were about to fall out. Red curls drooped around her ears.

Sylvia sat back in the booth. "Okay, but I'd prefer to work up on it from the sides. You know, to get in practice before I have to start worrying about missing the 'subtle clues' Dusty keeps talking about."

"You'd better not miss anything," Dusty said as he picked up his Guinness, walked over, and set the salad bowl on the table next to the chocolate cake. "You're the one who's been taking all those religious studies classes. You ought to be able to recognize witchery before anybody else out there."

Sylvia blinked like he'd just said something truly astounding. "You bet, boss, absolutely, so long as it deals with Aboriginal Australian metaphysics, I've got it covered. My last class delved really deep into that stuff."

Dusty gave Sylvia a reproving look as he started filling plates and handing them around the table. "Well, just keep your eyes open. There must be similarities between Aboriginal and Puebloan witchcraft."

Sylvia scowled. "Like what? The uses of witchetty grubs and rattlesnakes?"

Maureen smiled. She and Sylvia had become close friends during the excavations at 10K3 and had worked together at Pueblo Animas. Sylvia's keen wit included neither piety nor good taste, but Maureen had watched her work endlessly in the hot sun, muscles rippling under smooth sun-browned skin. She'd had a really tough childhood—much tougher, Maureen suspected, than Agent Nichols knew. After all these years, Sylvia still slept with a baseball bat just in case. Everyone who'd ever worked with her knew you did not surprise Sylvia when she was asleep.

Michall Jefferson, on the other hand, was a new element in the equation. A sober-eyed redhead, she had an Irish phenotype, short in frame but with the broad shoulders of a swimmer. In addition to being a principal investigator with her own antiquities permit, she had just finished the coursework for her PhD and had turned in the first draft of her dissertation. She wore a hooded gray sweatshirt with UNIVERSITY OF COLORADO stenciled across the front.

They ate in silence for a few minutes; then Sylvia said, "Hey, Dusty, what do you really think about all this?"

He looked up from his plate. "What do you mean?"

"Well"—she lifted a shoulder—"I mean, I don't know how to feel about digging this site."

Dusty swallowed another bite of tamale and wiped his mouth on his sleeve. "Don't feel, Sylvia. Don't think. Just dig. Every year dozens of archaeologists excavate murder sites. In places like Bosnia and El Salvador they have to dig up mass graves, a lot of them filled with recently murdered children. You're just excavating a site. Do it the very best you can."

Sylvia chewed a mouthful of salad and reached for her Coors Light can. She pressed in the sides, then released the pressure so that the aluminum popped out with a *tink*.

"You know, you couldn't do that with a real beer," Dusty said.

"Yeah, but the only difference between Guinness and ninety-weight gear lube," Sylvia responded, "is the price."

"And the creamy fizz." Dusty lifted a bottle of Guinness to the light. "This has fizz, and it's like oatmeal, it'll stick to your innards."

Sylvia *tinked* her Coors can again. "I always knew you were constipated. That's what gives you your peculiar personality."

Dusty pointed at her with his beer bottle. "You'd better be thankful I'm not in charge of this project. I'd make you dig the trash midden."

"Fortunately, this is Michall's project, and she says I have to dig the kiva."

Michall's pale eyebrows lifted. "Yep. It's just me, Sylvia, and the FBI." She shook her head. "God, I can't believe I'm actually doing this, digging the site where Dale was killed." Her face worked, communicating her upset.

In a soft voice, Dusty said, "Well, just do it like he'd have wanted: perfectly. Imagine him looking over your shoulder the whole time."

Michall's expression tightened. "Thanks, Dusty. It's creepy enough as it is."

"It's not the dead that you have to worry about." Maureen held her teacup in both hands. The pleasant aroma of mint was a welcome change. "It's the living."

"Damn right," Sylvia said. "I watch TV. Murderers always return to the scene of the crime. Who knows what sort of monster might come walking up to us out there?"

"I won't even notice," Michall said. "Not when I'm excavating the place where Dale was murdered."

"I'm glad you're the one digging the site," Dusty told Michall. "Dale would have appreciated the fact that you were in charge. He had a lot of respect for you."

She smiled at that. "God knows where I would have ended up but for Dale. I'd probably be married, with two-point-three kids, a mortgage, a house in the suburbs, and a harried life juggling kids, household, and husband."

"Well," Dusty chimed in, "you do have the SUV."

Michall drove a Dodge Durango, but somehow the blue four-wheel drive Maureen had seen that afternoon with its big meaty rubber-lugged tires, spattered mud, and heavy-duty winch evaded the "soccer-mom" model.

"Yeah," Sylvia said. "I can just see you as a housewife watching *Days of Our Lives* at noon every day."

Michall chuckled. "I came out here four years ago to escape my boyfriend. You know, one last fling with life before I married him. I had my BA in hand, and wow, what a rush! I could use my degree and go dig in the Southwest before I moved into a nice house in Chelsea."

"Where?" Dusty gave her a puzzled look.

"Boston. My degree was from Boston College. How was I supposed to know that Dale was waiting out here for me like a big brooding bird of prey." Michall's voice dropped to mimic Dale's. "Ms. Jefferson, you have a rare sense for archaeology. You are one of the truly gifted. However, if it is your desire to return to Boston and function as a bipedal set of ovaries, that, too, is a noble profession. The species does need to be propagated."

Sylvia smiled appreciatively. "God, Dale had such a way with words."

Michall shrugged. "How do you respond to that? I mean, of all the people on earth there was something about Dale that made you want to do your best. I would have rather crawled across broken glass than have disappointed him."

"As I recall," Dusty said, "he worked things out behind your back."

Michall had a thoughtful look. "Yeah, it was coming

up on fall, and Dale asked if I wanted to start my MA in January. He said Colorado was going to have an opening. He'd even lined up a couple of scholarships for me. There it was, a cut-and-dried decision."

Sylvia cocked her head, asking, "Do you ever regret not marrying that nice young man and having all those rug rats?"

Tears sprang to Michall's eyes. "The only thing I regret is that Dale won't be in Boulder next spring to see me hooded. We had a bet. If I finished my PhD in two years, he bought dinner."

A heavy silence descended. The only sound came from the hissing lantern.

Sylvia tossed off the last of her beer. "Yeah, well, I'm headed for the dormitory room that Rupert assigned us behind the park headquarters. It's going to be a long day tomorrow, and a nasty one if there's frost in the ground. That means swinging a pick." She stood up and slid out of the booth.

"I could always wander over to make sure you get up on time," Dusty offered.

"No, thanks," Sylvia replied. "My eardrums haven't recovered from your last shotgun blast."

"Yeah, thank God there are no guns allowed on national monuments," Michall added.

Sylvia's expression turned suspicious as she eyed Dusty. "You didn't bring that big ugly-assed revolver, did you?"

Dusty's blue eyes widened innocently. "With the FBI watching my every move? Come on."

"Yeah, right." Sylvia turned to Michall. "Hey, Mick, you want to follow me back? Just in case my Jeep blows the transmission on the way?"

Michall stood up. "Sure. No problem."

"Good night, all." Dusty locked the door after they'd stepped out into the night.

Maureen tossed the last of the forks into the dishwater and scrubbed them, then rinsed with hot water from the teapot. The paper plates went into the trash. Dusty used paper towels to wipe out the Teflon-coated pans and stuffed them into the cupboard.

He leaned against the counter, staring down at the floor. Maureen slipped back into the booth to finish her tea. She watched the interplay of emotions. As tough as it was going to be on her, it would be harder on him. They would only be spectators, sidelined while others uncovered the soil that held the key to Dale's last hours on earth.

"Michall seems like a sharp woman," Maureen said.

When he looked at her, pain lay behind his eyes. "Dale was right about her. Too good to waste as breeding stock. God, Dale was right about so many things. Michall, Sylvia, Steve, you...and me." He smiled at that, and said, "Good night, Maureen."

Caught off guard, she watched him step back and close the door to the small back bedroom. She could hear him as he undressed for bed. The little trailer rocked slightly under his weight.

She sat quietly for a time, finishing her tea, then pulled on her coat and stepped outside to head for the rest room. The campground was empty. She stopped, staring up at the sky. The stars seemed to pulse. Had she ever seen them so clearly?

"Yes, Dale," she said plaintively. "You were right about Dusty and me."

When she finally returned, excited by the chill of the clear night, she found the trailer silent. She folded out the front bench bed and tried to think. Her movements were slow, preoccupied, as she rolled out her sleeping bag, undressed, and turned the knob on the lantern.

The light sputtered, yellowed, and died.

As she rolled onto her side the silence dropped around her like a weight. With only the ticking of the cooling lantern, Dusty's face filled her mind. She could sense him, his presence oozing out from behind that thin door. Was he lying awake, staring into the darkness as she was?

Was he hurting?

Maureen wished she had the courage to go back there and ask, but she was too afraid of what might follow. They were growing ever more intimate, and she wasn't sure how she felt about it. On the one hand, it soothed something inside her to be close to a man again. On the other, it scared her to death. She still missed John, and deep inside her, she knew she always would. But what did that mean? Did it mean she would never have a normal relationship with a man again?

She punched her pillow to fluff it up and flopped her head down.

John had been the love of her life. He still filled her dreams. Sometimes she thought she would never truly love again. And, the way she was going, that was likely to be a self-fulfilling prophecy.

She exhaled hard and tried to go to sleep.

"How did we miss them?" Horned Ram demanded. "Our warriors searched Kettle Town from top to bottom. All that they found were dead First People, pack rats, and bats."

Blue Corn grimaced. "You're assuming that they really are there."

Horned Ram fingered his chin as he paced back and forth in the room. He and the rest of Blue Corn's warriors had turned the abandoned town of Center Place into the center of their hunt for the missing Mogollon warriors and the traitor Browser. The great building had once been the home of First People priests, the ones who conducted rituals for pilgrims traveling the Great North Road. From the town's high third-story roof, the Blessed Sun's war chiefs had sent and received signals that spanned the First People's empire.

Rain Crow stood in the corner, his arms crossed as he considered his young scout. The youth had only seen fifteen summers and seemed terrified of Horned Ram. "You're sure it was Pigeontail?"

"Yes, War Chief. He came from War Club village,

walking straight for Kettle Town. He and his two dogs. He was inside for at least two hands of time. Then, when he left, it was straight back to War Club village."

Rain Crow arched an eyebrow as he met Blue Corn's eyes. "That isn't exactly proof that Browser is hiding the Mogollon in Kettle Town."

"He's there," Horned Ram insisted. "I can feel him. His presence is like an owl's on the roof. I say we take our force, surround the town, and search it room by room."

"I thought you did that last time?" Blue Corn asked.

"That place is a rat's maze. They could have scurried around behind my warriors."

"Well, this time, make sure you find them. Then when you've driven them into the back, fire the place. Kill anyone who runs out."

"You would burn Kettle Town to get these few Mogollon?" Rain Crow asked. "Some of my ancestors built that place."

"If your ancestors were pawns of the First People, that is not my concern." Horned Ram gave Rain Crow a cold look. "Burning Kettle Town is just another way of stamping out more of the First People's perverted works."

Blue Corn weighed her options, then said, "As soon as our warriors return from scouting the lower canyon, prepare them for an assault on Kettle Town. Let us finish this. The gods alone know what is happening with our Katsinas' People hostages in Flowing Waters Town while I chase phantom Mogollon around Straight Path Canyon."

Rain Crow's ruined face reflected nothing of his thoughts. "Yes, Matron."

Blue Corn studied Horned Ram from the corner of her eye. The Red Rock elder had a grin on his frog face, as though he already smelled blood on the wind. He and his Flute Player warriors liked the killing and death. It fed something in his breath-heart soul the way a simmering buffalo stew did a starving man's stomach.

She wondered whether her calculations for the future should include the elder. He was brash, effective, and totally without scruples when it came to the destruction of those who did not share his beliefs. Such a man and his warriors could be utilized as a terrible weapon. Assuming, of course, that they could be controlled. What good was a weapon that was as dangerous to its wielder as it was to her enemies?

Blue Corn chewed on her lip as she considered. This alliance had seemed a golden opportunity when Gray Thunder first appeared, but she now feared it might prove more frightful than she had ever dreamed.

Blue Corn had never been one to turn down an unexpected opportunity, but she hoped this wouldn't be like having a rattlesnake in a pot. You always had to hope you could continue to keep it locked inside.

PIPER

A nest of snakes squirms in Piper's belly as she crawls along the bottom of Straight Path Wash as fast as she can. Her knees are raw and bleeding, like they've been rubbed with sandstone, but she cannot stop. She must hurry! Hurry!

She'd found the trail two hands of time ago. Mother was very careful, her sandals barely scuffing the sand, but Piper knew those steps. She had tracked her mother many times.

Was Mother looking for me? Did she try to find me?

Tears choke Piper.

When the wash cuts deep enough to hide her, Piper stands up and runs with all her heart, flying down the bottom of the wash. The small rocks scream and shoot out behind her feet.

"I'm sorry I ran away, Mother!" she sobs. "I'm sorry!"

If Grandfather can't get Aunt Obsidian's heart, he will take Mother's heart. She knows he will.

A burning flood gushes up Piper's throat. She stumbles

and retches onto the shining sand. She retches until her belly aches and twists, and she can't get enough air.

For a few instants she stares at the world through blurry eyes, then Wind Baby blows up the wash and strokes Piper's face with strong icy hands, and she runs again. Fast!

Hurry, hurry...

Dusty stuck his thumbs into the back pockets of his jeans. Three FBI guys stood on the other side of the yellow tape, clipboards in hand. They had just handed out white sheets of paper with the "rules" for handling evidence. Rupert Brown and Michall stood reading the sheets with quizzical expressions.

It wasn't bad enough that the government dictated how even normal archaeology was conducted, but here it was down to directives concerning everything including the sharpening of trowels.

To her credit, Michall took it all in stride.

"So, what do you think, Stewart?" Sam Nichols walked across the site and gave him a penetrating look. He had the collar of his brown canvas coat pulled up, and his horn-rimmed glasses rode low on his nose.

"I think this is bullshit."

Dusty gestured to the pile of rubble beyond the tape; the cold wind tugged at the brim of his brown western hat. "Very soon, your people are going to realize that this crime scene is also an archaeological site. It has its own special problems and needs that don't fit anybody's rules."

"Maybe, but your people aren't trained in forensic evidence recovery."

"And your people aren't trained in archaeological data recovery," Dusty reminded. "But it's okay, Nichols. They'll be on the same page by the time they get down to the intact levels."

Nichols gave him a disbelieving look. "Intact levels? Anything worth getting is going to be around where Dr. Robertson was buried." Nichols pointed to the frosted dirt, still readily visible where it had been turned.

"I'm sure that's how it works in most modern murder cases, Agent Nichols. I don't think that's what we'll find here."

Rupert Brown left Michall's side and walked toward Dusty and Nichols. He wore a green nylon coat with the Department of the Interior patch on the shoulder.

Nichols said, "You really believe that the person who killed Dr. Robertson buried something here?"

"Or something was already buried here, and that's why he picked this spot. Kwewur may be playing with us, Agent Nichols. I think he—"

"Dusty's right." Rupert shoved his hands in his coat pockets. His six-foot-six-inch frame towered over Nichols. Even Dusty, at six feet even, had to look up to meet Rupert's eyes. "I think it's like a turnabout on the old European trick of having illiterate natives sign a treaty they couldn't read. Kwewur is betting you can't decipher the message he left here, Nichols."

Nichols studied Rupert as if just seeing him for the first time. A faint look of hostility lit his eyes. "You seem to know a lot about him."

Rupert shrugged. "You grew up in Baltimore where witches showed up for Halloween. They were make-believe characters. I grew up in the Southwest, where witches were not only real, but you knew who was and was not a witch. You knew people who had died from their evil spells, or someone who almost died, and had to pay the witch to break the spell. Then, lo and behold, they got well. I was attacked by a witch once, Nichols. Because of that, I've spent more than half of my life studying Southwestern witchcraft. I know it works and I can tell you the key to a witch's survival these days. He wants you to disbelieve."

"You mean he thinks I'm a fool?"

Rupert shook his head. "No. Just the opposite. He's playing a game with you. The difference is that he knows that his rules are different from yours. But you think the rules of the game are the same."

"Meaning?"

"Meaning he believes in you, but you don't believe in him."

"But you do?"

Rupert gave a slight shrug as he watched the crew pulling stakes, strings, and a transit from the dig box.

Nichols's mouth pressed into a tight white line. "You have a PhD, Brown. And you really believe that crap?"

"Kwewur believes it, Agent Nichols, and Dale is dead."

"Yeah. Right. That's why I'm in this godforsaken place."

Rupert gave the agent a small smile. "If you wouldn't mind, I'd appreciate being addressed as either Dr. or Superintendent while I'm in the park."

"Sure, Superintendent Brown." Nichols frowned off into the distance. "That's your grandson out there, isn't it? Driving that pickup?"

"Yes. He's doing rounds. Picking up trash."

"Maybe I'll go down and talk to him." Nichols paused. "Does he believe in witches?"

"Go ask him."

Nichols nodded to Dusty before walking off, a thoughtful slouch to his shoulders.

Dusty gave Rupert an askance look. "Are you okay?"

"God, no." Rupert shoved his hands more deeply into his pockets. "On top of everything else, he's driving me crazy. Nichols has been throwing his weight around, reorganizing every park employee's schedule, tearing down tape, putting up tape, blocking roads, opening roads, giving orders, pointing his finger. That's what I really don't like. The finger-pointing thing." He shook his finger in Dusty's face to illustrate, then tucked it back in his pocket. "See?"

Dusty smothered a smile. "I think he's just being thorough, Rupert."

"Sure, I know what he's doing. He's got people just sitting, watching to see who does what. For the past couple of nights he's had agents out here, watching the site. The murderer returns to the scene of the crime. Maybe it'll work, but if he wasn't such a *koyemshi,* a clown, with his head stuck in the regulation book, he might have already figured this thing out. He really hates being out here, and it shows."

Dusty pushed windblown blond hair out of his blue eyes and decided he ought to change the subject. "Did you hear that Carter Hawsworth dropped by to see me. I wasn't there, but Maureen was."

Rupert's brows lifted. "Really? Is he still as much of an asshole as he used to be?"

"Well, Maureen wasn't impressed with him."

Rupert shook his head. "Don't get tied up in messes, Dusty. If you and I meet again twenty years from now, I'd like it to be one of those 'good to see you' kinds of meetings rather than the 'you asshole' kind."

"What kind of messes did you have in mind?"

"The kind that gets your friends killed." He used his

chin to point to where Michall and Sylvia slipped under the ribbon and began hammering in a datum stake, then setting up the transit to grid the site.

Dusty scuffed at the dirt with a worn boot. "Speaking of friends, I saw Lupe last time I was here."

"He's making flutes, can you believe it? Good flutes. He's selling them to tourists. He's even got a CD and sells them in the boutiques up in Taos and over in Durango." Rupert seemed genuinely pleased. "But then there's Reggie.

"Don't ever have a grandkid, Dusty. The boy's still not talking to his mother. That's bad. I don't care what she did to him, she's still his mother. But Reggie's trying. He's pretty well dried out and cleaned up. He's even been going down to Zuni to attend the sacred rituals. I think he's going to be okay."

"Not everyone has your gumption, Rupert. It's up to Reggie what he makes of himself."

"Yeah, but I have to try to help. He fell apart when Sandy died. She was the only mother he'd ever really known. I swear, Reggie was so high on drugs, he didn't know what he was doing when he broke into all those houses."

"Well," Dusty said, and his eyes tightened, "grief makes you crazy."

Rupert's wife, Sandy, had died from cancer four years ago. She'd been a good, kind woman. Dusty remembered her shaking a spatula at him one very hungover morning at breakfast and saying, *"Don't let nobody tell you that you're a bad boy, Dusty, 'cause you're not. You're just really stupid sometimes."*

He smiled at the memory. He'd been sixteen and what Dale had called "his worst nightmare."

Rupert watched Nichols reach his car and drive off to

intercept Reggie. "You know, sometimes all a kid needs is a chance."

"Yeah, I do know. I hope it all works out for him."

Rupert nodded, then a smile brightened his face. "Reggie's been talking about Maggie. Can you believe it? I guess he's trying to get up the nerve to ask her out."

"She'd be good for him," Dusty said. But deep down inside he wasn't so sure about that. Maggie was a traditional with deep-seated Keres beliefs. Not the hell-raiser that young Reggie was. Although, if Reggie really had been trying to get his spiritual life in order down at Zuni, maybe things would work out.

Dusty looked back as Maureen drove into the Casa Rinconada parking lot. She parked the blue Bronco beside Michall's Durango and stepped out. Even over the distance, Dusty felt his heart lift as she started down the interpretive path past Tseh So and toward the ridge overlooking the Casa Rinconada great kiva.

"I think maybe she's good for you, too," Rupert said, his brown eyes measuring Dusty's expression.

"She's just a friend." He tried to wave it off.

"I thought you were sharing the trailer?"

"'Sharing' is the key word, Rupert." Dusty tried not to squirm under that intense gaze.

"Does she know how you feel about her?" Rupert asked.

"How do *you* know how I feel about her?"

"I have this sixth sense. It's an Indian thing, very mystical. All I have to do is see your face light up and, bingo, I can read your mind."

Dusty folded his arms protectively over his heart. "Well, keep it to yourself. I'm not going to turn a nice friendship into a disastrous romantic interlude that will leave us hating each other." He paused. "Besides which, she's still in love with her husband."

"I remember Dale talking about that." Rupert kicked at the cold soil. "How long have we known each other?"

"All of my life. Why?"

"All of your life." Rupert paused and gazed off into the distance. "In many ways, you are like my son, Dusty. You and Lupe. I remember how the two of you used to play together."

"So do I. I remember the time Lupe almost knocked me unconscious with a rock. Great fun."

Rupert laughed. "Yeah, well, when ı see you and Maureen, I say to myself this looks like the right one. Maybe you should listen to your elder, for once? You don't want to end up like me, old, bitter, and alone."

Dusty studied Sylvia as she walked across rubble with the transit rod. Her freckled face had gone red in the cold wind. Then his gaze shifted back to Maureen. She lifted a hand and smiled.

Dusty said, "I won't, Rupert. I promise you that. If the time is ever right, I'll do everything I can."

"Make the time right, Dusty." Rupert paused. "Don't let her get away."

"Yes, Dad."

He studied Dusty thoughtfully. "So you'll really understand, I'm going to tell you the same story I told Lupe and Reggie when they were involved with good ladies, ladies I knew would make them happy. Are you listening to me?"

"Yeah, Rupert. Okay."

"The only woman I ever loved with all my heart left me for another man. I'd like to think it was because I didn't make enough of an effort to let her know how much of my heart and soul she really had. When she went, I came within a whisker of destroying myself. I wrote to her for years, but all my letters came back marked 'Addressee Unknown.' In all of my life, I've never completely recovered from what happened with her. Don't live your life like I've lived mine, wasting away over a woman you didn't do enough to win."

Dusty looked at Rupert from the corner of his eye. "I thought Sandy was the love of your life."

"Sandy was my best friend, Dusty, and I loved her very much. But it took Sandy and me years to learn to love each other. Those first few years, every day was a fight. We worked through it. We raised a good boy. I ate out my own heart when she died. But, no, she wasn't the love of my life."

Rupert smiled faintly as a flock of crows wheeled over their heads. His eyes had gone tight. "Don't think you have all the time in the world, my other son. Because you don't."

The White Moccasins warrior named Polished Bone watched the two shabby elders as they stepped out from behind Kettle Town and made their slow and laborious way down the road. As the afternoon sun bore down on Polished Bone's back, the high canyon rim sent its shadow across the crumbled sandstone below. He'd been placed here, on the high buff sandstone rim to keep watch on the massive structure across the canyon. Distant though it was from the southern rim, he'd be able to see anyone who entered or left the great house.

"When did they get there?" he wondered.

Surely these were not the tricky Mogollon he'd heard of from the tortured youth's screaming mouth. No sane warrior would wander out into the open knowing that he was being observed the entire time.

And then one of the elders fell.

Polished Bone lifted a lip in a sneer. Made People refugees, no doubt. Perhaps someone Old Pigeontail had told to flee while he was in talking with Browser and his warriors.

Browser, now there was a man Polished Bone would

love to meet. Perhaps he'd get his chance tonight, as soon as the cover of darkness masked their white capes.

Browser couldn't have known that by killing Ten Hawks and Bear Dancer, he had sealed his fate, and the fate of the Katsinas' People.

One of the elders was stumbling, leaning on the other as they made their way to the crossing where Straight Path Wash cut into the flat canyon floor.

Polished Bone sharpened his attention. The only place they might be able to escape would be in that wash. If they didn't immediately emerge, then it was a ruse, a party seeking to escape down the sheer-sided arroyo to one of the side canyons.

"Two people," he murmured thoughtfully to himself. Were they really old men? "Or Browser and Catkin? Cowards! Are you running?"

But no, here they came, struggling up out of the arroyo and staggering onward, their ratty clothes whipped by the west wind. It tugged at their loose white hair.

Polished Bone smiled in grim amusement. That was like Browser, no doubt desperate to save two old derelicts so that they wouldn't get hurt in the ensuing battle. Shadow had said he was quick of thought, but vulnerable when it came to those under his protection.

The two elders continued their irregular snail's pace down the road. The journey had taken them nearly a hand of time. Polished Bone shook his head. Fools, they should stop at Talking Stitch village and take cover for the night.

If they didn't, the White Moccasins surely weren't going to allow them within the safety of High Sun's walls. Not with what they might learn. And sleeping up on the mesa beyond the rim was brutal this time of the sun cycle.

To his surprise, the two elders didn't make for any of the small houses that dotted the canyon floor under the cliff. Instead they came straight on for the stairway that he guarded.

"Silly old fools!" Polished Bone left his comfortable vantage point in the cleft in the sandstone and took a more open position where he could see down the stairway. Sure enough, here came the elders. He could see them more clearly now: a man and a woman, old and frail, their clothing mere rags. Poor things, they were literally pulling each other up the stairway, panting with effort. The man looked the worse for wear, old and crippled, his back bent. An expression of agony marred his wrinkled face. The wind whipped his white hair.

Polished Bone squatted on his heels, absorbed by their struggle up the stairway. He fought the sudden urge to go down and help them. They were going to be coyote meat anyway: either the frost would get them; or the wind would freeze them; or they'd collapse from exhaustion by the time morning arrived. Besides, they were Made People. Let them take whatever fate the gods decided.

A third of the way up, they stopped, wheezing and panting. The old woman looked up, seeing him sky-lined. She waved and called in a feeble voice, "Young warrior! Come help your elders!"

"Make it on your own," he answered. "Unless you'd like to tell me about who is staying in Kettle Town."

The old man looked up, a hand to his heart. Pain filled his eyes, and the set of his mouth betrayed a desperation that Polished Bone could understand. It was the look that came when hope had vanished like dew in a hot summer drought.

One by one, the elders struggled up the stairs carved so long ago by their ancestors. Arms flailing, the old man missed a step, and the woman caught him a hairsbreadth from falling.

Polished Bone shook his head. He needn't worry about

them discovering his fellows at High Sun. They'd never make it that far before nightfall.

"Why...won't...you...help?" the old woman gasped between breaths as she neared the top.

"You are not of my clan," Polished Bone answered, the irony of that being his own personal joke. "Ask your ancestors when you see them."

Step by step, they made their way up until the old man reached the worn sandstone flat. There he seemed to melt, curling into a fetal ball. Wind Baby picked heedlessly at his tattered clothing. It looked dusty and moldy, so old that the patterns had faded from the material. Once, the garments had been of high quality, many seasons past.

Polished Bone lifted his eyebrows as he watched the old woman bend down to whisper to the old man. In his bony hand, the elder clutched something as though it were the most precious of possessions.

"Warrior," the old woman said, reaching out to him. "If you will help us, take us to shelter, and feed us, this is yours." When she opened her hand, Polished Bone started. There, in her palm, lay a polished copper bell.

"Where did you get that?"

"It's yours if you will help us," the old woman pleaded.

Polished Bone bent and reached for the bell, but she pulled it back in a miserly motion. "Help," she repeated, her old sad eyes on his.

"Give it to me." With his right hand outstretched, he fumbled for the war club on his belt with his left. "If you don't, I'll just take it from your clubbed bodies. You—"

The old man's movement caught him by surprise. The elder's hand whipped up, the clenched fist driving a deer-bone stiletto deep into the hollow under Polished Bone's ribs. He staggered back, stunned by the pain. Could feel the depth of the damage in his chest. His terrified reaction was to slap both hands to the wound as though to press the hot gouts of blood back into his ruptured heart.

"Well done," the old woman said, her voice clearer, the accent thicker.

"And with pleasure, White Cone." The old man stood straight now, a smile on his thin brown lips. "Arrogance and foolishness make a poor mixture, don't you agree?"

White Cone tossed the polished copper bell into the air and snatched it away as it fell.

The world spun and wobbled as Polished Bone stumbled backward and sat down hard. The pain searing his chest became unbearable. His blood, so much of it, spilled over his hands. Hot, thick, it soaked the front of his war shirt. The edges of his vision were going gray, hazy. The world whirled sideways, and his cheek was against the cold sandstone.

"Give your ancestors my regards," the accented voice said. "Tell them you are a gift to the Land of the Dead, courtesy of the Bow Society."

"Well, that's one," the old man said. "If you're up to it, we have two more to go."

"Next time, you're the old woman with the bell."

Polished Bone felt them push his quivering body over the edge, but he didn't feel the fall or the smacking impact he made as he landed on the rocks a bow shot below.

Not much happened on the first day of digging, which didn't surprise Maureen. Michall placed her grid over the site and, with the help of the ERT people, got most of the scrubby rabbitbrush and salt-bush cleared from the tumbled stone that marked the Bc60 ruin. Surface mapping of the features, the collapsed kiva, and surface artifact recording and collection took the rest of the day.

She watched Dusty pace the perimeter marked by the yellow crime-scene tape, up and back, biting off comments as Michall and her crew followed the instructions of Nichols and the ERT team members.

The next time his path brought him close, Maureen said, "It's a good thing they couldn't hire you to do this job, eh?"

"What?" he said, irritated. Wind waffled the brown brim of his cowboy hat and flicked the hem of his denim jacket.

"I mean, if you were in charge, this excavation would take twice as long since you'd be arguing every step of the way with the ERT people."

His blue eyes narrowed. "I'm not that bad. Yet."

Maureen crossed her arms against the wind's bite. "Don't you think Michall's doing a good job?"

"Of course she is. I trained her."

"Then just relax and let her work." She walked up and took his arm, feeling the tension in his swelling muscles. "Let's take a break. I want to see the sites down here. You can tell me all about the Casa Rinconada great kiva, and why it doesn't have a great house attached to it."

Reluctantly, he let her lead him down from the humped shale ridge to the Casa Rinconada kiva. The subterranean ceremonial chamber stretched more than sixty feet across. Snow lined the kiva bottom; it had swirled through the red and black sands to create a beautiful abstract design. Concave drifts scalloped the bench that encircled the structure.

Dusty said nothing. She could see how upset he was; his mind seemed to be locked on some perplexing problem.

"What's wrong?" she asked.

He forced his gaze away from the kiva, deliberately avoided her eyes, and glared at the rimrock. "Rupert said something this morning that's been bothering me."

"What?"

"I'm not sure I want to tell you."

Maureen shifted. "Then don't."

As he turned to face her, a gust flipped his blond hair around beneath the brim of his hat. He squinted against the onslaught. "He seems to think that we're perfect for each other."

Taken aback, she smiled uncomfortably. "Really? What does he know about us?"

Dusty jammed his hands deeply into his coat pockets. "That's the problem. He doesn't know anything. It's not like Rupert to say something like that. He minds his own business. Always has." His fists strained against his pockets. "Maybe it's Dale's death. We're all strung out."

She nodded, relieved that he hadn't said what she'd expected him to.

"That's something we have to watch out for, Dusty. During times of crises people are naturally drawn together. But when the crisis ends..."

The lines at the corners of his eyes crinkled. "Right. The Florence Nightingale effect. I only think I'm falling in love with you."

Maureen had to force herself to take a deep breath. "Dusty, I have feelings for you, too, but this isn't the time. Maybe in a few months, when your heart is intact—"

"But not now." He exhaled in relief, smiled, and said, "Thank you, Doctor."

"You were hoping I'd say that, weren't you?"

"Very much."

Maureen laughed and looked across the canyon to the road that led to the Park Service headquarters and Rupert's office. She could see Nichols's car where it had pulled up beside Reggie's green pickup. Strange how memories connected without any apparent rhyme or reason. The feelings stirring within her had reminded her of a phone conversation from long ago. She'd been sitting on the sofa next to John in his tiny apartment in Quebec when he'd called to tell his mother they were going to be married. John had pulled the phone away from his ear when his mother had shouted, "But she's an *Indian,* dear! Why would you do that?"

Maureen said, "I appreciate the compliment, though."

"Well, you earned it. Believe me."

Dusty took his hands from his pockets and crossed his arms over his broad chest, like a barricade. "I'm worried about Rupert. I think this thing may have affected him more than any of us know."

"He said he'd known Dale for more than forty years. It must be hard."

Dusty nodded, as though glad to be speaking of something else. "Dale once told me that Rupert was about the smartest man he'd ever known. That once he got over being Indian and Hispanic and just let himself be Rupert, he'd make something of himself. And look where he is now, Dr. Rupert Brown Horse, park superintendent. About to retire with full pension. And he's been smart, invested wisely. You ought to see the house he has west of Cuba in the foothills. It sits on twenty acres surrounded by timber, has a little creek running through it, and even has a small pueblo that he's going to dig in his retirement."

"Good for him." She stared down at a swirl of snow blowing around the kiva bottom. "Mixed blood is common among my people. We've been intermarrying for four hundred years. We just accept it. But in the West, both the western United States and western Canada, it's different. I think it's because it's still new here."

"We don't think in...the..." Dusty frowned down at the kiva bottom.

"What's wrong?"

"That's not *right*."

Dusty trotted around to the south and descended the steps down into the kiva. His boots crunched through the snow that filled the hollows of the steps.

Maureen followed him, ducked under the lintel, and stepped onto the kiva floor.

Her first awareness was of the masonry, straight, beautiful, so intricately placed. Each of the small square wall crypts might have been an eye from another world, watching her. The kiva seemed to pulse with the voice of the wind.

She turned around, gazing up at the sky. Her senses seemed to be on fire. There was a presence here. Old and powerful. Across from her, she could see through the T-shaped northern entrance to the bleak anteroom beyond. The stone bench was empty, but for the snow, lonely now where once it had supported dozens of finely dressed people. Their ghosts watched as she walked past the raised fire box.

Dusty stopped dead center between the foot drums and the four round roof supports; there, he knelt.

"What was the trench for?" Maureen asked, pointing at the shallow circular trench that ran around the end of the exposed tunnel in the kiva floor.

"We don't know. It was Chacoan, filled in by later Mesa Verdean people when they refinished the kiva in the mid-1200s. But this...this shouldn't be here."

She looked down. "You mean the sand? Why not?"

"In a kiva cut out of gray shale, where do you get red, black, and white sand?" Dusty stiffened as if stung. "There was a sand painting here."

He lurched to his feet as though he'd just seen a coiled rattlesnake. When Maureen looked, all she saw was a thin green yucca leaf.

"Step back," Dusty said. "Move your shadow."

Maureen carefully retreated and circled. She was looking now, forcing herself to see, to catalog and interpret what lay before her on the ground. The dark stains, weathered and bleached by the melting snow, had a familiar brown—"Oh, god, Dusty."

"What?" He spun around.

She pointed. "That's blood. Blood is delicate, it decomposes rapidly in sunlight and the moisture feeds soil organisms."

Dusty pulled his pen from his pocket and used the tip to whisk multicolored grains from the brown stain. His hand started to shake. He slowly rose to his feet.

"Maureen, move back." His breathing had gone

shallow and rapid. "Step on the tracks you made on the way in. Call Nichols. I want him in here right now."

"What did you find?" She tried to look around him, but his body blocked her view.

"Just go! Now."

Maureen headed toward the stairs; when she reached the top, she looked back.

Dusty stood with his feet braced and his fists clenched at his sides. The shiny black stone he'd uncovered glinted in the light.

20

The Flute Player warrior named He Sees watched the old people emerge from Kettle Town and proceed with painful slowness on their way south across the canyon. They had provided a grateful distraction from his boring duty. Rain Crow had placed him here, atop the stone stairway just north of Kettle Town, to "keep watch on things," and report back.

He Sees got to do this a great deal. Not everyone, especially in Red Rock country, had eyes like his. He couldn't see very well close up, but far away, he had eyes like Hawk. It seemed as if he had spent his entire life on high lookouts either half frozen from the cold wind or baked and blistering from the summer sun.

But two old people...

They weren't worth the energy to run back to Center Place with a report. A sentry, especially one such as himself, developed a sense for what was important. Why the two would have left in the middle of the afternoon was problematic, but then, who knew what the Trader had said in there? When they began their fumbling ascent up the far stairway, He Sees watched, alarmed when one nearly fell.

He was still watching when, to his surprise, he saw the distant figure of a man step out of a fissure in the rock. The man moved like a warrior, and though he couldn't be sure given the distance, He Sees thought the fellow had a war club at his belt.

When the two elders made the summit and the old man collapsed, He Sees waited. Why didn't the warrior help them? The fool, he...but then, yes, the man was stepping closer, his hand outstretched.

He Sees frowned when the old man suddenly leaped up, and the warrior backed away, stumbled, then collapsed and fell.

"What is this?" He Sees whispered.

Shading his eyes, he struggled to see, cursing the distance for the first time, and wishing that his eyesight was even better. He stood up, rising from the protection of an old shrine, unable to believe what he witnessed. The two old people rolled the young warrior's limp body to the side; then they tumbled him off the edge of the cliff.

The body fell, hitting the rock ledges on the way down.

"Ambush!" He Sees said. "They were not..."

Sand trickled below him, making a distinctive *shishing* sound. He lowered his hand from his eyes and looked down.

She was no more than fifteen steps from him, a bow in her left hand, an arrow drawn back in her right.

He Sees met the woman's eyes, and their souls linked. She was beautiful, tall, with wide cheekbones and an oval face. In a flash, he knew her: Browser's deputy, Catkin. But how had she—? Gods, while he had watched the old people she'd climbed up right under his nose.

A sliver of sunlight flashed down the arrow when she let fly.

The impact was silken. The sharp point sliced through him. His mouth fell open and he started to pant as though he'd been running forever. In all of his imaginations of this moment, he had never thought of the cold. The arrow was icy where it lodged inside him.

He stepped back and turned toward Center Place to cry a warning. The second arrow shocked him. Staggering on his feet, he stared down at the stone point protruding from the middle of his chest. Blood bubbled into the back of his throat and sprayed from his mouth with each desperate exhale.

His knees buckled.

His last sensation was hearing her feet as she sprinted up the road he was supposed to be guarding.

Dusty stood with his back to the wind, the collar of his Levi's coat pulled up to keep his neck warm. Gray clouds scudded out of the northeast, marking the arrival of a cold front dropping out of Utah. He stood at the western lip of Casa Rinconada, just back from the interpretive sign, and watched as the ERT team crawled over the kiva bottom on their hands and knees. They had taken samples of the sand, of the bloodstains, and collected the glittering basilisk. Now they were inspecting every square inch of Casa Rinconada's floor.

Twenty feet away, to Dusty's right, Maureen and Nichols stood. As she talked, Nichols took notes.

He heard Nichols say, "So it may have happened here, and he moved the body?"

"Maybe," Maureen said in her professional voice. "But we need more information. It snowed on the blood; then it warmed up and melted. I hope you can get something, but it's going to be tough."

"And," Nichols said pointedly, "we don't have any tracks down there but yours and Stewart's from today." He peered down into Casa Rinconada. "I can see how you picked that sand out. It is different. But what made you think it had anything to do with Dr. Robertson?"

"I'm an archaeologist," Dusty said as he turned. His tone implied that that explained everything.

"Right. So?"

Dusty shoved his hands into his jeans pockets and walked toward Nichols.

"The very first hafted axe head I found was in a Moenkopi sandstone outcrop. It was a crummy thing, battered, and badly weathered. No one in their right mind would have looked twice at it. It lay on the sandstone, in a pile of rocks."

"How'd you know it was an axe head?"

"It was granite, and the nearest granite source was forty miles away. It's the same with the sand down there. When I saw it, I knew someone must have carried it in."

Nichols squinted at him with his one good eye. "Dr. Brown told me that lots of tribes use this kiva for ceremonials. Maybe the Navajo held a Sing here?"

"Maybe," Dusty agreed. "Did Rupert tell you he'd scheduled one? You have to have permission to do that in a national park."

Nichols shook his head. "He didn't say anything, but maybe somebody—like young Reggie out there—didn't want to get permission and came here anyway."

Dusty knotted his fists in his pockets. "That's possible. I'm not the only one who hates government regulations, but no one—not even Reggie—coming here for a sacred ritual would have a basilisk, Nichols. They're evil. Pure witchery."

"He's a thorny kid, isn't he?" Nichols said. "You interrupted my little talk with him. He's what I'd call a very angry young man with a chip on his shoulder."

"He's had it tough."

"Do you know anyone who hasn't? I'm starting to

think all of your friends are basket cases." Nichols jotted something in his notebook and stared balefully down into the kiva. "A kiva, huh? It's sure a big thing, isn't it?"

Dusty waited until the gust of wind passed before answering, "Imagine digging that much soil out of the ground. Hammering down through the sandstone and shale with stone-headed mauls and digging sticks. No backhoes in those days."

"Impressive." Nichols looked around. Pointed to the north. "What's that? Those big ruins over there?"

Dusty looked across the canyon. "That's Pueblo Bonito. An Anasazi road ran right across there"—he used his hand to illustrate—"from Casa Rinconada's northern anteroom over to the southwest corner of Bonito. And the next ruin to the east is Chetro Ketl. If you get time you might want to walk through them. They were built between A.D. 900 and 1150. North America wouldn't have buildings this large again until the 1830s."

Nichols gazed across the canyon, wind-whipped now, and cold. Chaco looked dreary in its winter clothes, the rabbitbrush and grass turned tan to match the soil.

"Why would the Anasazi have come here? This is a barren place." Nichols was shaking his head.

"It was different then," Dusty said. "You're standing in the capital of an empire that covered one hundred thousand square miles. But if you need to put that in perspective, next time you're in Washington, DC, imagine what it will look like in five hundred years, after the buildings fall down and the trees are growing out of the rubble that's the Capitol building."

Nichols shot him a sober glance. "You think it will come to that?"

"Sure." Dusty shrugged. "It always does. Persepolis, Greece, Ur, Rome, the Maya, the Khmer, the Anasazi, or the Cahokians, they all follow the same pattern: They go through a warm wet climatic episode, overpopulate, build their cities, cut down all the trees, and overuse the soil. Then the climate changes, turns cold and dry, or hot and dry, and they can't feed their people. Some critical supply runs out. People feel deprived. Deprivation is the single most powerful human motivation. It feeds rage. Someone goes to war to win resources, and the system breaks. It cascades like a house of cards with ethnic hatred, religious war, and crusades. The trade routes are cut and the people fall into barbarism."

Dusty's gaze drifted over the ruins before him, imagining how glorious they must have been one thousand years ago. "Why should we be any different?"

"Aw, come on. This is the twenty-first century." Nichols examined him like a hawk with prey.

"How much oil do we import from foreign countries? How much wood? You know that plum you had for lunch yesterday? It probably came from South America."

Nichols grunted and flipped through his notebook. "There's something I've been meaning to talk to you about."

"Okay."

He ran his finger down the page. "We were doing some background on you." He glanced up to read Dusty's reaction when he said, "'The Mad Man of New Mexico'? Where does that come from?"

Dusty winced. "I hate that name."

"After what happened to your father, being locked up in an asylum, I can see why."

"For what it's worth," Maureen said, "Dusty's nickname comes from his unorthodox field methods; it has nothing to do with his father's illness. His methods generate some professional jealousy."

"Yeah, I figured that out," Nichols replied. "You, on

the other hand, Dr. Cole, are highly thought of by most of your peers."

Maureen spread her feet, as though preparing for a lecture. "Physical anthropology is more of a traditional science, Nichols. It isn't as bloodthirsty as archaeology."

Nichols returned his attention to the kiva. "Mr. Stewart, why do you keep finding these basilisks?"

Dusty felt light-headed. "I'd never seen one until we dug 10K3. We found a murder victim with one on her chest. Our monitor, Hail Walking Hawk, wanted me to rebury it." Dusty shrugged. "God, I wish I had."

Nichols perked up. "You've still got it?"

"It's cataloged," Dusty told him. "In the collections at UNM. We also found a second one at Pueblo Animas."

"You found it," Maureen corrected. "Dusty has a thing for finding them. We've tried curing him twice." She gave Dusty a hard look. "You're not going to start having nightmares again, are you?"

"I didn't touch this one."

"Could it be the same one?" Nichols asked. "Or do these things turn up all the time?"

"It's easy to check whether or not it's the same one," Maureen answered. "Get on your phone and call the curation facility at UNM. They can look up the catalog number and trot back in the stacks to find it. If it's there, well, I guess we've answered the question."

Dusty said, "To answer your question about how common they are, they're not. The 10K3 basilisk was the first pre-Columbian one ever found. They're more common in modern societies, but still not abundant."

"How many people know about this pre-Columbian basilisk?"

"Anyone who was on the 10K3 project." Dusty frowned. "Michall, Steve, Sylvia, Maggie, Dale, Maureen, and me."

"Don't forget," Maureen reminded, "that you described the artifact in the final report. Anyone in the profession could have gotten it through a simple request through the SHPO or Park Service."

"Anyone?" Nichols had his pen poised to write. "Like Carter Hawsworth?"

"Of course," Dusty said.

"Where is this report?" Nichols asked. "I'd like to see it."

"There's one over in the headquarters building." Dusty pointed across the canyon. "And another in Washington, one at the National Atmospheric and Oceanic Administration in Boulder, Colorado, another on file with the National Park Service in Albuquerque, one on file with the State Historic Preservation Office in Santa Fe, another—"

"Whoa." Nichols put his hand out to stop Dusty. "In other words, there are copies everywhere. So, it wouldn't have been hard for someone like, say, Dr. Hawsworth to have read it."

"All he had to do was drop by the university," Dusty admitted.

"Which he did quite frequently." Nichols seemed to be talking to himself. "Interesting."

"How's that?" Maureen asked.

"Oh, nothing. Ruminating, that's all."

"Nichols!" one of the agents in the kiva called. He held up a piece of paper he'd dug from under the snow. Weathered and soggy, Dusty could see the printing on it even from where he stood.

"What is it? One of the interpretive brochures?" Nichols called.

The agent, holding his prize up with forceps, shook his head. "No, sir. It looks like a fax. It's addressed to Dale and signed by...Jesus. How do you pronounce this? Kweee...Kaw..."

"Kwewur," Dusty said, barely audible.

Nichols stepped to the edge of the kiva and called, "Bring it up here! I want to know what it says."

As the agent got to his feet and carefully made his way to the stairs, Dusty looked at Nichols. "So Hawsworth has been a frequent visitor at the university. Have you searched his house?"

"I don't have cause to search his house, Stewart. So far, I can't prove he's done anything wrong. But why? What would I be looking for?"

The agent climbed the stairs and headed toward them.

Dusty said, "Dale's missing journals."

As he ran south on the road toward High Sun House, Browser looked down at his white cloak and white moccasins. They flashed silver in the dim evening light. Even at night, he would make a perfect target. He tried not to think about it. He had to have faith that the plan would work, that they would still believe him to be too incompetent to have thought up something this clever and daring. He forced his legs into the distance-eating trot he had developed during the sun cycles of warfare.

High Sun House dominated the southern skyline. He cast a glance over his shoulder and there, a hard hand's run to the north, Center Place projected like a dimple from the mesa north of the canyon. No signal fire yet.

Gods, this wasn't going to be his last run, was it? He reached up to massage the slight ache that lay behind the scar on his forehead. He could feel the dent left by Elder Springbank's war club.

Elder Springbank, in reality, the witch, Two Hearts—he had been coiled in their midst the whole time. That was the trouble with witches, they hid and worked their evil from unsuspected places. Two Hearts had brought Browser here, to this most desperate gamble of his life.

This was by far the most delicate part of the plan. He had to get close, but not close enough that they could see his face. Then, he had a hard run to make, at least a hand's worth, in which he could not be caught.

High Sun House was a compact three-story town built on a high point with a view for four days' run to the south. From here the First People had tied their southern empire together. Distant rebellions were reported, and important visitors were heralded days before they could physically arrive.

Browser concentrated on his pace and thought about the fires that once had been lit, and the mirrors that once had flashed the Blessed Sun's messages to the distant towns and houses. How odd that he, a descendant of the First People, was about to lure his relatives out into the open so that they could be killed.

A secret part of him wondered what his great-great-great-grandmother, the Blessed Night Sun, would have thought. Would she hate him for this?

As he approached High Sun, his skin began to prickle as though swarmed by insects. Where it dominated the heights, High Sun looked like a square bastion of purple against a bluish-yellow evening sky. Browser slowed as he neared the northern wall. Gods, they wouldn't have a guard outside, would they? Some warrior who would rise from one of the piles of stone toppled from old shrines?

To his relief, a voice called from the wall above, "Who comes?"

"Hurry!" Browser cupped his hands. "War Chief Browser, of the Katsinas' People, is searching the towns below the staircase. He and his warriors are tearing Pottery House apart! Two Hearts is at risk. It is only a matter of time before they find him!"

Then Browser turned and ran as he had never run before. His white cape flapped like monstrous wings behind him.

The man yelled, "Wait! How many warriors does he have?"

Over his shoulder, Browser called, "More than we thought!" and ran harder.

The road took him straight north.

How long did he have? Against trained warriors, who had certainly been preparing for a night raid on Kettle Town, he doubted he had one hundred heartbeats before they pelted down the road after him.

And if Springbank is really there, inside High Sun, they will know this is a ruse.

Would they still come boiling out after him? Were they even now perched on the high walls, watching his white cloak disappear into the darkness, laughing at the absurdity of a War Chief who could pitch so lame a diversion and then run away?

As if to allay his fears—up in the distant north—a twinkle of fire blazed to life near Center Place, now nothing more than a dark hump on the distant mesa.

Catkin! He was sure of it. She had done it! Her diversion must be working. It had to be working.

He hadn't had the time to worry about her until now. But as he ran, fear traced fiery lines through his veins. He might die tonight, and if he did, it didn't matter. But if she died, and he lived...

Browser shoved the thought away. Fearing for loved ones sapped a warrior's strength. Instead, he forced himself to dream—to dream of what it would be like to run away, just he and Catkin, Uncle Stone Ghost, and maybe some of their trusted friends. Could they find a place with fertile soil, a small supply of water, and live in peace? Gods, was that so much to ask? Not fame, or power, or prestige, just the simple peace to raise corn, love Catkin, and perhaps see a couple of their children survive to become adults?

A shout broke the silence, and Browser shot a look over his shoulder. Dark shapes lined out on the road behind him. He almost laughed with relief. Two Hearts must not be at High Sun House. This desperate scheme might work after all.

If he lived. If Catkin did her part. If...

If only they had had time to love each other that afternoon.

With his life balanced by a thread, the world depending on his next actions, why did that one thought lodge between his souls?

The shouts grew louder, and he could hear them coming, their feet pounding out his doom.

Browser ran with all his might.

PIPER

"He took it from me! He...took...it! Where is he hiding it? I must have it!" Grandfather cries.

They are in the old place, a single-story building consisting of five rooms surrounding a small plaza and a kiva. Down in the kiva, Piper crouches against the dark northern wall, under the bench. She is scratching shapes into the crumbling plaster with her fingernails. The plaster screeches its upset. She scratches harder to cover Grandfather's wheezing voice.

"Piper. Where's...your mother? Go find...your mother!"

Grandfather thrashes from side to side. His arms are a dying bird's wings, flopping, trying to fly.

She scratches in time with the thumping sounds, making them go away.

Mother was not here when Piper arrived.

But there were three warriors. Grandfather ordered them to pull the ladder up through the rooftop opening so Piper couldn't climb out again and run away.

She grits her teeth and scratches so hard that her finger-nails break and bleed. Red streaks the wall.

She looks at it and thinks how beautiful it is.

Red on white, like the blood on Grandfather's cape.

"Piper! For the sake of the true gods! I need...water. Bring me water!"

Piper glances at the canteen leaning against the fire pit stones, then scratches harder and hums, making the scratching sound with her mouth, making it very loud.

Grandfather wheezes and can't seem to catch his breath. Baby bobcat mews are coming up his throat.

"Piper, I-I'm witching your breath-heart soul...putting it in a rock...a-a pendant...that was buried long ago."

Piper's hand freezes. She can feel her heartbeat slowing, and her lungs struggle for air. She reaches down with both hands and holds tight to the turquoise necklace Stone Ghost gave her. He said it would protect her. He said it was very Powerful.

"Yes," Grandfather whispers. "You can feel it, can't you? That pendant...rests on a dead woman's breast...locked in darkness...just as your breath-heart soul will be...forever. Forever in darkness."

Grandfather reaches out to Piper with a claw-like hand. "Bring me water!"

But Piper can't.

She can't move at all.

While Maureen chopped up the makings for a salad, Dusty cooked dinner. Pots filled with macaroni and cheese—southwestern style—bubbled on the stove. Dusty's version of the dish contained a large amount of diced Ortega green chilis, and several crumbled chunks of extra sharp cheddar. Additionally, tonight's fare included fried potatoes, sliced thin and cooked in butter in the cast-iron frying pan. He'd sprinkled chili powder instead of salt on top.

A real vegetarian delight.

Sylvia sat in the back corner of the booth, a thoughtful expression on her face. She alternated between munching on cheesy fishes and sipping from her can of Coors Light. Though she'd washed her hands and face after the day's work, dust still coated her brown hair and green T-shirt.

Michall, to her nutritional credit, snacked from a bag of unsalted sunflower seeds. She sat across the booth from Sylvia with her red hair pinned up. A thin line of mud showed just above her brown turtleneck.

"This is so bizarre," Sylvia said. "I mean, I've run bits

and pieces of dead people through screens for years. But, I mean, wow. This is Dale's dirt."

"Yes," Dusty added seriously, "and don't forget it."

"I wonder why the UNM field schools didn't dig this site," Michall asked.

"I don't know," Dusty said as he stirred more cheese into the macaroni. "They dug most of the Rincon small sites between 1939 and 1942."

Michall frowned. "As I recall, it caused a lot of problems when they discovered that the small houses were occupied at the same time as the Great Houses, but either by different people, or the same people living differently."

"The former," Sylvia said. She accented her point with a handful of cheesy fishes. "If you buy Steve LeBlanc's warfare theory, and Christy Turner's Chaco hypothesis, then the country bumpkins from the hinterlands came to Casa Rinconada to be impressed by the grand Chaco priests. The priests put them up in the small houses and, after dark, showed them miraculous wonders."

She stuffed the cheesy fishes into her mouth and slurred, "Tha's why the trench is in the floor. The priests could rise up out of the underworld right before the hicks' eyes."

"Your mother taught you never to talk with food in your mouth," Dusty said irritably. "Show us some common courtesy."

Sylvia washed it down with Coors and answered, "Courtesy is never common. Especially around you."

"It's the basilisk." Maureen shot her a warning look. "It's eating at Dusty. Me, too."

"I thought you didn't believe in it?" Sylvia studied her fingers, dyed yellow from the crackers. "Or has experience changed your mind?"

"I don't believe in it," Maureen said with certainty.

"It's just a carved stone. But it gives Dusty nightmares, and I have to consider that."

But as she started to cut up tomatoes for the salad, she wondered why—if she didn't believe—the little fetish worried her so much.

"What's even more weird is the FBI finding the note buried in the snow. I'm never going to feel the same about Casa Rinconada." Sylvia shook her head. "It used to be one of my favorite sites. I mean, you walk down there and you can feel the power, you know? Even after all these years. It still hums."

Dusty slammed his fork down and braced his hands on the counter.

Sylvia jumped. "What did I say?"

"Nothing. It—it's not you. I just keep thinking. Those dark stains on the dirt. The fact that Dale was killed—"

"We don't know that for sure," Maureen cautioned, wondering if Dusty was finally going to shatter into a thousand pieces. "Let's wait for the blood analysis before we come to any conclusions about what happened down there."

"But...the note..."

Sylvia came to attention. Her green eyes narrowed. "What about it? You haven't told us anything."

Dusty didn't reply for a while; then finally he said, "It said something like: 'Dale. Hello, old friend. Almost two cycles of the moon have come and gone since that terrible night. What you took from me cannot be forgiven. On the night of the Masks, when the Dead walk the world, come to the great corner kiva, old friend. I shall be waiting.'" Dusty picked up his stirring fork again and aimed it at the pot like a knife. "It was signed Kwewur."

"Who's Kwewur?" Michail asked with wide eyes.

Dusty said, "A katchina from a dead clan. From Awatovi."

Sylvia nodded. "I read about this. The Hopi burned Awatovi to the ground because they thought the village was filled with witches. Then, at Polacca Wash, they chopped up the captives."

Maureen finished the salad, set the bowl aside, and went to refill her coffee cup from the pot on the stove. She glanced at Dusty, judging his mood, before she asked, "Two cycles of the moon? How long is that?"

"A little more than thirty-seven years," Dusty replied. "But I have no idea what happened at Casa Rinconada in 1964."

"Dale took something from Kwewur. At least that's what the note says. Something that couldn't be forgiven. What could it have been?" Maureen slid into the booth beside Sylvia and set her coffee on the battered old table-top. "It's all so cryptic."

Headlights flashed through the trailer windows, and Sylvia put her hand against the glass to block the glare. "Hey, it's Magpie!"

Dusty stepped to the door and opened it. "Hi, Maggie. Come on in."

"Hi," Maggie said, but she'd stopped short of the door and was holding something in her hands. "Losing things already, Stewart? I'm glad this is a report and not a bag full of sacred artifacts."

She handed him a thick booklet, the kind copy places made with plastic binders. It was paper, eight and a half by eleven.

"This isn't mine." Dusty took it, squinting down at it in the lantern light. "Wait a minute. This was just lying outside?"

"Yes, on the ground." Maggie pulled her coat off and hung it on the peg by the door. "Smells great. Was I smart enough to get here in time for dinner?"

"This is a joke, right?" Dusty asked, still holding the

bound pages. "You didn't really find this on the ground outside."

Maggie lifted an eyebrow, catching the serious tone in Dusty's voice. "I saw it when I pulled up and stopped. I thought it was yours, so I picked it up. It was lying right outside the door, on the ground. Want me to go put it back?"

"What is it?" Maureen got to her feet and walked. She read the front sheet and whispered, "Dear God."

Dusty swallowed hard and handed it to her. "Please guard this while I get the pistol and take a look around outside."

Dusty went to the rear of the trailer and came out with his pistol.

Maggie's eyes went wide. "Stewart, that's not what I think it is, is it? You know the rules about firearms."

He gave her a steely look. "You, of all people, know what we're up against. You didn't see a thing, Maggie. And neither did anyone else in this trailer. Right?"

Maggie jerked a worried nod as he shouldered by and slipped out into the darkness. She took a deep breath, shook her head, and leaned sideways to read over Maureen's shoulders. "What is that? It looks like..."

"Dale's handwriting? Yes. This is one of his private journals."

Sylvia came over and took it from Maureen's hand. "How did one of Dale's private journals wind up outside the trailer on the ground?"

Maureen rubbed her arms, a sudden chill in her spine. "More to the point, who left it there? And *why*? What do they want us to read?"

An arrow rattled in the rocks a body's length from Blue Corn. She ducked and almost lost her precarious footing on the canyon rim. A cold wind blew out of the starry west, teasing her hair and fluttering her dress.

"That way!" Rain Crow pointed with his war club, sending four of his warriors scrambling off to the east. A misstep meant a fall from the rimrock to the canyon bottom a bow shot below them.

This was madness, trying to fight a running battle in the rimrock above Straight Path Canyon. Boulders jutted from the canted bedrock, and could hide one, two, or no assailants. Three of her warriors had been wounded, perhaps some were even dead by now. When she looked back over her shoulder, she saw the flickering on the rooftop where some thrice-cursed fool had built a fire.

Another arrow hissed into the rocks at her feet. From instinct, she bent down, despite the pain in her leg, and picked it up.

"There!" Rain Crow cried. "No, you fools, off to your right. Just below the crest of the cliff!"

"It's a diversion," Blue Corn said as she inspected the thin wooden shaft. She stumbled painfully in the gloom. "They want us off balance. This is a willow stave. Probably a piece taken out of an old sleeping mat."

"It may be a diversion, but some of those arrows are real. We must run these rats down, before they pick us all off." Rain Crow watched his warriors as— bent double to decrease their target area—they charged forward. At the slow rate of their advance, the mysterious archers would have more than enough time to abandon their positions and retreat.

"No, pull back," she ordered. "Rain Crow, this is meant to wear us out, to keep us from the canyon."

He stopped short, and she could feel his gaze as he considered the situation. To date they hadn't had a clean shot at one of the darting, weaving targets.

"But Matron—"

"Fall back!"

Rain Crow called, "Pull back! Regroup at the stairway."

"Gods know, Rain Crow, climbing down that stairway is where we will be the most vulnerable. We need every archer we have." She turned and picked her way back over the rocks and loose soil. Her aching hip sent fire up her side, but she couldn't limp, not on this rotted slope.

Rain Crow came to offer his hand, and with his help she made her way back to the roadway. The rising sandstone hid Center Place from her view, but below, part of Kettle Town's walls were visible.

"What happened?" Horned Ram stood, guarded by his Red Rock warriors. They had arrows nocked in their bows.

"A diversion. Phantoms shot splinters at us, then fled." She offered the willow stave.

Her warriors reformed, eyes on the eastern edge of the rim where their tormentors had disappeared.

Rain Crow studied the dark rocks warily as he started to say: "I think we—"

They rose from just under the lip of the stairway, four of them, loosing arrows from beneath their white cloaks.

The ambush came as a complete surprise. Blue Corn instinctively dropped to her belly, trying to wiggle down into the worn sandstone. But she could only cover her head and listen to the screams of her warriors.

"By the gods, how did this happen?" Horned Ram bellowed. *"We had to practically step on them!"*

"Rise!" Rain Crow shouted. "There are only four of them! Follow me!"

"Black Stalk is shot through the guts!" someone cried.

"Go!" Blue Corn ordered. "I'll tend to him. Avenge him! In the Flute Player's name, *go!*"

Blue Corn watched her warriors rise, hunched figures with bows, ready to loose deadly arrows as they scampered to the top of the stairway.

Rain Crow's voice carried, "Where did they go?"

"Careful. Watch out."

"I don't see anything!"

Blue Corn crawled over to Black Stalk and rested his head in her lap. The young warrior gripped the arrow shaft that stuck out of his abdomen just below the navel. Despite the darkness she could see the spreading blackness of gut blood as it soaked the panting warrior's shirt. She ran cool hands over his hot face.

"You're going to be all right, Black Stalk," she soothed. "Just hold on."

"Matron?" he asked through clenched teeth. "Blessed Flute Player, it burns like fire."

"It's the gut juice," she said.

On the night breeze she could smell the sour stench of punctured intestines.

He shivered, his feet kicking slowly, futilely as his sandals slid across the gritty stone.

"Matron," he whispered. "I would ask a favor?"

"Of course, Black Stalk. Anything within my power."

Sweat trickled down his face to dampen her shirt. With a trembling and bloody hand he unhooked the war club from his belt. Offering it, he said, "Kill me, Matron. Quickly. I've seen wounds like this. I don't want to die slowly. And if you pull this arrow out, you'll take half of me with it."

"Black Stalk, I—"

"Please, Matron. You've seen gut-shot men die before. You *know* what it's like."

At the pleading in his voice, she took the heavy war club, and eased his head down so that he stared up at the glistening Evening People.

"It's a...good club, Matron," he said through gritted teeth. "My father...made it...before he...died. Straight... and true."

"Yes, a good club," she answered, deadening her heart.

Was this the Black Stalk she remembered as a little boy? The one she had watched grow tall and strong? She had seen him on the day he had walked across the plaza, no more than thirteen summers in age. It had been spring, and despite being frightened half out of his wits, as all little boys were, he carried his head high as he went for his first kiva initiation.

Now I must kill him.

She shifted, rising onto her knees. The shaft of the war club was cool and thick in her hands. The smell of Black Stalk's blood and guts hung like a miasma in the air.

What brought me here, to this place, to do this to such a nice young man?

She lifted the club, her muscles suddenly rubbery and weak. A constriction, like a tightening band of rawhide pinched her chest. She couldn't find her breath.

"Please, Matron?" Black Stalk whimpered. "You have no idea how this hurts."

Her heart might have been a stone as she raised the war club high and with all of her might brought it down on his head. The impact carried up the wood, into her hands, arms, and shoulders. She heard as well as felt the sickening snap of the bones in his skull. His body spasmed, then went still.

She flung the club away and couldn't stop the sudden rush of tears. For long moments, she sat there, in the middle of the abandoned road, and sobbed as she hadn't since she was a young girl.

"Matron?" Rain Crow's gentle voice broke through her misery.

"Yes, War Chief." She ran a sleeve over her hot, wet face and straightened.

"There are four of them. They're headed south, past Kettle Town. I'd say they were heading straight across the canyon."

Blue Corn looked at Black Stalk's crushed skull, and her souls seemed to wither.

"Find them," she ordered. "Kill them. Kill them all, and bring me their heads, War Chief."

"I'll leave a few warriors to keep you—"

"No! Take everyone. No prisoners, War Chief. You have your orders. Go! Just get away! *Leave me alone!*"

She heard the eerie shriek in her voice. Soul sick, she bent double, holding her stomach, hearing Rain Crow barking orders as he and his men clambered down the staircase after the white-caped assailants.

26

The only sound was the hissing of the Coleman lantern and the flipping of pages as Sylvia read Dale's journal.

"Get a load of this." Sylvia's green eyes widened. "Who was Melissa? A graduate student?"

"That's enough, Sylvia," Dusty said, and held out a hand.

"Why? Don't you want to read it?" Sylvia asked as she handed him the photocopied journal, open to the page.

"No." But his eyes were inevitably drawn to the name.

"Melissa has been sleeping in my tent for a week. The crew's starting to talk. I have to end this. I should have never started it to begin with. She's so young and beautiful. And brilliant. She's asked me to oversee her dissertation research. Do I dare put myself in the position of being close to her for another two years?"

Sylvia's hand hovered in midair. "Yeah. I thought you'd want to read it, and you didn't even have time to get to the juicy stuff?"

Dusty closed the booklet and set it on the kitchen counter. He couldn't look at Sylvia, couldn't meet her eyes. So what if Dale had had an affair with a graduate student? That didn't mean he'd made a habit of it. Field affairs happened. Generally, they didn't mean a thing.

Dusty said, "Nobody touches this from here on out. It's evidence."

Maggie and Maureen sat at the rear of the table with their eyes on Dusty, while Michall craned her neck to peer out the windows into the darkness.

"Uh, Dusty," Michall said. "You know, right, that the person who left that is probably the person who murdered Dale?"

Dusty contemplatively walked into the kitchen and placed the bound copy on the counter. "That's the point, Michall. We're supposed to play along, pick out the clues."

"Well, if that's so," Michall said as she jerked the curtains closed, "he's one sick son of a bitch."

"If it's a he." Dusty smoothed his hand over his beard while he studied the ominous papers. He had the over-whelming desire to sit down and read every word—but damn it, he hated being led around by the nose. The diary had been left because something in it incriminated a specific person, which meant...what? That the incrimi-nated person was *not* the murderer?

He glanced over at Maureen. She sat with her elbows braced on the table, staring at him. Dusty said, "What do you think we should do?"

"Despite all the manhandling you, Maggie, and Sylvia have given it, Nichols might be able to pull fingerprints, fibers, or other incriminating evidence from it." Maureen pulled her cell phone from her shirt pocket. "Nichols might also want to set up roadblocks, have his people scout around the trailer for tracks."

Dusty nodded. "Call him."

Just the sight of Dale's handwriting brought an ache to his heart.

"Agent Nichols?" Maureen said. "It's Dr. Cole. Someone just dropped a copy of one of Dale's stolen journals at our trailer."

A pause.

"Yes."

Another pause.

"We won't move until Rick and Bill are here."

Silence.

"Maggie Walking Hawk Taylor found it on the step when she arrived for dinner."

Maureen frowned.

"Yes, somebody did open it. Sylvia."

Another pause. Maureen nodded.

"Yes, I think you'll find her fingerprints on a number of the pages."

And then, "We won't step out until they arrive."

Maureen punched the END button on the phone.

Sylvia said, "Oops."

Dusty's stomach twisted. What was Nichols thinking? That Sylvia had just covered her tracks?

Maggie said, "You think the murderer is a woman?"

Dusty slid into the booth, forcing Sylvia to scoot over next to Maureen, and said, "There was a woman at Dale's funeral. Do you remember, Maureen? I didn't see her, but you said—"

"The one who touched Dale's ashes and hurried away? Yes. I remember." Maureen searched Dusty's face. "In her thirties, wearing a black fur hat and dark glasses."

"Maybe just a colleague." Dusty shrugged. "I didn't see her."

Sylvia stared wide-eyed at the windows. "Damn! She's here. Or he's here? In the park. Just watching us?"

"Playing with us, you mean," Dusty said. "How long till the FBI's here?"

"Five minutes," Maureen replied, a distance in her gaze.

"Aunt Sage says that the witch is like Coyote and he's teasing us like he would a family of rabbits trapped under a rock," Maggie said soberly. She poked at her macaroni and potatoes with her fork.

Dusty immediately gave her his full attention. "What else did your aunt tell you?"

Maggie took a bite of macaroni, chewed, and swallowed. "She said that he's powerful. Maybe the most powerful witch in a hundred years."

"Him? As in a man?"

"She didn't say. But it could surely be a woman." Maggie was frowning, hiding something. A terrible confusion lay behind her strained expression.

"Could she find him? Figure out who he is?"

Maggie's voice broke as she said, "Dusty, she's dying."

He took a deep breath and nodded. "I-I'm sorry, Maggie. It seems like the whole world is dying around us. Everyone we love."

"Aunt Sage said that he has to be stopped." Maggie jabbed her fork at her food. "That something is happening, changing in the witch's life. If he isn't caught he's going to keep hunting."

"Not Coyote," Dusty corrected. "Wolf. It's Kwewur, the Wolf Katchina. And if it's a woman, she-wolves are the worst."

"No, Dusty." Maggie gave him a warning look. "Not the Wolf Katchina. We're talking about the Wolf Witch, who has taken the katchina's name and fouled it, the way witches do. Aunt Sage is worried. She says that Grandma Slumber and Aunt Hail have been talking to her."

Sylvia had turned so pale her freckles stood out like brown dots. "From the Land of the Dead?"

Maureen had narrowed her eyes but said nothing. For that, Dusty really appreciated her.

"What did they say?" Dusty asked without missing a beat. "Did the elder tell you?"

Maggie nodded. "Aunt Sage told me they were worried that an old evil had escaped from the past and was released into this world. That we touched it at 10K3 and at Pueblo Animas, but it is centered here, just like it was in the old days when the white palaces fell."

"Okay, right," Michall said as she finished off her dinner and laid the fork down. "Ancient witchcraft loose in the modern world, guys?"

Maureen raised a hand. "Michall, before all else, I'm a scientist. You were there for the beginning of the work on 10K3. Whether you believe in the spiritual aspects or not, there is a link between that site and the things that are going on now."

Dusty and Maggie stared at each other. "Did Hail tell you anything at all about 10K3?"

"She told me that the evil was too strong there. She said, 'The witch has won again.' That's all she'd tell me. That's one of the reasons I made Aunt Sage go to the healing up at Aztec when Washais called."

"Who?" Michall asked.

"Washais is my Seneca name," Maureen told her. "Hail Walking Hawk preferred to think of me that way."

"It means bloody scalping knife," Sylvia said with aplomb.

Maureen's brows lowered. "You Whites are so inventive."

Sylvia grinned.

"Getting back to the witch?" Dusty said, his attention on Maggie.

"Think, old," Maggie said. "Aunt Sage said she couldn't really hear what Slumber and Hail were trying to tell her from the other side. Just that the witch had found something here, in the canyon, and it has been growing inside him."

"Or her," Maureen interjected.

"Did Aunt Sage say if it was a woman?" Dusty asked.

"No."

Sylvia whispered, "Did you see *The Blair Witch Project?* If I hear something like popcorn popping outside of the dormitory tonight, I'm going to come looking for you two." She pointed at Dusty and Maggie.

Maureen said, "I don't know much about witches, or witchcraft. I've only just begun studying it. But I do know something about death rituals. For example, my people, the Iroquois, keep our dead close until the Feast of the Dead when we send them to the Village of Souls. The southeastern tribes, the Cherokee, Choctaw, Chickasaw, and Creek, build shrines and keep the corpses of their ancestors literally in the back yard. The Apache and Navajo are dreadfully frightened of the dead. Among the Navajo, you can tell a witch because they dig up corpses and loot graves."

She turned her gaze on Maggie. "Among the Pueblo people, witches are known for eating the flesh of the dead, aren't they?"

Maggie nodded uncomfortably. "That's right."

Dusty asked, "Where are you going with this, Maureen?"

Maureen had a puzzled expression. "I'm not sure, yet. But it has to do with motivation. Like that photocopied journal in front of you. It doesn't make sense. Why is this happening the way that it is?"

"I'll bite," Sylvia said. "Why?"

"That's what we have to figure out." Maureen steepled her fingers, mind knotting around the problem.

Dusty thought she looked stunning, her eyes animated in the lantern light.

"So you don't think it's an ancient evil that got let loose?" Maggie asked.

Maureen shrugged. "Maybe that's part of it, but what does a witch want? What are the things that motivate them to do what they do?"

"Power," Maggie answered. "A witch wants to amass wealth and gain status. He wants to be looked up to, to be noticed and feared. He wants to be important."

"So, what's the worst thing you can do to a witch?" Maureen pursued.

"Stone him to death and bury him under a rock," Sylvia supplied.

"I don't mean how do you punish him, I mean how do you really piss off a witch?"

Dusty smoothed his hands over Dale's journal. "Humiliation is the worst thing you can do to a witch."

"Think back to that note that they found in Casa Rinconada today," Maureen reminded. "Something happened in the past that can't be forgiven. Something worth waiting more than thirty-seven years to avenge. Humiliation?"

Dusty's eyes went to the photocopied diary. He exhaled hard. "No matter what, we're supposed to read it. Kwewur wants us to read it."

Lights shone outside.

"We will," Maureen promised. "Just as soon as Bill and Rick dust it for prints and check for fibers." She narrowed her eyes in thought.

"What?"

"Something Rupert said...about witches and how they are into misdirection. If I could only..." But she shook her head, dashing his hopes.

War Chief Bear Lance charged northward along the dark, starlit road. His white moccasins flashed in the night as he sprinted in pursuit. He could see the runner when he crested the high points. The man's white cape flashed. It had to be Polished Bone or Puma Silk, one of the two sentries left to watch over Elder Two Hearts and the canyon.

"But what if it isn't?"

Could this be a ruse? Were they being led into a trap?

"What was that?" Stone Lizard, where he ran close behind, asked between panting breaths.

Bear Lance cast a glance over his shoulder. Eighteen men lined out behind him, running in their distance-eating stride with their white capes flapping like wings.

"I'm worried about being ambushed."

Stone Lizard replied, "Then let us be careful."

Bear Lance had succeeded the great Ten Hawks after his death and become War Chief for the Red Lacewing Clan in Straight Path Canyon. The awesome responsibility had fallen onto his shoulders at the most difficult of times. The existence of the White Moccasins was now openly spoken of among the Made People. Elder Two Hearts, descendant of the Red Lacewing Matrons, lay wounded, slowly dying, and now, if his scout ahead could be believed, was being hunted by War Chief Browser. Not just an enemy, but also one of the First People.

As he ran, Bear Lance couldn't help but feel the wrongness of this. Why hadn't Polished Bone, if that's who that was, run inside to deliver his message?

Maybe because the situation in the canyon is too critical? He knows he has to get back quickly.

Bear Lance thought of Two Hearts lying in the lone small house, guarded only by a warrior and Shadow Woman. He hadn't liked the idea. No, he hadn't liked any of it, but the elder had ordered—and as War Chief to the man he considered the Blessed Sun, that was enough. But Shadow, even after all these sun cycles, frightened him.

She had been his lover, his enemy, his greatest desire, and his utter despair. On rare occasions she still crawled into his blankets and stroked his body into a throbbing fountain of ecstasy. Then, not more than a hand of time later, she would shrivel his souls by eating raw flesh stripped from one of her Made People victims.

"A light." Stone Lizard pointed at the heights in the north. The tiny flicker came from Center Place.

"A signal fire?"

Stone Lizard said, "Perhaps. But signaling what?"

Bear Lance gripped his war club. "You are sure that was Polished Bone up there?"

"Blood Axe thought so, but he wasn't absolutely positive."

Bear Lance wet his lips and sucked in a deep breath, forcing his legs to move faster. "If that is not one of our warriors, and he gets to the Blessed Elder with so much as his bare hands, he can end all our dreams."

Night deepened around them as they ran. Bear Lance

passed the familiar shrines and felt the road begin to slope down to the canyon and the stairway.

"Careful," he called, raising one hand. "I want arrows nocked. I don't want us to be taken in ambush here. Spread out and keep—"

"About time!" a familiar female voice hissed.

Bear Lance shied away from the shrine at the side of the road where a dark figure arose, ghostlike in the darkness. Her long black hair shimmered with a silver fire in the starlight.

"I didn't—"

"*Fool!* What took you so long?" Shadow demanded. "A war party is coming! You must hold them or destroy them."

"The Blessed Sun, is he—?"

"Being moved to a new location. The Blue God curse you for standing here talking while our elder is at risk!" She flung an arm toward the trail. "*Go. Now!*"

As the last of the White Moccasins charged down the stairway, Obsidian slumped to the ground. Her bones shook like sticks. But she had done it. At the last moment, as the warriors slowed, something had risen from deep within her, and she had found a part of herself she never knew existed.

Gulping deep breaths to cool her fevered body, Obsidian forced herself to her feet and started down the stairway in the wake of the departed warriors.

Gods, why did it have to be so dark?

Placing her feet, she lowered herself step by step, desperate at the feeling of unseen eyes in the darkness. When she reached the road, she slipped off to the side, making her way through the tumbled boulders below the cliff.

She heard the sudden cry, and then shouts and howls accompanied by the sound of battle.

If she could only make it back to the safety of Kettle Town, she'd never...

Silky laughter seemed to seep from the rocks. "Why, *Sister,* what did you just do?"

Dusty crouched next to Maggie at the edge of the tape, watching Michall carefully screen the last of the disturbed fill that had surrounded Dale's body. Nothing had been recovered from the dirt except several potsherds.

"Nothing" was the key word. Just like nothing had been recovered from the FBI search around the trailer the night before. Not that that surprised him. Were he Kwewur, he'd have sneaked up on the pavement, left the diary, and slipped away. Asphalt left no tracks.

The gray November day was cold. Rupert had thoughtfully provided tarps and straw bales to keep the excavation from freezing at night.

"Let's go deeper," Michall called as she finished the last of her notes. "It's kiva fill so I say we take twenty-centimeter levels until we come down on the roof." She shot a glance at Dusty, as if seeking his approval. He nodded, aware that in another time, he'd have instinctively looked to Dale for similar concurrence.

He missed Maureen. She'd been gone for only an hour, taking the propane bottles to Cuba to get them refilled, but it seemed like an eternity. He was genuinely worried about her.

Gravel crunched when Maggie shifted to sit down cross-legged on the frozen soil. "It's odd, isn't it? Being on the outside of the excavation?"

"It's driving me crazy."

In a low voice, Maggie said, "Dusty? I've got to talk to someone. If I tell you..."

"Sure, Maggie. You don't even have to ask."

"Remember that night? Back at 10K3? The night when you first called me out to the site to tell me you thought you had uncovered a witch?"

"Uh-huh."

"You trusted me."

"Yep. I still do."

She stared thoughtfully at the excavation where Michall's crew was working. Finally she said, "About last night...at the trailer. I said that Aunt Sage was telling me those things."

"She's not?"

"Some. The rest of it has been coming to me." She gave him a sidelong glance, as if to measure his response. "Sometimes I catch an image, like a phantom in the half-light. I know it's Grandma Slumber and Aunt Hail. And they're gone, just like that."

"What does your aunt Sage say?"

"That I need to let myself go, allow myself to see."

He considered that. "So do it."

She shivered despite her coat. "I'm afraid I'm going nuts. What if it's schizophrenia?"

"Being nuts isn't so bad. People have called me crazy for years."

"Don't joke."

"Okay. Maggie, I think you need to talk to your aunt.

That's what elders do, they help people find their gifts. They guide them down the road to Power."

She made a face. "I started talking to Reggie about it, and, God, maybe it was the wind, but I'd have sworn I heard Dale's voice telling me not to."

Dusty studied her, his heart skipping. "You think?"

She shrugged. "I don't know. Maybe it was my subconscious. I got to thinking about it later, and, well, there was something about the way that Reggie was looking at me. Almost like he wanted to devour me on the spot. You know what I mean?"

"No. Look, the only advice I can give is that you trust yourself, okay? That, and go talk to Aunt Sage about it."

"As soon as I can. I'm worried sick about her. And things are so tense here these days, I can't get away."

Dusty picked up a handful of soil and poured it from hand to hand as he watched the white Ford Explorer pull into the parking lot beside the crew vehicles. A tourist? At this time of year? A brave one.

Dusty said, "I thought Nichols had closed the road."

"He did; then he reopened it." She lifted her eyes heavenward in a gesture of exasperation, and added, "You think I'm going crazy. You should have to work with Rupert these days."

Dusty smiled but wondered about that. Had Nichols reopened the road to allow the murderer to return to the scene of the crime? Were the openings and closings some sort of clever FBI trap?

Maggie scrutinized the woman who got out of the car wearing a thick down coat with the tan hood pulled up and said, "I'll take care of it if she gets too close."

He nodded.

Maggie's brow furrowed as wind tugged at her shoulder-length black hair. "Dusty, the morning I found Dale's truck, I saw an owl. He was sitting in the road. I stopped, and he just vanished." She paused, letting that sink in. "Then, over by Casa Rinconada, I would have sworn that I saw Dale walking up the trail."

Dusty tried to keep his heart from leaping. The wound in his soul opened. "God, I hope you did. Did he look all right? I mean, you know, happy?"

She shivered inside her brown Park Service coat. "He did. He looked just like the old Dale. I think he was telling me he was all right. That he was still with us."

"That makes me feel better."

"I wish I felt so good about it. I'm worried what people will say if this gets out."

Dusty brushed his hands off on his pants. "You just need more time, Maggie. I think your people will accept it. You have to open yourself up, give them a chance."

"Easy for you to say. You don't know the things that are being whispered about Aunt Sage."

"What things?"

The worry in her face couldn't be hidden. "All of my aunts had Power, Dusty. They could see the dead. Sometimes just having the ability scares people, if you know what I mean. They don't understand."

"You mean there's talk that she might be a witch?"

"Shh!" Maggie said and looked around to make sure no one could overhear them. She murmured, "Yes, now let's talk about something else."

"Okay," he said, but the news stunned him. Maggie's aunts were the only truly holy people he'd ever known. He brushed at the dirt on his pants and looked toward Casa Rinconada. The woman had her back to them, looking down into the kiva. "Where did you see Dale?"

Maggie turned and pointed. "There. He was walking out of the morning, looking just fine, Dusty."

Dusty smiled.

Maggie's gaze rested on the tourist, probably seeing

that the woman didn't step onto the ancient walls or throw trash into the kiva—which tourists were prone to do; it was just a big hole to them.

After a long silence, Maggie said, "What do you know of Reggie Brown Horse?"

"Rupert's grandson?"

She nodded. "He seems nice. He's been coming by my place a lot, bringing me things. You know, gifts he's found, pretty stones. Last night, he brought me a single rose."

Dusty shrugged. "He's on probation. Breaking and entering, burglary, fencing stolen goods, I don't know all of it. Maybe he's changed. I'm sure being up here with Rupert has helped."

"He isn't the first kid coming out of that background to get a little off track. Especially since he and his mother don't get along. You know Reggie's father, right?"

"Lupe. I hear he's making flutes and selling them. I always liked Lupe." Dusty smiled at the memories. "We had a couple of wild times when we were both kids."

He hoped she wouldn't ask him to explain that. If she thought the stories about him dancing with strippers and freezing his nether portions to Wyoming trucks were bad...

"We're all so fragile," Maggie said. "Reggie most of all."

Thankfully, she turned her attention to the FBI team. They pitched rocks out of the kiva, while Michall and Sylvia shoveled dirt into screens. "What is it about men and women that makes us so dangerous for each other?"

"Bad genes," Dusty said. "It's that X and Y chromosome crap."

Maggie laughed, then carefully asked, "What's happening between you and Maureen?"

"Nothing."

"Why not?"

"God," Dusty said, annoyed, "give us some time."

"The way the two of you look at each other, I'd think your souls were getting sticky."

He laughed softly. "Not yet. Well...maybe a little. We'll see what happens after all this is over."

Maggie smiled and tucked her hands into her pockets. "Good."

The tourist climbed from the trail below. She had her head down, and her tan hood waffled around her face, hiding it.

"Here comes your charge," Dusty said. "As the resident tourist herder, maybe you'd better go empty the potsherds from her pockets and send her back to the established trails."

Maggie stood up and called, "Pardon me, ma'am, but this area is closed to the public. You'll have to stay on the prescribed trails."

"Indeed?" she called in that precise New England accent. "I think your administrator would approve of my being here. I believe he would consider it, well, let's say professional courtesy."

Dusty put a hand out to restrain Maggie. "Oh, shit. It's Ruth Ann Sullivan."

"Your *mother?*" The note of incredulity and the look on Maggie's face were precious.

"In the flesh. Now, what was it we were just talking about? That thing with men and women?"

"Forget I said it," she muttered. "Want me to go warn Rupert that she's here?"

"He's got papers to shuffle and a park to run. I'll make sure she doesn't flip cigarette butts into the carbon samples and keep her from collapsing the ruin walls."

Maggie gave Ruth Ann a skeptical look, then turned to hug Dusty, as though she thought he might need it. She whispered, "Thanks for listening."

"Yeah, Magpie, anytime. See you." He let her go and watched her give Ruth Ann a wide berth as she headed down the hill.

Ruth Ann Sullivan wore a thick coat, the sort sold by upscale sporting goods stores. Her hiking boots looked brand new, slightly dusted from the walk up to the site. A knit cap was pulled over her shining silver hair. She looked somehow disheveled, her blue jeans wrinkled.

"You must have risen at four A.M. to make it out here this early."

"I slept in the Explorer last night." A faint smile crossed her lips as she looked back at Maggie, who picked her way down the ridge. "Another one of your women, I take it? You surprise me. You're more of a lothario than I would have thought. What happened with you and the good doctor, the one with the black eyes and the killer figure? Did she finally come to her senses?"

In a curt voice, Dusty asked, "What are you doing out here?"

The wind teased strands of her silver hair as she turned toward the dig. "That's where they found Dale?"

"It is."

"What have you discovered?"

"Nothing yet."

She let out a breath as though relieved, or maybe disappointed, Dusty couldn't tell for sure.

"Slept in the Explorer, huh?" he said and crossed his arms, anticipating an argument. "You didn't, perchance, drop a photocopy of one of Dale's journals by my trailer before you came out here, did you?"

Ruth Ann turned slowly. Her eyes resembled cut diamonds, hard and glittering. "You have a photocopy of one of Dale's journals? I'd very much like to see it."

"Why?"

"Did you read it, William?"

"I will as soon as Agent Nichols gives it back."

She didn't say anything, as though waiting for him to continue, but her gaze affected him like a knife in his belly, carving him apart. "Nichols must have read it by now. And he hasn't found the killer, or the dig would be closed. Oh, come on. You must have sneaked a glance at the pages? What did it say?"

Dusty matched her stare. "He said you were a ruthless bitch who would stop at nothing to get your way."

Ruth Ann's left brow arched. "Amazing, your mouth still quirks when you lie. Just like it did when you were five years old."

She walked away, toward the site.

Browser skipped and skidded down into Straight Path Wash, his fevered lungs burning for breath. They were still behind him. He'd seen them less than fifty heartbeats ago. He unpinned the white cloak he'd taken from the body of the scout killed by his uncle and let it drop into the dark mud. Then he bent down and stripped the white moccasins from his feet. He quickly replaced them with his own worn brown buffalo-hide pair and slogged downstream through the runoff.

The cold air felt wonderful. It dried the hot sweat on his skin and cooled his lungs.

He heard shouts, but from the north. Browser hesitated only a moment, listened, then ran again. Blessed Gods, was it working?

He trotted forward on unsteady legs and hunkered down beside the roadway. He could hear labored breathing. He lifted himself and peered over the bank. They wore white cloaks, but not the fine cloaks of the White Moccasins; these had been dyed with white clay and ash, but the effect was the same in the darkness.

"Here!" he called.

"War Chief?" Yucca Whip led his party toward Straight Path Wash.

"Yes. Take your cloaks off and toss them into the wash. Then follow me."

As they tossed their capes into the mud, the gasping Yucca Whip managed to say, "You should have seen it! Masterful! They were looking everywhere except at their feet. I'd have never believed it!"

More shouts.

"Quickly, this way." Browser led them westward, then dropped onto his belly on the cold ground. They lay down behind him. "Look!"

There, running northward, they could see the shining cloaks of the White Moccasins. Angry shouts broke out from Blue Corn's warriors when they, too, picked out the bobbing white cloaks.

"Holy Thlatsinas," Yucca Whip whispered. "It's going to work."

"Where's Catkin?" Browser asked, scanning the group.

"I don't know, War Chief. Her party drew the warriors off to the east, but as soon as they figured out it was a diversion, they returned. If the deputy or any of the others was wounded, none of the Straight Path warriors spoke of it."

Browser returned his attention to the closing warriors, but a knot of worry drew tight in his chest.

R uth Ann Sullivan stopped at the edge of the yellow tape and watched Sylvia screening the dirt that Michall shoveled up to her. The FBI team had started to sweat. It beaded their faces, collected dust, and ran down their necks. Sylvia kept giving Ruth Ann questioning looks, obviously wondering who she might be, but Michall barely seemed to notice her. Dusty walked over to stand beside his mother.

"So, this is where they left him?" Ruth Ann said.

"What do you mean, they? You think it was more than one person?" Standing there in the wind, Dusty tried to decide what he felt for this woman, but he didn't seem to feel anything. It was as though a big blank hole opened up inside him when he looked at her.

"Dale was a big man."

"Not that big. He was seventy-three. Bone and muscle mass decreases with age. He'd lost a lot of weight. I'd say he might have weighed one-thirty or one-forty, somewhere in there." He was looking at her, remembering the way she'd walked up the hill—as though she owned the world.

As if reading his mind, she said, "You don't like me, do you? Not that it matters, God knows."

"I don't know you well enough to dislike you. Give me another day."

She laughed, the sound of it dry and brittle. "No wonder you got along with Dale. I must admit, I thought about killing him once upon a time, and I sure as hell would have if he'd been behind those faxes."

Dusty studied her face, and for a moment he could see her as she had been when he was four or five. Ravishingly beautiful, smiling, her long blond hair whipping around her face in the wind. Where had that been? What dig? One of the excavations out at Zuni? A sensation of happiness spread through him.

He marveled at that. All these years he'd believed she'd never really done archaeology—yet he had memories of her on excavations. Memories he'd apparently locked inside himself and forgotten. Or perhaps Dale's words that she'd never "sunk a trowel" had tricked his memories into retreating?

He said, "Why are you still here?"

"Your friends at the FBI asked me not to leave." Her squint wasn't just the wind. "And I'm interested. I thought I'd see where this investigation of yours goes. I've just about come to the conclusion that Carter's at the bottom of this. He always was a vindictive son of a bitch."

"Why would he kill Dale?"

"Envy, William. It's a hideous emotion. Dale was everything Carter wanted to be: famous, respected, powerful, charming, and virile. He got along with people. All Dale had to do was turn on that charm, and even his enemies liked him. He was a big man in every mannerism and aspect. Carter Hawsworth, for all of his show, is small-minded." She shook her head. "It must have come as quite a blow to Carter when he returned here to find just how important Dale had become."

Dusty nodded. "The governor even gave him an award last year, for his contributions to understanding New Mexico's past."

"In Carter's mind, that's reason enough for murder."

Dusty watched Sylvia pick something out of the screen. She examined it, then tossed it aside. Probably a rock. "You're pushing this 'Carter the Murderer' thing pretty hard, aren't you?"

She slipped her gloved hands into her pockets. "The human muscle tissue that you said they found in Dale's mouth—"

"Had been taken from a cadaver; it had preservative in it."

She rubbed the back of her neck, and whispered, "A cadaver," but it sounded like a question. "So, the murderer must have had access to a medical school, anatomy lab, or mortuary."

"Or graveyard. If you know about southwestern witch-craft, you know how important graveyards can be."

"And Dale was killed right here?" She was staring woodenly at the excavation. "But why kill him..." She turned slightly as she examined the surrounding canyon. He saw her finger moving, marking off the landmarks, and then she stiffened at some thought in her head.

"Something just tripped your trigger?" Dusty asked.

"Nothing, I just...are you *certain* he was killed here?"

"Actually, we just found out yesterday that he was killed in Casa Rinconada." Dusty was watching her. "The bloodstains are still there, on the kiva floor."

She swiveled around to look back at the great kiva.

Something about her expression, the odd tension in her face, the hardness at the corners of her lips...

Dusty said softly, "But then, you knew that, didn't

you? That's the first place you went when you arrived. You stopped there and looked in for a long time. What were you seeing? The way Dale looked in his last moments?"

She swallowed hard. If anyone ever looked guilty, Ruth Ann Sullivan did. He saw the fear in her eyes as she turned away and started down the hill.

"Wait!" Dusty started after her. "How did you know he'd been killed there? Did someone tell you? Or did you—?"

She spun around, panic and tears mixing on her face.

"I *didn't* kill him, you simpering little bastard!" She broke into a hobbling run.

"Wait. Come back!"

When she hit the graveled path, Ruth Ann Sullivan broke into a flat-out run, headed back to her parked vehicle. When she finally reached it, she slammed the door, the engine screaming to life.

Dusty watched her speed away down the dirt road. Only when he happened to glance back at the dig did he notice that Michall, Sylvia, and the FBI guys were watching, wide-eyed and silent.

The White Moccasins boiled up from Straight Path Wash. Rain Crow blocked the first blow with his war club; then the battle disintegrated into a mad chaos of slashing, hacking warriors.

"Kill them! Kill them all!" The cries of the White Moccasins carried over the grunting pants of men fighting for their lives.

Screams rang out as warriors were battered senseless, or some archer drove a shaft into a sweating body.

"Orphan scum!" "Dirty killer!" "Bastard born of a slave!" Curses were hurled as the melee swirled. "Kill our Blessed Elder, will you? He'll eat your liver!"

"Die, you pus-licking First worm!"

Rain Crow twisted his ruined face into a grimace and blocked yet another of the raining blows that were being showered upon him. Sun cycles of practice stood him in good stead. He ducked, and his assailant's momentum carried him past. Rain Crow thrust his war club into the man's crotch with enough force to send him howling and reeling. A follow-up stroke crushed the man's ribs.

Pivoting on his foot, he split the fellow's skull with a meaty smack.

Somewhere to his right, a man let out an eerie blood-curdling scream as he died.

Around him, warriors swirled in a blur. The white cloaks of the enemy mixed with his darker-dressed warriors.

Rain Crow charged headlong into another white-clad warrior. The impact of their bodies thumped hollowly. Rain Crow recovered first, but his enemy skipped back and blocked his savage attack. An eternity passed as they swung at each other. It might have been a macabre dance, each step and movement part of Death's mating ritual.

An arrow whisked past Rain Crow's cheek. The White Moccasin flinched; Rain Crow slammed his club into the man's shoulder and kicked him hard in the belly. The shocked warrior staggered back, and Rain Crow broke his neck with a quick swing of his club.

For a heartbeat, he stared down at the man, his eyes blinking, surprised to be still alive. Then he glimpsed movement to his right—and a brilliant yellow bolt blasted through his vision like lightning on a summer night.

Yellow lantern light pulsed over the interior of the battered camp trailer, reflecting from the wood veneer walls and the heaping plates of enchiladas on the table. The scents of melted cheese and cumin filled the air. Dusty ate another bite of blue corn enchilada.

"You should have seen it," Michall told Maureen as she tucked a loose strand of red hair behind her ear. "We didn't know who she was. We figured she was cool because Maggie hadn't chased her away. Then she and Dusty started yelling at each other."

Michall scooped up a forkful of food, and continued, "Turns out he's reaming Ruth Ann Sullivan. The *real* Dr. Ruth Ann Sullivan, of Harvard fame. Right there in front of us!"

"Yeah." Sylvia thumped her Coors can and squinted at Dusty. "Talk about a dysfunctional family. You guys wouldn't even have made it to the waiting room on *Leave It to Beaver*."

"Sylvia," Dusty warned, "give it a break."

Michall gobbled down a big bite of dinner and continued, "The FBI went crazy, taking notes, talking on their cell phones. The excavation came to a dead halt."

Dusty glanced at Maureen; She gave him a sympathetic look, and kept eating. He'd added whole coriander to the sauce, giving the enchiladas a real tang.

Sylvia took a sip of Coors and thoughtfully changed the subject. "You know that FBI guy, Rick? He's a pretty good hand. Bill, however, is a worthless sack of shit. I can't figure how a guy like that gets by. He doesn't like to get his fingers dirty. How do you think he deals with a bleeding corpse?"

"Lots of rubber gloves," Dusty answered. He didn't feel like talking. The day's activities had left him drained and irritable. He ate another bite and crunched a cumin seed. He should have let the sauce simmer longer, but damn it, he'd been hungry—and in a hurry to be done with the day.

Michall covertly watched Dusty as she finished her enchiladas. He could feel her gaze on him. His mood had put a damper on everyone's spirits.

When they had all finished eating and sat around sipping their drinks, Sylvia gave Dusty a knowing look, and said, "Come on, Mick, let's get out of here. Every bone in my body is crying for sleep, and I still have field notes to finish."

Sylvia slid out of the booth.

Michall opened her mouth to say something, caught Sylvia's look, and said, "Sure. Okay. I'm finished with my beer." She tipped the can and gulped the last ten swallows. "Good night, Dusty. Night, Maureen."

Michall pulled on her coat. At the door she said, "See you guys tomorrow."

Through the window, Maureen watched them drive away, and stood up. She dropped her paper plate in the trash, washed her fork in the sink, and rinsed it off with hot water from the teapot. Then she set the half-full enchilada pan on the ice block in the cooler. It would be fodder for breakfast in the morning.

While she worked, Dusty walked his fork across his plate in a rocking motion. The tines left patterns in the damp paper—a sort of punctate indented design, just like that found on a lot of ancient pottery.

"She really got to you, eh?" Maureen asked.

Dusty shrugged. "I think I got to her more than she did to me."

"Did you believe her when she said she'd slept out at Chaco in her Explorer?"

"Yeah, she looked it."

"Then she didn't leave the diary."

Dusty's voice softened. "She could have paid someone to leave it for us, Maureen. Who knows what that woman is capable of?"

He put his fork down and started massaging the muscles at the back of his neck. They really ached.

Maureen dried her hands on a paper towel and slid into the booth beside him. "Let me help you with that."

Uneasy, Dusty turned slightly, and Maureen started massaging the muscles.

"Oh, my god, that feels good," he sighed and leaned into her hands.

"Well, don't get any ideas, I'm just doing this because I can't stand to hear the air crackle."

Dusty could feel his anxiety seeping away, his headache even eased. "You're good at this."

Maureen smoothed away a lock of his blond hair. "I took a massage course in college. The same semester that I had macrame."

"Tough load."

She smiled. "For what it's worth, Ruth Ann had the same effect on me. When she walked away from my table at the Loretto, I would have loved to have run after her and wrung her neck. I didn't because I was surrounded by people, but out here...?"

Dusty closed his eyes, and images of Dale flashed through his mind. The grief that he held locked deep inside him wriggled up and shot through his chest like tiny fiery lightning bolts. What had Dale ever seen in his mother? "Ruth Ann called you my girlfriend, the one with the black eyes and killer figure."

"Well, I like the last part."

He reached up to touch her right hand. "I told her we were friends. Only."

Maureen patted his fingers and continued massaging his ironlike muscles. "I doubt that she believed you. She seems to think you're some kind of Casanova."

"She called me a leather rio."

"That's 'lothario.'"

"Whatever." He lowered his hand and wondered what he was going to do. Dale had been the center of his life, the one person he trusted. "I worried about you today. I'm not sure you should be running around alone—even to go to the grocery store. I kept wondering what it would be like if you didn't come back, and it scared me."

Maureen stopped massaging, hesitated, then leaned forward to wrap her arms around his broad shoulders. Dusty was afraid to move, afraid she might let go.

"Are you all right?" she asked in a tender voice.

He exhaled the word "No," then shook his head. "I don't think I will be for a long time. I keep hearing Dale's voice."

Maureen tightened her hold. "What is he saying?"

"I can't make out the words, but his tone is angry and frightened, as though I'm missing something right in front of my eyes, and he can't understand why I'm so blind."

Headlights cast white on the trailer windows as a vehicle pulled in beside the Bronco.

Dusty pulled away from Maureen. "If it's Sylvia, I'm going to brain her."

"We both will," Maureen added with a smile.

The motor outside shut off and a door made a soft thump. Seconds later there was a knock at the door.

"William?" Ruth Ann's voice called stridently. "May I come in?"

Dusty squeezed his eyes closed. "Oh, god."

Browser slid forward on his belly and peered over the low rise at the two dark figures. They walked among the dead and wounded like silent specters.

"Let's go get them," Fire Lark whispered.

"Wait," Browser cautioned. "We have just avoided one trap, let's not walk into another."

"Blessed Thlatsinas," Yucca Whip whispered. "I wish it had been daylight."

Browser hissed, "The losing side would have broken and run, knowing they were beaten. They were fighting in the dark, that's why they slugged it out until only two were left standing."

"But, to have—"

"Shhh!" Browser could barely see the two standing figures now. They had walked to the edge of the battle-ground and stood talking in low tones, gasping for breath as they turned and slowly began to walk northward toward the lumbering darkness of the cliff. In their wake, occasional groans and moans could be heard among the wounded.

Then a single scream rang out.

"Who's there?" a frightened voice called. "Get away! Don't—" The voice was choked off by the hollow thunk of a war club against a human skull.

Yucca Whip whispered, "Who is that out there? Is he going around killing the—"

Browser clapped a hand over his mouth, barely exhaling, "Silence," as he struggled to see through the night.

He and his warriors lay like the dead while the evening chill settled on their cold flesh. The wait seemed eternal as the faintest glow built on the eastern horizon and finally surrendered to Sister Moon.

Still, Browser wouldn't allow them to rise. They shivered until their teeth began to chatter. Blow after blow silenced the cries of the wounded. Browser allowed a hand of time to pass before he tapped Yucca Whip on the shoulder and rose. He led them forward. At the edge of the road, he surveyed the dead.

"Who did this?" Fire Lark whispered. "I never saw anyone!"

Browser knelt by one of Blue Corn's warriors. The man lay on his back, his half-open eyes gleaming in the moonlight. The arrow through his guts, though fatal, should have allowed him to linger for at least a day or two. The red stain on his chest, however, betrayed the wound that had killed him.

"Stiletto," Clay Frog said woodenly. "Someone went through and made sure."

The hair at the back of Browser's scalp started to prickle. He spun around, searching. "Yes, and if she's not hunting us now, she will be soon."

"Who, Blue Corn?" Clay Frog asked.

"No," Browser replied. "Keep your eyes open."

Slowly, painstakingly, he led them across the battlefield, weaving between the bodies. He almost tripped over a man who lay sprawled in a narrow drainage. Moonlight bathed the exposed arms and legs, each of which had been sliced open. Cuts of meat had been taken from the bone.

"Blessed Gods," Clay Frog whispered, pointing at the head; like a broken pumpkin, the insides had been scooped out. "The killer took his brain, along with the steaks!"

Browser squinted into the darkness. She was out there, somewhere, maybe looking at him this instant. "She's taking meat back to Two Hearts."

"By the Blue God," Clay Frog whispered, one hand against her flat stomach. Her short black hair glinted in the moonlight. "And I thought that what she had done to Gray Thunder—"

"She didn't need meat that night," Browser replied grimly. "Come. Let's go find the rest of our party."

He hadn't made three steps when he saw the man. Somehow in the darkness, Shadow had missed him. He had crawled away on his hands and knees. Browser could see that much from the scuffed soil and the blood trail he'd left.

Browser kicked the man's foot and got a low groan.

"Watch him." Browser grabbed the man's foot and pulled him backward to see if he held a weapon. His hands were empty. Despite the clotted blood on the man's face, Browser knew him. He knelt at the War Chief's side. "Rain Crow? It's Browser. Can you hear me?"

The War Chief murmured, his movements weak and aimless.

"Kill him." Yucca Whip hefted his war club. "It will be a kindness. Sometimes, when men are hit in the head, their breath-heart souls flee."

Browser hesitated and glanced around, unnerved by Shadow's work. "No, we must bring him along. Let's hurry. I don't want to be out here longer than we have to."

Catkin had gone to divert Rain Crow and his warriors.

Where was she? Had she escaped the fighting on the cliff top? With a sudden desperation, he bent down, pulled one of Rain Crow's arms over his own shoulders, and lifted.

"Here, War Chief." Red Lark and Yucca Whip stepped forward. "You've done enough for the night. We will carry him."

The memory of the dead warrior with moonlight shining into his empty brain case hovered about him like foul mist.

He tried not to think of Catkin, and what Shadow Woman would do if she caught her.

SHADOW

My souls dance, twining up to spin as the Blue God laughs.

The party of warriors walks away, heading north. I lift my head and sniff the cool wind. I cannot smell them. The odors of blood, entrails, and death are too strong.

Then I turn back and run a slender finger along the side of his jaw, feeling the chill that has leached into his flesh.

"Didn't I tell you I was the Summoning God, Bear Lance?"

I reach beneath his war shirt, and my fingernail traces a path around his testicles before I grip his cold penis. Unlike times past, he does not gasp and tense. Reluctantly I withdraw my hand and return to stroking his slack face. My dark hair spills over him.

The breath-heart soul lingers near the body after death, so I know he is watching me, hating me, but unable to do anything.

"*You knew this would happen eventually,*" *I whisper.* "*Ordinary men cannot touch the flesh of the chosen and survive.*"

I kiss his cold lips, then rise and sling my blood-soaked shirt, heavy with meat, over my shoulder.

36

Maureen leaned against the kitchen counter, watching Ruth Ann and Dusty toy with their coffee cups. They sat on opposite sides of the table, facing each other like predators over the carcass of a fatted calf. Ruth Ann tugged at her gray wool turtleneck. She appeared to be having trouble breathing and sweat shone on her bladelike nose. Fragments of grass dotted her silver hair. Had she been sleeping on the ground?

"I will make this succinct," Ruth Ann began. "I came here because I did not kill Dale. I knew nothing about it until I heard it on the news. I am here because I was *summoned.*"

"What does that mean?" Dusty held his coffee cup in both hands.

"I'm not entirely sure myself, William. I was halfway to the highway before I turned back." She sipped her coffee, looked surprised, and sipped it again. "There's something I need to ask you."

"Whatever I thought has never mattered to you before."

"No," she said straightforwardly. "It certainly hasn't, but it does now. These messages from Kwewur, Dale's death, the missing journals—they all point to something long ago." She cocked her head. "Are you sure that your father is dead?"

Dusty jerked as though he'd been struck. He stared at her through hard unblinking blue eyes. "He was in a mental institution. I assume they know who occupies each room. He was examined by a coroner. There was a funeral, notices in the newspapers, along with articles about Dale going through the proceedings to be declared my legal guardian. If Dad faked his death, he did a damn fine job of it. And I would have heard from him."

"I'm sure your childish mind thought you'd hear from me, too," Ruth Ann countered. She looked around the trailer, as though cataloging every speck of dust. "William, I'm just trying to cover the bases here, that's all."

"Let me get this straight," Dusty said, and leaned across the table. "You think Dad faked his death, then hid out all these years just to kill Dale. Why would he do that?"

"Sam was a very patient man, and Dale took everything Sam had."

"Everything?" Maureen asked. "More than just you?"

Ruth Ann gave her a condescending look. "Everything means everything."

"Ah," Maureen said with a nod, and her stomach turned. "I see. You were married to Samuel, but you were still sleeping with other men, and Sam knew it."

"I knew it, too," Dusty said.

Ruth Ann didn't even blink. "Well, don't blame me. They called it erectile dysfunction, William. Sam was so desperate, he took off one weekend and went to Mexico. There was a surgeon down there. He told Sam that the problem was caused by scar tissue around a nerve and performed some hocus-pocus procedure."

Maureen closed her eyes. "What happened?"

Ruth Ann jiggled her coffee cup. "Absolutely nothing. I don't know what the surgeon did, but Sam was completely incapable after that. That's when he really went overboard with his archaeology. As if the harder he worked, the more we would have to share professionally, since we had nothing to share personally."

"When did you get pregnant?" Maureen fit the pieces together. "Before or after Mexico?"

Ruth Ann shrugged. "I honestly don't know. Neither did Sam. On occasion I tried things with him. Sad sort that I was, I thought it was partly my fault."

"Wait a minute." Dusty's breathing had gone shallow. Maureen could see the truth sinking in as his blue eyes widened. "What are you saying?"

Ruth Ann held his stare. "You wanted to know why I stopped and looked down into Rinconada today? For all I know, you might have been conceived there. I went there often enough."

"When you weren't at La Fonda," Maureen pointed out.

"We only went there in the beginning." Ruth Ann leaned back. "Santa Fe, especially in those days, was still a small town filled with gossip."

Dusty looked as if someone had just kicked his guts out.

Maureen walked over and slid into the booth beside him.

Dusty stammered, "That's why you think D-Dad might be alive? Because you—"

"If Carter didn't kill Dale, Sam is the only other person who would have had a reason."

Maureen leaned back. "Why have you dropped Hawsworth from the suspect list?"

"Who said I dropped him? Professional jealousy *might* be enough, even for Carter, and"—she lifted a finger—"I've heard him threaten to kill people for less reason than that. Unless he's gone way overboard and begun to believe he really is a witch. In that case, Dale, who's innocent for the most part, just got in the way. It's me that Carter really wants dead."

Maureen thought back to the conversation she'd had with Hawsworth. "But why would he be after you?"

"He has recently discovered that beyond the old reasons, he has ample new ones." Ruth Ann shifted wearily. "Lord knows, he does."

"Did you ever leave a man behind who didn't hate you?" Dusty asked.

"It was the sixties," Ruth Ann said, as if that was sufficient. "I don't make any excuses for what I did or why I did it. I wanted to be an anthropologist, to step outside of the roles I'd been enculturated for. So, I did. I turned the tables on my culture and made my own way."

Maureen returned to the subject at hand. "So Sam said nothing. He claimed Dusty because not to would have exposed his impotence. But tell me, did you ever tell Dale that Dusty might be his?"

"Of course not. First, I couldn't be sure. Second, I didn't want to. When I heard later that he had taken over legal guardianship of William, I was fairly sure that Dale believed the boy was his son. It made a great many things easier for me."

Dusty's voice was like silk. "You're good at easy, aren't you?"

Stiffly, she answered, "I don't care for the censure in your voice, William."

He burst to his feet, staring down into her startled

eyes. "I don't give a *damn* what you care for. You just waltzed in here to tell me that *Dale* was my father? Why?"

Ruth Ann leaned back, frightened by his physical presence. "I thought you'd like to know."

Dusty suffered a sudden weakness, as if all the nerves had been cut in his body. He straightened and stepped away. "Damn it, this is going to take some time to get used to."

"Time?" Ruth Ann asked and laughed. "I hope you get it."

The knock, when it came, was tentative. Nevertheless, it brought them to a sudden and complete silence. Maureen's stomach knotted, adrenaline surging.

Dusty, the first to recover from the start, called, "Come join the party!"

Maureen was expecting Carter Hawsworth, not the young woman who opened the door and climbed up the aluminum steps.

She stood perhaps five-eight, slender, with ash hair. She wore a black wool coat. Slim black boots—the velveteen type more common to Fifth Avenue—made her feet look delicate. She had a long but pleasant face, and hauntingly familiar dark eyes.

When she spoke, it was with a delightfully modulated English accent. "My, this is the absolute *end* of the earth!"

Ruth Ann's hands clenched to fists on the table. "Why, Yvette, fancy meeting you here."

"I know you," Maureen said, her heart leaping. "You were at the funeral. I saw you reach down and touch Dale's ashes. Who are you?"

"I'm Yvette Hawsworth, Dr. Cole." She turned to Dusty and extended her hand. "Hello, dear brother. If I'd known you existed, I swear I'd have knocked you up for a chat long ago."

Dusty, speechless, gaped at her.

Yvette said, "Mum didn't tell you about me, did she? No? Pity. It makes my father's reasons a bit more understandable."

"Reasons?" Dusty said. "Reasons for what?"

Yvette removed her gloves. "For wanting to kill her."

37

S tone Ghost gingerly lowered himself to the pile of stones—part of a collapsed third-story wall—and peered out the window at the small party that straggled up the south road from Straight Path Wash. In the hazy moonlight, he had difficulty keeping count, and his eyes were not what they used to be.

"It looks like five walking and a sixth being carried," White Cone told him, the Mogollon elder shading his eyes.

"I think so, too." Stone Ghost sighed. "We will know soon enough."

The sounds of battle had carried to them, though they had seen nothing in the darkness. For long hands of time, worry had eaten at Stone Ghost's stomach with needle teeth.

So many things could have gone wrong. Battle plans rarely survived the release of the first arrow, and Browser was the only family he had left. Through the hardships of the last two summers, a bond had grown between them that was even stronger than that of blood.

As the staggering party approached, a figure rose from

the shadows of the outer wall. Slim and agile, she rushed out toward the leader. For a long moment they clung to each other.

Stone Ghost smiled in the moonlight. His world was still intact. Catkin and Browser were alive.

"Come," Stone Ghost said. "Let's go down and see who is hurt."

White Cone grunted and rose, favoring his left hip. "Do you think they could be carrying Obsidian?"

Stone Ghost hobbled past White Cone and out into the dark hallway. "I pray that's who it is. She should have returned many hands of time ago."

Dusty lay in his sleeping bag, staring out the window at the moonlit darkness, wondering about Dale. If Ruth Ann had been right—that Dale had taken Dusty into his life because he'd believed Dusty was his son—why hadn't Dale ever spoken of it? Obviously, he wouldn't have told Dusty when he was a grief-stricken boy still wounded over his mother's defection and his father's suicide, but what about later? Maybe by putting off the discussion for so many years, it had simply become impossible.

And it didn't matter. He was my father, and he knew it.

Dusty flopped onto his back, trying to find a comfortable position.

As the trailer shook, Maureen called, "Dusty? Are you all right?"

"This is like a bad mescaline hangover."

Her voice returned, "Really? I wouldn't know. Drugs are too scary for me."

"After tonight? Are you kidding? Drugs don't seem scary at all."

To his relief, she chuckled.

He draped an arm across his forehead. "What did you think of sister Yvette?"

"She likes the 'good life,' that's for certain. London, New York, Paris. Her clothes are not made in the good ole USA. They're very expensive."

Dusty turned his head slightly, as though he could see her through the wall. "You mean, like L.L. Bean expensive?"

"No, like Versace or Vuitton expensive."

Dusty's brows raised. The only "labels" he knew were Carhartt, Wrangler, and Levi's.

Dusty tossed to his left side and glared at the wall. "Do you think it's true? That Dale's my father?"

Maureen was silent for a moment. "You don't really look like Samuel Stewart. I don't know. There are ways of finding out. Blood tests. DNA. Things like that."

"It's just so strange. When I was growing up, I used to wish with all my heart that Dale was my father—as though that would have somehow changed our relationship."

"And now?"

"It's going to take some time to come to terms."

She took a deep breath. "You know, all of this: Dale's death, the investigation, the revelations, the heartache and grief...it will pass."

"I know." He paused. "I've been trying to imagine what it must have been like for Dad...I mean Sam. There he is, watching Ruth Ann's belly grow, knowing it isn't his, and Dale, his best friend, is slipping away to screw his wife. I feel like I'm in a soap opera."

He heard the cushions on her fold-down bed shift, as though she'd sat up or rolled over. "Well, don't hold it against Dale," she said gently. "The guilt must have nearly killed him. Not only had he betrayed his best friend, he'd also sired a child on the man's wife. Then, after Ruth left, Dale took care of Sam as best he could. Think about how hard it must have been to commit the man he helped destroy. Imagine how he felt after Sam's suicide." Maureen paused. "No wonder he never had a steady woman in his later years."

"Afraid to, eh?"

"Maybe."

Dusty ground his teeth for several seconds, then said, "But it would have helped so much if Dale had just said, 'William, I'm sorry. The man you think was your father couldn't get it up, so I had an affair with your mother. You were the result.'"

The floor creaked as Maureen walked down the hallway. She appeared in his doorway dressed in a white T-shirt that fell to the middle of her thighs. Her long black braid stood out against that pale background. She leaned against the doorframe and said, "Dale was a very good person, Dusty. He loved you. If he hid things from you, it was because, in some way, he thought he was protecting you."

"Protecting me from what? Finding out my mother was a slut? Or that my father was impotent? I might have cared when I was twelve, but when I was thirty, Maureen?"

She folded her arms as though the night's chill was eating into her flesh. "Personally, I think Dale knew you inside out. Children tend to feel guilty about things that aren't their fault. I suspect he wanted to spare you that."

Dusty sat up and leaned against the cold wall of the trailer.

Maureen's eyes glistened in the darkness, watching him. "Dusty, do you think Samuel Stewart is alive?"

"Good Lord, how do I know?" He lifted a hand uncertainly. "Even if he could have faked his death, why wait until now to deal with Dale? A really pissed husband usually picks up a pistol and settles the dispute immediately."

"Tell me about what happened after your mother left? Did your father hate Dale? Throw him out of the house, shout at him, that kind of thing?"

Dusty shook his head. "No. I don't know how, but they were still friends."

"Do you think he knew that Dale and Ruth Ann were lovers?"

"My guess, and it's only a guess, is that even if he did, he blamed himself. He probably thought his sexual problems had sent her running to Dale."

Maureen stepped over and sat on the foot of his bed. Her long legs shone in the moonlight streaming through the window. She stared at the floor for a time, then turned to Dusty. "May I ask you a tough question?"

"What tough question?"

"At Dale's funeral, Yvette touched Dale's ashes in a very tender way. She ran her fingers across them, looking sad, and then turned and left. It didn't make sense at the time. But now..."

Dusty gave her a quizzical look. Then, as her meaning dawned, he blurted, "You mean, you—you think..." He searched for the right words.

Maureen nodded. "I'm sure Ruth Ann told Carter Hawsworth the child was his, and he believed it—that's why Yvette carries his name—but I'm not so sure Yvette believes it. She touched Dale's ashes like she was saying goodbye to a father she had never known."

Dusty rubbed a hand over his face, as if to wake himself from a nightmare. "But what could have happened to suddenly make her think Hawsworth was not her father?"

Maureen shrugged. "I assume someone told her."

Dusty's thoughts jumped around, trying to figure out

who and, more important, why someone would have done that after all these years. Who would want to stir a thirty-year-old pot?

Dusty said, "I noticed that there was no real love lost between Ruth Ann and Yvette."

"So did I."

Maureen looked out the window and seemed to be examining the moonlight on the cliff. "How old do you think Yvette is?"

"Younger than I am."

"That's what I thought, too." She tilted her head. "After the 10K3 site, I did some research on Ruth Ann. Dale's comments had piqued my interest. There's a sizable body of literature about her, but none of it mentions a daughter. Nor does a daughter appear in the much more limited information on Hawsworth. That's strange, don't you think?"

"Uh-huh."

Maureen grabbed the blanket folded at the foot of Dusty's bed and spread it around her shoulders. "She does look like Dale, don't you think?"

"Especially her eyes."

"If Hawsworth just recently found out he'd raised Dale's child, would he take it out on Dale? Is that motivation for murder?"

"Possibly."

She let out a breath that frosted in the moonlight. "There's another question I'd like to ask you, Dusty, but I've been dreading it."

"It's the perfect night for awful things. What do you want to know?"

She turned and moonlight slivered her face. Her aquiline features—the straight nose, full lips, and dark eyes —gleamed an eerie white. "Dusty, please answer me honestly. Are you *certain* that Dale never had a relationship with Sylvia?"

Dusty's hands turned to fists as he felt his anger rising —and wondered why the very idea coaxed such rage from his heart. "Dale knew about Sylvia's childhood, Maureen. He would never have risked hurting her. I *am* certain of that."

"When Sylvia opened Dale's journal and asked about 'Melissa,' your eyes immediately went to the passage. Who was she, Dusty?"

He ran a hand through his blond hair. "A graduate student he was having an affair with. Dale knew he had to end it, but she had apparently asked him to be on her dissertation committee. He was trying to figure out whether or not he could stand being close to her for another two years."

Maureen's gaze drifted over the bedroom while she absorbed that. "By now, Nichols knows that Dale did have affairs with students. He will be watching Sylvia like a hawk."

"I know."

"Is that what the murderer wanted us to find in the diary? Or is there something else there that only you would understand?"

"I've been waiting for Nichols to return—"

"I don't think he's going to, Dusty. Not until this is over."

Dusty nodded and let his chin rest on his chest while he waded through the morass his insides had become. "Well, he can't trust me. I guess I understand that."

She stood up, pulled the blanket from her shoulders, and spread it over the foot of his bed again. "I think it's time we both got some sleep. Tomorrow is going to be another long day."

"Good night, Maureen."

She disappeared down the hallway, and he heard her bed groan as she settled on the old foldout.

But he couldn't close his eyes. He stared out the window at the cliff and the stars that gleamed above the rim and wondered why he had reacted so emotionally to her question about Sylvia. It was as though, just by asking, she had soiled Dale's integrity.

Which is ridiculous, she did no such thing.

But somewhere deep inside him, he'd felt she had, and he'd defended Dale. Would he always feel compelled to do that?

Probably.

For despite all the things he had learned, he could not believe Dale would do anything to deliberately hurt another human being—and certainly not for his own gain. Dale did not use people. Not even Ruth Ann's stories would change Dusty's mind about that. Dale was a decent human being. Period.

Or was it just that Dale had been decent to Dusty?

Did a person ever really know what another person was capable of?

His thoughts returned to Sylvia, and Rupert's words: *"A witch hides by misdirection."* Dusty knew the stories. A really good witch, one filled with power and evil, could stand right beside you, and you'd never know.

Sylvia wouldn't have had any trouble carrying Dale's weight from Casa Rinconada up to Bc60. She was studying witchcraft, for God's sake. And if that deep-seated terror that lived inside her had sneaked out...

Dusty bit his lip. *Yes,* he admitted to himself, *Sylvia could kill someone if they hurt her badly enough.*

But then, so could he.

The fire in the cracked gray bowl had burned down to a red glow. Matron Blue Corn pulled again at the tight cords binding her wrists. Catkin hadn't shown either respect or sympathy when she'd knotted them.

Blue Corn winced as she tried to shift, and the pain shot up her leg. The way they'd bound her ankles and run a cord up to the wrists left her in burning agony.

"My warriors will be back to rescue us," Horned Ram promised from across the room. He, too, looked like a macaw bound for travel. When traders brought the brightly plumed birds north, they often tied them up into bundles to keep from being bitten and scratched.

Blue Corn snorted her derision. "You didn't acquit yourself well. It wouldn't surprise me if they didn't set you free just for the privilege of knocking your brains out of that worthless head of yours."

A smile displaced the pain on Horned Ram's frog face. "My people know my value. And it isn't as a corpse laid out on the ground after some fight."

She grunted, wondering what was happening, how it

all could have gone so wrong so quickly. Gods, she'd been sitting there like a wounded goose when they had surrounded her. She had looked up through tear-blurred eyes to see Deputy Catkin and three armed Fire Dogs standing over her.

She had opened her mouth to scream and stared down an arrow shaft pulled back to its head.

Catkin's soft "I wouldn't do that" had carried more threat than a vile shout.

With nothing but death as her lot should she resist, she had meekly let them drag her to her feet, bind her hands and feet, and stuff a rag cut from Black Stalk's bloody garments into her mouth.

Only after darkness masked their movements did they ease her down the stairway; that process had left her blind with terror. In the charcoal blackness, a misstep would have meant a fall and death.

They had been at the bottom when Horned Ram had run straight into their arms. In his fear and excitement, he just assumed they were allies, crying out, "Quick. The fighting is that way. They are White Moccasins! First People! Hurry so you don't miss the opportunity to kill some!"

The next sound had been Catkin's war club breaking his shoulder.

The journey to Kettle Town had been punctuated by the distant sounds of fighting, the faint clacking of wood, the screams and angry cries.

"What happened out there?" Blue Corn shook her head.

"They'll be coming for us." Horned Ram winced as he tried to shift. "Gods, this hurts. I'm too old for this."

"Is that why you ran?"

"I was coming for reinforcements."

"All of our unwounded warriors were committed." Blue Corn stared her hatred at him.

"You couldn't tell friend from enemy out there. It was the middle of the night." He moved and his broken shoulder bones grated. Horned Ram shuddered, gasped, and went white with pain.

Blue Corn told herself, "It will take them a while. They'll return to Center Place. When they don't find us, or the wounded tell them we didn't come back, they'll come here."

"I wouldn't count on that." Browser stepped into the room. Behind him came a throng of Mogollon warriors followed by Jackrabbit and Catkin.

The first thing the deputy did was step over, expression serious, to check Blue Corn's bonds. Catkin tugged them to make sure of their strength.

"What happened?" Blue Corn snapped. She might be trussed up like a captive bird, but by the Blessed Flute Player, she was still a Matron. Then she saw Rain Crow, his limp and blood-soaked body supported by two Fire Dogs. They laid him carefully by the heating bowl while others ripped apart another of the willow mats and began feeding sticks to the embers.

As the flames leaped up, Blue Corn caught glimpses of Rain Crow. His head looked shiny from the blood in his hair. It had dried into crack-like patterns on his face.

Browser crouched before her. An absent part of her realized that his hands weren't even blood-smeared.

"Matron? They are dead."

"Who won? The White Moccasins?"

Browser's eyes dropped. "No one, except perhaps Shadow Woman. She killed the last two of your warriors."

"But there should still be wounded! Not everyone—"

"*Yes, everyone,*" Browser said, and his voice sounded

deeply weary. He took a deep breath. "Matron, why are you here? Why are you placing yourself at risk?"

She glared up at him. "You, or your friends, killed my warrior. You spat upon my hospitality."

"We killed no one," Stone Ghost said as he hobbled into the room, supporting himself with a juniper walking stick. The dark wells of his shining eyes reflected the firelight.

"Liar! My warriors will be here s-soon!" Horned Ram sputtered. "They'll see what you've done to me. How you've treated me, and they'll take their revenge!"

Browser's response came so softly Blue Corn almost couldn't hear it. "They're dead, Elder. All of them. Dead."

Blue Corn blinked, trying to understand. "Killed by White Moccasins? They're real?"

Browser nodded and let out a tired breath. "You asked for proof once. Upset that I had no dead White Moccasins to show you. Now I have enough bodies to glut an army of crows. But, Matron, I don't have the will to show them off."

She watched, hearing the truth in his weary voice. The reality left her too stunned to speak.

Browser turned to Stone Ghost. The elder knelt beside Rain Crow, examining his wounds. "How is he?"

Stone Ghost gently felt the bloody matted hair on Rain Crow's head. "The war club crushed a small part of his skull. From the hair that's torn off, I'd say it was a glancing blow." Stone Ghost turned Rain Crow's head and peered into his eyes. "But his pupils are two different sizes. His brain is swelling with evil Spirits. They'll be feeding for days. If he lives through the next quarter moon, his souls might come back."

"He's tough." Blue Corn looked up at Browser. "What are your plans for me, War Chief?"

Browser rose and stared at Horned Ram. The old man

squirmed, testing his bounds. "You allied yourself with those who stir hatred, Matron, and look what has become of it." He turned back to Blue Corn. "If you give me your oath that you will not retaliate against me or the Katsinas' People, I will release you. We are not your enemies. We never have been."

"I still have wounded up at Center Place."

Browser nodded. "I will send someone for them at first light. I will not risk my people at night with Shadow prowling around."

"*Your* people?" She arched an ironic eyebrow. "I mostly see Fire Dogs here."

"We are Katsinas' People, Matron. All of us."

She narrowed an eye, taking his measure, seeing the terrible fatigue that weighed his souls. "Come, Browser, do you really believe in the katsinas?"

He smiled humorlessly. "There is only one thing I am certain of, Matron. If we don't stop killing each other, it won't matter who is right. In the end, we will all be dead."

He gestured toward the south. "The only one left from tonight's battle is a witch. I greatly fear that when all of this fighting is done, witches will be the only survivors."

"The Katsina religion is witchery!" Horned Ram cried. "You are all a vile pollution in the sight of the gods. They will destroy you, you and your—"

"Cut me loose, Browser," Blue Corn interrupted and held out her hands. "I don't know where we will go or what we will do, but I will not fight you." She glanced at Rain Crow. "If for no other reason than you brought my War Chief back to me."

He pulled the hafted chert knife from his belt and sawed through the cord that bound her ankles and wrists.

As he stood, he looked at the warriors standing around the room and said, "I'll take the first watch."

"No, War Chief," a young Mogollon warrior said, and

stepped forward, chest out, eyes level. "Jackrabbit and I will take the watch. Sleep soundly, War Chief, and know that we are alert and watchful."

The Fire Dogs were on their feet, lithe and deadly, hands on their weapons. Blue Corn wouldn't have believed it had she not seen it with her own eyes. Flute Player take her, they worshipped him.

"Shadow is out there," Catkin said. "Never forget that."

Yucca Whip nodded. "Yes, Catkin."

Blue Corn rubbed her wrists, amazed as Catkin led Browser from the room. Horned Ram, still trussed, watched them go, his eyes filled with hatred.

Dusty awakened at the sound of Maureen's voice: "Good morning, Yvette. Care for coffee?"

"Yes! Smashing!" the cultured English voice responded with too much enthusiasm as the trailer rocked with her entry. "I feel bloody beastly. I swear, I'm half frozen and every joint in my body is screaming."

Dusty sat up, yawned, and reached for his jeans. The chill of the morning left his breath frosty in the air. He pulled on a sweatshirt and his boots, stood and studied himself in the mirror. His blond hair stood out at odd angles, and his puffy eyes made it look like he hadn't slept at all, which he hadn't.

He combed his hair with his fingers and headed down the hallway.

"Good morning," Maureen said. She stood at the kitchen stove with a spatula in her hand, turning over eggs and chilis.

Dusty stopped very close behind her and said, "Sorry about last night. I didn't mean to sound—"

"You didn't," she said and smiled. She wore a blue turtleneck underneath an oversized gray sweatshirt. Her freshly washed and braided hair was still damp and smelled of shampoo. She pointed to the coffeepot. "Have a cup. You'll feel better."

He poured a cup of coffee and stepped over to the table. "Good morning, Sis," he said as he slid into the booth opposite her.

In the morning light, Yvette Hawsworth was an attractive woman, and yes, he could see Dale in her long face, thin nose, and most of all in her eyes. The rest of her, the ash-blond hair, the fine bones, all seemed to be Ruth Ann.

"Ever slept in a truck before?" He smiled, trying to set her at ease.

"No, and I must say, it's a bit of an experience." Her laugh betrayed a sudden insecurity. "But for your blankets, I'm quite sure I would have died."

"You wouldn't have. If it gets too bad you can always turn on the engine and pray you don't asphyxiate before dawn." He took a sip of the coffee and let the rich dark brew soothe him. "I was born in a truck. At the side of the highway south of Tuba City."

She lifted a slim eyebrow, as if trying to determine how much of what he was telling her was bullshit.

He wrapped his fingers around his coffee cup. "Is this as much of a shock to you as it is to me?"

She laughed. "You have no idea. Tell me...William? Is that what I should call you?"

"The only person on earth who called me that was Dale. When Ruth Ann does, it makes my nerves grate."

"Dusty?" She placed her palms together in a prim gesture, her eyes searching his. "Did you send me that fax?"

He slowly lowered his cup to the table. He could hear the eggs sizzling in the pan in the kitchen. "What fax?"

"Two weeks ago. The fax telling me that my life was a lie."

"Yvette, until you walked in here last night, I didn't even know you existed."

"No one did," Maureen said as she separated three paper plates. "I take it you're eating with us? There's no other breakfast out here. The closest source of food is the cold locker at the gas station in Crownpoint." She shot a scathing look at Dusty. "And believe me, you don't want to try it."

"I told you," Dusty protested, "I didn't know you then."

"Yeah sure, eh?" Maureen shook the spatula at him. "The enchiladas at the Pink Adobe almost, I said *almost,* make up for that sandwich."

"I feel rather a fool," Yvette said, shifting nervously in the booth. "I followed Mum until she took off on that dirt track. I was just bloody determined to see where she'd got off to, what great secret was hidden out here.

"A number of times, I thought I'd lost her. It's a good thing I rented that bush vehicle."

"Bush vehicle?" Dusty asked. "Where'd you learn to call a Jeep that?"

"On safari," she told him, and shook hair out of her eyes.

"Hawsworth took you on safari?"

"Oh, god no." She seemed uncomfortable. "I went to Africa while Carter was working there. But mostly I went with my first husband."

"First?" Dusty asked. "How many have you had?"

"Three. Currently I'm between."

Dusty silently sized her up again. She didn't take after her mother, did she?

"You went on safari, and you didn't have any idea about backcountry?" Maureen asked.

"Well, you see, Africa isn't like this. At least not the places I went. People imagine tents and *Out of Africa,* but it's really quite civilized. The lodges have running water and gourmet food."

Maureen scooped eggs onto the paper plates, and brought two to the table, along with forks wrapped in napkins. She set one plate in front of Yvette and the other in front of Dusty. The glorious aroma of cheddar and chilis wafted up.

Maureen went back for her plate and said, "You're a real mystery woman. Your name doesn't appear in any of the biographical material about Ruth Ann Sullivan or Carter Hawsworth."

Yvette wet her lips. "They were rather Machiavellian about that, weren't they? Believe me, growing up between them wasn't any picnic. I raised myself, bouncing from boarding school to boarding school." She lifted her eyes. "Tell me, did Dale Robertson...did he have any idea that I existed?"

Dusty shook his head and toyed with his cup, moving it around the table, remembering what Maureen had said last night. "And he would have told me, Yvette. Why do you ask?"

"Well, I was born in Geneva, Switzerland, in '70. Isn't that a rip? I have dual citizenship, Swiss and British. Right off I was bundled away into a facility while they ran off to the Pacific. Auntie Vi did most of my raising when I wasn't in school."

"Is that why you came here? To find Dale?" Dusty asked as he took his fork from his rolled napkin.

"The fax came two weeks ago. When Mum refused to talk about it, it made me suspicious. Not that we ever talked, but this was worse. She had never been part of my life, and after she and Carter split, he hadn't much of a care for me either."

She frowned as she sipped her coffee. "Then a couple of days later, a letter arrived with an old newspaper clipping from an Albuquerque paper. There was a picture of Mum, not much more than a girl, and Dale Robertson. They were at an archaeological dig. A note penciled at the bottom read: *'Meet your real father.'*"

Dusty guessed, "Could Hawsworth have sent it?"

Yvette shrugged. "I called Auntie Vi for Carter's address. My father and I hadn't been in touch in years. We don't share much in common, you see. Imagine my surprise when I discovered he was in Taos." She pronounced it Tayos.

"So, what did he say?" Dusty ate a mouthful of *huevos rancheros* and gave Maureen a thumbs-up sign.

She smiled and slid into the booth beside him with her plate and coffee cup in hand.

"He told me flat out that it was ludicrous, that of course he was my father, but after he said it, he hesitated for a long time, and finally said he'd ring me back."

"Did he?"

"No, it was Mum who rang me up, asking where I might have gotten the bright idea that Carter wasn't my father. I told her about the fax and the news article. She was quiet for a moment and then asked if Carter had returned my call. I told her no."

"Did you talk to Dale?" Maureen asked and dipped up a forkful of eggs.

She nodded. "I got his answering machine. At the beep, I couldn't say anything. Bloody hell, what does one say? 'Hello, are you my father?'"

Dusty sipped his coffee and gave her an askance look. "A newspaper article and a fax don't mean he was your father, Yvette. It just means someone wanted you to think he was."

"Yes, I—I know." She looked at him soberly. "But the letter I received from Carter, FedEx, the following day, informed me most tersely that to his mortification, I was *not* his daughter. Apparently he had received a fax asking how I might have blood type B when Mum and he were both type O."

Maureen's fork hovered over her plate. Her eyes narrowed as she looked at Yvette. "Dale was AB." She turned to Dusty. "And you're type B."

Dusty took another bite of breakfast and around a mouthful said, "Yeah, so?"

"If Ruth Ann and Carter are both type O, they can't have a child who is either type A or B." She scowled at her eggs. "You wouldn't possibly have any idea of Samuel's blood type, would you?"

Dusty blinked. "I'm not sure I ever knew his blood type."

"Then Dusty and I share the same blood?" Yvette looked surprised.

"It's an exclusionary test," Maureen told her. "It only means that if you are type B, Carter Hawsworth cannot be your father, eh? Not if he's an O."

"But Mum is an O."

"Yes, and an O crossed with another O results in type O blood in one hundred percent of the offspring. If Ruth Ann is an O and Dale was an AB, then fifty percent of their children would have been type A and fifty percent would have been type B." She used her fork to point first at Dusty, then at Yvette.

Yvette frowned. "Mum told me she left the US six months before I was born."

Maureen looked at Dusty. "Dale told me that Carter and Ruth Ann were together for two weeks before she left. Does that ring true?"

Dusty nodded. "You thinking what I'm thinking?"

Maureen answered, "It looks like she was pregnant again with Dale's baby, couldn't stand Sam's guilt, and—"

Dusty finished, "Along came Hawsworth, and she was on him like a leech."

Yvette seemed to be stunned by the loathing in Dusty's voice. Her shoulders hunched forward. "But what of Dale Robertson? He just bred Mum like a prize mare, and sod the poor bloke stuck with the child?"

Dusty ate the last of his eggs, wiped his mouth with his napkin, and leaned back. "If he'd known about you, Yvette, he would have done something. And when he did, it would have been classy, up front, and honest. Just like he did with me."

Dusty tossed his napkin on the table. "I don't know what our mother or Carter have told you, but you could do a hell of a lot worse than having Dale Robertson as a father."

Maureen's dark eyes fixed on the window, but she didn't seem to be looking at anything outside. She murmured, "Why bring the children into it? Why does the murderer need you and Yvette here?"

Dusty replied, "I didn't get any faxes."

"No," Maureen said, and slowly turned to face him. "He expected you to be here."

SHADOW

I star at her in wonder. Raising my head, I sniff cautiously, drawing in her scent. She and I are so much the same—and so very different. I search for the odor. Has she been with him? Is he hers now? But my nostrils fail to detect the musk that lingers on a woman after she's coupled with a man.

Sister looks at me, distress in her large dark eyes. She has never had my strength. "He is coming for you, Shadow. For you and Father."

"Of course he is," I reply. "I am the Summoning God. They all come to me. Some sooner than others."

I place a hand to my belly, aware of the glow within. Father's power never ceases to amaze me. Where others leave only the faded memory of pleasure, I am his fertile soil.

"Shadow," Obsidian says, looking anxiously across the kiva to where Father lays moaning in his blankets, "you have no need of me here."

I throw my head back and laugh.

Piper lies frozen, her breath-heart soul paralyzed in the air above her. What did Father do to her this time? How did he witch her so completely. Was it the turquoise necklace? When, and where, had she gotten that? Is Piper truly so weak? I expected more from her.

"Ah, Sister, I may have great need of you. Tell me, in what should I place more value? In your heart, or your body?"

Her face has become a pale mask.

"Tell me of Browser."

"I think he knows where you are. Were I you, I would leave, Sister. Now, while you can."

"I see."

"Don't take him lightly."

"Browser?" *I smile, remembering the times I have tempted him, fondled him, seen the battle in his eyes as his heart struggled with his manhood. Yes, he desires me. All I need is a little time.* "He's the most dangerous man I know, Sister."

"You continue to overestimate him. You should have seen him, worry dripping from his skin like sweat. The desperation in his eyes was overpowering when he asked me to help him."

I watch her, and she squirms, unable to meet my eyes. She is smart not to challenge my stare. I would reel her breath-heart soul out of her the way a hunter does a yucca cord string from a rabbit hole. Instead her eyes are fixed on the fragments of bone littering the kiva. She is particularly fascinated by a section of shinbone. It gleams like polished shell, stark against the ash-stained earthen floor.

"His name was Carved Splinter," *I tell her, gesturing at the length of broken bone.* "I sucked the marrow from it for supper last night."

She swallows hard, the color draining from her face.

"He was a Fire Dog. Not a real human like you and me, Sister."

"I know..."

She is so weak. I hide my anger, saying, "I am disappointed with you, Sister. But for you, Bear Lance and so many others would still be alive. Perhaps you don't understand, living as you do in the midst of Made People, but we are fewer as a result of your actions last night."

She hears the wrath throttled deep in my throat. She glances at the bloody cloth, heavy with meat where it hangs from one of the pilasters. I watch the shiver pass through her soft flesh. It pleases me. I know what she has been trying to do. But for my appetite, I would seek to take her place. It would not be such a bad life, sharing Browser's bed, being his wife. But it is only fantasy. The Blue God has other plans for me.

"How will you make this thing you have done right, Sister?" *I tap my chin with a long finger and hide a smile as her gaze slides again to Father where he lies dying.*

"He wanted your heart from the very beginning, Obsidian. Yours or Piper's. But I had such high hopes for Piper." *I glance at my daughter again, seeing her empty eyes, and wonder if indeed, I shouldn't cut her chest open.*

My sister swallows as if her throat is too tight. "I have something better to offer you, Shadow. If you will let me speak with Old Pigeontail, I'm sure that I—I can arrange—"

"Indeed?" *She cannot see the smile that lights my breath-heart soul.* "You still amaze me, Sister."

Catkin sighed as she gazed at the morning light that cast a glow into their room. A warming bowl rested an arm's length from their bed, the coals cold and gray.

Browser made one of those male sounds of indescribable contentment and hugged her.

Through the window, he could see the half-moon-shaped bulk of Talon Town. He stared at it, wondering at the twists and turns of life.

It had started on the morning of his dead son's funeral, an entire sun cycle ago, with the discovery of a desecrated grave. Then came the wounding of his lover, Hophorn, and his wife's disappearance. It wasn't until now that he could understand that everything started, on that cold and blustery morning. One after another, each event had unfolded to bring him, the Katsinas' People, and his Mogollon allies to this place at this time. It had brought him here with Catkin, in love and craving a future that he could just barely feel with the fingertips of his breath-heart soul.

But it would cost something. What? The gods never

granted happiness without a price. As his ancestor, Poor Singer, had known, there was always a payment to be made.

He propped himself on one elbow and gazed down at Catkin with thoughtful eyes. At the feel of the cool air on her sweat-damp chest, she tugged up the blanket, and smiled.

His hand crept to her breast. She slipped one of her long legs over his. "Are you all right?"

He smiled. "I have finally made peace with life. I understand now."

"Understand what?" She toyed with his short-cropped hair.

"That the most important thing isn't clan, or honor, or status, or wealth, or any of the things our people believe. The only things that truly matter are having a full stomach, a soft warm wife, and the knowledge that you'll see the sunset." He tipped his round face and sunlight flashed through his thick black brows. "Catkin, when we are finished here, I want to go south."

She studied the longing in his eyes. "What's in the south?"

"It is far from the First People's kivas and towns. I'm thinking of the mountains. Maybe a green valley halfway between the Fire Dogs and the Hohokam. A place where a man and woman can build a little house, grow some corn, and love each other."

"Just one soft woman?"

He smoothed a hand over her hair. "I'm not fool enough to put you and Obsidian under the same roof. You'd kill her."

She stared at him with glistening eyes. "You are not a wise man, Browser, discussing a beautiful woman immediately after sharing my bed."

He studied her with genuine amusement. "I don't love

her. I love only you." The blanket fell from his muscular brown shoulders, and he tugged it up again. "Do you realize that last night's battle was a miracle?"

"I do."

"A War Chief lives all his life dreaming of conducting a fight like that. We tricked two war parties into fighting each other. We didn't take a single loss. No one was even wounded. We destroyed two enemies and didn't suffer a scratch in the process." His smile turned meloncholy.

"Then why are you sad?" She took his hand and held it to her heart. "You were brilliant. You should be proud."

"I'm more proud of sharing your blankets than of that fight last night. After my wife..." Pain tensed his expression. "I wasn't sure I would ever be able to share a woman's blankets again."

Catkin slipped her arms around him and pressed her naked body against his one more time. "My blankets are always open to you."

"And mine to you."

They held each other until Father Sun's light filled the room and their blankets became too hot.

As he rose and reached for his war shirt, Browser gazed out the window. Some of his warriors had gathered on the first-story roof, pointing.

Browser looked out, seeing the lone figure with two dogs trotting stolidly toward Kettle Town. "Old Pigeontail is coming. He seems to be in a hurry."

"Anyone with him?"

"No. Just him. But somehow, I don't think we can take any comfort from that."

Maureen stared out the Bronco's passenger-side window as Dusty drove past the interpretive signs for Pueblo Bonito and Pueblo del Arroyo and then crossed the bridge over Chaco Wash. In the mirror he could see Yvette's rental Jeep following him.

"Why do you think she wants to see the place Dale died?" Maureen asked.

"She thinks he was her father. I guess that's enough of a reason," Dusty said, and squinted at the road, wondering just where Maggie had seen the owl. The Casa Rinconada parking lot was just ahead, it had to be somewhere in here.

Maureen said, "Have you thought about the actual mechanics of the murder?"

"What do you mean?"

"I mean Ruth Ann couldn't have killed and buried Dale by herself. How would she have gotten his body out of the great kiva and up the hill to the place where he was buried? She doesn't look strong enough."

"I hadn't thought of that." Dusty parked the Bronco and gazed up the ridge to where Michail, Sylvia, and two

FBI men peeled away the black plastic that had covered the site. Yvette pulled in beside them.

They got out of the Bronco and met Yvette on the trail. As they walked, Dusty gestured to the great kiva. "Dale was actually killed at the ceremonial chamber in front of us, but he was buried up there where you see the people standing. Do you think Ruth Ann could have carried a one-hundred-forty-pound body up that slope?"

Yvette's eyes widened. "Perhaps. She goes to the club every week. She used to run in marathons. Finished respectably at Boston a couple of years ago. I wouldn't have known, but Collins was in New York on business."

Dusty pulled his collar up against the wind. "Who's Collins?"

"My third husband. He faxed me the sports page of the *Boston Globe*. It said: 'World-famous anthropologist to run Boston Marathon.' I came to the States straightaway. I wanted to see her."

The wind whistled up the slope and ate into Dusty's exposed face. "Did she know you were coming?"

"Yes, I called first, but it was a terrible trip. The traffic was beastly; they shut down the city for the Marathon, you know. I got to her home just after Mum did, she was still hot and sweaty, wearing her tracksuit. It didn't go well. I left twenty minutes later."

Dusty decided not to ask what that meant.

"What happened with Collins?" Maureen asked.

"He died," Yvette said evenly. "Killed on the motorway. He crashed his Jaguar." She pronounced it Jag-u-waar.

Maureen's expression went from evaluative to concerned in a heartbeat. "How are you doing?"

Yvette replied cautiously, "I'm whole, actually. Life goes on."

In the silence that followed, Dusty led the way past the Tseh So ruins and walked to Casa Rinconada.

He stood at the edge of the kiva, staring down into the sunlit depths. The place had changed. He would never come here again without wondering if Dale's screams had echoed from the cold stone walls.

"You can see some of the sand," he said. "We think it was a sand painting. Maybe used by Kwewur to trap Dale's soul."

Dusty glanced at her. She looked a lot like him. She had his jaw, and he could see his nose on her, scaled down, more feminine. The biggest difference in their faces was her thoughtful brown eyes. Dale's eyes.

"All that was left was the blood?" she asked in a small voice.

"That and a note. The FBI has it. Apparently it was sent to Dale to get him to come here on Halloween night. After the witch killed him and mutilated him"—it surprised him how easily he could say that now—"he carried Dale up there." He pointed to the excavation on the ridge to their south and headed in that direction.

She followed him up the slope, walking carefully in her funky black suede boots with their high heels. She stopped beside him at the police tape.

"Michall, Sylvia," Dusty called, "this is Yvette Hawsworth."

Michall climbed out of the chest-deep kiva and shook hands. Sylvia just leaned on her shovel and waved.

Rick and Bill perked up at the Hawsworth name. They walked around the kiva and eyed her carefully.

"Does Agent Nichols know you're here?" Bill asked after introductions.

"He's scheduled to talk to her later," Dusty said, preempting anything unpleasant. To his relief, Yvette didn't fumble it. She just nodded.

"This is where they found Dale." Dusty pointed. "Buried there. So we're digging. Trying to find out why the killer chose this spot."

"Any clues yet?" she asked.

"Talk to Michall. She's the Principal Investigator here." He stepped around to study the profile where the pit transected the kiva. "Hey, what's that discoloration?"

"The coyote hole where the site was potted." Michall hopped lithely back into the pit and pulled a trowel from her back pocket. Using the point she outlined the intrusive dirt that funneled down and disappeared into the pit floor. "It's been a while, Dusty. But not that long ago."

"How do you know that, Professor Jefferson?"

She walked to the side of the kiva and reached into a brown paper sack to pull out a rusty beer can. "Coors," she said. "Steel. And look at the top." She turned it to expose the characteristic triangular punctures made before poptops.

"Late fifties through the sixties," Dusty said.

"Hey, you're good at this. Have you ever thought of doing it for a living?" Sylvia asked.

"Careful," he said. "Your next excavation is going to be a cat box."

Sylvia grinned and used her shovel to start chunking out the next twenty-centimeter level. "I once knew a guy who found a Folsom point in a cat box," she said. "'Course it had fallen out of his shirt pocket when he bent over to...whoa!" She laid her shovel to the side and got down on her hands and knees. "We got bone here, boss."

Maureen leaned as far over the police tape as she thought she could get away with, and called, "What kind of bone?"

"Hold on." Sylvia brushed sand from a brown sliver. A white gash marked where the shovel had cut it.

The FBI guys were on her like vultures, staring over her shoulder as Michall bent down to look.

Dusty knotted his fists. He couldn't see anything except a cluster of backs.

"Washais?" Sylvia called. "I think we need you in here."

"Wait a minute." Bill stood up, one hand out. "She's not cleared."

"Right," Sylvia said. "Can you tell me what this is? You've been doing great for a cop. You've actually proved you could learn how to dig like an undergraduate. You haven't torn out the strings, and you haven't collapsed the pit walls. Now, we can shut this down for a week while you guys get an ID, or Washais can tell us in five seconds. Which is it?"

Rick, his dark blue FBI jacket mottled with dust and smeared with dirt, took the bone from Sylvia and studied it for a moment. Then he looked up at Maureen. "Dr. Cole, I'm only asking for an opinion. I'll have this analyzed later to ID it for certain. Do you think you could—"

Maureen was under the tape like a hound after a rabbit. She took the bone from his hand and turned it over and over again.

Yvette shook her head. "My mum did this once upon a time? Mum, who wouldn't take a chance on opening a car's boot for fear of cracking a nail?"

"Well, if it's any consolation, she told me she hated archaeology. The Zuni used to call her The-Woman-With-No-Eyes because she never looked at them, she just looked at her papers," Dusty said. "But that was before she got famous. She wasn't—"

"Human," Maureen said. "What we have here is about fifteen centimeters of the distal portion of the tibia—the shin bone—right side. Probably male from the robusticity of the bone. The spiral fracture was perimortal. It occurred around the time of death."

She lifted the fragment to the gray light filtering through the cloudy sky. "I can't tell you here, but from the looks of it, I'd say this was butchered."

"Butchered?" Rick asked. "You mean they cut him apart?"

"Probably," Maureen said.

"Is it prehistoric?" Rick asked. "Or is this one of our unsub's previous victims?"

"Don't be a dork," Sylvia said, leaning on her shovel handle. "Look at it, Rick."

Rick took the bone, slightly cowed by Maureen's amused expression. He studied it for a moment and said, "Prehistoric, right?"

"Why?" Michall asked. Her red hair blowing about her face in the wind.

"Because if it was modern, you wouldn't be jacking me around like this."

"That's a smart cop." Sylvia nodded, dug another shovelful, and artfully tossed it up into Michall's screen.

"Seriously," Michall responded, "why's it prehistoric?"

Rick scowled as he studied the bone. "Uh, the discoloration?"

"Right." Maureen pointed to the patterns on the dirt. "And what's this?"

"It looks like marks left by roots," Rick guessed.

"Very good, Rick. Acids in roots etch the bone's surface. It takes time. If this was a modern forensic specimen, the roots wouldn't have had time to create this effect on the bone's cortex."

"Hey! Wait a minute," Dusty called. "What's the provenience on that tibia?"

"Pot hole backfill," Sylvia called back. "Disturbed. It's out of context."

"Damn," Dusty said.

"What's that mean?" Yvette asked.

"It's been moved. Probably dug out when the site was potted in the sixties and then shoveled back in when the hole was backfilled." He paused, frowning. "Hey, Michall? You've read all the Parking Service's notes on this site. Did they ever mention backfilling this?"

"Parking Service?" Rick looked confused.

"It's derogatory," Sylvia told him. "A term used to refer to the National Park Service, which is part of the Department of the Inferior."

Michall ignored them as she looked up from the screen where she was processing the dirt Sylvia had tossed her. "According to the records, the Park Service has never touched this. It's just recorded with its original Be number."

Dusty shook his head. "That can't be right."

"Why not?" Yvette was watching him with Dale's eyes. It was almost spooky.

"The beer can. The lack of documentation of the backfill, a chunk of human bone that big. It's not the sort of stuff the Chaco Rangers would throw back in a hole."

He looked out at the canyon before him. "In the sixties? This isn't the kind of place pot hunters would hit. It's open. You can see this ridge from the entire west end of the loop road."

"Unless it was done at night," Maureen said as she walked up with the precious tibia fragment in her hand. "Maybe it was a summer temp working on his own after hours?"

"Yeah, maybe. It's certainly happened before." Dusty frowned down at the tibial shaft. "You think it was butchered?"

She used a fingernail to trace the thin line incised in the dirt-encrusted bone. "I need to clean it and look at it under the microscope, but yes, I'd say that cut mark was made when someone disarticulated the foot."

"Cannibalism or disarticulation for secondary burial?" Dusty asked.

"If they cut the body apart to make it easier to carry to another place for burial"—Maureen's dark eyes challenged —"how do you explain the spiral fracture?"

"What about the spiral fracture?" Dusty crossed his arms. "The tibia might have gotten broken when the pot hunter dug up the site."

Yvette looked over Dusty's shoulder as Maureen pointed to the dimple where the bone was broken. "Remember? The fracture was perimortal? That dimple marks the hammer impact right there." She turned it over. "And if this was cleaned, we'd see scrubbing from the anvil right here."

"Pueblo Animas all over." Dusty took a deep breath. "Sylvia?"

"Yo, Boss Man." She looked up.

"When you get to the kiva roof, keep a sharp eye out. I'm betting you a case of Coors we're going to cut the same McElmo ceramics that we did at 10K3 and PA. You get my drift?"

Sylvia stopped her shoveling. The wind whipped her brown hair around her freckled face. "Yeah, Dusty, I got you."

Rick was looking even more confused as he mumbled, "What's McElmo ceramics?"

"She didn't sound happy," Yvette noted. "What did you mean?"

Dusty shoved his hands into his pocket. "It's hard to explain unless you—"

"Got charcoal!" Sylvia sang out and dropped to her knees in the pit. "We're coming down on a burned layer."

"Surprise, surprise," Dusty whispered, remembering the charred ruins and burned bodies at Pueblo Animas.

Browser and Stone Ghost stood with Old Pigeontail in the room where Horned Ram lay bound. The Red Rock elder had turned a shade of gray, and his shoulder, swollen and bruised, looked terrible. Blue Corn knelt at his side, mopping his face with a damp cloth.

Pigeontail's faded red cloak swayed around his tall body as he walked over to Horned Ram to examine his injuries. The man's tawny eyes gleamed in his long face.

"If you do not cut his bonds soon," Pigeontail said, "he will lose this arm. It's already turning purple." He bent down and gestured to Horned Ram's bad shoulder.

Browser rested his right fist on the hilt of his belted war club. Casually, he said, "I plan on freeing him before that happens."

But only just before. Every time he looked at the old man, anger pumped brightly in his veins.

Pigeontail straightened and gave Browser a worried look. "I came to talk with you about Obsidian."

"What about her?"

Stone Ghost gripped Browser's forearm. "I didn't tell

you last night," he said softly, "because I thought she still might return, and you needed your sleep desperately, but she is gone."

"Gone?" Browser started. "You mean she never came back?"

Stone Ghost nodded, and his wispy white hair caught the morning sunlight. "Since the battle went as you'd planned, I assumed she had succeeded in luring the White Moccasins down the staircase, but something must have happened after that."

Pigeontail took a deep breath and said, "I don't normally bend my rules, War Chief."

"But you are going to this time," Browser replied stiffly, and his fingers tightened around his club. "Let us hear it."

Pigeontail held out both hands in a gesture of surrender. "Obsidian apparently climbed down the staircase after the fight. Made it as far as the canyon floor...and Shadow captured her when she started across the battleground."

Dusty sat on the Bronco's tailgate, his legs swinging. He, Maureen, and Yvette were lunching on cold enchiladas. Two vehicles down, Michall, Sylvia, and the FBI guys sat in Michall's blue Durango and worked on sandwiches and cans of pop. From the corner of his eye, Dusty studied Maureen, trying to read the thoughtful expression. She kept glancing curiously at him, as if probing for his response to the morning's findings.

The odd one out, Yvette, stood to one side, chewing thoughtfully on her enchilada. She used copious amounts of Coke to soften the impact of the spices. Evidently jalapenos and red chili weren't common fare in London.

"Beer and bones," Yvette said, a perplexed look on her face. "It's just so blinking peculiar." Her gaze took in the canyon, tracing the cold sandstone walls. "All of this is. It's hard to believe that people lived here, let alone that they still do."

"You're just not used to it," Maureen said. "I grew up in Ontario, in the forests. My country is cool and green, and I live on one of the largest lakes in the world. The first time I stepped off an airplane in Albuquerque, it was complete culture shock. From Toronto to Chaco in one day, slap, bam."

"But this place, it's so bizarre."

"It's pretty normal to me." Dusty bit off another hunk of enchilada and washed it down with a swig from his soda can.

"But it's so bloody far from anything like civilization!" Yvette cried.

"Hip hip, hooray," Dusty answered. "That's the whole point."

Yvette gave him a blank stare.

A mud-splattered automobile was making the curve on the loop road, its top just visible across the winter brush. He could hear it, slowing, making the right onto the Rinconada road.

"Company." Dusty pointed with his enchilada. "This guy's got guts to do it in a two-wheel drive vehicle that's that low to the ground. From the looks of it, he just hammered the accelerator and blasted his way through the mud puddles on a hope and a prayer."

The Chevrolet pulled into the parking lot, swung wide, and pulled up in front of the interpretive sign. Two semicircular arcs had been left by the wipers as they sloshed the mud from the windshield. The hood, grille, doors, and even the roof were mud-coated. Gunk on the side windows darkened the interior, shadowing the single occupant.

"Heads up," Maureen said cautiously. "If that's who I think it is..."

Dusty took another bite of enchilada. At the same time his nerves started to tingle. No, this wasn't going to be some tourist out to see the sites.

The man who opened the door had a beanpole figure, his white hair pulled back in a ponytail and clipped with a silver clasp studded with turquoise. His thin face, long nose, and startling blue eyes gave him a mature look. Dusty figured him for his early sixties. He wore a brown canvas duck coat—the kind sold in places like Eddie Bauer stores where the trendy bought "outdoor" clothes in Santa Fe. A garish silver belt buckle with big chunks of turquoise snugged a woven leather belt around his slim hips. Expensive ostrich-skin boots were on his feet.

"Bloody hell," Yvette whispered.

"You know him?" Dusty asked.

"Hello, Father," Yvette called. "I fancied you'd show up eventually."

Her father? It took a moment for the meaning to sink in.

"Want to go meet Carter Hawsworth?" Maureen asked. "Just promise me you won't do anything dumb—like get yourself thrown in jail for murder, eh?"

Dusty set his half-eaten enchilada down, wiped his fingers with a paper towel, and swung down from the tailgate.

Hawsworth stepped up to Yvette, his head cocked, a pinched expression on his face. His first words were, "I want you to know, I don't hold it against you personally."

Dusty almost recoiled at that familiar English accent. He'd listened to it enough on the answering machine tape. He could still hear that voice saying, "*I'll be your worst nightmare.*"

"Thank you, Carter. It's not like I was consulted, you know." Yvette had crossed her arms, the posture something a wounded child might have adopted.

He studied her with angry blue eyes. "Over the years, you cost me nearly two hundred thousand pounds. Isn't that an incredible amount to lose to fraud? Had your mother swindled that sum through fraudulent FTSE investments, I could have her locked away for life. But since you were a child, I have no real recourse."

Dusty blinked, asking Maureen from the side of his mouth, "What's a pound worth?"

"About a buck fifty, US."

Yvette's expression had cooled even more. "Did you come to present me with a bill, Father?"

Hawsworth finally smiled, the expression anything but warm. "In the first place, I'm not your 'father' as we both now know. In the second, I would, if I thought I had a dog's chance in hell of collecting." His eyes narrowed. "But I wouldn't bill you, Yvette, I'd send it to your foul bitch of a mother."

"And have a right jolly time getting her to pay," Yvette replied bitterly.

His eyes seemed to burn as he said, "Oh, fear not, Yvette, your mother shall have her comeuppance. From now on, I'm the cunning spider in her life. And she knows it. No matter what it takes, I *will* destroy her. And, why, yes, you can tell her that. See what sort of expression you get?"

"Sod off. Your squabbles are your own."

"You're not the least bit sorry for poor old Mum?"

"If you recall, we've both been lied to. Very well, what do we do now, you and I?"

"Nothing." Hawsworth stuffed his long fingers into his back pockets. "The nice part is that we don't have to perpetuate the lie anymore, Yvette. Don't you find that liberating?"

She had gone rigid. "In more ways than you could know."

He shook his head. "I must say, it's quite something to

discover that one has been a cuckold. I swear, I'd kill Dale for doing this to me—but some bastard beat me to it. Were it me, I'd have made him suffer a bit longer before I put him out of my misery."

Dusty's universe collapsed, tunneling itself into the image of Hawsworth's face. A vague comprehension of the man's expression imprinted: the transition from loathing and anger to downright fear...

"Dusty! *Dusty!*" Maureen was screaming into one ear. The words intruded, bringing him back to the here and now. Her frantic hands were tugging on his arm, trying to break his hold. He was standing, his fists knotted in the lapels of the thick duck coat, his knuckles pressing together as he lifted Hawsworth up on his tiptoes and half choked the man.

"Dusty, let him down!" Maureen was screaming.

Despite heart-pumping anger, Dusty forced himself to relax his hold and step back. His hands kept grasping and knotting in the air.

"You son of a bitch," Dusty whispered. "You'd better be glad I'm not—"

Hawsworth stumbled back, face white, a hand to his throat. "You *assaulted* me!"

"What's the trouble here?" Bill asked as he advanced from Michall's Durango. He was still chewing some of his sandwich as he wiped crumbs from his blue FBI coat.

"Hey, Bill," Dusty managed through gritted teeth. "Meet Carter Hawsworth, returning to the scene of the crime...just like Agent Nichols figured he would."

Bill was watching them, a hard expression on his face. Rick had come to back him up. Michall and Sylvia, large-eyed, followed behind them. Sylvia held a handful of cheesy fishes; Dusty could hear them crunching in her tightening grip.

"Please, don't hurt him, Dusty," Yvette said from the side. "He may be an ass, but he was fair with me."

"Dusty?" Hawsworth asked, and his mouth dropped open. "Oh, of course. You're Sam's little snotty-nosed boy. The one Ruth couldn't wait to be rid of."

Dusty's universe had begun to narrow again, but Maureen reached out, dragging him back as he started forward.

Carter looked at Dusty as though he were a species of insect. "Yes, breeding will tell. The nasty little boy becomes a burly bully."

"Father"—Yvette stepped in front of Hawsworth—"stop trying to provoke him."

"You grew up with him?" Dusty asked Yvette. "You're lucky you're not a basket case."

"Like you, Mr. Stewart?" Hawsworth asked. "You should have seen yourself as a child, dirty, whining, forever with your finger in your mouth. When I think of you, I associate you with the stench of urine. I do hope you finally grew out of that."

Maureen's grip tightened on his arm. "Leave it be."

Bill stepped up. "What are you doing here, Dr. Hawsworth?"

"I came to see where Dale was killed." Hawsworth shifted his attention to the FBI agent. "This is still public property. I am violating no law."

"Just came for a look-see, huh?" Bill reached into his back pocket and pulled out a notebook. He checked his watch and noted the time, jotting down notes. "It's not exactly an easy place to get to, is it?"

"No. And I have little to say to you. I gave my statement to your Agent Nichols. If you have any other questions, I refer you either to that document or to my lawyer."

"Yeah." Bill cocked his head. "I read your statement. I

was fascinated by the fact that you couldn't account for your whereabouts on Halloween night."

"As I told Agent Nichols, I was out on the Navajo Reservation. Doing research."

"I read that. On plants." Bill gave him a quizzical look. "I couldn't pronounce the name."

"*Toloache,*" Hawsworth said condescendingly.

Dusty exhaled hard, immediately drawing Bill's attention.

"Tolo—" the agent began.

"*Toloache,*" Dusty finished, his hard gaze on Hawsworth. "I'm sure that poor Agent Nichols, like a good East Coast city cop, had no idea what you were talking about." He reached over and eased Maureen's hand from his sleeve.

"What is it?" Bill asked, his pen poised.

"Sacred datura," Dusty replied. "It's a pretty common plant out here. Normally it's hard to find this time of year, but we hadn't had a freeze up until Halloween. The monsoon season was good and rainy this year. Lots of moisture, lots of blooms. Let me guess, Dr. Hawsworth, when you're not busy seducing other men's wives, you're an ethnobotanist, right?"

Hawsworth crossed his arms, head back. "My, you really are a younger edition of your mother."

"Yeah, that's me," Dusty said, "and I have a very long memory. It goes back to the times when you couldn't keep your hands off Sam Stewart's wife. Along with memories of you, I have a good imagination. I can visualize poor Sam as he crawled up on the sink and stuck his finger into the light socket."

"Well, I didn't make him do it!" Hawsworth replied.

"Maybe not. But you made it a lot easier."

"You *do* have a good imagination." Hawsworth chuckled and waved a hand at Yvette. "Can you also imagine your mother with lots of different men? Even Dale? Yes, the good Dale Robertson, planting the sweet young Yvette in your mother's belly."

Yvette blinked and pain lit her eyes.

Dusty said, "Why did you say that to her?"

"Wait until you're stiffed for two hundred thousand quid and made into a bloody fool before the world. It sours the milk of human kindness."

"While you're feeling sour, I have something else to bring up."

"What would that be?" Hawsworth looked amused.

"A tip for Bill, here. He needs to write it down in his little book. It's interesting that you told him you were out looking for *toloache* Halloween night."

Bill waited for Hawsworth to comment, then said, "I'll bite. Why is that interesting?"

Dusty was watching Hawsworth, their eyes locked in mutual loathing. "Because he could have called it 'sacred datura,' or 'western jimsonweed,' or 'Indian apple,' or 'moon flower.' Even *Datura meteloides,* but he didn't. You see. sacred datura is an interesting plant. The blossoms were used historically to put infants with colic into a drugged sleep. Just the fragrance can make you dizzy, impair your ability to think and walk. Sometimes *curanderas,* medicine women in the back country, will use it to deaden pain before setting broken bones or pulling teeth. It doesn't take much, fifteen to twenty seeds, to kill an adult. But even a nonlethal overdose can cause permanent insanity."

"But Dr. Robertson wasn't poisoned," Bill reminded.

"That's not the point," Dusty said.

"Then what is?" Bill sounded irritated.

"*Toloache* is the word witches use for the plant. Witches, Bill. No one else calls it that."

"That doesn't prove anything," Hawsworth said shortly. "I'm an anthropologist. I know the names!"

"Yes," Dusty agreed. "And the FBI doesn't. You were counting on that, weren't you? What's *toloache* to Agent Nichols? Nothing. Just another weird anthropological word. One he couldn't easily cross-reference. Witches survive through misdirection. They like being clever, thrive on outsmarting their opponents. They like working at night—whether they're collecting *toloache* or sucking a man's soul out through a hole in his head."

This time Hawsworth stepped forward, his bony fist rising to shake under Dusty's nose. "You're just like Dale: an arrogant loudmouth. You don't know the half of it, Stewart. Well this time the trickery is over. The stakes have risen.

"Kwewur will get you, just like he got Dale, and it will fill my soul with joy when it happens." Hawsworth stalked away.

On impulse, Dusty called, "Too bad about Cochiti! Watch your step around cliffs, Carter. It's a long way down."

Hawsworth gave him a look that would have splintered bone. The tall man folded himself into his Chevrolet, slammed the door, and started the engine. Throwing the car into reverse, he swung around and roared off on the way to the loop road. Tires squealed as he made the turn onto pavement and accelerated.

"Someone ought to tell him the park speed limit is thirty-five," Sylvia noted as she fished more cheesy fishes from the box.

Yvette swallowed hard, struggling to keep her composure. "Excuse me. *Toloache?* Cochiti? Did I just miss something?"

Maureen's expression was thoughtful. "Dusty just

accused your father of being a witch—and he didn't exactly deny it, now did he?"

"That is one dangerous man," Dusty whispered.

"I don't think you did yourself any favors here today, Stewart," Bill noted as he scribbled furiously in his notebook. "He doesn't strike me as the forgiving kind."

"That makes two of us," Dusty replied.

By late afternoon, the sun began to break through the clouds, and shafts of golden light bathed the cliffs, but the west wind had a real bite to it. No one complained because no one even seemed to notice the cold.

Dusty stood beside Yvette, clasping his fleece collar beneath his chin, as he studied the progressing excavation. The fallen kiva roof lay exposed, the soil black with charcoal. When it had burned, the south side had fallen in first. The northern half, which they were excavating, had hinged, so the roof poles and cribbing sloped downward, disappearing into the unexcavated south half of the kiva. Michall had taken, stabilized, and bagged core samples for tree ring dates; then she'd collected soil samples and mapped in and photographed the burned beams.

Dusty prowled the rim of the kiva like a hungry coyote, staying just behind the yellow tape. In the center of the rich black earth, a round brown spot marked the location of the old pot hunter's hole.

"Hey, Bill?" Dusty called. "I want you guys to consider something."

"Yeah? What?" The FBI agent looked up from his notebook where he jotted observations.

"Dale was laid in that hole upside down. The person, or people, who buried him didn't dig a new hole. They reopened this old one. I mean, Dale's head was right over that brown intrusion down there in the kiva roof."

"Uh-huh." Bill studied him. "What's your point?"

"If that hole was dug in the sixties, your unsub and the pot hunter may be the same guy."

"Or girl," he added. "Sure, Stewart, maybe. Or it could be a wild-assed coincidence. Maybe the dirt was softer here, because it had been dug up before."

"Yeah, well, it would have been, but—"

"But that's the point. If I'd just murdered someone and was looking for the easiest place to bury them, I would not have spent my time stabbing a shovel into sand that's been filtering into the kiva for the last eight hundred years." He offered his hands for evidence. Swollen red blisters dotted his palms. "It's hard as Hades. I would have tested a few places and dug where it was the softest. Right here." He pointed to the old pot hunter's hole.

Yvette leaned toward Dusty and asked, "Could Dale have done this? Dug this hole back in the sixties? Maybe the person who killed him buried him here as a payback for digging this hole? Or for taking something he found."

Her once immaculate black wool coat was covered with wind-whipped sand. She must have been freezing. She had her arms wrapped around herself, toughing it out.

Dusty shook his head vehemently, then abruptly halted.

That was an interesting idea. Not about Dale, but maybe someone he'd worked with.

He turned to look back at the Casa Rinconada kiva and recalled the things Ruth Ann had said, about how often she'd come out here in the sixties. Sunlight blazed from the kiva's perfectly fitted stones. Dale would never have dug a hole in a site unless it had been gridded first and excavated according to accepted scientific methods—but Ruth Ann was another thing. She'd gotten out of archaeology because she'd hated it: *"I wanted the good stuff quick, so I could get out of the dirt."*

As he turned back, Dusty saw the green Chevy Suburban coming up the road toward them. Dusty had been wondering where Nichols was.

He looked at Yvette. "Dale never potted a site in his life. And this was a pot hunter, a looter. Somebody who wanted the good stuff quick. Even if an archaeologist had dug that hole and the records were lost, it would have been excavated differently. The walls would have been square. Not only that, Dale was immaculate when he dug. He'd never have backfilled it with a beer can and a big chunk of tibia."

Bill had been listening and taking notes. "Okay, Stewart, what's your take on why this hole's dug in the north half of the kiva? Why not smack dab in the center?"

"The center is generally where the roof entry is. The fire pit sits below that so that the smoke goes straight up and out, right? The only thing pot hunters find in fire pits is charcoal. Prehistoric charcoal doesn't sell for squat on the open market. The best chance for pottery or artifacts is on the north or south next to the wall. That's what our pot hunter was doing."

"Are many pot hunters women?" Yvette asked.

Dusty paused, glancing at Maureen. She inspected some burned fragments of bone that Sylvia had recovered from the screen.

Dusty shook his head. "Not usually. Women pot hunters in the Southwest are generally in their fifties or sixties, and married to men who are the true aficionados. They mostly run the screens and do the surface collecting.

They're the types who hand out cups of iced tea and wear fluffy sun hats."

"I daresay you don't much approve of them," Yvette noted.

"Not even slightly." Dusty glared at the hole. "But this wasn't dug by a weekend pot hunter. This is much more to the point. It's focused."

"How can you tell that?" Maureen asked as she looked at the brown soil so perfectly outlined in black. "It's just a hole."

"No, it's not. The pot hunter had some archaeological savvy. He knew where to dig to get to the good stuff the fastest."

"Would Carter Hawsworth have known that?" Maureen asked.

Dusty shot Yvette a sidelong look to catch her reaction. "Yes. He would have."

"Oh, my god, this floor is..." Then Sylvia yelled, "*Shit!*"

Dusty jerked his head up in time to see Sylvia drop the shovel and claw at the air as a section of pit floor collapsed beneath her. A sodden thump followed, and dust fountained up. The ragged hole had the same rough diameter as a fifty-five-gallon drum lid.

Dusty screamed, "*Sylvia!*"

Old Pigeontail's light-brown eyes seemed to bore right through Browser's body as he said, "It's a bit more difficult than you think, War Chief. You see, Shadow sent me. She wants you to know that Obsidian has been taken to High Sun House."

To one side, Catkin shifted, her moccasins grating on the room floor. She had crossed her arms, the fingers of her left hand tapping a nervous cadence on the wooden handle of her war club.

Blue Corn and Horned Ram watched in silence from the rear of the room, their eyes wide.

Browser stroked his chin, glancing at Stone Ghost. "Why there?"

"I assume," Pigeontail said, "that Shadow is going to pull Obsidian's heart out there. Two Hearts is convinced that it will save his life."

Browser's gaze sharpened. What was Pigeontail's hidden motive here? Why was he doing this? And he recalled something with a start.

In the eye of Browser's soul, he could see that sunny day as he, Redcrop, and Uncle Stone Ghost had walked across Longtail village's plaza to the small fire. There, Matron Ant Woman huddled beside the flames as she ate corn cakes. It had been the day after Matron Flame Carrier's funeral, during the Feast of Mourning.

The image was so clear: Ant Woman's age-creased expression, her dark eyes seeing so far into the past. Stone Ghost had asked about Flame Carrier's early life, about the time when she was a young woman. The old woman's reedy voice filtered out of Browser's memory...

"Old Pigeontail was from somewhere near Green Mesa. He frequented our village. He's still around, charging outrageous prices for his trinkets. He may know. And your Matron was married to him for a few summers." And then she had admitted: *"...Spider Silk ordered her to marry him. I never knew why."*

Browser felt a cold chill run down his back as he studied the old Trader, noting the bones underlying the loose flesh on his aged face. And suddenly he knew why the Blessed Spider Silk had ordered that long-ago marriage.

"Catkin," Browser said softly, "remove your war club." As she quickly complied, Browser said, "Thank you. Now, at my command, I would like you to break Pigeontail's shoulder."

Catkin said, "Yes, War Chief."

Pigeontail swallowed hard, then asked, "What are you saying, Browser? You know the rules under which I must work."

"I think my nephew understands that, Trader," Stone Ghost replied evenly.

"Then what is this about? Why would you have the deputy strike me?" Pigeontail raised his hands in supplication.

"So that it would hurt more when we bound you," Browser answered. "And binding you would be a necessary process before we dangled you upside down over the fire. Not a hot fire, mind you, but rather a bowl of glowing coals. If we do it correctly, we can sear the skin off your skull, and as it blisters, the brain will begin to boil beneath the charring bone. Handled correctly, it doesn't kill, but I've heard that it will leave the survivor mostly demented and in the most horrible pain."

"You are not frightening me, War Chief." His head high, Pigeontail's nostrils flared with disdain. "If you do this thing, you will reap nothing but trouble. Traders will walk three days out of their way to avoid you and the Katsinas' People. You will be shunned by all good people. Maybe even murdered in your sleep for breaking the Power of Trade. That threat of retaliation has protected Traders since the beginning of time."

Browser removed his own club and slid his hand up and down the shaft. "Our world is dying around us. I've seen graves robbed, and the bodies of dead friends butchered as if they were deer. What is one tortured Trader in a time of famine, death, and man-eating White Moccasins? What is your pain compared to entire kivas full of children being incinerated because their parents believe in the wrong gods?"

"War Chief, I don't think—"

"That I care?" Browser inspected the stone warhead; the chert cobble that he had lashed there so long ago was nicked along the edges, bits of dark matter in the deep cracks where he'd been unable to clean it. "Tell me, Pigeontail, how many summers were you married to our dead matron? Two? Three?"

The question seemed to catch Pigeontail by complete surprise. "Married to..."

"Flame Carrier. The Blessed Spider Silk ordered you to marry her. As I recall the story, you were younger than our dead matron, and the two of you fought like beasts."

Pigeontail's expression drooped. "Who told you about that? I've tried to forget it my entire life."

Browser slashed a blinding backhanded blow, the war club whistling through the air, its passage whipping Pigeontail's white hair. *"How many summers?"*

"Three," Pigeontail cried as he flailed backward, only to have the tip of Catkin's club jam hard into his back, propelling him forward with a jolt.

Stone Ghost stepped to one side and said, "Trader, we do not do this lightly. As you are no doubt aware, my nephew and I are descended from the Blessed Night Sun. You see, since most Traders are Made People, they would not retaliate against the Katsinas' People for murdering a First People's spy—especially one working for the White Moccasins."

Stone Ghost stopped, cocking his head to study Pigeontail's reaction. "What does Shadow really want?"

A slight sheen of sweat had broken out on Pigeontail's forehead. "She wants revenge. The destruction of Two Hearts's warriors last night has thrown her into a violent rage. Beyond that, Two Hearts is dying. He is desperate for two things: Obsidian's heart and the turquoise wolf that War Chief Browser stole from him."

"And you?" Browser asked as he swung his club. "What is your place in all of this? That you are the eyes of the White Moccasins, I understand, but—"

"I am *not* their eyes," Pigeontail hissed. "I go where I will, and do as I please. I serve no master but myself. They have their own eyes, and believe me, they are everywhere."

A faint sneer bent his lips. "What about you, War Chief? Whom do you serve? The Made People? The ones who hunted your ancestors as if they had been but rats or other vermin? Or do you serve the katsinas?"

"I serve my people," Browser said and thrust his war

club into Pigeontail's face to stifle the man's rebuttal, adding, "I'm just trying to find out who my people are, Trader."

"So, tell me, War Chief," Pigeontail mumbled past the club shoved against his lips. "What do you *really* believe?"

"I believe in Poor Singer's prophecy," Browser said truthfully. "I believe the words that Gray Thunder spoke in Flowing Waters Town: That we will only survive if we lay our differences behind us. Myself, I have never seen a katsina. I don't know if they exist or not. But Gray Thunder's words were of hope, of a way to live together. The Made People hunted us down because we made slaves of them and committed terrible atrocities. Maybe the horrible deeds of the past must be paid for, but the ways and means of the White Moccasins, Two Hearts, and Shadow are wrong, and I will destroy them."

"You would turn against your own kind?"

"My kind!" Browser thundered, bulling forward and pushing the old man back against Catkin's club. "My kind doesn't eat the flesh of men! My kind doesn't murder entire villages of men, women, and children. And most of all, *my* kind doesn't burn kivas filled with children!"

"The gods demand these things, Browser!" Pigeontail roared back. "The Blessed Flute Player, Spider Woman, and the Blue God, like the First People, are in a battle for their lives!"

"Then let the gods fight their own battles," Browser fumed.

Pigeontail met his glare. Eye to eye, they stood; then, several breaths later, Pigeontail shrugged. "Why should it matter? You are one man. Very well, pack up and go. Take your Fire Dogs and leave. If you won't fight for your people, at least promise me you won't fight against them."

"You think it's that easy? That I can just walk away? That I can forget what Two Hearts and Shadow did to my wife? Forget the friends they have killed? Am I supposed to leave the ghosts of those hideously burned children to wail in lonely pain? To ignore the way they killed my Matron—your one-time wife? What they did to her body? The soul they stole by drilling a hole in her living head? And leave Obsidian for that monster and his misbegotten spawn to murder?"

"If you stay, it will cost you your life, Browser." Pigeontail was watching him, searching his expression... for what?

"My life?"

"And that of your party." Pigeontail smiled. "Although Shadow's warriors might want Blue Corn released."

"Blue Corn?" Stone Ghost asked.

Pigeontail gave him a curious look. "She is one of us. I don't think she knows it, but she is. Most of her lineage is descended from the First People. She is not pure, having intermarried with Made People, but enough of the blood remains that it is worth keeping her alive."

"I don't believe it!" Blue Corn blurted.

Pigeontail shrugged. "What you believe doesn't change the way things are. Your great-grandmother made the decision not to tell her children. At the time it seemed prudent. The Made People were at the height of their power. Prospects for our kind were dim. It was a way to maintain control of Flowing Waters Town. The place, as you know, was important to us. It was supposed to be our new beginning, a fresh start after the Blessed Featherstone led us out of Straight Path Canyon."

Blue Corn's eyes slitted as she studied Pigeontail. "I'm supposed to believe that? That I'm descended from First People?"

Pigeontail shrugged again. "I have no care what you believe."

Stone Ghost stepped forward and examined Blue Corn's face. "What is your clan?"

"She is descended from the Red Lacewing Clan," Pigeontail answered. "Of the Blessed Weedblossom's lineage." He gestured around. "Ironically, Kettle Town was once theirs."

"Weedblossom?" Blue Corn whispered, her thoughts knotted around the revelation. And in that instant she looked suddenly unsure, casting an unnerved glance at Pigeontail.

"So my entire party can just leave?" Browser asked. "We can walk out of here without being attacked?"

"That would be permitted...provided you turn that little turquoise wolf over to me." Pigeontail's curt nod guaranteed it. "As to your safety, I will make the case to Shadow." A curious amusement lay behind his eyes. "She has a certain, well, softness for you, War Chief."

"Why do we need anyone's permission? I thought the White Moccasins were killed in the ambush last night?" Under Catkin's critical gaze, Pigeontail might have been a mouse beneath Coyote's nose.

Pigeontail lifted an eyebrow. "That is today, Deputy. What do you think will happen tomorrow, or a moon from now? You have dealt the White Moccasins a stinging blow. Had it been your pride that was slapped so ignominiously, would you just let it go?"

Browser made a face against the sinking sensation in his stomach. "What of Obsidian? May she go with us?"

"I told you, War Chief, she's in High Sun House, being prepared for the ritual sacrifice."

Browser read that slight gleam in the Trader's odd eyes, as though he were waging a desperate gamble.

Browser nodded at his deputy. "Break his shoulder, Catkin."

She was well into her swing when Pigeontail ducked

away, yelling, "Wait!" He rolled sideways as Catkin's blow sailed through empty air. "Gods! You'd do this thing? Hang me over fire?"

"Deputy," Browser said in chastisement, "you're losing your skill. I told you—"

"Wait!" Pigeontail screamed as he skipped to the side on his old legs. He had his hands up as Catkin circled, preparing for another blow. "Blessed gods, War Chief, are you mad?"

Browser growled, "I'm tired of being made a fool of! Perhaps your death will show them I'm serious!"

Catkin deftly chased the old man back into a corner of the room and lifted her club to strike.

"In the name of the Flute Player!" Pigeontail wailed as he looked into Catkin's implacable eyes, "What do you want to know?"

Browser roared, "I wish to know where Obsidian is!"

Pigeontail wearily slumped in the corner. "Telling you won't make any difference. The rituals are almost finished." Catkin lifted her club again, and Pigeontail rushed to say, "She is in Owl House! In the kiva, bound across from the Blessed Two Hearts!"

"How many warriors does Shadow have?"

Browser's blood ran hot and swift in his veins, eager for the battle. His enemy was just over there, across the canyon, poorly guarded and vulnerable.

"Two. The sentries who had been assigned to guard the elder. They keep watch from the rooftops. There were three, but Shadow sent one of them to Starburst Town for reinforcements."

Browser shot a glance at Catkin. "Then we must hurry."

He noticed that Blue Corn had a dazed look, as if she had come adrift from the world, eyes focused on some distance in her head.

Catkin watched Pigeontail with narrowed eyes. "This is a trap, Browser, and you know it. Is one life worth the risk?"

Keen anticipation lit Pigeontail's eyes. Where did that come from? What did it mean? What was he waiting for?

Browser turned to Stone Ghost.

Perspiration had glued his uncle's thin white hair to his wrinkled forehead, but his black eyes blazed. Stone Ghost said, "Catkin is right. This is certainly a trap. Which means you must make certain, Nephew, that you are smarter than Two Hearts, and few have ever been. That's why he's still alive, though we've tried to hunt him down many times."

Stone Ghost stepped toward Browser and looked up. "You must also make certain that anyone who chooses to accompany you on this raid knows he is going there for one reason, to kill the most dangerous witch in the land. There is a good chance that all of you will die at Owl House."

Blue Corn added, "There is one more small thing to consider."

Browser turned to face her. She looked suddenly frightened. "Yes, Matron?"

"Two Hearts is a very powerful witch. If there is any chance that Obsidian's heart can extend Two Hearts's wicked life—"

Browser spun around. "Catkin, find Straighthorn and Jackrabbit! The time has come to end this."

"**C**areful!" Dusty cried as he leaped the yellow tape and ran. "Stay back! The whole roof can go at any second!"

No one questioned his unexpected authority as he shouldered through the gaping FBI agents to get to Michall and shouted, "Give me your flashlight!"

She pulled it from the sheath on her belt and thrust it into his hand. Dusty dropped to his hands and knees and crawled forward until his head cleared the hole. "Sylvia? Do you hear me?"

"I'm okay!" she called up.

Flipping on the flashlight, he shot the beam around the interior and saw her, sitting about four feet below. Dust covered her from head to toe.

Sylvia coughed and shielded her eyes against the light while she looked around the interior of the kiva. "Oh, Dusty, you're not going to believe this." She lifted a long tan object and pointed to the floor in front of her. They were everywhere.

"What does she see?" Michall asked.

Through the swirling dust, he made out the bones, and a portion of the curving kiva bench that buttressed the north wall. Plaster still clung to the stone in places. Dusty swiveled to look at Maureen. "Sylvia is sitting in the middle of a bone bed."

Maureen hurried toward him, and Dusty slid backward, gave her the flashlight, and said, "Be careful not to collapse the rest of the roof."

"I'll be careful." She took the light, got down on her belly, and slid forward to look. Her long black braid snaked through the dirt at her side.

Yvette and the FBI guys looked wary and uncertain, obviously expectant, but without the feeling of pure ecstasy that shone in Michall's wide eyes.

"It's intact," Dusty said to her unasked question. "The roof hasn't completely collapsed onto the living floor on the north side."

"Dusty?" Maureen twisted her head around to peer at him. "We have...let's see...one, two, three, at least three femora that I can see. From the looks, it's probably two individuals. Well..." She paused, as though confused. "This is strange. You can't have three different sized lefts, and that fourth femur is smaller."

"What does she mean?" Rick asked.

Dusty wiped his brow with his coat sleeve. "She means there are probably more than two individuals."

Michall said, "Okay, how do you want me to do this? I'm not a physical anthropologist."

Dusty studied the slanting pit floor, and for the first time since Dale's death, he felt whole, excited, happy to be alive. "If we can get Sylvia out without bringing the whole thing down, I think you should drop back. The smart way is to trowel this down to the burned beam." He cocked his head, reading the pit floor, seeing through the soil. "The best entry is right there in the middle of the pot hunter's hole. We have to assume that he fell through, too, just like Sylvia. And both of them have destroyed the context. Which means we can—"

"Huh?" Rick asked as he photographed Maureen's butt where it hovered over the hole.

"The pot hunter and Sylvia had to put their feet somewhere," Dusty said. "That means that they either crushed or kicked the bones aside."

"That's bad." Bill was holding a tape recorder where he'd been dictating notes. "Sylvia just destroyed evidence."

Dusty said, "But we also have about a third of this kiva floor intact! The pollen, the phytoliths, the artifacts, everything's there."

"Except what the pot hunter took," Michall corrected. "It's not like it's pristine."

"Yeah, but this isn't the thirties, almost-a-doctor Michall. For now, this is pretty spectacular."

"What the *hell* is going on here?" Nichols's unexpected voice demanded harshly. "Stewart! You consider yourself under arrest for interfering with an investigation!"

Sam Nichols stood at the edge of the kiva in his brown canvas coat, breathing hard. His thick black hair was sticking out at angles from under his gray knit cap. "Is that Dr. Cole in that hole?"

Dusty smacked dirt from his hands. "Agent Nichols, we've hit the mother lode."

"I hope that means you have a damn good explanation, Stewart."

Dusty helped Maureen out of the kiva as she crawled back, a glow in her eyes. "I could see two adult skulls, a male and a female."

"Uh, Sam," Bill said, his tape recorder held out in

Maureen's direction. "We've had some interesting developments. I wouldn't file charges on Stewart or Dr. Cole yet. We'd probably better take Stewart's advice and excavate as he recommends, or we'll collapse the rest of it. Stewart says that—"

"Hey!" Sylvia yelled, her arms extended from the hole. "Somebody get me out of here! This is spooky!"

Michall said, "Give me my flashlight. I want to go look."

Dusty handed it to her, and watched Michall slide forward on her belly until she could shine light into the hole.

"Hey, swamp rat," Michall greeted. "You look picturesque squatting there amid the bones."

Sylvia replied, "Come on. Get me out. There's something really strange about these bones. It's as though I can feel them crawling all over me."

Michall panned the beam around for a while, then asked, "Is that a wall crypt over there?"

Sylvia answered but Dusty couldn't make out the words.

"All right." Nichols fixed his good eye on Dusty. "Assuming that I'm not dragging you off to Albuquerque and one hell of a stiff fine, what's going on here?"

"We don't know for sure yet," Bill said from behind. "Sam, there's a kiva full of dead people here. You just missed the collapse of the hole in the roof."

Dusty caught movement from the edge of his vision and spun around. "Yvette? Where are you going?"

She was headed downhill, her black coat flapping.

"I'm cold!" she called over her shoulder. "See you later."

"Yvette?" Nichols asked. His horn-rimmed glasses flashed as he whirled to take another look at the woman.

"Yvette Hawsworth," Dusty said. "She just showed up at my trailer last night—"

"And you didn't call me immediately!" Nichols roared. He waved an arm. "Rick, would you kindly run down and detain Ms. Hawsworth. Stewart, Cole, get in my car! Let's find a place to talk."

Browser stood in the windswept plaza, the ruins of Kettle Town rising around them. The long-abandoned town felt oddly remote, as if the place watched through the dark windows and doorways, waiting for some great event to unfold.

Rubbing a hand down the back of his neck, Browser could feel the eyes of the old ones—his ancestors—upon him. He addressed his small party: "First, I need two volunteers to make sure that Matron Blue Corn gets safely to Flowing Waters Town."

Two of the Mogollon warriors trotted forward, expressions grim. "Yes, War Chief. Upon our lives, the Matron will be delivered safely."

"You need not do this," Blue Corn said, a grudging respect in her eyes. "Just get me back to Center Place. I left three wounded warriors there. They will be wondering what has happened. They can get me home. Or, rather, we can get each other home."

"See to them, too, if you will," Browser charged the warriors.

"Yes, War Chief."

"I do not think this is smart," White Cone said from the side. "It is not the time to divide our forces."

Browser cast a sidelong glance at Pigeontail, aware that the old Trader seemed to soak up each word the way a wadded fabric shirt absorbed water in a rain puddle. "We must move rapidly, Elder. If not, Shadow's reinforcements will arrive from Starburst Town before we can rescue Obsidian and be on our way south."

Stone Ghost added, "Time, my friend, is the one thing we do not have."

"Those who jump too quickly fall into fires or floods," White Cone countered. "But, very well, what of Elder Horned Ram? He is failing."

"We'll take him with us." Browser took in Catkin's stunned expression, then turned to Blue Corn. "He wanted us dead, didn't he?"

"He did," a gravelly voice called.

Browser turned to see Rain Crow propped in the doorway, a war club hanging from his hand. He squinted against the daylight, and his expression reflected the terrible agony inside his head. He took a step forward, wobbling, and had to use his war club like a cane to brace himself.

Blue Corn asked, "War Chief? Are you fit to travel? Are you ready to start home?"

Rain Crow swallowed, his negation the faintest shake of the head, as if any more would have split his skull. "No, Matron. I wish to remain here for a time. Browser is going after Two Hearts, correct?"

"I am." Browser nodded.

"Then I am going with you." Rain Crow lifted his ruined face and glared at Browser.

"I need you at home," Blue Corn said shortly. "And beyond that, you're not fit to fight a mouse, let alone

White Moccasins. You look like a passing butterfly could blow you over."

Rain Crow smiled. "Matron, while I have been sick, tongues have been loose. The talk is that the White Moccasins were responsible for Gray Thunder's death. None here has let slip, or even hinted, that my guard was killed in retaliation."

He almost toppled, jamming his war club down to keep his balance. "I would know who caused my guard's death." He shot a veiled look at Browser. "You, War Chief?"

"No," Browser insisted. "My suspicion is that Shadow did it."

"I share your thoughts." Rain Crow took another step. "And I think you are right to keep Horned Ram close. He is the sort of serpent you are better off keeping in a cage. At least when you can see him you have an idea of what he's up to."

"Why would I want you with me? You look like you're about to fall over dead yourself," Browser said.

The grim smile played about Rain Crow's pain-racked lips. "I relieve you of any obligation for me, War Chief. I will make my own way. Should I fall behind, you have my leave to abandon me. I have sworn an oath to find and kill the culprit who murdered my guard. It is something I must do, that is all."

Browser nodded, remembering how disoriented he had recently been when Two Hearts had cracked him in the head. The pain had to be like watery fire running through Rain Crow's brain. "Very well, but you are on your own if you come with us."

"I understand that," the War Chief replied.

Catkin stepped in front of Browser, her back to the others in the room, and whispered, "We can't take an old man and a wounded warrior with us! Are you trying to get us all killed?"

He gazed into her dark, panicked eyes and said, "I have reasons. Please—"

"They will slow us down to a crawl, and if Horned Ram has the chance, he will scream out our location to our enemies! Have you lost your wits?"

Browser put a hand on her shoulder and felt the bunched muscles. "My wits are the only thing I have left. I can't explain right now. You must trust me."

She didn't wish to. He could see it in her expression. The cant of her jaw, the way her nostrils flared. But she nodded and stepped back.

Browser called, "Red Dog? Fire Lark? Please find a ladder and lay Horned Ram on it. I want to be out of here in one half-hand of time."

"What will Straighthorn and I do?" Jackrabbit asked.

"Come with me."

Browser turned toward Old Pigeontail. "Tell me one last thing, Trader? Are you certain Carved Splinter is dead?"

Pigeontail gave Browser a sympathetic look. "Only bones remain of the young warrior. And most of them have been boiled and splintered, if you understand my meaning."

Jackrabbit's throat worked.

Browser looked at the young warrior. "I have special duties for the two of you. Gather your things and meet me at the front entrance of Kettle Town. We will discuss it there."

"Yes, War Chief."

The conference room at the Chaco Culture National Historic Park visitor center measured about sixteen by twenty feet and had artsy photographs of Chaco Canyon on the pale-green walls.

Nichols leaned back in the chair at the head of the long rectangular table and glared at Dusty and Maureen, who sat side by side to his left. Stewart appeared a little insecure, but Cole stared right back at Nichols, as though she'd endured a thousand such interrogations and wasn't intimidated in the slightest. Nichols took out his notebook and slapped it on the table.

"This is a criminal investigation, for God's sake. Are you two particularly dense?" He loosened his tie and reached for the cup of weak coffee Rupert Brown had provided; it steamed on the battered government tabletop.

"Not at all, Agent Nichols." Maureen crossed her arms. "And neither are your agents. Both of your men are conscientious. They wouldn't allow anyone to compromise evidence."

Nichols squinted at her. "They've assured me of that,

but your involvement *appears* to be a conflict of interest, Dr. Cole. Do you understand that?"

"They needed the input of a professional archaeologist as well as a board-certified forensic anthropologist. That's all it was. Unofficial Q and A."

Nichols shoved his glasses up on his nose. "Not when those specialists are potential suspects in a federal homicide, Dr. Cole."

"Oh, come on," Maureen said. "We have a dinner receipt from the Pink Adobe the night Dale was killed. I think our server was Maria. We sat in a corner table. She can place us there. You have a telephone log for Dusty's trailer. Or you should have. If you don't, you can subpoena it. You know that we answered Sylvia's call from Albuquerque. Not only that, neither of us would have wanted Dale dead. Neither motive nor opportunity."

Nichols shoved his notebook around the table. "That's the problem. I have no *real* suspects, folks. Every lead has petered out to nothing, which means *you* are still suspects."

"What about Carter Hawsworth?" she asked.

"I don't have anything I can take to a prosecuting attorney. The same with Dr. Sullivan. No one in Dr. Robertson's department sticks out. Stewart looks to inherit, but it's not a huge chunk of change, just enough to pay the estate taxes and leave him something comfortable for the future."

Maureen braced her elbows on the table, and her black eyes gleamed. "What about the lab work? The notes? The blood tests? The fax they found in Casa Rinconada?"

He said nothing, frowning. Finally, he grudgingly offered, "The fax was printed on Dr. Robertson's machine. The phone company records sent us to the Marriott. The same one we stayed at. At five thirty-seven on Halloween night, someone used the business center to send it. They paid cash for the service. No one remembers what the sender looked like."

"Just like Carter Hawsworth claims happened to him." Maureen frowned.

"Could he have sent them to himself?" Dusty asked. "You know, as a cover?"

Nichols swiveled his chair back around to face them. "The basilisk on the business card from Stewart's office? Same thing. No prints but yours and Stewart's. It was Bic ink." He sipped his coffee. "The diary that was left outside of your camp trailer? Professionally done at a print shop in Albuquerque. We're still following up on that one. Maybe we'll get lucky. But, again, no prints outside of yours, Maggie's, and Sylvia's."

She considered him for a moment. "That in itself says something."

"Enlighten me, Dr. Cole."

"In my part of the world, we call him a 'player,' someone who knows the rules of the game. He's done this before, Agent Nichols. He knows how to hide evidence, and he likes doing it. He's baiting us. He knows what he can get away with. You just have to hope he'll get bored with the easy stuff and take a chance, give you a dare."

Nichols glared at her with his squinted eye. "I thought of that, but you're the only person out here who 'knows the rules.'"

Maureen shook her head. "What's my motive? Why do I want to murder one of my best friends?"

He sat back, dull gaze on his coffee cup.

"No idea, eh?" she asked.

"No, and it pisses me off." A slight tic jerked in his cheek. "I feel like I'm chasing my tail."

Dusty said, "Remember when Rupert said this wasn't a White crime?"

Nichols nodded. "I do."

"You're looking for White motives. That's why you're getting nowhere."

Nichols leaned across the table and almost shouted, "That's anthropological bullshit, Stewart!"

"Then how did you miss *toloache?*"

"What?"

Dusty went on to explain that Hawsworth had used a witch's term. "It went right past you. Just like Hawsworth wanted it to."

"Look, we've put the guy under the microscope. So, he used a term from the Native language. Dr. Cole has flipped out more bone terms in the last couple of hours than I've ever heard. You guys talk that way."

"It's not a White crime," Dusty insisted doggedly.

"Motives are motives. I don't care whether you're Navajo or Hindu. Besides, none of my sources in the traditional community picked up a single red flag. The only Indian suspect I have"—he held out a hand to Maureen— "is sitting here in this room."

Maureen laced her fingers on the tabletop. "Then why haven't you arrested me?"

Nichols felt like throwing his notebook at her. "All of my evidence is circumstantial. I've decided I'm not even going to charge you with interfering with an investigation. Bill and Rick spoke up on your behalf, and Rick said he'd do it in a court of law. Which also pissed me off!"

A knock came at the door, and Rupert Brown leaned in. His gray temples accented his brown hawklike face. "Sorry to interrupt. I thought I'd check to see if you needed anything."

"No, Dr. Brown, we're fine, thanks," Nichols said.

"Okay. Then I'm off for DC." He lifted a hand to Dusty and Maureen. "See you when I get back."

"DC?" Nichols said. "Whoa! As in Washington?"

"Yeah. Big high mucky-muck meetings." Rupert smiled. "It's the annual policy implementation and general bullshit session that the Department of the Interior makes us endure each fiscal year."

"Have a nice trip," Maureen called as Rupert started to shut the door.

"Hold on!" Nichols shouted. "Who said you could leave town?"

Rupert opened the door and leaned against the frame. "I didn't realize I needed your permission, Agent Nichols. But if I do, *please* make me stay here. I beg you. No, I beseech you. I might even forgive you for screwing up my park."

Irritated, Nichols flicked his pen open and closed several times, then said, "No. Go. I'm sure I can find you if I need you."

Rupert smothered a smile, saluted, and shut the door.

"So, getting back to this dig," Nichols said.

"Look, Agent Nichols"—Maureen leaned forward—"you have a kiva littered with human bones. No one out there—not Michall or Sylvia, and certainly not your agents —is prepared for the kind of analysis that will be required over the next few days."

Nichols jotted down a note about her manner:

Dr. Cole is insistent, authoritative, abrasive. Thinks we're incompetent.

He said, "You want to do it, huh?"

"I'd love to. But I think it would be better if you conscripted Sid Malroun from OMI. He's used to bodies in the flesh, but if he needs me, I can crawl over the tape and give him a hand with the cannibalized bone."

In the middle of jotting another note, Nichols's pen stopped. "The what?"

Dusty smoothed his hand over his blond beard and said, "We found a cannibalized leg today. Someone had carved the flesh off the bone. We saw the same treatment of bodies at the 10K3 site and at Pueblo Animas. Believe me, mister agent, sir, there's a relationship between Dale's burial site, the basilisk, and those two sites. Each is rife with witchcraft and cannibalism."

Nichols studied their expressions. Both appeared excited but rational. "Didn't Rhone work on those sites, too?"

Stewart straightened slightly. "Yes. What of it?"

Nichols shook his head and finished his note. "Nothing...just correlating."

The line of people stretched behind Browser like a slithering snake. As each person exited Kettle Town and came to meet them, Catkin's eyes narrowed to ever thinner slits. She thought he was mad. And he wasn't so sure she was wrong. He was gambling on legends. A thing no one sane would attempt. "Clay Frog, please help Rain Crow."

"Yes, War Chief."

She trotted back. Rain Crow limped along behind them, his lopsided face looking worse for the contorted expression he had adopted to grit back the pain.

Clay Frog offered an arm to the burly War Chief from Flowing Waters Town. He took it gladly.

Rain Crow had to be in excruciating agony. Having suffered a similar, if less threatening wound recently, Browser had to admire the man's courage and endurance. Not only must he have a skull-cracking headache, but his balance and coordination were slightly off, as well. Worse, after a blow to the head like that, a man's souls could slip away before he realized it. Nevertheless, Rain Crow doggedly walked forward.

"Why am I still a prisoner?" Old Pigeontail asked from where he proceeded a half pace ahead of Catkin. "I've told you enough to get myself killed should Shadow or her allies ever find out."

"Then we are your best hope for a long and happy life," Stone Ghost told him. He plodded along on stumpy thin legs, his wrinkled old face set with determination. White Cone walked at his side. "Be content, and keep your mouth closed."

"Where are the two young warriors?" Old Pigeontail asked.

"I sent them back with a message for Matron Cloud-blower." Browser pointed his war club at the withered Trader. "And my uncle told you to be quiet."

Catkin looked at the elders, and her jaw clenched.

In her gaze, Browser could read the tracks of her souls. She could not believe he was actually doing this.

She was right. The elders ought to be up on the mesa top with Blue Corn, headed for safety; it had been impossible to convince either of them. For Stone Ghost, this was the end to a journey he had begun many sun cycles ago when he'd mistakenly blamed a young warrior for a crime he did not commit. Until Stone Ghost stood over the corpse of Two Hearts, he could not say, "Here, it ends."

Old Pigeontail looked over his shoulder, fully aware that Yucca Whip and Red Dog followed immediately behind him. After Pigeontail's story about Carved Splinter, either warrior would gladly crack his skull open, and he seemed to know it.

Browser glanced back. Badger Dancer and Fire Lark bore old Horned Ram on his litter. They had looted the ladder from a collapsed room on the fourth floor, padded it with blankets, and made a platform to carry the Red Rock elder. Horned Ram looked gray and pale; each step that jolted his broken shoulder reflected in the corners of his constantly tensing mouth. When he met Browser's eyes, it was with a look of loathing.

Yes, soon you will tell me what you know.

They headed south onto the road. When they had gone far enough, Browser turned to stare up at the cliff behind Kettle Town. Blue Corn's party labored up the stairway, climbing for the mesa top. It was the first step on their journey, and the Matron was already lagging behind.

"Do you think she believes it?" Catkin asked. "That she's descended from First People?"

"It doesn't matter," Browser murmured. "So long as she never tells her people."

"You think they will kill her if they find out?"

"I think they might."

Browser looked back at Kettle Town. With the plaster cracked off of its once-pillared portico, the town looked like a squat grinning head with too many teeth. The image wasn't macabre, or sinister, but rather reminded him of a perplexed and exhausted observer.

Blue Corn's party reached the top of the cliff. For a few brief instants, they stood skylined, then one by one, they disappeared.

Well and good. The Matron was out of harm's way.

The flat, washed clay of the canyon bottom ahead reflected the sunlight. A bow shot in front of them, irregular dots marked the roadway where it dived down into the wash.

Browser slipped his fingers along his war club. He and his club had become old companions, survivors of many desperate battles. The touch reassured him.

An ominous silence settled on the party as they approached the battleground where the bodies of the dead warriors lay as they had fallen. Even as they closed, Browser could hear the muffled gurgles and occasional faint hiss as the corpses warmed in the morning sunlight.

"Blessed Gods," Rain Crow muttered as they drew up. "Did no one survive?"

"Only you, War Chief," Browser said. "And that is a miracle. If you hadn't crawled as far as you did, today you'd be a wandering and homeless ghost searching futilely for your ancestors."

They passed the first of the bodies; the blood had dried black. Expressions on the faces of the dead ran the gamut from tranquil, as if blissful in death, to contorted grimaces. Men with dried sunken eyes and receding lips watched them pass.

"Blessed Gods," Fire Lark hissed, pointing with his war club. "That one. Look. He's one of them. A White Moccasin. He's been..."

"That's Shadow's work, my young friend." Old Pigeontail shot a leering smile at Fire Lark, enjoying the young warrior's discomfort. "The man you see there is Bear Lance, one of Shadow's old lovers. Sometimes I wonder whom to pity more, her enemies, or those that she takes a special liking for."

The Mogollon and Rain Crow stared at the few dead who showed evidence of butchery. The bones looked oddly thin where they protruded from the thick muscles of a carved leg.

Browser ordered, "Move."

As they started away, White Cone asked, "What sort of monster is she?"

"A monster as terrible as any in the legends of your people or mine," Stone Ghost said.

Browser pointed ahead. "Yucca Whip, check the bottom of the wash before we cross and make sure that no ambush is waiting for us. Then guard the other side of the crossing and ensure our safety."

"Yes, War Chief." Yucca Whip charged forward,

smoothly withdrawing a fistful of arrows from his quiver and nocking one.

"I wouldn't believe it," Old Pigeontail said under his breath.

"Believe what?" Catkin asked, sparing him a quick sidelong look before returning her attention to the crossing.

"That Fire Dogs would follow a Straight Path War Chief. More, that members of the Bow Society—of all the Mogollon—would follow Browser."

"Perhaps Poor Singer's prophecy is more Powerful than you thought it was. Perhaps this alliance is just the beginning," Catkin said.

"And perhaps," he responded, "you are just a small group of fools who think that you are more than you are."

Browser looked down into the vacant eyes of one of the dead White Moccasin warriors. Lightning patterns of blackened blood streaked his face.

Browser said, "We will soon find out, Trader."

As the sun dipped toward the western horizon, the cliffs in Chaco Canyon shimmered the color of pure gold. Dusty added another stick to his campfire and looked around the canyon. Clouds filled the eastern sky, slowly heading west. He watched them for a time, seeing how their shapes changed; then he took a deep breath and savored the pungent scent of burning juniper. Maggie leaned back in one of the lawn chairs, her legs out straight, her eyes locked on distant thoughts.

Maureen had gone back to the dig and said she'd return at sunset with Sylvia and Michall. He'd told her he'd have dinner ready, but it would still be a while before he'd bring out the grill and the buffalo burgers. He wanted a good solid bed of coals to roast them over, slowly, very slowly. It wasn't every day a man had the pleasure of eating rich, succulent buffalo. Maureen had found the burger at a specialty food store in Santa Fe. He'd been saving it, hoping to cook it to celebrate a significant find—like today's intact kiva floor.

Dusty walked back to the trailer, opened the squeaky door, and went to the little closet in the rear, where he pulled out two more folding lawn chairs. He grabbed the small ice chest filled with beer on his way outside.

As he unfolded the chairs before the fire, Maggie said, "Dusty?"

"Yeah?" He heard the worry in her voice.

"Aunt Hail came to me in a dream last night."

"She did?"

"She's worried." Maggie avoided his eyes. "She thinks the danger is closing around us. These words stuck in my mind. 'Can't you see? The witch is right there, looking over your shoulder and laughing as the yucca hoop drops around you.'"

"Did she say who the witch is?"

Maggie shook her head, lost in thought. "No. Maybe it was just a dream. I mean, how do you tell the difference?" She looked up then, pleading. "Was it *really* Aunt Hail, or just my imagination?"

"I think you should ask your aunt Sage. Maybe she could help you."

Maggie gestured impotence. "I'd love to. I'd call her, but she won't trust the phone lines when it comes to talking about spirit things. She doesn't trust electricity. What she means by that is that she's unsure if witches can monitor it. It's still so new that no one knows if witches can hear things through telephone lines."

"Yeah, like the FBI. Think there's a similarity?"

Maggie smiled at that. "I'd drive down there, but with Rupert leaving, I can't."

"He took off already?"

She nodded. "He left me in charge. I didn't get a complete briefing. He was in his office with Dr. Hawsworth for about an hour. And after Hawsworth left, Rupert didn't look happy at all."

"Yeah, Hawsworth has that effect on people. He's sort of the human form of Kaopectate."

He saw Yvette's Jeep coming and let out a soft groan. She'd looked like a skewered rabbit ever since seeing Hawsworth. He flopped into the chair and reached into the ice chest for a bottle of Guinness.

Yvette stopped at the edge of the camp site, and dust boiled up behind her Jeep. The instant she got out, she cried, "I can't bloody believe it!" She tramped toward him like a woman on a mission.

"What?" he called sociably.

"First I have to deal with my father, and then the FBI! I'm a suspect! In the death of a man I never even knew! Agent Nichols has been raking me over his own proverbial coals!"

Dusty gestured to the remaining lawn chair. "So, you want a Guinness or a Coors Light?"

"What?" she asked as though startled by the question. Her ash-blond hair looked like it hadn't been combed since dawn, and she'd been sweating. Tiny curls framed her forehead. "Oh. Right! Damn. Set me up, Landlord."

Dusty reached into the ice chest and shared a quizzical look with Maggie. "Who?"

She unfolded the other lawn chair and sat down. "Barkeep? Is that the word you use out here in the wilderness?"

"This isn't a wilderness. That's over by Kayenta."

He popped a top on a Guinness and handed it to her. The way she upended the bottle and chugged made his brows lift in admiration.

"What a sodding miserable day this turned out to be."

"What did Nichols want?"

She glared at him over the bottle. "Everything! He wanted to know when I entered the bloody country. All about the faxes and emails I'd been sent. How I came to know about Dale. What I felt when I found out. Did I hate him for being my mother's lover? What did Fa...

Carter do? What did he say? Did I have any reason to think Carter would have killed Robertson. And on and on and on!" She shivered and tugged the collar of her black coat closed. "Good Lord, Stewart, what are you and Maggie doing sitting outside on a night like this? It's freezing."

"Pull your chair closer to the fire." He threw another piece of juniper on the flames. "You'll be warm soon enough."

"And as to me," Maggie said, standing and stretching, "I have a park to run. I'd better get back to the office. If Agent Nichols is up to his usual tricks, he's got one of the bathrooms closed off and everyone's in a panic."

"Good night, Maggie," Dusty and Yvette said in unison, and then turned to stare curiously at each other.

Yvette dragged her chair closer as Maggie climbed into her pickup and drove off.

"Maggie seems like a gem." She rubbed her face, as though massaging the fatigue away.

"Yeah. She's a real special friend." He looked at her. "You okay? I mean after some of the things Hawsworth said to you. I can't believe that guy. I wanted to choke the living daylights out of him."

"That's just Father. I mean, Carter. Bloody hell, this is going to take getting used to." The firelight cast an orange gleam over her face.

She did look like Dale.

Dusty lowered his gaze and pretended to study the Guinness label while he hurt. Flames crackled up around the new tinder, and sparks spiraled into the cold air. "Yvette?"

"Right here." She gestured flamboyantly with her hand. "And going nowhere since that tight-knickered bastard took my passport."

"How do you feel about all this?"

She chugged more of the Guinness, before she replied, "I feel like bloody damned Alice falling through the looking glass."

Dusty smiled. "Sorry. I'm feeling pretty confused myself. I can't imagine having someone like Hawsworth for a father and Ruth Ann for a mother. And then there's Nichols sniffing around like a starving coyote."

"Well, it's not going to be pleasant, you know."

Dusty frowned. "What isn't?"

"What they find out about Collins."

"Your husband? The one who died in the crash?"

She pursed her lips, hesitated, and finally shrugged. "There were questions about the crash, Dusty. The people who saw it said he accelerated like a crazy man. He never even touched the brakes. Just smashed himself under the back of a stalled lorry."

Dusty didn't quite know what to say. He toyed with his beer, then said, "My father committed suicide, too."

"Well, it would be nice if it was all so clear, dear brother. Unfortunately, when the widow collects over a million pounds of insurance, on a policy that was taken out the week before..." She gave him a knowing look and handed him her empty Guinness bottle. "I don't suppose I could trouble you for another? This one is quite done, and after the day I've had, all things considered, I think I could stand getting a little pissed tonight."

"Nichols get a rock pissed," Dusty agreed.

"Since when do rocks become inebriated?"

"Huh?" Dusty gave her a confused look and pulled out a fresh bottle. As he popped the cap for her, he said, "Well, why would Nichols care about your ex? It's not his jurisdiction."

She looked at him as though he must be joking. "Why would Nichols care that I'm a suspect in another suspicious death? I can't imagine."

Maureen awakened at the graying of dawn, and though they slept in different sleeping bags, she found Dusty comfortably pressed against her on the foldout couch in the trailer. Her face felt icy, and she could see frost on the aluminum frame surrounding the window. Her breath rose in the cold.

At her movements, Dusty opened one blue eye. "Is it morning?"

"I think you can sleep for another hour if you want. I'll get breakfast started." She unzipped her bag and sat up.

"Wake me when Yvette gets up?" he asked.

"If it's before noon, you mean?" she asked with a smile. "Speaking of which, how are you feeling?"

"Perfectly fine. There's an intact kiva waiting for me."

Maureen rose, fully dressed since she'd slept in her jeans and a black sweatshirt. As she slipped on her hiking boots, she peered down the hallway toward the bedroom. Yvette lay snuggled under the blankets like a caterpillar in a cocoon. Only her hair protruded. She'd been in no condition to drive, and she certainly could not sleep in her

Jeep. She'd accepted Dusty's offer of a bed without the slightest hesitation.

Dusty rolled to his side and said, "I wager Yvette is not going to have a pleasant morning."

"I suspect not."

Maureen stood up, went to the kitchen. First she poured water into the coffeepot, then filled the basket with coffee. While she worked, she gave serious thought to the shower in the dormitory behind the park headquarters where Michall and Sylvia were staying. The problem with life in the field, and the one thing she still could not abide, was the lack of hot water. Maybe tonight she'd take them up on their offer for a hot shower.

Maureen slipped on her coat and stepped outside into the shimmering morning. The trucks, the trailer, the rabbitbrush, and the picnic tables carried a quarter-inch layer of frost. She walked hurriedly down to the restroom and, with great stoicism, exposed herself to the cold. At the same time she reminded herself that her ancestors had withstood colder temperatures than this, for much longer periods of time, and without the benefit of Duofold and Hollofil.

She made her way back to the trailer and found Dusty gone and Yvette sitting at the table.

"Where's Dusty?"

"Went to the loo." Yvette had a pained look on her face. Her hair was mussed, and her white turtleneck looked the worse for wear. Through puffy eyes she watched Maureen check the coffee and unpack eggs from the cooler.

"I feel bloody beastly," she muttered.

"There's orange juice in the cooler," Maureen said sympathetically. "That or a can of Pepsi."

"Pepsi?" Yvette screwed up her face. "That sounds positively sadistic."

"Trust me. It'll help."

"Plenty of experience, Dr. Cole?" She narrowed an eye. "I didn't see you sucking down pint after pint last night."

"I don't drink."

"That doesn't mean I'm going to get a lecture, does it?"

Maureen smiled. "I wouldn't dare to lecture anyone, Yvette."

As Maureen melted margarine in the frying pan, she thought about how she'd fallen apart after John's death, and how Yvette didn't seem to show any of the normal signs of grief she would have expected. After everyone had gone to sleep last night, Dusty had told her a few of the details of Yvette's husband's death, and Maureen hadn't been able to get them out of her mind.

Cautiously, Maureen said, "You seem to have survived your husband's death much better than I survived mine."

"Yes, well..." Yvette looked down at her hands. "I think Collins and I were together just because we didn't have to be someplace else. The investigators, sod them all, tried every trick to pluck that out of me."

Maureen chopped up the last of the fresh poblano peppers and added them to the pan. "Were you together long?"

"Too long," Yvette said, and looked around at the shabby interior of the trailer. "You'd jolly well never catch me living in a shoddy caravan like this. Just where the hell are we? Is this Chaco place even on maps?"

While Maureen peeled an onion, she replied, "Chaco Canyon is on lots of maps. This is actually a popular tourist attraction."

"Really, well, good on them." She propped her hands on the table and twisted them, appearing distracted.

"You don't really look like much of an outdoors type. Why did you stay so long yesterday?"

"I just couldn't make myself leave. I kept watching, wondering, and then to see the bone and the burned wood..." She smiled. "It was really fascinating. Though, you can be sure, had I known that Father and then your blasted Mr. Nichols were going to arrive, I'd have been long gone."

She stood up and groaned. "You don't really expect a girl to walk down to that cold toilet when there's a perfectly good little water closet right behind you?"

"This caravan, as you call it, has no running water because the pipes would freeze this time of year." Maureen pointed at the camper door. "I'm afraid your only choice is a tall bush or the restroom down the way. Welcome to the Wild West."

"Bloody hell," Yvette muttered and pulled on her long black wool coat. "So, how long have you and Dusty been together?"

Maureen used the spatula to dig *refritos* from the can and added them to the simmering pan. "We're not together, Yvette. Just friends."

"Oh, sorry 'bout that. But he's handsome, isn't he?"

"Yes, and he knows it, too. He has quite a reputation as a lady killer."

"Too bad he's my brother." She paused, her hand on the door handle. "Tell me, did he have a lonely childhood?"

Maureen met Yvette's curious eyes. "After his mother left, it was pretty tough on him. But, later on, he had Dale, and Dale loved him very much."

Yvette nodded. "We're not that different, he and I. Except I never really had anyone."

Yvette opened the door and stepped out onto the rickety trailer steps.

Maureen watched her pass the window; then she

poured herself a cup of coffee and leaned heavily against the counter.

Sunlight shone golden on the rimrock as they stepped out of the Bronco, but shadows still clung to the canyon bottom, creating a well of cold air.

Yvette parked beside them and climbed out of her Jeep.

"Yvette?" Maureen asked as she put on her gloves. "Do you have any other clothes?"

Looking a bit uncomfortable, she said, "I'm afraid everything looks like this."

"Then," Dusty said as he buttoned up his denim coat, "I think you had better take a day and go shop for something more practical. A down coat and some hiking boots for starters."

Yvette sighed, "I suppose I should at that."

When the first gust of wind hit Maureen, she jerked her wool hat from her coat pocket and slipped it on her head. "Michall is going to be very glad that Rupert provided that tarp and those hay bales. That freeze last night went deep. I wish I'd..."

Dusty blinked at the hill where the site nestled.

"What is it?" Maureen followed his gaze to the irregular shape on the hilltop. She didn't remember it, but maybe it was just the poor light.

The sound of a truck motor made her turn. Michall and Sylvia's vehicle led the FBI Suburban around the turn from Loop Road onto Rinconada Drive.

"What is that?" Dusty whispered and started up the trail.

Maureen gripped his sleeve to hold him back. "I think we should wait for the FBI to get here."

"Why?"

"If it's something unusual, you want them to find it first. That way it doesn't look like we did it. Understand?"

"Oh. Sure. Okay." Dusty tucked his hands in his coat pockets. His gaze was fixed on the ridgetop site.

"Good morning!" Sylvia called as she climbed out of the truck. Brown hair stuck out from beneath her gray knit cap. She lifted a gloved hand to wave.

Dusty waved back, but he'd started grinding his teeth, obviously eager to be at the site. He folded his arms and gave Maureen an irritated look when the ERT people climbed into the back of the Suburban and began handing out equipment. Dusty leaned sideways to whisper, "If my crew took this long to get to the site in the morning, I'd fire them."

Yvette chuckled. "They're bloody government employees. What do you expect?"

Finally, they started up the trail toward Dusty, Maureen, and Yvette.

Dusty looked at Maureen. "You think it's safe to go up now?"

She took his arm. "Why don't we let them lead the way."

He muttered something unpleasant under his breath, but he waited.

Sylvia climbed the hill first. As she approached, she

called, "Hey, Washais. How are you this fine morning?" She had her pack slung over one shoulder and a thermos in her other hand.

Maureen waited until Sylvia came closer, then said, "What's the strange shape at the site?"

Sylvia stopped and squinted, and her expression slackened. "I don't know. Let's go find out."

"Now you're talking," Dusty said, and headed up the hill beside Sylvia.

Everyone else followed.

The black plastic was not as Michall had left it the night before. Two of the straw bales were set neatly side by side on the ground, making the strange shape seen from below.

"Somebody's been here." Michall looked at Bill and Rick. "Did you guys bring Agent Nichols up here last night."

"No." Rick had his camera out. "Don't touch anything. Stewart, you, Dr. Cole, and Ms. Hawsworth just arrived?"

"Five minutes before you did."

"We waited for you," Maureen told him. "We didn't want another tongue-lashing from Nichols."

"Good." Bill knelt to study the black plastic tarp. "Okay, let's take this one step at a time. Rick, you keep shooting as we take this apart. If someone's been dicking with our evidence, I want it thoroughly documented."

"Uh, guys," Sylvia pointed. "Someone has also been in our back-dirt pile. Look at the hole scooped in the side."

The shovel, its handle frosty, still stood, stuck in the hollow that someone had excavated. Bill pulled Michall away and gestured Rick over. "See if you can get photos of the tracks." He looked back at Dusty and added, "I want everybody else to stay put. Don't move an inch. Do you understand me?"

Dusty nodded. "Yeah."

The two agents donned gloves and carefully peeled back the black plastic. The kiva depths remained in shadow, the other straw bales barely visible.

As the light filtered in, a mound of dirt like a cinder cone appeared in the center of the kiva floor. Rick and Bill pulled the plastic back farther, and Sylvia's breath caught. She stumbled backward, hissing, "Oh, Jesus!"

Michall whispered, "Son of a bitch."

Maureen stared, unable to move.

Dusty murmured, "Dear God, don't let it be anybody we know."

Two human feet, bloody and sand-matted, protruded from the fresh earth. They looked small. Too small to be a man's feet.

Maureen closed her eyes, afraid of the worst.

Browser led the way past Corner Kiva, slowing only long enough to stick his head inside and ensure that no party of warriors lurked there to ambush them. With worry upsetting her guts, Catkin followed behind, her war club thrust against Old Pigeon-tail's back to keep him moving. She kept glancing this way and that, expecting attacking warriors to materialize out of the very ground. As they climbed the slope, she peered down at the abandoned villages of Pottery House and Spindle Whorl. Fallen stones and bits of cracked plaster covered the ground.

It had taken them longer than Browser had planned to get here. Time was their only advantage. The elders, Rain Crow and the wounded Horned Ram, had slowed their pace. Would they have time enough to rush Owl House, kill Two Hearts and Shadow, and still make an escape? That *was* what Browser was planning, wasn't it?

A sudden whirlwind sprouted from the washed clay, lurching and dancing as it toyed with the weeds and wavered its way across the canyon floor. Before them, the sandstone rim jutted against the southern horizon. The deeply eroded cliff looked almost tired in the late fall light. How many pairs of eyes watched from up there? Catkin's skin started to crawl. They turned away from Corner Kiva and began the last climb up the ridge toward Owl House.

The small U-shaped block of rooms stood on the ridgetop. It seemed to waver in the clear light. As they climbed, the cold grew deeper and more bitter, forcing the elders to huddle together with their capes clutched at their throats. Stone Ghost hobbled up the slope behind Pigeon-tail, grunting softly. His thin white hair whipped around his wrinkled face. White Cone struggled up behind Stone Ghost.

"Fire Lark, break right," Browser ordered. "Red Dog, take the left. Let's make sure we see all sides as we approach."

At his words, the warriors tapped their weapons in acknowledgment and split off from the party, advancing along the slope at a trot.

Catkin walked up to stand less than a handsbreadth away and whispered, "We're just going to walk up the hill to the Owl House?"

"Yes."

"There must be a way around, Browser."

His thick black brows had pulled into a single line over his flat nose. "By now, they already know we're here, Catkin. Being clever isn't going to help us. We must strike before Shadow and her warriors have time to move Two Hearts or get reinforcements from Starburst Town."

Catkin's gaze lifted to the rim and she searched for the guards Pigeontail had said would be here. She saw no one. But they must be there.

Owl House had a commanding view of the canyon bottom. Not even a rabbit could have hidden in the flat expanse that stretched from Corner Kiva to Straight Path Wash, much less a war party. The only cover was in the tumbled rimrock that had broken off and accumulated beneath the cliff face several bow shots to the south.

Catkin glanced at Old Pigeontail. Something about him wasn't right. He looked smug and self-confident—as though proud of himself for leading them into this trap.

She looked around the canyon. Nothing, only the deteriorating houses and the pale barren silts of the canyon bottom could be seen. Above, on the rim, nothing moved, no heads rose against the skyline.

It couldn't be this easy, could it? Just walk up and storm the house? Kill Two Hearts and Shadow and set Obsidian free? She stepped closer to Browser, lowering her voice to say, "I'm worried."

"Why?" His gaze remained fixed on the single-story structure they approached.

"I don't like the way Pigeontail is taking this. He doesn't seem the slightest bit concerned even though he has betrayed the White Moccasins and Two Hearts."

"That's because he lied to us back at Kettle Town."

"Lied?" Catkin whispered. "You know this to be true?" She shot a hot glance at Pigeontail.

"He gave in too easily."

She shifted and clutched her club more tightly. "Then he got us to do exactly what Two Hearts and Shadow wished."

"He did, but we're ahead of schedule. Ordinarily, I would wait until nightfall to go in, hoping darkness would cover our approach. Two Hearts knows this."

"You are telling me that we're walking into a trap?" she asked, searching his face.

"Of course."

Catkin gripped his sleeve and pulled him back to stare hard into his eyes. "What is your plan?"

Browser smiled at the commanding tone in her voice. "Just promise me: When I give the order, kill Two Hearts.

His death and Shadow's are the two most important objectives. Everything else—Obsidian, you, me, the elders, the Mogollon—is secondary."

He gave her a look that melted her heart. "Do you understand?"

She twined her fist in his sleeve as though to rip it from his arm and said, "I understand."

He smiled. "Thank you for your loyalty, Catkin. Because this is a turning point."

"What do you mean?"

"I mean that if we are successful, killing Two Hearts will be the beginning of the end."

"The end of what?"

"Of this war, of clan against clan, of the katsinas against the old gods. It might take generations for the hatred to dissipate from the people, like rings on a pond, but in the end the waters will be still again. As they were before the katsinas came to Sternlight. Someone must show the world a beginning—that we can all live together: Made People, First People, and Mogollon."

Catkin studied the blocky shape of Owl House on the hilltop. "Who will win, Browser? The old gods, or the katsinas?"

"I don't know," he whispered. "But let us go and stamp out this evil now. Let us make a beginning to the end." He walked up the slope.

Catkin reached into the quiver that hung down her back and pulled out two arrows. She thought she caught sight of a head lifting ever so slightly from the rooftop of Owl House.

"They're watching us," she said.

"Good. It is time to spring their trap and see how they plan to kill us."

"The three of you were together all night?" Agent Nichols asked for the fifth time as he paced up and down the yellow tape in front of the murder scene.

"All night," Maureen said. "We didn't hear anything. There was frost on both our vehicles this morning. So we didn't drive anywhere. We didn't do it."

Nichols had that look in his eye. He wasn't a man a sane person wanted to cross. His fists worked for a moment as he read the truth in Maureen's eyes, then turned away and stalked to where Sylvia and Michall sat on a small sandstone ledge. Spooked and cold, they obviously longed to be anywhere but here with a corpse in their dig.

"Jesus," Dusty whispered. "Why is the killer doing this?"

Maureen felt a sudden chill. "He's taking it to the next level of the game."

"What do you mean?"

"This is the dare," Maureen murmured as she watched Nichols pace. "And Nichols knows it."

Yvette said, "Since I have a good solid alibi, I suppose I'm off the good inspector's list of suspects. But given his mood, I don't fancy asking him for my passport back. At least not in the near future."

Dusty smoothed his hand over his beard. "Who do you think the victim is?" He tipped his blond head toward the hilltop. "Could you see anything?"

Maureen shook her head, not willing to tell him what she'd thought about the size of the feet, because if she was right, Dusty was about to lose someone else. "We're not going to find out until Sid gets here."

"From Albuquerque? That's late afternoon at the earliest. Won't Nichols try to..." Dusty turned at the distant chatter of a helicopter.

"I think"—Maureen looked toward the southeast— "that when Agent Nichols gets pissed, things happen."

Dusty's eyes narrowed as he shifted to watch Nichols question Sylvia and Michall. Both women looked like they wanted to throw up. "Think I ought to mosey over there and eavesdrop?"

"Not unless you want to spend the next couple of nights in a cozy little cell learning the intricacies of body-cavity searches, good cop/bad cop interrogations, and the ins and outs of the lawyer-client relationship."

The helicopter cleared the rimrock and settled over the parking lot. Dust whirled as the bird spooled down. Moments later, the doors opened and Sid Malroun and four men in blue FBI coats ducked out. In a knot, they hurried across the parking lot toward the trail that led up past Casa Rinconada.

"Dusty?" Maureen asked and gave him a frightened look. "If this site has been disturbed, do you think—?"

It took a second before her meaning dawned, and his gaze went to the great kiva where Dale had been killed.

"Oh, my God."

"Nichols just said we weren't supposed to go back to the trucks," she reminded. "And I ought to say hello to Sid. It would look perfectly natural if we walked down to meet him, then you could—"

"I hear trouble in your voices." Yvette leaned closer to join their conversation. "Are we off somewhere?"

Maureen said, "We're just going to take a walk down the hill."

Yvette followed them, tagging along.

They reached the great kiva at the same time Sid Malroun and the FBI men came walking up the interpretive trail. The FBI call must have pulled Sid out of bed. Brown stubble covered his face, and the sparse hair on his mostly bald head stood straight up. His glasses had frosted when he'd stepped out into the cold air so Maureen couldn't see his eyes.

"Good morning, Sid." Maureen walked forward to shake his hand while Dusty stared over the side and into the depths of the kiva.

"Maureen, good Lord, are you still mixed up in this?" Sid asked as he shook.

"Apparently."

"Okay. Tell me what I'm looking at today?"

"I don't know." Maureen frowned up the hill at the displaced straw bales. Everyone, as she'd expected, turned to follow her gaze. "The FBI won't let me near the body. I've been trying to tell them that—"

Dusty turned, cupping hands around his mouth to shout: "Nichols? I think you should see this! The blood down here is already frozen, but it's a safe bet that it matches the corpse on the hill!"

Nichols spun around where he stood on top of the ridge and squinted across the distance to where Dusty pointed into the dawn-shadowed great kiva. The agent left the ridge at a run. Maureen had to hand it to him. He vaulted the sage and rabbitbrush with grace that belied his age. When he stopped at Dusty's side and stared down at the dark stain on the kiva floor, his face reddened. "Bill? Rick? Get over here and photograph this!"

Maureen and Sid hurried to stand beside Dusty. Maureen stared down at the large bloodstain on the frosty kiva floor.

"See that sand pattern that's just barely visible through the frost?" Dusty pointed to the left of the blood. "It probably matches the samples you took out of here a few days ago."

"Meaning?" Sid asked.

Dusty said, "I wager he gets it from the same place, Dr. Malroun. Probably a sacred place."

Maureen studied the footprints that led from the stain, across the kiva, and up the stairway. Small prints, like those of a woman, or a diminutive man. The murderer hadn't been so careful this time. Or maybe she couldn't be. Perhaps she hadn't anticipated the frost, or it had happened in the middle of the murder.

"Well, Sid," Maureen said through a long exhalation. "You have your hands full."

"Yes." He nodded. "As of today, our man is a serial killer."

"Brilliant," Yvette said unhappily, "and I was pissed out of my gourd. He could have driven right up, opened the door, and lifted me out with no one the wiser."

She shoved her hands in her coat pockets and stalked up the trail toward the excavation.

Maureen quietly said to Sid, "You really think it's a man?"

Sid rubbed his stubbly jaw and studied the footprints. "Not necessarily, but I think it's prudent to keep saying so in public."

He turned slightly to watch Yvette climb the hill.

Then his eyes drifted to Sylvia where she knelt looking down into the excavation. His brows lowered.

In a low voice, he added, "I'm not even sure it's one person we're looking for."

As the day ground on, Dusty's patience wore thin. Maureen sat on a rock and watched him pace along the yellow tape like a caged tiger, watching the FBI team secure the scene, record the evidence, and carefully dig the corpse from the loose sand and the straw bales that the killer had used to prop his victim's body.

Preliminary inspection revealed that the soles of the feet had been skinned, but hastily, as though the killer feared discovery. The toes had been hacked off to make the skinning faster—which is why the feet had looked so small. A yucca hoop encircled the man's body. Then, as the knees were uncovered, Maureen could see the yucca leaves that pierced them. The man's genitals had been sliced from the pubis with a sharp blade.

When the technicians finally lifted the body from the soil, Yvette let out a soft cry and put a hand to her lips. Tears glistened in her wide eyes.

It took Maureen a moment longer. Blood and filth matted the face, and gore ran from the hole that had been sawed in the rear of the skull—but she saw his silver ponytail.

Yvette whispered, "Oh, no. God."

"Who is it?" Dusty asked.

Yvette took an involuntary step backward. She was shaking. "It's...I think it's...my father. Carter." Her voice broke.

Dusty turned back to scrutinize the body as they carried it across the kiva and said, "Are you sure?"

Yvette nodded. "Yes."

Maureen put a hand on Yvette's shoulder. Carter Hawsworth may not have been a good father, or even her biological father, but for most of her life she'd thought he was. Softly, Maureen said, "I need to go tell the medical examiner. It will cut the time it takes to verify the ID. Will you be all right?"

In a breathless voice, Yvette said, "Where's my mother? Does anyone know?"

As Maureen walked toward Sid Malroun, she heard Dusty answer, "I suspect Agent Nichols will have her picked up within the hour."

O wl House consisted of five single-story rooms with a contiguous kiva on the south side. The long axis of the edifice ran northeast-southwest along the ridgetop. To take it, Browser had split his forces, sending Badger Dancer around to the north and west with Split Beam and Clay Frog. Meanwhile, he, Catkin, Yucca Whip, and Fire Lark charged in from the south and east. White Cone and Stone Ghost stood just out of range, guarding Pigeontail and Horned Ram, with orders to kill the Trader should anything go amiss and make their escape as best they could. Rain Crow, practically wavering on his feet, gripped his war club and staggered forward, his cloudy eyes fixed on Owl House.

Browser zigzagged as he ran. From the corner of his eye he could see Catkin sprinting up the slope, her long legs pumping. Sunlight flashed off the polished wood of her bow. She had never been so beautiful. Gods curse him, why had he wasted so much time mourning the dead when he should have been sharing her blankets?

Heart pounding, he charged up to the wall, more than a little surprised that no arrows whistled down from above.

Catkin flattened herself against the wall beside him, followed a half breath later by Fire Lark.

"Up!" Browser said, raising his right foot.

Catkin and Fire Lark cupped their hands, lifting as Browser straightened. They almost threw him, despite his weight, onto the roof. He caught the lip, nearly falling as the plaster crumbled under his fingers, and flipped himself onto the flat earthen roof.

In a split heartbeat, he was on his feet, surprised to see...nothing. No enemy waited to club his brains out. The only movement was Red Dog being boosted in a similar fashion to the opposite side of the roof. Eyes wide, panting, the warrior scrambled to his feet, his war club up to deflect a blow.

Browser stepped warily to look down at Catkin. "Hold your position but be on guard. Red Dog and I will check the rooms."

Browser tiptoed lightly to the dark roof opening. The ladder's two weathered gray upright poles stuck up against the sky. He tested the roof near the entryway and quickly pulled his war shirt over his head. Red Dog was watching with a sudden frown, baffled as Browser took a quick wrap of his shirt over the head of his war club. Then he ducked low and shoved the cloth bundle over the lip of the entryway before jerking it back in the manner of a peeking head. Nothing. Again he feinted with the bundled cloth.

Red Dog had finally caught on and pulled off his own blue war shirt, mimicking Browser as he feinted at the next room opening. Generally, if a warrior were waiting in ambush within, their nerves would be pulled as taut as damp rawhide in a hot sun. At the first movement they'd loose an arrow.

Browser circled, grasped the ladder in both hands, and pulled it out of the room. He lowered it over the side of the building and Catkin swiftly climbed up.

"It's too dark to see into any of the rooms," Browser told her as he slipped his war shirt on. "Let's pull up all the ladders. Anyone inside will stay that way until we decide to let them out."

"Or until they knock a hole in the wall," Catkin said. "What about the kiva?"

"That's our next stop."

Catkin whispered, "He's here, Browser. I can feel him, like a cold wind whispering around my souls."

Catkin led the way to the south roof. From there they could look down on the kiva—a round disk raised to knee height above the ridgetop. A faint twist of blue smoke rose from the hole in the kiva roof.

Browser met Catkin's knowing eyes and took a moment to touch her shoulder. That one light touch, the feel of her body, sent warmth through him. Her reassuring smile was just for him. And with that, he squatted, swung his legs over the side of the wall, and dropped lightly to his feet on the kiva roof. Two heartbeats later, Catkin thumped down beside him. Stepping to the side, he motioned to his warriors who waited beside the walls. In single file they trotted along, forming up on either side of the kiva entry.

Browser turned, gesturing to Red Dog to stay on the high rooftop. With his index and middle fingers he pointed to his eyes and made the "keep watch" sign.

Attacking a kiva was a relatively straightforward problem. All an attacker need do was pull out the ladder and drop burning brush down the entry hole. The next move was to throw hides or damp cloth over the hole. The smoke, flames, and heat finished the job without exposing the attacker. If you wanted the occupants out, however, the ladder was left in place as the flaming brush was dropped in. Provided the ladder didn't catch fire too quickly, the defenders would eventually be driven out, crying, coughing, and blinded. It was an easy matter to simply wait at the top of the ladder with war clubs and beat their heads in as they emerged. The problem Browser now faced was how to retrieve Obsidian from the kiva before he set fire to it.

"Browser?" a woman's gentle voice came from the kiva.

He glanced at Catkin and answered, "Obsidian? Is that you?"

"It is." Something about the sensual tones warned him.

"Come out, Obsidian. We're here to take you away." To Catkin, Browser silently mouthed: "Shadow Woman?" and shrugged his shoulders.

Catkin tightened her grip on her war club.

"I'm tied up. Please come and get me!"

A muffled voice rose, like a woman trying to scream with a hand over her mouth. Then a child let out a high-pitched roar of sheer terror, which was abruptly halted by the sound of a fist striking flesh.

"Bone Walker?" Stone Ghost cried, his eyes suddenly huge. "Bone Walker, is that you?"

The old man rushed forward, but Rain Crow gripped his arm and held him back. They spoke to each in quiet harsh tones for several moments; then Stone Ghost reluctantly stepped back. But he stood as though poised to charge the instant he could.

Browser considered, then said, "Shadow? Do you remember the turquoise wolf? The one Two Hearts lost when he attacked Hophorn outside of Talon Town. The turquoise wolf that belonged to the Blessed Night Sun? I'm setting it here on the kiva roof, and then I'm coming down. If I don't call back to Catkin, she'll take her war club and smash it into dust."

Silence, and then Browser recognized Two Hearts's

weak voice. "Don't, Browser." A faint cough and a groan. "We can work this out."

"Yes," Browser agreed. "You send Obsidian up, and I'll send the wolf down. Do we have an agreement?"

He could hear whispering from below.

"Browser!" Red Dog shouted. "War parties! Several of them, White Moccasins, they're boiling out of Straight Path Wash and from War Club village to the east!"

"How many warriors?"

Red Dog straightened. "Five there. Ten, no...ten and two there." He turned slightly. "From the west, there are more. Five...seven in that band."

Twenty-two at least. Not to mention any that might be down in the kiva with Two Hearts.

"Find the best positions to shoot from—then take cover!" Browser ordered, pointing toward Owl House's roof with his war club. "Make sure that Stone Ghost and White Cone are lying down on the roof, safe. Pull up the ladders. We can hold them!"

White Cone glanced down from above. "With your permission, War Chief. I will handle the defense from up here."

"You have my blessing and appreciation, Bow Elder. Now sit down and rest. We have some time before they arrive. Reserve your strength and mind for the challenge to come."

"Browser?" Shadow's sensual voice drifted from the kiva. "It doesn't have to be this way. Let us talk."

They had maneuvered him into coming here, then left the place unguarded. If he did only one thing today, he could kill them. Surely they knew that. Which meant they had risked everything to get him here. Why?

"I'm listening, Shadow," he said as he strode to the edge of the kiva roof. The seven warriors from War Club village ran full tilt to cut off the stairway that led out of the canyon.

"You have us, we have you," she called. "I think we can bargain."

"Red Dog," Browser called, "any activity in the rooms?"

"No, War Chief." The young warrior stood looking worriedly at the closing warriors.

"Good. If this turns against us, kill Pigeontail. In the meantime, find anything that will burn. Pull the roof apart if you have to and get the kindling to me."

"Yes, War Chief." Red Dog bounded away, and Browser could hear the scraping of a ladder.

"Browser?" Shadow called. "If you harm us, neither you nor your Made People friends will leave here alive. You know that, don't you?"

"We came here to die, Shadow. You and Two Hearts have destroyed everything we hold dear. You killed and butchered our friends, killed our Matron. You burned innocent children to death in the Longtail village kiva. The only thing we care about now is your deaths."

"We had our reasons! You are one of us, you should know!"

"Reasons?" he shouted. "You are witches! You—"

"*Browser?*" Red Dog called from above. "The White Moccasins will be in range soon, should we shoot at them? Slow them down?"

Browser shook his head. "Wait, Red Dog. There's no sense in wasting arrows."

Browser took the ladder that Red Dog had lowered and raced to the roof. From the vantage point he could see the closing ring of warriors, taking their time, moving into position.

Cupping his hands to his mouth, he called, "Stop where you are! I am War Chief Browser, of the Katsinas'

People. The witches, Two Hearts and Shadow Woman, are in the kiva. If you attack us, we will set fire to the place and burn them alive. If you would see your leaders alive again, you will withdraw."

One of the warriors stepped out, the breeze fluttering his white tunic. "I am Thorn Fox, of the Red Lacewing Clan, War Chief of the Starburst warriors. You are surrounded. Your only hope for survival is to surrender."

"Piece of filth," Rain Crow growled.

Browser called, "War Chief, we will not surrender, and you will not attack."

"Why won't I?"

"Because, I told you, if you do, your elders will be burned to death."

"If you kill them," Thorn Fox warned, "we will kill you—then we will hunt down and kill your families! Your clans will be cursed!"

"Hold your position!" Browser called.

Turning he strode to the kiva opening. "Shadow? Thorn Fox is out here. Tell him to stay back, or I will set fire to your kiva this instant!"

aggie pulled up and shifted her green pickup into park. She stepped out as Dusty opened the camp trailer's door. The rimrock on either side of the canyon had turned brown and foreboding beneath the gray clouds that obscured the late afternoon sky.

"What's up, Maggie?" he called. His blond hair was mussed, and his blue eyes were red-rimmed.

Nichols had run everyone through the mill that morning, and Dusty looked it. Worse, when she'd called Rupert in Washington that morning, he'd told her that under no circumstances was she to interfere with Nichols's investigation. The FBI agent had had her jumping through bureaucratic hoops all morning.

"Hi, Dusty." She walked over and climbed the aluminum steps. Inside it was warm and the air smelled of coffee and green chili.

Sylvia and Michall sat on the foldout couch up front. Maureen and Yvette were in the booth. Maggie could tell Yvette had been crying. Her eyes were swollen and her face puffy.

"Hello," Maggie greeted, taking in the sister who had just magically appeared in Dusty's life. It would never cease to amaze her that Whites treated relatives so cavalierly.

She has a wounded soul. Be wary until you know what she is.

The words popped into her head, as if whispered from another place. Was that Grandmother Slumber's voice?

Dusty said, "What can I get you to drink, Maggie?"

Maggie looked around, confused by the voice she had just heard. Maureen and Yvette had coffee. Dusty clutched a half-empty bottle of Guinness and Sylvia had her traditional Coors Light. Michall cradled a can of cherry soda.

"Coffee would be great." Maggie slid into the booth near Maureen. Her nerves were humming. Was her grandmother trying to warn her from the other world?

"So, are we all under arrest?" Dusty asked as he poured a cup of coffee and set it in front of her.

"Not yet," she told him. "Rupert's on his way back. I called him on his cell phone. Got him out of a life-and-death budget meeting. He said he'd explain the situation to the deputy director and catch the first flight he could."

Maggie turned to Sylvia. "You okay after Agent Nichols put the screws to you?"

Sylvia nodded, her face pale. "Can you believe that guy? God, he took me into that conference room, and I thought I was in the hands of the Gestapo. He must have spent every dime the Bureau has to rake up all those nasty things from my childhood. God, you'd think I'd killed Dale, the way he was asking questions."

"It's all right," Michall soothed, reaching out and punching Sylvia's shoulder. "I told him if you'd done it, the skull would have exhibited blunt-force trauma—I also told him where to find your baseball bat."

"Thanks," Sylvia said. "That's all I need. The FBI looking under my pillow."

Michall jiggled her half-empty soda can. "That was a grueling experience, answering all those questions. Nichols kept staring at me with that funny eye of his. I thought my oral exams were tough. After what he put me through this morning, my PhD dissertation defense is going to be a piece of cake."

"What about you?" Dusty asked and pinned Maggie with tired blue eyes. "Did Nichols take a chunk out of your hide, too?"

She nodded. "I just got out of my 'interview.' Once he established that I didn't know Hawsworth, he seemed to lose interest in me, but he sure quizzed me about you."

Dusty pulled back in mock surprise. "You mean he thinks I have a motive? Just because Hawsworth ran off with my mother and ruined my life?"

"It always seems to come back to that, doesn't it?" Yvette asked.

Maggie cocked her head. "Are you *really* Dusty's sister?"

She studied Maggie through eyes that looked fragile. "Same mother," she said in a small voice.

"You have my condolences," Maggie said before sipping coffee. Then she added, "The reason I'm here, outside of the good coffee, is that Agent Nichols has a dilemma."

"No shit," Sylvia said. "For one thing, I'm out of here! I have just established new standards for my work. I won't excavate any kiva unless the bodies have been dead for at least a week."

"Damn straight," Michall agreed. "Sylvia and I talked it over. We're finished with this."

"That's part of Nichols's dilemma." Maggie cradled her coffee, grateful for the warmth on her fingers. "He's more convinced than ever that the site needs to be dug, that some important clue is there. His problem is that each of you are now potential suspects."

"So," Dusty finished, "where's he going to find a crew? Write an RFP and put it out to bid?"

Maggie tilted her head uncertainly. "I told him that if he doesn't get it dug in the next couple of weeks, the frost is going to make it impossible for him to finish the excavation before spring." She took a deep breath. "I asked him to call Steve."

Dusty nodded. "Good choice. If Steve can find a crew."

"He's bringing four graduate students, leaving this afternoon from Tucson. He says he'll be here in the morning." She winced. "Dusty, I went out on a limb and told him he could use your equipment. Is that all right?"

"You were worried about that?" Then he nodded, eyes warming. "Of course you were. I'm not thinking straight. I'll gladly loan him my equipment, unless Nichols thinks my screens and shovels will bias the investigation."

Maggie stared into the depths of her coffee. Her grandmother had once told her that Dreamers could see things in black liquids. "Dusty, I need to check on Aunt Sage, but I'm in charge while Rupert's in Washington. I can't go. I have a terrible favor to ask. Would you mind—?"

"Not at all," he cut her off. "I'll leave as soon as we eat. Are you up for burritos?"

Maggie smiled her relief. "Sure. I haven't eaten since six this morning. I'm starved." She added, "Thank you, Dusty. About Aunt Sage. I've just got a bad feeling, that's all."

The faint voices, barely audible in her mind, whispered in assent.

Catkin spread her feet, eyes fixed on the rooftop kiva entry.

It took ten heartbeats.

Shadow emerged from the kiva like First Woman from the underworlds. As she climbed onto the roof and looked around, the wind pressed her soft white dress against her perfect body. Turquoise, coral, and jet beads were woven into her shining black hair. An inhuman gleam filled her black eyes. She moved with the grace of a mountain lion across the rocks, sinuous and sure, each motion fluid.

She smiled when she walked up to Browser, and Catkin's arm muscles tensed, ready.

Browser didn't even flinch as Shadow's slim fingers ran along his chin. Gods, how could he do that? Catkin would have been cringing under that witch's faintest touch.

In a soft sensual voice, Shadow said, "Two Hearts has a bargain for you, War Chief."

"What is it?"

Shadow spread her arms, the gesture visible to the warriors below and Browser's own warriors on the rooftops. "All of this was orchestrated just for you, War Chief—your journey from Flowing Waters Town, your stay in Kettle Town, your 'attack' on us here at Owl House, everything was designed just to get you here today. Isn't it lovely? Aren't you pleased?"

Browser's gaze thinned. "What are you talking about?"

"You simple fool! Two Hearts brought you here because he wishes *your* heart."

Browser's hand involuntarily went to his chest. "My heart?"

"Of course. You are both descended from the Blessed Night Sun. You are one of his relatives, and you are a strong young man. Your heart is much better than that feeble organ beating in my sister's chest."

Catkin's stomach turned. She took a step forward with the intent of bashing in the foul camp bitch's skull.

Browser lifted a hand to stop her. To Shadow, he said, "You are a liar."

"I am?" Shadow raised a slim eyebrow.

Browser smiled grimly. "You never planned to sacrifice the White Moccasins in a fruitless battle. Are you trying to tell me that you didn't think it would be easier to simply surround me in Kettle Town, thus saving your warriors and lessening the risk that I might just burn you alive in Owl House and figure on fighting my way out?"

Her eyes had narrowed. "Nevertheless, *we* brought you here and Two Hearts will have your heart."

"What does Two Hearts offer in return?"

Shadow laughed softly as she walked around Browser. Her white dress conformed to each curve of her lithe body and swirled about her sandaled feet. "You are surrounded. If you fight, you will surely all be killed." She aimed a slender finger at Catkin. "Including the woman you love. So think carefully before you give me your answer."

Browser looked at Catkin with his whole heart in his dark eyes.

"Yes," Shadow hissed in Browser's ear. "I will roast her alive and feed her body to my daughter, then—"

"I ask one thing," Browser said a little too quickly.

Shadow stopped. "Name it."

Before he answered, Browser met the eyes of every warrior, and took a long look at Stone Ghost. "If you will allow everyone else to leave, I will willingly lay down my weapons and be your prisoner."

Catkin stared, speechless. A hoarse chuckle, followed by a cough, came from inside the kiva.

Shadow studied Browser with luminous eyes. After a moment, she stepped over to the kiva wall and looked down the slope to where the White Moccasins waited. "Thorn Fox! Most of these people will be leaving. They are to be allowed safe passage up the Great North Road. You will detail one warrior to follow them and make sure it is so."

"Yes, Blessed Shadow," Thorn Fox called back.

The form of address sickened Catkin's souls. *Blessed Shadow?*

Shadow stepped back to Browser's side and said, "You have the wolf? That was not a lie?"

Browser touched the bulge sewn into the hem of his war shirt.

"You will have to give it up," Shadow told him.

"Then he is that close to death?" Browser asked.

"He is." Shadow paused, and a small smile tugged at her lips. "Just in case your heart is not enough to save him, he must have a Spirit Helper to guide him through the underworlds."

"And afterward," Browser asked. "What of the leadership of the White Moccasins?"

Catkin's gaze went from Browser's face to Shadow's,

and back again. Had Browser lost his mind? She kept trying to fathom his plan. He must have one. Right?

Shadow moved forward until her breasts touched Browser's chest. "Leadership will pass to the man I choose." Then she turned abruptly and climbed down like a serpent into the kiva.

Catkin crossed the space in two strides. "What are you—"

Browser's sharp gesture stopped her short. Anger flashed in his eyes. "Take everyone north to Flowing Waters Town and rejoin the Katsinas' People."

Catkin began a protest when Browser shot a meaningful glance toward the kiva entrance. She didn't need to look to understand that Shadow's head must have been just below the roofline, listening.

"War Chief, as your deputy—"

"I'm sorry, Catkin. I can't let you die. And you know that's what will happen."

"Browser, for the sake of the gods, let's fight!"

"No, Catkin. This is best for everyone." His eyes burned into hers, emphasizing his meaning. "You were right earlier. One life is not worth ten."

What in the name of the monsters of the underworlds was he doing? She searched his face.

"Browser? Please, don't do this, I can't—"

"By doing this, I have given you extra time, and I expect you to be a better War Chief than I have been. Remember, the roundabout way is often better than a direct assault against superior numbers. Victory goes to those who are swiftest, and allies can appear from the most unexpected places." He smiled, touched her face lightly with a gentle finger, and ordered, "Now go. *Quickly!*"

"No, Browser, please—"

"Do not disgrace me in front of others by disobedience."

Shadow appeared on the ladder a moment before Obsidian did.

In the light, they might have been identical but for the curious sheen in Obsidian's eyes. She wore a tan cotton shift that was loose, smudged, but her glossy hair hung to her waist. She cast a sad look at Browser, a wistful longing in her eyes. She walked up to him, saying, "Don't you wish now that you had taken me away? None of this would have had to happen."

Browser's lips curled. "You didn't have to join them. I would have seen to your safety."

Obsidian shrugged. "They are my family, Browser. My People. I made my own bargain with them. Your heart instead of mine. I'm the one who sent Old Pigeontail this morning."

Shadow told Obsidian, "Go down and wait with Thorn Fox's warriors where you will be safe, Sister. I'll call you when we are ready for the ritual feast."

Obsidian gave Browser a seductive smile as she passed, and Catkin took a step, her war club raised.

Browser gripped her shoulder and pulled her back, whispering, "Catkin, go *now!* You may not have much time."

She swallowed hard and met Browser's eyes one last time. Perhaps if she just looked at him long enough, she would understand his plan. Browser would not just offer himself up like a sacrificial deer! She whispered, "I'll be waiting for you at Flowing Waters Town."

"All right. Yes, if I can. Now, go. Hurry. And leave Horned Ram."

Catkin gave him one last incredulous look, then gestured to the warriors on the rooftops. "Come. Let's get out of here!"

Her heart hammered like a foot drum on dance night as the Mogollon filed off the roofs and came toward her in a murmuring knot. Disbelief strained their features. White Cone seemed the most baffled of all of them.

"You heard the War Chief," she ordered. "Let's go."

She started down the hill, but Stone Ghost's voice stopped her.

The old man called, "I'm staying."

"No!" Browser shouted and whirled to look at the old white-haired man. "Uncle, please."

To Catkin, Stone Ghost said, "Tell Matron Cloud-blower we wish her well in her search for the First People's original kiva."

Rain Crow appeared on the roof above, leaning heavily on his walking stick. Sweat coated his pain-racked face. Through gritted teeth, he said, "I will be staying also, War Chief. I will just slow Catkin down."

Browser hesitated only a moment, and Catkin swore she saw a slight smile on his lips as he waved her away. "Go on! Leave!"

Catkin led the way out of Owl House and down the slope.

They passed unmolested through the ranks of the White Moccasins, and at the last opportunity, she looked back. Browser and Stone Ghost watched from the kiva roof. Shadow and Thorn Fox stood a short distance away, their heads together, as though in deep conversation.

Rain Crow perched on the roof, like a lonely owl waiting for night to fly far away.

What just happened there? Why don't I understand what Browser's doing?

"I know it's here somewhere," Dusty said as he peered at the weed-filled fence line that bordered the road. He drove slowly on the asphalt, looking for a break that would mark the two-track dirt road leading to Sage Walking Hawk's home.

"I'll take your word for it." Yvette leaned forward anxiously in the backseat. "You say she's dying?"

"Breast cancer," Maureen answered. "I think the gene runs in the family."

"Nasty lot that. Maggie seems like a gem."

"She's a deaer friend," Dusty said. The glow of the Bronco's instruments seemed dimmer tonight than usual. He probably needed a new battery, as well as a new truck, but both would have to wait. "We've seen a lot of tough times together."

Yvette was silent for a moment. "You've a great many friends, don't you, Dusty?"

"I guess I've never thought about it."

"That's a gift, you know."

"You don't have many friends?" Maureen asked.

"I grew up in a different world," Yvette said bitterly.

"If you value friends, God help you if come into money. Old companions vanish overnight. Everything changes."

"Yeah, well, I've never had that problem." Dusty pulled over onto the shoulder of the road as a pickup appeared out of the night and sped past them with the engine roaring. It careered down the road in front of them.

"One really pissed Native, I'd say," Yvette commented. "I hope he makes it home."

"What makes you think he's mad and not just drunk?" Dusty wondered.

Maureen chuckled nervously. "Among the Brits, pissed means drunk."

"Oh." Dusty pulled onto the asphalt again. Drunk drivers were common out here, especially right after payday on the first of the month, but he hadn't liked Yvette's tone. It was superior, as though she'd seen too many TV shows about reservation Indians.

Maureen seemed to sense Dusty's discomfort. She turned around to look at Yvette. "You've had a tough day. How are you faring?"

Yvette shook her head and ash-blond hair fell into her eyes. Dusty watched her brush it away through the rearview mirror. She said, "Stunned."

"I'm sure," Maureen said gently. "He was your father."

"Is that what he was?" Yvette asked plaintively, and when Dusty and Maureen didn't answer right away, she continued, "He was a cold man. Somehow I ended up in no-man's-land between him and Mum." Her face twisted. "But he deserved better than that. Oh, dear, I swore I'd not break down and bawl like a babe."

Dusty said, "There's a roll of toilet paper in the bag under my seat, if you need it."

"Thank you," she said in a slightly stronger voice.

"Both of you. For letting me tag along these last couple of days."

Dusty slowed at the break in the fence. In the distance, off to the right, a yard light illuminated the dilapidated old trailer nestled at the mouth of the side canyon. Dusty turned and rattled over the cattle guard onto the track.

Yvette hesitated for a moment, gazing at the rusty car bodies and broken appliances that hunkered in the weeds, then said, "I truly can't believe people live like this. It's barbaric."

"Barbaric?" Dusty gave her a curious look over his shoulder. "Living in a place where you can hear coyotes howl and eagles cry? Where you can walk for days without seeing another human being? Personally," he said as he shifted gears, "I think city life is barbaric. Hundreds of thousands of people per square mile, living on top of each other? God, how do you live like that? It's not even *human.*"

He pulled up in front of the trailer house, shut off the Bronco, and turned off the lights. As he opened the door, he said, "We don't knock on doors in this part of the world, so just do what I do. It's considered polite to give the people inside time to prepare before they open the door."

Maureen walked around to stand beside Dusty. Her gray coat and black hair blended so well with the darkness she was almost invisible.

Yvette stared at the trailer as though in disbelief. Weak yellow light gleamed in the living-room window. The rickety front porch leaned precariously to the right, and rusty tin cans and windblown plastic bottles lay beneath it. "This place is a bloody junkyard."

Dusty shoved his fists in his pockets and replied, "I doubt that Sage Walking Hawk shares your value system,

Sister. Her wealth is not in things, but in family and clan, the animal world, and the Spirits."

"Spirits?" Yvette said the word as though she'd never heard it before. "She believes in Spirits? Like ghosts that roam the world haunting people?"

"Like Spirits that live in the stars and trees, and beneath the water. It's a beautiful belief—one I share. I also believe in witches and Buffalo Above."

That completely silenced Yvette.

Dusty added, "Remember, Sister, Sage Walking Hawk has spent her entire life enriching her soul." He gave her a hard look. "Can you say the same thing?"

"Are you implying, dear brother, that I've spent my life enriching my bank accounts?"

Dusty walked toward the trailer and, from inside, a wavering voice called, "Door's open."

Dusty climbed up the creaking steps and pushed the door ajar. "Elder Walking Hawk? It's Dusty Stewart. I'm here with Washais and my sister, Yvette. Magpie wanted me to check on you."

"Come on in, Dusty." Sage coughed and wheezed as though she couldn't get enough air.

Dusty walked in. The trailer smelled of stale urine and old grease. The knickknacks, the trophies of a lifetime, that sat everywhere cast shadows on the shelves. A giant loom covered the wall to his right, the masterpiece rug unfinished.

Sage turned on a lamp. She sat in a worn recliner, her body emaciated; her pain-bright eyes sank deeply in her wrinkled face. Flakes of dandruff dotted her sparse white hair. The faded picture of a uniformed World War II airman lay crooked in her lap, the young white man smiling out from the past. A cane lay out of her reach on the floor next to a fallen plastic drinking glass.

"Elder?" Dusty asked, walking over and kneeling in front of her. "Are you all right?"

Sage's mouth opened in a toothless smile. "The ghosts haven't got you yet?"

"Not yet, but I'm still worried."

Sage chuckled and it sounded like brittle autumn leaves blowing in the wind.

"Have you eaten, Elder?" Dusty took her hand, and it felt cold. The musky smell of urine clung to her. "I packed a pan of leftover enchiladas in the ice chest in my truck. Can I bring them in and warm them in your stove?"

Her faded old eyes slipped off to the side and she gasped. Dusty felt her hand tense, then relax as she smacked dry lips. "Never felt pain like this. It clouds the mind."

Dusty turned to Maureen. "Maureen? Could you bring in the cooler?"

Maureen turned and her quick steps sounded as she trotted down the steps and out to the Bronco.

"I'd drink," Sage whispered. "Could I have water?"

Dusty went into the kitchen, pulled a glass from the cupboard, and filled it. He knelt in front of Sage and held it to the elder's lips. Yvette was standing to the rear, watching with wide brown eyes.

"Thank you," Sage said after sipping half the glass. "I haven't been able to get up. Legs won't work."

Maureen returned with the ice chest and headed directly for the kitchen. Dusty heard her pull the enchilada pan from the chest, then open and close the squeaky oven door. She came back into the living room and pulled a chair up beside Sage's recliner.

Dusty put a hand to the old woman's forehead. "Elder, please let us take you to the hospital. You're dehydrated, and they can give you something for the pain."

"I'm not going nowhere," Sage insisted. "He's close."

"Who is?"

Sage smiled. "That Flute Player in the black shirt with white spirals. Been calling to me for days. Comes and goes." Her frail hand trembled as she lifted it to her throat. "Got a pretty necklace shaped like a turquoise wolf." Sage's hand dropped to rest on Maureen's shoulder. "What do your people call the evil one?"

Maureen seemed to hesitate, as though not certain what Sage meant. Then she said, "Do you mean *Shon-dowekowur*? The faceless one?"

Sage chuckled, her mouth falling open to expose a pink tongue. "The faceless one's laughing at you, Washais." Her expression tightened as she listened to a voice none of them could hear. "I'll tell them."

"Tell us what?" Dusty asked.

Her crooked fingers waved in the air, pointing. "I see... shadows on the kiva wall, running together and pulling apart. And a heart so black...filled with anger. But power-ful. Close to death, they dance..."

"She's delirious," Yvette said. "Wouldn't it be best to call for medical assistance?"

"Shhh." Dusty held up a hand in irritation. "Elder, who is the evil one?"

Sage's eyes began to close. "Yes, yes. I hear you, Slumber."

Dusty's stomach muscles clenched tight. *Her dead sister.*

Sage's neck weakened, and her head rolled to the side. "Kwewur's ears are laid back. You can hear the sandals crackle in the dry grass."

Dusty asked, "Is Kwewur a he?"

Sage's chest barely rose with her breath. "My bones are breaking apart...hurts."

"Elder," Dusty said as he brushed white hair from her hot forehead. "Please let us take you to town. If you don't want to go to the hospital, we'll take you to Magpie's house in Chaco Canyon."

She blinked, her eyes glassy, and her mouth opened and closed like a fish out of water. "All I have to do is step through...but Kwewur is waiting. Waiting right there. For Magpie. Can't...can't warn her. Sick...too sick."

"I'll warn her for you," Dusty said softly.

He released her hand and walked over to the cell phone—probably a gift from Maggie—and ran his finger down the phone list taped to the wall. He saw Maggie's number first, but a nurse's number was listed right below it. Nurse Redhawk. Her number was underlined.

Dusty picked up the phone and dialed.

Sage's old hand trembled in Yvette's direction, and she smiled again. "The Shiwana were there," she whispered. "When you were conceived...in the kiva...in the moon-light." Sage swallowed hard.

Yvette looked shocked, her eyes wide, like a deer in the headlights. "What are Shiwana? Ghosts?"

"No," Maureen whispered. "Spirits."

Yvette backed up, then turned and walked out the door.

Dusty was about to go after her when a voice said, *"Hello?"*

"Hello, this is Dusty Stewart. I'm out at Elder Sage Walking Hawk's house. She's very ill. I'm afraid—"

"I'm on my way! But it will take me an hour to get there. Keep her warm and give her fluids."

"We will. Please hurry." He hung up the phone and turned back to Sage. Maureen had a damp cloth and was washing the elder's face. "Someone's coming, Elder."

"Got to...go..." Sage whispered.

Dusty's heart ached at her pained expression. Sage was looking into the distance, seeing something outside of this world. He could barely hear her when she said,

"Shadow Woman's...with him...*el basilisco*...on her breast."

Sage faded again, gasping from the pain.

To Maureen, Dusty murmured, "Can't we do anything for her?"

"Not without drugs." Maureen shook her head.

"Flying," Sage whispered and sounded suddenly happy. She chuckled again. "Flying...in a big bomber..."

Sage Walking Hawk died forty-five long minutes before the nurse from the Indian Health Services arrived.

Dusty carried her to her bed, gently covered her with blankets, and sank onto the foot of the bed.

He stared blindly out the little window to the starlit desert beyond. Shadow Woman? Who was she? Kwewur? Didn't matter, the evil one was hunting again, and Maggie was in danger.

62

Catkin's mind raced as she looked back across Straight Path Wash. What was Browser thinking? What curious errand had he sent Straighthorn and Jackrabbit off on, and how had he allowed himself to walk into a trap?

Blessed Katsinas, Browser, did you outsmart yourself this time?

True to Shadow's word, only one lone scout followed. The White Moccasin's cloak caught the midday sun as he trotted behind them. Surely Shadow would not let them off that easily? But no pursuit was in evidence, rather it seemed that Shadow wanted Browser surrounded by a ring of warriors. Why? Wouldn't it make more sense to just kill him, take his heart, and send the rest of the White Moccasins to destroy Catkin's party?

What did Browser know that she didn't?

She led the way past the sprawled corpses of the battle. It struck her suddenly that all the arrows were missing, the quivers of the dead completely empty. When had that happened? Who had taken them?

White Cone began wheezing. They had come such a

short way and already the elder was falling behind. Sweat trickled down his wrinkled face. Was that what Shadow was banking on? That they couldn't travel rapidly with an exhausted elder? In that case it would be easy to run them down long before they could make the safety of Flowing Waters Town. Cunning and heartless as Shadow was, she had to be planning exactly that.

And following along, just out of bow shot, came the one lone White Moccasin scout, to mark the trail and make sure that her party could be found when the time came.

Clay Frog growled, "What was the War Chief thinking?"

"About Gray Thunder's prophecy," Catkin said. Memories stirred of the time he'd rescued her from the Fire Dogs. "The prophet was right. This insanity must end somewhere."

"But how will this end it? We should have fought!" Clay Frog's young face betrayed her frustration. "He offered his life for ours!"

"Yes," Catkin agreed. "He did."

A chorus of assent rose from behind Catkin. They would all die for Browser now. Not because of the Bow Society's honor, but because Browser had won their hearts and souls by his willingness to sacrifice his life for theirs.

Browser's words echoed in her head: *"By doing this, I have given you extra time, and I expect you to be a better War Chief than I have been. Remember, the roundabout way is often better than a direct assault against superior numbers. Victory goes to those who are swiftest, and allies can appear from the most unexpected places."*

As they neared the hulking mass of Kettle Town, Catkin turned, looking back at the party following her. White Cone's old face twisted in agony. He'd started to stumble and weave on his feet. Three bow shots to the rear, the White Moccasin scout followed in his shuffling trot.

Catkin slowed to match her pace with Fire Lark's. The young warrior glanced curiously at Catkin as she remarked, "It is said, Fire Lark, that you are the best bow shot among your party."

"I am, Deputy."

"I want you to do something for me."

"Yes, Deputy?"

"The timing must be just right, do you understand? And then you are going to have to run very hard to catch us. Can you do that?"

"Yes, Deputy."

"Good, because all of our lives are going to be in your hands."

"Then," Fire Lark asked hopefully, "we're not going straight back to Flowing Waters Town?"

"No, warrior, we're not. We're going to see what it's like to have the heart of a cloud. Today, Warrior, we are going to make legends."

63

The fringed end of Agent Sam Nichols's black muffler whipped around his neck as he walked. He had his shoulders hunched against the wind and his hands deep in the pockets of his brown canvas coat. He turned to Dusty as he led him up the trail toward where Maureen stood, overlooking the excavation. "Steve Sanders says two of the burials are still articulated, but that's not the really curious thing."

Dusty thought about that. What Steve had meant was that the bones were still in the exact positions they'd been in at death. Nothing had disturbed the burials. Then what about the scattered bones Sylvia had seen when she'd first fallen into the kiva?

"What's the really curious thing?" Dusty asked. Clouds filled the sky, and it felt like snow, but he'd seen no flakes yet.

"There was a beer can and a pack of cigarettes in the northern wall crypt. That pot hunter's hole led right to it."

"Hmm."

Wall crypts traditionally held sacred artifacts, items left for the gods. Pot hunters, like all vandals, often desecrated such things. "Is that why you brought me out here? To tell me that?"

"No," Nichols said, and wind flipped his thick black hair around his ears. "I'm taking a calculated risk. I brought you out here hoping you might see something that we haven't."

"Okay."

Dusty felt empty. Sage Walking Hawk's funeral had been a wrenching experience. Maggie had stood through the whole thing, smiling and comforting others, but Dusty had known her heart was breaking. To make matters worse, when it was all over, he'd felt obligated to tell Maggie that her aunt had said Kwewur was waiting for her. And that she might be Shadow Woman. But Maggie had no clue who Shadow Woman might be, or if, for that matter, Kwewur and Shadow Woman were one and the same.

Since her return to the canyon, Maggie hadn't stepped out of her office, and Rupert was acting like a protective bear, refusing to allow anyone to disturb her.

Rupert, himself, seemed distracted after his return from Washington. Something was eating at him, something that had turned his brown eyes somber. When Dusty asked him how he was doing, Rupert replied that he was the only park superintendent in nation with an unsolved murder investigation. And was that to be his legacy in the Park Service?

Was it Dusty's imagination, or did Rupert look thinner, as though he'd lost weight over the last couple of days?

Evil was loose on the wind, and as Dusty climbed after Agent Nichols, he could sense the final pieces about to fall into place.

Nichols ducked under the yellow tape and walked toward Maureen and the kiva rim. Dusty followed. In seven days, Steve's five-person crew had excavated to the floor of the kiva, even the south half that Michall had decided against touching. An aluminum ladder led down to an earthen pedestal. Fragments of human bone lay scattered on the kiva floor and near the fire pit, but Dusty's gaze fixed on the two skeletons. They lay on their backs with their arms and legs spread. Sandstone slabs the size of manhole covers rested beside the skulls. Big stones. Heavy.

Someone took extra care to make sure those souls stayed locked in the earth.

Maureen turned when they approached and said, "The body to the left is male; the female is on the right."

Steve, bundled like an Eskimo in a gray knit cap and red down coat, was working with a brush to clean and record bone fragments before removing them for stabilization and collection. Concentration marred his handsome face so mindful of a young Billy De Williams'.

Dusty thoughtfully examined the bodies, then shifted his gaze to the square hole in the north kiva wall. "That's the crypt where you found the beer can and cigarettes?"

"Yes." Nichols jammed his hands into his pockets.

"Let me guess," Dusty said. "A steel Coors can, the old kind that had to be opened with a can opener?"

"Right, and the cigarettes, Stewart?"

"Now there, you've got me."

"Parliament." Nichols looked annoyed. "My people tell me that that particular package design was manufactured in the midsixties."

Dusty nodded. *About the time my mother was taking her lovers to the Casa Rinconada kiva five minutes' walk away.*

"Dr. Sanders," Dusty called. "Who flipped the rocks off the heads of those two skeletons?"

Steve looked up, confused. "What makes you think I moved the slabs?"

"I can see the indentations and soil discolorations where they originally rested."

"Right." Steve wiped his face with his coat sleeve. "My guess is that the pot hunters moved the slabs. Back when they potted the site, we figure the roof was another twenty centimeters higher on the north side. So long as they stayed bent over, they could have duck-walked to the bodies. We also recovered several mid-thirteenth-century black-on-white McElmo potsherds, and a stone axe head, maybe for a war club. Last but not least, we found a beautiful ceramic spindle whorl, with a bit of the wooden spindle preserved. Cool, huh?"

"What about the pieces of bone, Sanders?" Nichols asked, kneeling to scrutinize the fragments he could see.

"Lots of partially calcined, cracked, and perimortally disarticulated bone, Agent Nichols. Preliminary analysis, as suggested by Dr. Malroun, indicates 'Turner events'— that the bodies had been 'processed as if for consumption.'"

Nichols squinted. "What the hell does that mean?"

Dusty answered, "That's the politically correct way to say it looks like cannibalism."

"What about the two skeletons?" Maureen asked. "Any evidence they were 'processed'?"

"Not yet, but the man would have been as tough as an old bull. He was ancient. I mean *really* old by Anasazi standards. Well past sixty. He's got some curious problems with his bones. Sid says he thinks he suffered from treponema."

"Really?" Maureen nodded thoughtfully.

"What's that?" Dusty asked.

"Syphilis," Maureen replied without looking at him. She was staring at the bones as if she might be able to tell that from up here. "Are there any lesions?"

For an answer, Steve carefully tiptoed across the bone

bed and picked up the skull. "See what you think. Maureen." He climbed the ladder and presented the skull to her.

She took it and gently turned it over in her hands while she inspected the outer table of the frontal bone, the forehead.

Dusty knelt beside her. Her braid smelled flowery from the shampoo she'd used that morning. "What do you see?"

Nichols stepped forward to listen. The tail of his black muffler fluttered over Maureen's shoulder.

She ran a finger over the pitted surface of the frontal bone. "I agree with Sid. Classic syphilitic lesions. Given the advanced stage of the disease, he was probably insane." She lifted the delicate skull to the sky. "And see the porosity?"

"Cribra cranii?" Dusty guessed.

"My god, Stewart," she said in mock surprise. "You've actually learned something scientific."

"Despite myself, Doctor."

"What's that mean?" Nichols asked.

"Poor diet," Maureen told him. "Generally we associate these kinds of holes, this porous look, with iron deficiency."

"But no cut marks?" Dusty asked, studying every line on the skull.

"No," Maureen answered.

"There's more," Steve called up from the bottom of the kiva. "Somebody caved in the old boy's ribs. Sid says they had started to callus, to heal, so the guy took the hit premortally, before he died. But the broken bones probably punctured his lungs."

"He must have been tough," Dusty granted. "He bled to death inside—but not for a while." He looked around.

"So, you're in NAGPRA land. Where's your Indian monitor?"

Steve grinned. "That's only for archaeology, Boss Man. This is a federal crime scene. Murder overrides the Native American Graves Protection and Repatriation Act."

Under his breath, Dusty sighed, "Thank God."

"What about the woman?" Maureen asked.

Steve shrugged. "Sid does facial reconstructions. He said she would have been a real beauty. We even found a few of her hairs preserved. Sid's going to run some comparisons at the OMI lab. The thing is, her hyoid bone is broken. Sid says someone strangled her."

Dusty pointed to the area above the woman's shoulders, where a forest of pin flags clustered. "What do all the pins mark?"

"Beads," Steve said. "Dozens of them. Turquoise, coral, jet, you name it. The lady was fixed for a night on the town. All she needed was a tuxedoed gent, a limo, and an American Express Platinum Card."

Maureen studied the woman's splayed pelvis. "Steve? Inside the innominates, is that what I think it is?"

"Yes, fetal bone," he said. "Sid figures she was just finishing the first trimester."

"Mom and Dad?" Dusty asked.

"Maybe. I doubt we'll ever know," Steve said.

Maureen looked at Nichols. "If Agent Nichols authorizes it, Sid could run some DNA tests on the bones. We might be able to answer that question."

Nichols tilted his head as though considering the idea.

"One last thing," Dusty said, remembering Sage Walking Hawk's last hours. He took a breath to gird himself. "Was the woman wearing a basilisk?"

Steve straightened and his dark eyes glinted. "No. At least not that we've found so far, but the man had one."

Steve pointed to the skull in Maureen's hand. "It was underneath him. He may have been wearing it as a pendant, but it wasn't finished yet. He'd carved the snake inside the broken eggshell but was still working on the inset for the eye. Other than that"—Steve propped his hands on his hips—"it was just like the one you curated from the 10K3 site."

As though someone had asked, Steve added, "And yeah, it's still there in the University of New Mexico collections. I called to make sure."

Maureen handed the skull back to Steve and pointed at the northern wall crypt. It was roughly two feet square and another two feet deep. "That crypt looks like it was dug out with a shovel."

"Probably," Nichols said and crouched down to stare at the destroyed crypt. "But the guy found something in it. It looks like he pulled a box out, then shoved the beer can and cigarettes in."

"Did you find anything else?" Dusty asked.

Nichols shrugged. "A couple of handprints, nothing we can really use except for palm diameter. Along with the beer can and cigarette pack, there was some cordage."

"Don't forget the butt." Steve was staring down at the skull in his hand as though he expected the dead man to suddenly comment on their theories.

"Right," Nichols added. "We found a single cigarette butt. The only problem is, it's been lying in the ground for nigh onto forty years. We'll probably never be able to identify the brand."

Steve turned the skull to look into the empty eye sockets. Unlike the hundreds of skulls Dusty had stared into over the years, this one looked eerie, malignant. Dusty shivered involuntarily.

"What about the cordage?" Dusty asked. "Anything interesting?"

"It was knotted in a loop," Steve answered. "You know, just lying there on the stone. It had apparently been around the box that the pot hunters slid out of the crypt."

Dusty closed his eyes.

"What?" everyone seemed to ask in unison.

"Probably a yucca hoop," Dusty said.

"Like the hoops around Robertson's and Hawsworth's bodies?" Nichols asked.

Dusty nodded. "That's why the slabs were left on their heads. Somebody killed two witches here, dropped slabs on top of them to keep their souls locked in the earth forever, and torched the place before they left."

"Then," Steve said uneasily, "a goddamn pot hunter dug them up again around forty years ago."

Maureen pinned Dusty with hard black eyes. "Are you suggesting Dale was murdered because the pot hunters dug up this site?"

Dusty spread his hands. "Dale must have known about this, Maureen. He came out here all the time in the sixties—usually in the company of my mother." He turned and gazed down at the enormous circle of Casa Rinconada. The beautiful stonework looked bleak under the gray winter sky. "And I wager he wrote about it in his journals."

Nichols stepped between them. "Why would it matter that two witches, murdered over seven hundred years ago, were dug up?"

Dusty looked past Nichols to the rimrock behind the site, and his soul seemed to glimpse something his eyes could not physically see. His heart went cold in his chest. Something terrible had happened here. He could sense it.

Softly, he said, "A stone is placed over a witch's head to keep the wicked soul from rising out of the grave and attacking the living, Nichols. You know, spirit possession, sickness, dying screaming. That kind of thing."

"So?"

"So." Dusty looked back at the agent and their gazes held. "After this site was potted, I suspect someone was attacked."

Nichols made a deep-throated sound of disgust and walked away.

Dusty looked back at the skeletons of the two witches and old Hail Walking Hawk's voice seeped from his memories: *"Many years ago, my grandmother told me about two witches who lived over at Zuni Pueblo. They could change themselves into animals by jumping through yucca hoops, and once they turned a man into a woman. Everybody said they were crazy, but people were too scared of them to try and kill them."*

They'd been excavating the 10K3 site, digging up the brutalized bodies of women who'd been dead for almost eight hundred years. One of the women had had a basilisk on her breastbone. Hail had been certain the women been killed by a witch.

Only now did it occur to Dusty to wonder how many years ago the two witches had lived at Zuni. Were they still alive?

"**D**rop your war club and climb down," Thorn Fox ordered and gestured at Browser as his warriors closed in.

Browser tossed his club to the side. "What about Horned Ram?"

The old man lay gasping on the blankets, his swollen shoulder black and mottled. Shadow crouched beside him. Browser kept his eyes on Rain Crow, watching the warrior's expression. His eyes had fixed on Shadow, anticipation there like a flame.

"Cut me loose," Horned Ram said. "This shoulder is killing me."

"Yes, Elder." Shadow reached into her belt pouch for a thin blade of obsidian. "This will only take a moment."

"Blessed gods," Horned Ram managed through gritted teeth, "I thought you'd never bring this to a conclusion."

"One thing you can rely on, Elder"—Shadow smiled down at him—"I always finish what I start." She leaned forward, her black eyes glittering, and her hand flashed.

Horned Ram's scream exploded in a guttering spray of blood. Shadow leaped away, but blood speckled the hem of her white dress. A rich red river flowed across the kiva roof as Horned Ram's severed throat sputtered and his limbs twitched. Browser watched the Red Rock elder's eyes dim and the pupils enlarge.

Rain Crow watched in horror. He frowned as Shadow stepped up to him, her head cocked. "Is there a problem, War Chief?"

"No," Rain Crow rasped.

"You always finish what you start," Browser repeated. "How did you enlist Horned Ram in the first place?"

Shadow shrugged and bent down to wipe the blood from her obsidian blade onto Horned Ram's clothing. "We have been working with Horned Ram for a long time. He had a fertile imagination. We always gave him information that fed his thirst for violence. Two Hearts actually brought him into our fold sun cycles ago. Fortunately, Horned Ram never asked questions about who we were, or why we would let him know the things we did. All he cared about was that we were against the katsinas. I'm sure it all came crashing down on him when your little trick led his warriors into battle against Bear Lance's warriors."

"So he ran," Stone Ghost said. He stood like a small, hunched animal, his turkey-feather cape flapping in the wind. "Not only did he discover that the First People existed, but that he'd also been working with the White Moccasins for sun cycles."

Shadow stepped up to him, smile ravishing. "Not all of our adversaries have your dedication to honor and duty."

Old Pigeontail had been leaning against Owl House's plastered wall. "What about War Chief Rain Crow?"

Rain Crow propped himself on his war club, his gaze fixed on the red pool of Horned Ram's blood.

"What about you, War Chief? Are you with me or against me?"

Rain Crow blinked hard, either from the blow to his head or from the sudden death of Horned Ram, Browser couldn't tell.

"With you," Rain Crow whispered. "I'm no fool."

"Good." Shadow paused long enough to run a finger down the side of his ruined face. Then she turned. "Browser? Stone Ghost? Would you be so kind as to climb down into the kiva? We have things we need to discuss."

Browser caught the desperate look in Rain Crow's eyes. The Flowing Waters War Chief didn't look as sick as he had. Some subtle communication passed between them, accented by a slight nod of Rain Crow's head. What had the War Chief been trying to tell him?

Tendrils of smoke coiled up past his shoulders, rising from the hearth below, but the air was strangely cold as Browser descended the ladder.

At the bottom, he stepped to one side, blinking to help his eyes adjust to the dim interior. Shadow immediately climbed down and took a position beside him.

Stone Ghost took the steps down one at a time, his gaze searching the kiva, probably looking for the little girl. When his feet touched the floor, he gripped Browser's sleeve to steady himself.

Rain Crow's stout body blocked the sunlight as he descended. He kept trying to stifle his ragged breathing but couldn't. The pain in his head must be overwhelming. When his feet touched the floor, he staggered over to collapse on the kiva bench. Then the ladder rattled as Thorn Fox dropped athletically to the floor.

Murals of the old gods had been painted on the kiva walls: the Flute Player, the Blue God, the Hero Twins, and Spider Woman stood to his right. On Browser's left, one huge painting depicted the First People climbing into this world, carrying enormous ceremonial knives in their hands.

"Who—who's there?" a thin reedy voice wheezed.

In the shadows, Browser made out the broken waste of a man lying on a reed mat. His features were recognizable, but just barely. Filthy white hair matted his head, and his skin—old and wrinkled—hung loose, as though insects had eaten the flesh out from inside him. The wall crypt above him held a beautifully painted rawhide box. A pile of wadded blankets lay at the foot of his bedding, as though kicked off when he'd grown too hot.

Browser caught the motion as Rain Crow flinched. The man's mouth gaped. His eyes had fixed on the pile of bones that gleamed around his feet. Human bones. They were scattered across the floor like litter.

When Rain Crow lifted his gaze to Shadow, it was filled with such horror that Browser wondered if he was hearing the screams of his wounded men as she killed them, then cut the flesh from their bodies.

"You didn't know?" Browser asked softly.

Rain Crow just shook his head, but the hardening around his mouth indicated that he'd come to some decision.

Browser turned his attention to Two Hearts and took a step. Thorn Fox moved with catlike quickness to place himself between Two Hearts and Browser.

Browser's gaze bored into Thorn Fox's. "Don't be an imbecile. If I had wished the elder dead, he'd be dead by now. I had plenty of opportunity before you and your warriors arrived."

Thorn Fox grinned; several of his teeth were missing on the right side. The broken roots could be seen rotting in pink and inflamed gums. "Killing you will be a pleasure."

Browser shouted in his face, "Move!"

Thorn Fox regripped his club in both hands but stood his ground.

"Obsidian," Two Hearts hissed. "Where is she?"

Shadow knelt and smoothed hair from Two Hearts's brow. "The warriors are holding her, Father. Like I said they would."

Browser frowned and exchanged a glance with Stone Ghost. Stone Ghost pursed his lips and shook his head. Not yet. Not until they knew more.

"The turquoise wolf? Where...where is it?" Two Hearts extended a skeletal hand and his fingers trembled.

Shadow stood and reached out. "Give it to me. Now!"

Browser pulled open his shirt hem, and the wolf slid out onto his palm. He handed it to Shadow, who put it in Two Hearts's hand and closed his fingers around it. "Here, Father. Feel it?"

The old man clutched the wolf to his heart, and relief slackened his face. His thin brown lips parted to expose toothless gums. He might have been caught in a moment of pure bliss.

As Two Hearts shifted his foot, a terrified squeak came from the wadded blankets, then soft babbling, like that of a demented newborn.

"Bone Walker?" Stone Ghost called and turned to Shadow. "Please, let me go to her."

"Bone Walker? Do you mean my daughter, Piper?" Shadow waved a hand. "Go. But she has lost her souls. She can't speak or even focus her eyes. I don't know what happened to her."

Stone Ghost gently pulled at the blankets until he'd uncovered the little girl, face dirty, her hair a tangled mass. She lay curled on her side. Her huge black eyes stared intently at nothing, as though focused on some terror inside her. She had both hands twisted in a turquoise necklace that Browser had seen Stone Ghost wear a hundred times.

Had he given it to the child, or had she stolen it?

Stone Ghost lowered himself to the floor and pulled the girl into his lap. Her body was limp, as though her muscles had stopped working. Her head rolled back over his arm. Stone Ghost hugged her to his chest and whispered in her ear in a comforting voice. The only words Browser could make out were, *"I'm here. I'm right here."*

Browser crossed his arms, shooting a look at Thorn Fox. "Very well, Shadow, I am ready to listen to your proposal."

Two Hearts coughed, and blood speckled his mouth. "Shadow...tell him."

Shadow said, "Browser, the Blessed Two Hearts does not wish to kill you. None of us has pure blood anymore, but you are one of only five men left to us whose blood is almost pure. By mating you with several of our purest women—"

"Like you?" Browser interrupted.

Blessed gods. That's why they let me live this long.

"Yes, like me," Shadow answered, "and a handful of others. It will not be unpleasant for you, I assure you. Because of our blood, we are all attractive and eager to mate with others of our kind."

Our kind. The words sickened Browser.

"We are the last," Shadow said as she strode up to face him. "We have only ourselves. Two small clans of First People. That's why it's so imperative that you live and marry."

Browser crossed his arms. "Then why were you hunting me at Dry Creek village? You were out there, weren't you?"

Shadow reached out to touch his shoulder. "I was that close to you. But for Stone Ghost's arrival, I would have killed Catkin that night." She cocked her head, the wealth of beads clattering in her long black hair. "How would that have looked, Browser? Your deputy dead within a body's length of you? Perhaps it would have been the impetus for Cloudblower to dismiss you."

"You are a most clever woman, Shadow."

"Yes, and patient."

"Why me? There's always Thorn Fox," Browser reminded. "From the number of warriors I've seen recently, it isn't like we're running out of White Moccasins."

A branch broke in the fire and the resulting swirl of sparks reflected in her black eyes. "We need them, yes, but a good deal of Made People blood runs in their veins. To regenerate ourselves, we must strive for purity."

"I don't think I understand," Stone Ghost said as he gently lowered the limp little girl to the floor. "If you wish my nephew to live, what of Two Hearts?"

"We still have Obsidian's heart," Shadow said easily. "And if that fails, he has the Blessed Night Sun's turquoise wolf to guide him through the twists and turns of the afterlife trails."

Through a tense exhalation, Browser asked, "What if I say no?"

A daring smile curled Shadow's full lips. "If you say no, the woman you love will die. She can't outrun Thorn Fox with that Mogollon elder panting at the rear. After that we will slowly, one by one, kill everyone else you care about, starting with the *kokwimu,* Cloudblower, and Matron Crossbill."

Browser's fists knotted. Even if Catkin hadn't understood his message, all they had to do was be patient, keep a close watch on her, and someday she would be vulnerable. All of the skill in the world could not save a warrior from treachery. He turned to look at Stone Ghost, and his heart ached.

Shadow folded her arms and her white dress swayed as she walked closer. "We are not fools, Browser. Just as you used the northern staircase to trap Blue Corn, by now your people are in our trap."

She looked up into his eyes and he sensed an unnatural hunger there, like that of a dying animal.

"You will either do as we say, or your friends will be stewed bones by the time the sun rises tomorrow."

"What if I want Obsidian?" Browser met stare for stare. "What if I wish to marry her? A woman can't very well bear daughters when her heart has been pulled out of her chest with a spindle."

Shadow stepped over to the bench and lifted a long slender spindle from the plastered stone.

Browser added, "You know she helped me ambush Bear Lance's warriors."

"Then turned on you when I captured her." Shadow twirled the spindle in her hands. "She's always been a disappointment to me."

Browser gave a slight shrug of the shoulders. "If you truly wish to save our people there is only one way. Stop all this murdering and destruction. I want Obsidian. Alive. I want Catkin and the Katsinas' People left alone. And I want my turquoise wolf back. It belongs to me. The gods made sure it fell into my possession."

He gave her a knowing look. "Do that, Shadow, and I will help you in any way I can."

Shadow's eyes seemed to enlarge, swelling in her face, as if they were peering into his very soul.

Yvette heard the auto pulling into the parking space outside Dusty's camp trailer but didn't think much of it. People came and went constantly. It didn't sound like Dusty's Bronco, but that didn't mean anything. He often arrived with other people.

She stared into her coffee cup, trying to sort out her emotions. She should have been prostrate with grief over Carter's murder. But he'd been more of a father in name than fact. They had always had an uneasy relationship, a sort of keep-your-distance-and-spar, instead of the sort of father-daughter intimacy she had always imagined proper. The fact that she still thought of him as Carter proved something.

Through the years, Yvette had analyzed and reanalyzed her relationship with her parents or, rather, the lack of it. Mum had been even more cold and indifferent than Carter. Yvette had always felt guilty around them, as if she were at fault for something terrible and she'd never understood what it was.

Then she had discovered this curious brother who

believed in Spirits and witches, and all sorts of things Yvette considered utter nonsense.

"I'm going bloody crazy," she whispered and absently listened to the vehicle idling outside.

The old Indian woman's voice kept echoing in the back of her mind. Over and over, she heard Sage Walking Hawk say: *"The Shiwana were there. When you were conceived...in the kiva...in the moonlight..."*

But what did it mean?

A door slammed outside.

At the knock, Yvette called, "Come in. It's open."

When Mum opened the door and stepped in, her appearance was shockingly out of place. She looked ravishing, wearing a full-length camel-hair coat, a wool suit jacket, tailored gray wool pants, and western-style boots. A silver concho belt snugged her waist, and she'd pulled her silver hair back into a ponytail that hung down to her collar. Her blue eyes had a predatory glitter to them.

"Been out stalking the wily male of the species again, Mum?" Yvette asked, reading that look she had grown passingly familiar with.

"I'd forgotten what Taos was like." Mum smiled. "I guess I never realized I'm getting old. It isn't so bad in Boston. I'm part of the society. Men know me. Powerful men, who can provide the things that interest me. Here, well, I'm afraid it's a younger crowd."

"Sorry 'bout that, Mum."

Yvette moved her coffee cup in little circles over the scarred tabletop while Mum looked around the trailer. Finally, Yvette asked, "What are the Shiwana?"

Mum gave her a speculative look. "That's an odd question coming from you. The Keres tribe believe that the Shiwana are spirits of the dead who climbed into the sky to become cloud beings. They bring rain, they watch over people. The Hopi call them Kachinas. The Zuni refer to them as Koko. Why do you ask?"

"Are they gods?"

"Well, that's debatable. Whites categorize them as ancestor spirits with supernatural abilities. What the people actually think is anybody's guess."

Yvette gripped her coffee cup. When she'd worked up the courage, she asked, "What happened the night I was conceived...in the kiva...in the moonlight? Were the Shiwana there?"

Mum started as though caught completely off guard, but she quickly recovered and leaned against the kitchen counter. "What are you talking about?"

"Just answer the question."

"I don't know what you're talking about."

"I'm talking about the spirits dancing the night I was conceived."

Mum laughed. "You've lost it, dear. A few days in the Southwest and you're a raving lunatic."

Yvette looked up. "Is that why you killed Carter? Was it the last part of the ritual you performed the night I was conceived? Or just plain witchcraft?"

Her mother's face paled. "Carter's..."

"Dead. Yes."

"When?" she asked breathlessly. "How?"

Ruth Ann eased down opposite Yvette.

"He was killed a week ago and dumped upside down in the same kiva where they found Dale Robertson. His feet had been skinned. I don't know much more about it. The FBI is still investigating."

Mum's fists clenched on the table. In a strained voice, she whispered, "Oh, my God."

Yvette watched her mother's eyes widen in fear. "Tell me what happened that night, Mum. I've a right to know."

Mum's fear turned to anger in a heartbeat. Her voice

cut like glass: "Do you want to know the whole of it, Yvette, or just the good parts?"

"The whole, please, Mum."

"Well, first of all, daughter of mine, let's get one thing clear: You don't have any rights when it infringes on my privacy. Second, I doubt you can stomach the people you'll have to deal with to hear the full story. I'm supposed to rendezvous with one of them in half an hour."

"I can stomach them, Mum. I've managed with you and Carter over the years. Might I go with you?"

Mum gave her the same murderous look she had when Yvette had been seven and accidentally knocked over a prehistoric pot Mum had displayed on her desk: *the careless hateful look of a stranger.*

"You want to know what happened the night you were conceived? No matter how frightening or ugly?"

"I do, Mum."

Ruth Ann shook her head as though disgusted with her. "All right, daughter, I'll make it short and sweet, and then I've got an appointment to keep."

"Fine, Mum. Let's hear it."

Her mother glanced around. "I came here to see your brother. Where is he?"

"He and Maureen went out to the site with that charming FBI agent, Sam Nichols."

"Well, too bad for him, then." Mum got to her feet and her necklace fell forward.

"New pendant?" Yvette asked.

Mum lifted the black stone from where it hung on her breast. "An old one, actually. I've had it for what seems an eternity. I used to swing it over Dusty's crib when he was a baby, to hypnotize him to go to sleep."

Mum tucked the pendant back into her jacket, leaving Yvette barely enough time to make out that it was a snake with a glistening red eye.

All in all, Yvette thought it a perfect match for Mum's personality. "Good, now I want to hear about that night."

"You won't blush, will you?"

"After so many years with you, I rather fancy that as unlikely."

"We'll see," Ruth Ann began. "Dale and I had been..."

S hadow stared at Browser as if across infinity. Finally, she nodded. "You will swear to me that you will act as I wish? I am the descendant of the Blessed Night Sun, as are you. We are Red Lacewing Clan. Just as in the days of our ancestors, were I to choose you, you would become the Blessed Sun, Browser, the ruler of the Straight Path Nation."

"I will do whatever you ask of me." A hollow prickling invaded his chest. How much time had passed? "But what about Two Hearts?"

Shadow ran her gaze up and down Browser's body and smiled as she pulled her white dress over her head and tossed it aside. She stood naked before him, beautiful in the soft glow from the fire. Challenge lit her large dark eyes. "His fate is up to the gods. Come. If you wish to seal this bargain, let us do it now. You and I, here, in front of these witnesses." She clasped his hands and drew him to her, pressing her naked body against him.

Any chance Browser might have had to delay had just vanished like the whisps of smoke through the kiva's open entry.

In a mocking and irreverent tone, Shadow said, "I, Shadow Woman, of the Red Lacewing Clan, choose you, Browser, as my leader, my chief." She spoke the ritual words with curious ease.

Browser's jaw muscles tensed, his heart thudding. Those were the words the Blessed Night Sun would have said to the man she had chosen to join with. To the man she had chosen to become the Blessed Sun.

Browser responded. "I, Browser, of the Red Lacewing Clan, accept the responsibility for our people, Blessed Shadow."

According to the ancient traditions, they had just become husband and wife. Browser's skin crawled when he looked at Shadow. An animal excitement lit her eyes.

"May Spider Woman bless our actions this day," he said, and put his arms around her in an iron grip.

Her lips opened, and he saw the pulse beating in her temple. In that instant, she read his souls.

Browser shouted, *"Now, Rain Crow!"*

Browser shoved Shadow off balance, twisted her around, and brought his muscular arm down across her throat.

The speed with which she reacted stunned him. He had no more than gotten hold of her when she sank her teeth into his arm and grabbed his testicles. A scream broke from his lips, and his frantic jerk pulled her teeth loose. She clung to him, trying to twist his scrotum off his body with one hand, while the other reached up and clawed for his eyes.

At the edge of his vision he saw Rain Crow swing his war club into Thorn Fox's stomach. Stone Ghost had stumbled back, dragging the little girl with him.

Browser used his forehead to butt Shadow hard in the face. At the impact, her head rocked backward and she staggered, overbalancing him. Together they crashed to the floor.

In the mad scramble that followed, she scuttled on all fours for the ladder. He clasped a handful of her bead-encrusted hair and punched her in the face. She flipped, catlike, powerful, stronger than any woman he'd ever known. Her knee shot into his throbbing crotch and yellow light blasted his brain.

Her hand flashed up from the side. Like a striking snake, she slammed him in the head with a hearth stone. Browser roared and threw himself on top of her.

To his left, he caught the bizarre image of Stone Ghost bending over Two Hearts with a broken shaft of human leg bone.

Shadow screamed as Browser clamped both hands tightly around her throat. She bashed his shoulder, arm, back, anywhere she could strike with the stone, but he kept his grip on her throat. Bucking like an elk in deep snow, she tried to throw him off. Each blow of the stone thumped hollowly, painfully, through his body, splintering the world. Doggedly he tightened his grip on her throat, hearing the liquid sounds of her protruding tongue against the back of her palate.

The image fixed in his brain: her parted lips and heaving breasts, her legs thrashing as she struggled for air.

When Shadow's flailing arm lost its strength and the stone fell to the floor, he stared down into her widening eyes, vaguely aware of the blood that dripped from his battered head to speckle her smooth skin. Between his knotted hands, he could feel her pulse as it slowed and see her eyes growing vacant. He felt the Blue God as she settled on his shoulders, hovering and expectant.

My wife. My wife. The disconnected words repeated in his brain. I *am killing my wife.*

"Browser!" Stone Ghost's voice barely cut through the

exaltation. *"Browser! Behind you!"*

Browser's gaze shot up, and he saw Stone Ghost—crimson-spattered— leaning over Two Hearts, a bloody bone in his hands.

"Behind you!"

Browser twisted, but not in time. The blow that was meant to crush his skull landed in the corded muscle of his shoulder, just below the neck, stunning him. Then a hard body slammed into him, toppling him to one side. Thick, muscular arms wrapped around his, breaking his hold on Shadow, prying him away from her.

Thorn Fox kicked him in the belly, and the blow of his war club numbed Browser's spine. He collapsed, dazed, to the dirt floor, unable to catch his breath.

As Browser fought to roll over, he caught sight of Rain Crow, lying on his back in the corner, his arms sprawled. Was he dead?

Thorn Fox's club raised again, and Browser saw a tiny form dart at the edge of his vision. Browser blocked the next blow with his left arm, heard the bone crack, and a searing flash of pain shot through him. He lurched up, grabbed the club with his right hand, and jerked with all his strength, pulling Thorn Fox off balance. The man fell, and Browser drove his fingers into Thorn Fox's eye sockets. He felt his fingertips rip through the tissue, and blood gushed out over his right hand and ran down his arm.

The silence that followed Thorn Fox's shocked scream seemed to deafen. Browser shoved the blind man off and stumbled to his feet.

Thorn Fox, whimpering, crawled away, his hands searching the floor for his lost war club. Rain Crow got to his knees and wavered. With one final swing of his club, he broke Thorn Fox's neck. Then Rain Crow slumped to the floor, panting.

Browser looked down at Shadow. He had made a

mistake once before, believing that he'd killed Two Hearts but not taking the extra moment to make certain. Browser walked to Shadow's blood-smeared naked body and reached out. He touched her wide, dark eye. She did not blink or flinch. When he withdrew his hand, only the bloody fingerprint marred the glassy orb.

"Uncle Stone Ghost, let's—"

An inhuman shriek rose from the little girl's throat. She raced forward and threw herself over her mother's dead body, clawing at her skin, squealing incoherently.

Browser staggered back, breathing hard. "Uncle, the warriors down below...will have heard the screams."

"Yes, but they may have thought they were your screams, Nephew."

Stone Ghost watched the blood pool from the lethal gashes in Two Hearts's throat and chest; then he dropped the spearlike bone onto the kiva floor beside Shadow's spindle.

Browser winced at the ache in his left arm. One bone was broken at least. Since it didn't flop, the other must have been intact, but, gods, it hurt.

The little girl rose and madly skipped around Shadow's body, humming a haunting song. Her filthy black hair bounced as though alive.

Browser went to Rain Crow, pulled the warrior over, and saw he was still breathing. "War Chief?"

Rain Crow whispered, "Gods, my head. I feel strange, Browser. Tingly, and everything's gray. I can't see...can't..." His eyes were wide, unfocused. "They killed my sister's..."

Browser put two fingers to Rain Crow's throat. He knew the instant the man's heart stopped. He shook his head and lowered his hand.

Stone Ghost asked, "What now, Nephew? It won't take long before they figure out..."

A shadow blackened the kiva entrance overhead.

"**W**here could she be?" Dusty asked as he and Maureen walked out into the evening, away from Maggie's cabin. When no one answered their knock, they'd found the door unlocked, stepped inside and called. But Maggie hadn't answered. The sound of voices came from the other cabins, soft and happy. Someone laughed. Dusty turned his gaze to the west and Chacra Mesa. The fading rays of sunset made the canyon walls gleam like varnished copper.

"We've tried the dormitory. Neither Sylvia nor Michall have seen her. We could try Rupert's," Maureen suggested.

Tired and frustrated, Dusty said, "I'd really like to find her."

"Dusty," Maureen warned. "Maggie has a lot on her mind: her aunt's recently dead; there have been two homicides in her park; Rupert just returned with a thousand questions. She probably needs time alone."

"Probably, but I still have to find her."

"Do you really think she has to immediately hear that Steve found two witches?"

"Uh-huh. Remember 10K3? Remember how Hail Walking Hawk reacted? Maybe a White person wouldn't care, but you can damned well bet that Magpie Walking Hawk Taylor wants a heads-up. Finding two witches has ramifications for the traditional community."

He led the way through the scrubby sage to the park superintendent's house. For Chaco Canyon standards, it was actually pretty nice. Dusty had been in it many times.

They followed the gravel walk around to the front and found a man already standing at the door. Dusty slowed, half irritated that some stranger had beaten him to Rupert. The man knocked. But no answer came. He knocked again, waited, then turned to leave.

"Hey, Lupe!" Dusty started forward, smiling. "Long time no see!"

"Stewart? Is that you?"

Lupe might have been in his forties but tonight he looked fifty. He wore a leather jacket and a black felt cowboy hat with a huge silver concho band. He took Dusty's hand, grasping it hard. "God damn, man. Good to see you! What's the latest on Dale's murder?"

"The FBI's still working on it. Steve found two Anasazi skeletons in the kiva today. They had stones on their heads. You get my drift."

Lupe's expression went tense. "Yeah. You be careful, huh? That's bad stuff."

"Hey," Dusty said with a sigh and changed the subject. "I hear you're bilking tourists for off-tune flutes these days."

"Yeah, man. I got my stuff in big-time galleries, and there are collectors, people with money, buying flutes these days." He glanced at Maureen. "Hey, Maureen, you still can't find a decent guy to hang around with?"

"There's a limited selection out here." She smiled. "How have you been?"

"Better," Lupe replied. "It's a tough time all the way around. But next time you need help getting this *cabron* in a truck, you call me."

Dusty said, "Lupe and I drank our first whiskey together, got in fights, and did all the things teenage boys aren't supposed to do."

"Yeah, god, we had fun. You remember that time we poached that deer up by Chama? Man, I thought we was dead when that highway patrol car stopped us."

Dusty playfully punched Lupe in the shoulder. "We had a taillight out. Lupe was cool as ice. He just acted like a perfectly mannered kid. When the cop asked him where he was going to school, he said, 'At the military academy at Roswell, sir. I'm going to start as a lieutenant when I enlist.' The cop told us to get the light fixed and sent us on our way with our deer safely in the trunk."

Maureen smiled.

"So, you know where Dad is?" Lupe hooked a thumb at the dark house.

"Nope. We're looking for him, too."

Lupe frowned and reached into his leather coat. "Hey, could you do something for me, man? These are for Dad. I gotta go. I gotta reception tomorrow in a gallery in Taos, and the radiologist said that Dad demanded a copy of these test results as soon as they were done. Could you make sure he gets them? And this"—he lifted a flannel bag—"is a flute I made for him. It's beautiful. Turquoise inlay. My best yet."

"Yeah. Sure." Dusty smiled and took the bag and the envelopes. When he saw the return address in the glow of the yard light, Dusty's head jerked up. He just stared at Lupe.

Lupe studied him thoughtfully. "He ain't told you?"

"No." Dusty felt sick to his stomach.

"God, that's where he was all last week. One test after

another. It's cancer, man." Lupe scuffed the ground with his shoe and glanced uneasily at Maureen. "But you don't tell Dad that I told you."

Dusty tucked the envelopes into his coat pocket. "Thanks, *amigo*. Really. *Cuanto tiempo?*"

"*Seis meses...mas o menos.* Reggie's taking it really hard. He won't talk to nobody about it, just sits in his room in the dark with that old painted box that he found way back when in Dad's basement, the one Dad kept his letters in."

Dusty reached for Lupe's hand again and held it in a strong grip. "Drive carefully getting up to Taos, okay. I don't want to lose you, too."

"Not me, man." Lupe grinned sadly. "Tell Dad I love him. I'm outta here."

Dusty waited until Lupe got into his car and started away; then he lifted a hand in farewell. Lupe must have seen him through the rearview mirror. He waved.

Dusty slowly lowered his hand. "I thought he was supposed to be in Washington. Cancer? For the love of God, is the entire world dying around me?"

Just as they turned to leave, a man stuck his head out of the cabin next door and called, "You looking for Dr. Brown?"

"Yes, have you seen him?"

"He jumped in his truck and flew out of here spinning gravel about a half hour ago."

Dusty lifted a hand, called, "Thanks! Hey, you don't know where Maggie is, do you?"

The guy shrugged. "She left to find Reggie about an hour ago. Him and his trash truck didn't check in at quitting time."

"Thanks, again. Good night."

The guy closed his door.

Dusty looked across the canyon. Headlights sparkled on the road leading to Casa Rinconada.

As he watched them moving toward the kiva parking lot, Dusty suddenly felt weak. A rush of information seemed to fall out of his brain. Things that Sage had said, that Lupe had just said, about Rupert and the old painted box, and Reggie being on parole, and working part-time for his grandfather.

Dusty opened the flute bag. The instrument was beautiful, made of red cedar with a turquoise inlay. In the center, just above the finger holes, surrounded by turquoise, a beautifully carved basilisk had been inset. The single coral eye would stare at the player.

An attached note read:

Dad, here's my best yet. If you need more of the little snakes, give me a call. They don't take but half a day to carve. Hope this flute makes you well. Love, Lupe.

A witch survives through misdirection.

"Dusty?" Maureen asked as she walked up behind him. "Did you hear a word I said?"

He tugged the laces closed on the bag and reached out, steadying himself on her shoulder. "Come on. We have to hurry."

PIPER

Owl is flying above Piper, his wings puffing air on her face where she huddles behind Stone Ghost.

She stares up, waiting in silence as a man's legs drop into the kiva. Browser shifts, as if a smoky shadow. For an instant she sees the Blue God—as Browser times the swing of his war club. The man coming down the ladder has just seen Mother's naked body, just realized that Grandfather's bedding is soaked in blood.

She watches the breath going into his lungs to shout as Browser's war club smacks loudly into the back of the man's neck. His eyes go blank and he falls to the floor.

Owl whispers, "You have been born to a time of war, little Bone Walker. Death swirls around you. Listen, listen for its soft footsteps."

She knows the sound. Mother's breath-heart soul hisses as it slips away past her tongue, then makes the faintest rasping as it scampers around the kiva, trying to get away from the body.

Stone Ghost lifts a heavy grinding stone, grunts, and drops it onto Grandfather's head.

As he staggers back, he says, "I need another stone."

Piper points to one of the bench slabs that is loose in its setting.

As Stone Ghost rocks it free, Browser lifts the dead warrior's body with his good arm and drapes it over his shoulder. Then he begins the hard climb up the ladder.

Piper jumps when Stone Ghost drops the big stone on her mother's head. Mother will never look at her again with dead flying squirrel eyes.

Voices call from outside.

Piper stares up at the hole in the roof.

Owl whispers, "The Blue God is feeding."

Piper swallows the sourness that rises into her throat. She's dizzy.

Owl whispers, "Shh. Shh. Shh."

69

O bsidian folded her arms and anxiously stared up at Owl House. As the twilight deepened, a chill settled on the canyon. She rubbed her cold skin. The screams had stopped, but no one had summoned her for the ritual preparations. Obsidian had no interest in seeing Browser's torture and death. She didn't want to witness his heart being extracted from his chest. Until Shadow had captured her, she had still hoped Browser might be her way out. She would have taken him for a husband. A woman could do worse. But now? She looked around at the White Moccasins, trying to see a future with any of them.

How did this go so badly for me?

What did Shadow think? That Obsidian would wait around down here until after dark? It was getting cold, and she was tired of being ogled. She wished the hungry-eyed warriors would look elsewhere.

"Something is wrong," she said to Old Pigeontail.

The wrinkles that wrapped his fleshy nose deepened as he frowned. "Perhaps." He was watching her with an unusual amusement in his eyes.

"Do you know something I do not?"

He shrugged, a smile hidden behind his thin brown lips. "The preparations took longer than usual, that's all. Browser was a strong man. He might have withstood the torture longer than anticipated."

"I don't see why they had to torture him at all. They wanted his heart. That should have been a simple matter of throwing him down, cutting his chest open, and pulling it out." Obsidian rubbed her cold arms again, then pointed. "You, young warrior, what is your name?"

The black-haired youth came forward and bowed respectfully, though his gaze was fixed on her breasts. "I am Star Knife, Blessed Obsidian."

"Good. Go up there and see what is happening. By now, Shadow should have Browser's heart boiling in her pot. This is taking too long."

Star Knife continued to stare at her chest as he nodded; then he turned and trotted the short distance up the hill. His white cape swayed with his gait.

Obsidian glanced at the other warriors in irritation.

They were all watching with speculative eyes, probably waiting for their turn to bed her, as they did her sister. Well, they would have a long wait.

Star Knife climbed onto the kiva roof. He cupped a hand to his mouth and called out, but Wind Baby had been gusting ferociously all day, Obsidian couldn't make out his words.

Star Knife climbed down and disappeared into the kiva.

He didn't come back out.

Obsidian had opened her mouth to shout to him when Pigeontail muttered, "Blessed Flute Player, something isn't right about this. Shadow should have had his answer by now, and that youth should have been sent scurrying."

"Answer?" Obsidian asked. "What answer?"

Pigeontail gave her a disgusted look. "You don't think this is just about you, do you? It's about the future. If Shadow can't turn him...oh, never mind. The gods made you to be beautiful, not smart." He raised his voice. "Something is wrong! Half of you, come with me!"

Pigeontail started up the hill toward Owl House with a cluster of warriors following in his wake.

Obsidian frowned. A pale blue finger of smoke rose from the kiva and twisted into the evening sky. Obsidian started forward, crested the ridge, but stopped when a body flopped out of the kiva's rooftop entrance. Then, a moment later, a second body was shoved out, and a man emerged.

"It's Browser!"

The White Moccasins in the process of surrounding Owl House stopped short, suddenly uncertain. Old Pigeontail pointed a hard finger and shouted, "Kill him!"

Warriors surged forward. One young man vaulted to the roof, his war club held high. In less than a heartbeat, an arrow sliced its way into the youth's chest. Sunlight flashed on the shaft as he staggered, eyes blinking, blood gushing from his mouth.

Obsidian waved both arms at the suddenly hesitant warriors. "Get up there!"

As the white-caped men dashed around her, she tried to understand.

Browser, half hidden by the smoke, helped old Stone Ghost from the kiva, then lifted Piper out. The three of them turned, making a run for the rocks under the rim, a bow shot south of Owl House.

"Stop them!" Obsidian shouted. The next warrior reached the roof—only to stumble backward, a fletched shaft piercing his abdomen. As he kicked and screamed, hands clasping the arrow that lodged in his guts, the others charged past.

Obsidian gaped when another warrior, no more than five paces ahead of her, screamed as an arrow lanced his arm. Obsidian leaped to the kiva's low roof and looked up the ridge to the rimrock.

Jackrabbit and Straighthorn were making good use of their bows from behind the tumbled rocks.

Obsidian grabbed one of the warriors who ran past. "There are only two of them! You can rush them!"

The young warrior gaped at her in panic.

"Go!" Obsidian ordered. "Now! Take them."

Flames crackled wildly inside the kiva. Smoke billowed, and tongues of fire leaped up the ladder and caught in the dry matting around the entryway.

Obsidian edged past the bodies to the entryway and bent down, waving at the smoke and heat. Someone had piled firewood around the base of the ladder and kicked coals from the hearth into the tinder. In the gaudy flickering glare, Obsidian saw the bodies with huge stones atop their heads.

Saved! I am saved!

A laugh came bubbling up from inside as she backed away, coughing, and stumbled to the edge of the kiva.

It took several instants before she could identify the cluster of warriors charging up the slope from Corner Kiva. A woman ran in front. "Catkin? What are you doing here?"

Obsidian ducked away from the acrid smoke and fire. The White Moccasins were pursuing southward along the rim, ducking arrows, as they chased Browser and his party.

Obsidian pulled herself up and shouted, "Catkin! Hurry! They have Browser trapped! You can still..."

She saw it coming. The sliver-like gleam of light flashing along the shaft. Then Catkin's arrow caught Obsidian in the chest. The force of the blow knocked her off her feet. She landed hard. For a couple of heartbeats, she sat dazed. The weird thing was that she could feel it, something hard, burning with pain, and resisting her efforts to draw breath. Looking down, it was to see the fletching and notched shaft protruding from swell of her left breast.

"No!" Obsidian clawed at the ground. When she coughed, blood bubbled from her mouth and soaked into the kiva roof's packed earth. Frothy. Bright.

Catkin and several of the Mogollon warriors pounded past. Over the shouts and screams, the crackling of the fire, Obsidian heard the impact as Catkin swung her war club and crushed the right side of Pigeontail's skull.

As her vision began to fade, Obsidian saw the White Moccasins break before Catkin's war party. One long shrill shout carried as they fled into the falling evening...

"God, I pray I'm wrong," Dusty called as he drove maniacally down the loop road.

"About what?" Maureen braced her feet for the next curve. "Tell me what you're talking about!"

Dusty pummeled the steering wheel with the palm of his hand. "Do you know what Reggie does? Why he's on parole in El Paso?"

"No, why?"

"He's a burglar, Maureen. Breaking and entering. He broke into houses in El Paso, loaded stuff in his trunk, and fenced it across the line in Juarez."

Dusty slid the Bronco onto the Casa Rinconada drive.

"What does that have to—"

"Reggie stole the diaries! I'm sure of it!"

Not only were two sickly green Park Service pickups parked in the Casa Rinconada lot, but so was a familiar Ford Explorer, as well as Reggie's trash truck. As Dusty pulled up and shut off the ignition, he just stared at the Explorer.

"What's your mother doing here?" Maureen asked.

"I don't know." Dusty opened his door and stepped out.

The moon hung, nearly full, over the canyon walls. The pewter gleam seemed to set the world afire.

Maureen zipped up her coat and cast a nervous glance at Dusty. What was running through his head?

He pulled a flashlight and his big Smith & Wesson revolver from under the driver's seat. He shoved the pistol down into the back of his jeans, then walked over to Ruth Ann's Explorer. With his hand he wiped some of the frozen mud and dust from the rear window and shone the light into the back.

"What are you looking for?"

"Bodies."

He stepped over to the first Park Service truck, opened the door, and reached for the coffee cup sitting on the dash. "Warm. Rupert hasn't been gone long. Come on."

"This is Rupert's truck?"

"Yes. The other truck is Maggie's."

"How do you know?" They looked identical to her.

"I just know, okay?"

Maureen now terrified, followed along behind him, aware of the darkness, the cold, and the silence of Chaco Canyon at night. Her heart beat a staccato in her chest. She kept sniffing the clear cold air, as if for a hint of Shon-dowekowa's foul breath.

"Dusty? Damn it, you're scaring me."

"Yeah," he said. "I'm scaring me, too."

After a second, he told her, "If anything happens, Maureen, promise me that you'll run straight back to the Bronco and get out of here."

"I will, but it would help if you'd tell me what you're afraid might happen."

"The same thing that happened almost forty years ago."

The electric feeling pounded with her blood. She'd never heard such fear in his voice. "Which is?"

"I'm not sure yet. A ritual. Something about witching souls."

They had passed Tseh So and started up the trail toward Casa Rinconada. The only sound was the gravel under their boots and the faint rasping of their clothing.

Dusty whispered, "I can't believe this. This is a nightmare."

"What?" Maureen asked.

"Rupert and my mother," Dusty said, voice husky.

Maureen's boot slipped off a rock in the dark trail, and she stumbled sideways before she caught her balance. "You think Rupert and your mother—"

"I think she's the woman he loved with all his heart. The woman he lost to another man."

They scrambled up the incline and Dusty shone the flashlight down into the great kiva. There, in the hollow stone box that once supported the foot drum, a bound figure looked up, eyes slitted against the light.

"Maggie?" Maureen called. Duct tape made a gray smear across her mouth. Maggie struggled to scream and thrashed back and forth against the foot drum.

On the kiva floor stood a wooden box, beautifully painted, measuring about two feet square. Inside were quart-size glass jars filled with different colors of sand, some with their lids removed. In the center of the kiva, a painting spread across the floor, the image indistinct, unfinished.

Dusty wheeled, flashing the light around, its beam revealing nothing but rabbitbrush and chamisa, though the brush could have hidden anyone.

"Come on"—Maureen tugged at him—"we have to cut her loose and call Nichols."

"Where's my mother?" Dusty flashed the light toward the low ridge to the south. "Oh, my god. Is that firelight? You don't think he already has her up there, do you? In the witch kiva?"

Maureen grabbed his arm. "One thing at a time. Let's turn Maggie loose, call Nichols, then we'll go up there and look."

They hurried for the southern stairway that led down into the great kiva. Maureen climbed down, ducked the lintel, and stepped out onto the dirt floor. She ran to Maggie and started untying the ropes on her hands.

Low laughter echoed from the kiva walls, as if issuing from the niches themselves, and a deep voice boomed, *"Get away from her!"*

Maureen whirled, eyes following the wavering flashlight as Dusty played the beam back and forth.

"Rupert!" Dusty cried where he stood over Maggie. "It's over!"

More laughter rolled down as if from the star-filled sky, and the voice sounded muffled, somehow inhuman. "Circles come full."

"Where's my mother?" He flashed his light up at the kiva rim. But no figure could be seen.

Maggie was shouting against the tape. Dusty paused in his search and reached down to pull it off.

"Don't!" the shout echoed. "If you do, I'll shoot you dead, Dusty. And her, too. The end of it all. Over with. Dale's seed dies here, where it was planted."

Maureen's blood ran cold. Even now he could be drawing a bead, centering a bullet on the middle of her back. She started to shake.

"Put the flashlight down, Dusty!" The hollow voice echoed around the kiva.

When Dusty continued to hold it, a gun cracked and the hearth burst into flame as though previously soaked in gasoline.

"Rupert, for God's sake!" Dusty threw the flashlight down. He stood defiantly beside Maggie, one arm up to shield his face from the heat of the roaring fire, while the other hand reached behind him for his own gun. "Let's talk! You're like a father to me. We could always talk!"

A figure moved on the kiva rim twelve feet above Maureen's head. He stood there, illuminated by the fire-light, a tall man, wearing what appeared to be an ancient wolf mask, the leather worn and cracked. Matted gray fur still clung to the collar. The eyes—irregular round holes—seemed possessed. The muzzle had been sewn on, the teeth, perhaps real, had cracked, and now hung by threads. The thing might have been brittle and antique, but it projected a menace that froze Maureen's soul. She could feel it, as though an ancient evil stalked the kiva around her.

"I am Kwewur," the man slurred the words and weaved on his feet. "I am reborn!"

Maureen could see that something was wrong with him. Drunk? Drugged? That's why the voice didn't sound quite right.

"Come on, Rupert. You don't have to do this. I know about the cancer! Let me help you! I've known you all of my life. That's got to count for something. We can make this work."

"You know nothing!" The wolf figure raised a small black pistol and aimed it at Dusty's chest.

Dusty spread his arms wide, and Maureen saw a swallow go down his throat.

In a reasonable voice, Dusty said, "Agent Nichols knows all about this, Rupert. He knows how much you loved my mother. How you wrote to her for years after she left you. He knows about h-how you were attacked by the dead witch after you potted the site up the hill. I'm sure you probably started studying witchcraft to defend yourself. Nichols knows you hired Reggie to steal the diaries. He-he—"

Dusty stuttered as though frantically putting facts together but not knowing the proper order. "They'll make him talk, you know, and Reggie will roll for them. Yeah, you were here that day, with us, but you damn well knew that Reggie had plenty of time to go in and take the diaries. Damn, you didn't even know they existed until you rode out here with us and saw the one in the backseat. So, you called Reggie and, piece of cake, he used Dale's keys, taken off his body, to drive up, open the front door, pack up the journals, and walk out."

"Nichols knows nothing," Kwewur slurred.

"Sure he does. Your name is on the park rolls. You were working here thirty-seven years ago. You were potting sites at night. Is that where you found the mask? Up the ridge? In the witch kiva? Let me guess, that's what was in the niche where you left the beer can and the cigarettes. What a sight that must have been. Two witches laid out on the floor, and a wolf mask in an old painted box in the wall crypt. Dale had a suspicion, didn't he? That's why he rode up Tsegi Canyon, and why he wouldn't let me come. He was afraid the Wolf Witch would be someone he knew."

"He deserved to die." The wolf extended the pistol again.

Dusty hesitated. "Why?"

"He took everything!"

"And Hawsworth? What did he do?"

"He *stole!* He—he stole my *secrets*...my *woman!*"

Maureen's heart thundered in her chest.

Carter and his witch. Hawsworth had been learning about witchcraft from Rupert.

Maureen edged toward the stairs.

The wolf cast a sharp look in her direction. "Don't try it, Dr. Cole."

Maureen moved back to Maggie and propped her hand on the stone foot drum near Maggie's face.

Dusty's voice broke. "For God's sake, what will this solve? Those things happened almost forty years ago!"

The wolf head tilted back, and the black eye holes looked like deep dark caverns. "Dale and Hawsworth took everything from me! They *humiliated* me. I loved her with all my heart! I wrote her a hundred letters begging her to come back. I knew someday I'd pay them back for what they did to me! That's when I started learning to be a witch. Two crazy old women over at Zuni taught me. And then the cancer...out of time. I'm out of time."

Dusty slowly walked toward the rim where the Wolf Witch stood. "Rupert, please listen to me. I know—"

"You don't know!" the man sobbed suddenly and choked it back. "I wouldn't be dying if it wasn't for your mother! She's the one who wanted to pot that kiva. Don't you understand? When I touched those old witches, took the basilisk from the skeleton's chest, the evil entered me. Your—your mother...she knew what I was, who I was becoming. She's the one who told me to take the box with Kwewur's mask! She was there at the birth of it all."

He desperately sucked in a breath as though his lungs were starving. "And then, just a few days later, I found them. Here! I heard them."

Rupert silently moved around the rim. The wolf mask bobbed, and the teeth flashed in the firelight. "There they were. Dale Robertson, my good friend, naked, screwing the woman I loved. Right there!"

He pointed with the pistol to the partially finished sand painting.

"I was heartbroken. How could anyone have done that? She was screwing four men at once! I wasn't strong enough to punish them then. But I am now. I'm going to kill all of you. Everyone who ever hurt me. You will all die before I do, and then I—"

"Grandfather, no!"

The deep voice came from the darkness up the hill.

Rupert spun around and almost lost his footing. He staggered. "R-Reggie?"

Maureen reached down and quietly pulled the tape from Maggie's mouth and whispered, *"Stay down!"*

M aggie blinked. Power, something ancient and glistening, flowed around her. Maureen's silhouetted body wavered in the firelight, surrounded by silvery traces of light, like a laser show she'd seen once in Santa Fe.

Toloache. That's what Rupert had told her was in the orange drink he'd let her sip on the tailgate of his truck before he'd grabbed her and tied her up. *Toloache,* sacred datura, a plant loaded with alkaloids. Atropine was flooding her system. Spirit power, or a drug? Medicine Power or science? Indian or White? She felt her soul swell.

Reggie walked into the fire's glow with tears running down his cheeks. His black ponytail shone in the firelight. "Put down the gun, Grandfather."

Rupert regripped the pistol.

Reggie stepped closer. "I wish I'd known why you wanted me to steal those diaries. I thought they contained some tidbit on archaeology that you wanted. Grandfather, please don't do this. You're a good and kind man. You saved me, and I love you more than anything in the world. Don't do this!"

The gun in Rupert's hand shook. "Don't try to stop me, Grandson! You know they all deserve—"

"They do *not* deserve any of this!" Reggie roared; then his voice dropped to a whisper. "I'm sure you're right. The evil in that thing is what caused your cancer. You should have left it in the kiva crypt where you found it."

Rupert said, "Those two old witches at Zuni told me the mask would make me the most powerful witch alive. That I would be able to make people do anything I wished. And look!" He lifted a hand to the people in the firelit kiva below. "I summoned them here from all over the world, and they came!"

Reggie dared to take another step closer. When he did, Rupert aimed the pistol at Reggie's heart.

Maggie blinked, seeing them as though through glistening water.

Reggie slowly lifted his hands as though in surrender. In a very tender voice, Reggie said, "You think these people hurt you, Grandfather? Right now, this instant, you are hurting me far more than any of these people ever hurt you."

Reggie extended his hand. "Give me the gun. Let's stop this now before anyone else gets hurt."

From the darkness behind Reggie, another form emerged, tall, half stumbling. She wore a long camel-hair coat and had her hair drawn back in a ponytail. The silver conchos on her belt flashed in the fire's gleam.

Reggie spun at the sound of footsteps.

"Ruth, stay back!" he shouted. "I told you not to come here!"

Rupert stumbled, and his entire body began to shake. "No! No! How did she get out of the kiva?" He screamed insanely and clutched the pistol as though trying to keep hold of a living animal that wanted to be free. The gun seemed to be fighting his grip. "Help! Help me!"

"Oh, good Lord, what's happening?" Reggie yelled and ran forward.

The pistol bucked in Rupert's hand, the report loud. Beside Maggie, the foot drum fractured. Stone chips showered the kiva, falling, falling like many-colored feathers.

Maggie shivered, her soul half scared, half in awe of the flying chips.

Maureen hit the ground on her belly and crawled like a madwoman for the safety behind the foot drum.

"Rupert, for God's sake!" Dusty stood defiantly in the middle of the sand painting, one arm up while the other hand reached behind him, clawing for something Maggie couldn't see. "Nichols is on his way! You don't want to do this! They'll put you away forever."

Maureen's hands were working on the ropes at Maggie's feet. With a sudden rush of relief, Maggie heard Grandmother Slumber's voice.

"Don't worry. We are here, Granddaughter."

The ropes came loose around her ankles. Maureen? Or Grandmother Slumber?

Maggie climbed out of the foot drum and rose unsteadily to her feet. Her hands remained bound, but she didn't need her hands for this.

"Maggie, get down!" Maureen's voice hissed from that other world and into the one where Maggie now found herself.

"No," Aunt Hail's voice said from behind her other shoulder. *"We are all here, Niece. Together we are stronger than he is."*

"I am Kwewur!" Rupert proclaimed.

"His *name is Two Hearts,*" Aunt Sage's soft voice came from behind Maggie. *"Tell him!"*

"You lie!" Maggie shouted, feeling Sister Datura flowing through her tingling veins. "Your name is Two Hearts!"

The Wolf Witch stopped short, staring at her. The black pistol in his hands wavered, then shifted from Reggie to her.

"We are guarding you," Grandma Slumber assured. *"He cannot hurt you."*

Maggie staggered sideways and struggled to stay on her feet. "We are all here, Two Hearts. Come down here! Come talk to the dead!"

"Maggie!" Maureen shouted from the darkness. "For God's sake, get down!"

Dusty said, "Come on, Rupert. You don't have to do this. I know you've had a tough time, but let me help you!"

"You know nothing!" The wolf aimed his pistol at Dusty's chest.

"He knows everything!" Maggie said. She swayed on her feet as she stepped forward to stand beside Dusty.

The world spun, shifting and slipping around her. By force of will, she managed to slow it, stabilize it. Power built deep in her chest, ebbing and flowing. "Two Hearts, the dead are coming for you! Look, there, beside you. See them?"

Maggie watched as phantoms appeared out of the kiva walls, ghosts of images that barely trapped a reflection in the flickering firelight.

Kwewur cocked his head and glanced around him. "What—?"

"They're reaching for you!" Maggie shouted, and her knees went weak. She had to lock them to keep standing. Dusty's hand clamped her arm, steadying her.

"There's no one here!" Kwewur shouted back, and the wolf teeth in his mask clicked together as he whirled to look at Maggie again.

Maggie bent forward. A pounding rush of nausea overwhelmed her, *and she could see him.* His wiry gray hair and mustache glowed in the firelight. He wore his old, battered fedora. "Dale? Dale, thank God!"

Dusty's grip on her shoulder tightened, and Maggie was vaguely aware that his eyes had gone huge and wide.

She called, "Kwewur! Dale is right there. Right there *beside you!*"

Dale's voice filtered between the worlds like a mist: "I'm sorry, my old friend, but I can't let you do this."

Maggie didn't know if anyone else heard, but Kwewur turned, looked out at the night, and shrieked, "Who's there? Show yourself!"

"They've come for you!" Maggie shouted. "Look at them, all around you!"

Maggie's stomach heaved. She threw up, and threw up, until she couldn't catch her breath, and she saw the dead dancing in the firelight on the kiva rim. Her grandmother and aunts, young again, moving between the katchinas like wisps of white smoke.

From a great distance, Grandmother Slumber's voice said, *"We're proud of you, Magpie. We love you so much."*

Maggie's soul was coming loose, twining up and out of her body. She surrendered to hot wavelike caresses of Sister Datura's hands and collapsed onto the kiva floor, where her body began to twitch uncontrollably.

Rupert swung the pistol forward, aimed at Ruth and then Reggie, or maybe at the Spirits he saw. The black steel shook wildly in his hand.

"Oh, my god, what are you!" Rupert screamed. "Shadow Woman? Is that you?"

Dusty screamed, *"No!"* He was tugging at something behind him in his waistband. Then the long-barreled revolver was dragged free.

Maggie saw Reggie leap in front of Ruth just as Rupert's pistol cracked, and a blinding flash of yellow swallowed the night.

The next muzzle blast from Dusty's gun shook the world.

Dusty sprinted for the kiva stairway, his pistol clutched in his trembling hand. He took the stairs up two at a time. Moonlight and firelight did a macabre dance on the cliff to his right. The old gods dancing. He swerved around the circumference of the kiva and headed for Reggie.

Reggie lay on his side, his chest blasted open, his left arm protectively across Ruth Ann's waist. Rupert lay almost on top of them, sprawled on his back. The black pistol lay six inches beyond his curled fingers.

Dusty's shot had torn through his right lung. Blood bubbled at Rupert's lips.

Ruth Ann sat up, shoved Reggie's arm off her, and peered at Dusty with drugged blue eyes. As she straightened, her blouse, unbuttoned, fell open; a basilisk pendant swung on its string to rest on her breast. The malignant red eye glared at Dusty.

"Is he d-dead?" she stuttered in terror.

When Dusty shot a look at Rupert, it was to see the man's pain-glazed eyes fixed on Ruth Ann. "Shadow

Woman?" The words were half-choked on blood. "Is that...you?"

High above them, an owl circled in the moonlight. It hooted four times.

Rupert jerked. Frothy blood ran from his ruined lungs. He coughed and stared wide-eyed at the sky. *"Dale, don't...don't!"* His fingers crept toward the gun.

Dusty kicked the pistol away and looked up. But he saw only moonlight. Moonlight and glittering stars.

When he looked back, Rupert Brown was dead.

Stone Ghost had to squint into the late spring sunlight to see Browser as he walked out of Streambed Town. The War Chief's muscular shoulders bulged through the yellow fabric of his shirt. Spring light was painting the sandstone rims that hemmed Straight Path Canyon in hard buff colors. A faint trickle of water ran in the wash just behind the town. A new summer lay just around the corner.

Bone Walker squeezed Stone Ghost's hand, and he looked down at the little girl. Her unfocused eyes would forever remind him of Shadow Woman's as they'd stared up at him in death. They were the eyes of an animal, huge and black, and empty. Bone Walker hadn't spoken a word in six moons, but he kept talking to her anyway, talking and telling stories, hoping that someday she would peek out of that black inner hole where she had locked her breath-heart soul and say something.

"Browser looks rested, doesn't he?" he asked Bone Walker. "It's all the new people flooding in. He doesn't have to stand guard as often now as he used to."

All morning long, Stone Ghost had been thinking

about what had happened at Owl House. Even after six long moons had passed, he could not get the images out of his mind. They had set the kiva afire. When the roof had burned through on the south, it had hinged and fallen in. A shower of sparks had twirled into the night sky. Had they carried the evil souls of Two Hearts and Shadow Woman off into the darkness?

White Cone sat in the sun at the base of the new tri-walled Kiva of the Worlds they'd built.

As Stone Ghost passed, he said, "Greetings, Bow Elder."

White Cone lifted a hand to shield his eyes from Father Sun's glare. Wispy white hair framed his thin face. "A pleasant morning to you, Stone Ghost. Are you ready to head south? I've been thinking of the perfect place for us. On the western side of the mountains. Where the rivers head before winding down toward the Hohokam lands."

Stone Ghost didn't answer for a time. There was a task he had to take care of before he could allow himself to rest. Somewhere out there, perhaps still in the rock shelter near Longtail village, a desiccated mummy lay on her side in the dirt. It was his duty to find Night Sun and give her a proper burial. Her soul had wandered the earth alone for long enough.

Stone Ghost nodded to White Cone and said, "As soon as Matron Cloudblower gives the order, the Katsinas' People will be on their way."

They shared a smile, and White Cone leaned his aged head back against the wall and closed his eyes. He seemed to be enjoying the spring sunshine on his wrinkled face.

Stone Ghost continued on toward Browser.

Just before their paths crossed, Browser lifted his gaze to the cliff where his wife, Catkin, stood guard. She was tall and beautiful, and her shoulder-length hair blew in the breeze. They were expecting their first child in four moons.

"How are you feeling, Uncle?" Browser asked as Stone Ghost and the little girl came closer.

"Alive," Stone Ghost said with a sigh. "And you, Nephew?"

"Better."

The pain and fear of that terrible day at Owl House had bound them like thongs of dried rawhide. The power of the White Moccasins had been damaged, but not broken. First People had begun to emerge from almost every village to join the White Moccasins. Their attacks on isolated villages had become brutal, inhuman, and frequent. So had the retaliatory raids. To Browser's horror, Matron Crossbill's people had split off, and began raiding Flute Player villages in the north.

But as the warfare escalated, the Katsinas' People grew. Fully one-third of Blue Corn's Flowing Waters Town's people had converted. It seemed that what Flame Carrier's search for the First People's kiva could not accomplish, a Mogollon prophet's death did. The Katsinas' People would survive. Poor Singer's prophecy would live—and somewhere in the future, the katsinas would dance with the old gods.

"I've been thinking about Owl House all morning, Nephew. I've never had a chance to ask how you knew that Rain Crow had been working with Horned Ram?"

"I first suspected him the night the prophet was killed. But when Rain Crow insisted on coming with us, I was positive. Neither he nor Horned Ram knew they were working for the First People when they allowed Shadow access to Gray Thunder's room. It must have shocked Rain Crow to see Obsidian in the kiva, having just seen her twin sister murder Acorn and Gray Thunder."

"Why did he do it?"

"That I cannot answer. I suspect that our defense of the Mogollon made Rain Crow suspicious. Then the reaction of his people to Gray Thunder's death, the prophet's instant popularity and the sudden interest in Poor Singer's prophecy, coupled with Acorn's death, left him uneasy. Since nothing was working the way it was supposed to, Rain Crow knew that he had been used. I think he came here to find out who had turned him into a puppet and who had killed his nephew."

Stone Ghost searched his belt pouch, then extended his hand. "Here, Nephew. I took this from Two Hearts's hand before we left. I believe it belongs to you."

The blue stone seemed to radiate a heat all its own. Browser reached out. Stone Ghost laid the beautifully carved turquoise wolf onto his palm. Browser let out a sigh and clutched it to his heart.

Stone Ghost turned his attention to the long line of people coming down the road from the north. Too many people. They couldn't remain here. The soil was so played out, the rain and runoff so spotty, they couldn't feed this many in Straight Path Canyon.

But they couldn't go north. Over and over he'd heard the same stories from refugees. They said things were so bad in the Green Mesa country that most of the people had moved east to the Great River. It was hard to imagine, the cliff towns deserted, nothing but pack rats and yellow-jackets living there.

Stone Ghost shot a sidelong glance at Browser. "Cloudblower is worried."

"Worried?"

"Yes, another twenty people arrived this morning, mostly Flute Player Believers who came to see the heroes who killed the most feared witch in the land."

Browser smiled. "I thought you liked all those hands touching you."

Stone Ghost gave him a disgusted look. "They just keep coming, either to see me, or you, or to see if we really can live together, Made People, First People, Fire Dogs, and all the rest."

"That's the strength of the katsinas, Uncle."

He pointed to the tall round Kiva of the Worlds that stood behind Streambed Town. They had finished building it just yesterday. "I thought the dawn dedication was beautiful, with the pure white plaster and painted katsinas."

"Yes," Stone Ghost sighed, "but no opening appeared to the underworld, Nephew. I wonder—"

"Nor will it," White Cone called.

Stone Ghost turned back to look at the Mogollon elder. "What do you mean?"

"That's not what Poor Singer meant!"

Stone Ghost led Bone Walker back to where the old man basked in the sunlight. Browser followed. "Do you know what he meant? Did Gray Thunder tell you his vision?"

White Cone folded his arms across his drawn-up knees. "Gray Thunder always said that the truth is never hidden. It is always right there before our eyes. We are just blind."

Stone Ghost grunted as he lowered himself to a rock beside White Cone. Bone Walker climbed into his lap and leaned her head against his bony old chest. Stone Ghost patted her back gently.

Life moved, as inconstant and fickle as Wind Baby, frolicking, sleeping, weeping, but never truly still. Never solid or finished. Always like water flowing from one place to the next. Seed and fruit. Rain and drought, everything traveled in a gigantic circle, an eternal process of becoming something new. But we rarely saw it. Humans tended to see only frozen moments, not the flow of things. Is that what White Cone meant about being blind?

"What did he tell you?" Stone Ghost asked.

Browser moved to stand behind Stone Ghost, listening. The fringe on the bottom of his yellow shirt danced in the wind.

White Cone smiled. "When Poor Singer said that you had to find the First People's original kiva, he did not mean the hole where they emerged from the underworlds in the Beginning Time."

"But he said we had to reopen the doorway to the Land of the Dead," Browser said and propped a hand on his belted war club. "What else could he have meant?"

"The doorway to the dead is not a physical hole in the earth, you young fool. If you wish to seek the advice of the dead you must have the heart of a cloud."

Bone Walker's fists twined in Stone Ghost's shirt. He lifted a hand to silence White Cone and looked down.

Bone Walker's lips moved, but no sound came out.

Very softly, so as not to frighten her, he said, "What is it, Bone Walker?"

She seemed to be struggling to find words. "Tears..." she whispered. "You have to live inside the tears of the dead."

Browser's face slackened and White Cone smiled.

Stone Ghost hugged Bone Walker tightly against him, and she tucked her head against his chest.

Stone Ghost's heart swelled until he feared it might explode. He kissed the top of the little girl's head and said, "I told you, didn't I, that if you worked very hard someday, you would be a great Singer."

Bone Walker smiled. A little girl's smile, frail and heartwarming. She looked up with sparkling eyes and focused on the cliff where Catkin stood. She stared hard for a time.

Finally, she said, *"He's* going to be a really great Singer."

"Who is?" Browser asked, looking up at Catkin and frowning.

Bone Walker sucked her lip for several instants, then whispered, *"That little boy in her belly."*

Dusty walked into the candlelit church and looked around. The place was quiet and empty except for one person: Maggie knelt in the second pew, her hands clasped prayerfully before her. Her gaze rested on the crucifix on the wall.

He walked forward, the paper bag crackling in his right hand, and slid into the pew beside her. The church smelled of melted wax and incense, things he found oddly comforting.

Maggie turned to look at him. Her eyes were swollen, and grief strained the lines around her mouth. She wore a white scarf over her black hair, knotted beneath her chin.

"You're not a churchgoing person," Maggie whispered. "What are you doing here?"

"I thought I'd surprise God."

Maggie smiled. "Speaking of God, how are you doing with the owl?"

Dusty gave her a startled look. "How do you know about the owl?"

"I talked to Sylvia this morning. She said you'd been

sleeping with your pistol because the owl follows you everywhere you go."

Dusty turned sideways to face her and propped his arm on the pew ahead. "It's the strangest thing. The owl kept me up, hooting outside my window when I was sleeping in my trailer in Santa Fe. So I moved to Dale's house, and he showed up there. Perched right on the kitchen windowsill and watched me eat breakfast. Gave me the heebie-jeebies."

Maggie let out a disappointed breath. "When a Spirit Helper comes fluttering at your window, you don't close it, Dusty. You open it as wide as you can."

Dusty made a face. He knew that. It was just hard to do in real life. He gripped the smooth wood of the pew and lifted his brows. "Yeah, well, I'm working on it."

They sat in silence for a moment, and Dusty absorbed the calm golden glow of the church.

"How are you doing, Maggie? Are you all right?"

"As well as can be expected after the things that have happened." She glanced at him. "I saw it all, Dusty. I was hovering there, above my body, and I saw you and Maureen and Reggie and Rupert." Her brow furrowed.

"Is that a problem?"

Her brown eyes pleaded with him. "I think the datura did something to me. I keep seeing between the worlds, and I know"—she swallowed hard—"that datura overdoses can cause insanity."

Dusty laughed, handing her the sack. "You're not insane yet, old friend. Of course, it's inevitable. Working for the government is bound to get to you sooner or later." He pointed to the sack. "That's in return for the fry bread you brought me that day. Those are my own special recipe super black bean burritos."

Maggie clasped her hands on the sack and squeezed it hard as though fighting grief. "Aunt Sage used to say that if you wanted to understand death, you had to have the heart of a cloud."

"Hmm," Dusty grunted. "Which meant what?"

Tears filled Maggie's eyes, but she smiled. "That you had to live inside the tears of the dead."

Dusty sank back into the pew and looked up at the crucifix. Jesus's body was emaciated, his face anguished. But his painted eyes seemed to be alive and looking at Dusty with a kind of curious benevolence.

Dusty held that gaze for a long time. It hadn't occurred to him before, but that's what archaeology was all about.

Living inside the tears of the dead so we can learn from them.

"Maggie? We have one more thing to do, that is, if you're up to it."

|||||||||||||||||||||||||||||||||||

Epilogue

Dusty sat on the kitchen counter in his Santa Fe trailer, his feet, clad in Nacona boots dangling. He sipped a bottle of Guinness while he listened to his mother.

Maureen and Maggie sat at the table across from Ruth Ann. Maureen had worn her long hair loose, combed to a rich sheen. Her white sweater did nice things to Dusty's imagination. Maggie had a strangely serene expression. A small cedar box sat on the table before her. On the couch, Yvette watched them through wary eyes. Over the last couple of weeks, Dusty and Yvette had come to share a warm but curious sort of relationship.

"Rupert said that we needed to talk, that he'd meet me at Casa Rinconada at nightfall." Ruth Ann propped her fists on the table. Her black cashmere sweater accented her silver hair. "I assumed he wished to tell me something about Dale's murder."

"You weren't afraid he was the murderer?" Maureen sipped a cup of coffee.

"God no. Why would I be? For years he wrote me love letters. I mean, hell, what would it hurt to see him again?"

Ruth Ann laced her fingers together primly on the table, intent on her story. "We had taken a walk up to the site you now call Owl House. We were sitting there, looking down into that kiva, and Rupert handed me a candy."

She smiled. "Hell, it was like old times. It was the sixties. Rupert and I used to go up on hilltops, drop a little acid, and watch the sun go down."

"You knew it was LSD?" Dusty asked.

"What do you think I am? A blessed virgin? Of course, I knew. I'm telling you the same thing I told your friend, Agent Nichols, in my formal statement."

"So you went down into the kiva?" Maureen asked, disbelief in her voice. "Knowing that Dale and Hawsworth had been murdered there?"

"In my state of mind, what did I care? Rupert and I pulled the tarp back and built a fire in that old hearth," Ruth Ann whispered, seeing it all again, "and I swear something happened. Firelight in that hearth for the first time in over seven hundred years, flickering on those little pieces of bone and those two skeletons. We talked of old times, of things Rupert and I had done, of things Dale and Sam and I did, and people we both knew. Rupert asked me if I had it to do all over again, would I? I said, 'God, yes. I'd sell my soul to be twenty-five again.'"

Ruth Ann paused, a gleam in her eyes. "That's when he tied me up, put on the wolf mask, and left."

Dusty contemplatively scratched off part of the label on his Guinness bottle. "It didn't occur to you that he was Kwewur?"

"No. Why would it? He sure as hell hadn't made any threatening gestures."

Yvette made a disgusted sound deep in her throat, and Ruth Ann glared at her.

"So, you just sat there?" Dusty demanded to know.

"While he turned Casa Rinconada upside down trying to kill us?"

"Have you ever done acid, William?"

"No."

"Well, you can just sit. It's wonderful." Ruth Ann smiled beatifically. "And I sat, feeling the nightfall, talking to that young woman and the old man. The light was flickering on their bones. It was quite pleasant."

"What about the gunshots?"

She spread her hands. "They were katchinas clapping their hands, making thunder in the night. You know, a mystical experience. I could have sat there until dawn, just me and those two people."

She gave Dusty a scathing glance. "I *would* have sat there if Reggie hadn't dragged me out of that kiva and untied me. He said he'd been working late and saw his grandfather's truck parked in the lot beside Maggie's and mine. He'd stopped to check on things, make sure everybody was all right, and that's when he saw the firelight coming from that old kiva." She twisted her hands on the table, and regret tightened the corners of her mouth. "I wish I'd known why he told me to stay put. I would have."

"But you didn't. You wandered down the hill to Casa Rinconada," Dusty said.

"Oh, come on, William. How was I to know I'd be walking into a maelstrom?"

Dusty ran his thumb down the side of his Guinness bottle. It felt cool and damp. He was so tired, he didn't have the strength to hate her. But he would always wonder what would have happened if she hadn't come walking in out of the night. Would Reggie have been able to talk Rupert out of the gun?

"Did those people tell you who they were?" Yvette asked. "The dead ones?"

"Just a man and his wife." Ruth Ann sighed contentedly. "Delightful people raising a family. She had several children by him. It was his second marriage. His first wife was killed in a fall. From the cliffs just south of Rinconada. It was icy."

Maureen arched an eyebrow as she met Dusty's glance. But it was Yvette who looked ready to reach out and strangle Ruth Ann.

"And that's it. That's my statement." Ruth Ann clapped her hands together. "Agent Nichols, after giving me a lecture about the use of controlled substances, has allowed me to plead guilty to a narcotics charge, a charge of criminal trespass, and a couple of misdemeanors. For that, I get two years of probation to be administered in Boston."

Dusty had no idea what was going to happen to him. Nichols hadn't arrested him. All the witnesses had said it was self-defense. But he'd killed his best friend's father. No matter what the courts did to him, it couldn't possibly be as bad as what Dusty was going to do to himself over the next forty years.

Dusty squinted at his half-peeled label. "But you'd never been there before? In the witch kiva, I mean?"

"No. Why?" Ruth Ann fixed hard blue eyes on his.

Dusty reached across the counter. He handed the photograph to his mother. "I came across this in Dale's file cabinet while we were replacing the journals recovered from Reggie's apartment."

Ruth Ann took it and looked at it with expressionless eyes. "I remember this. The barbecue in Dale's backyard. God, let's see. Sixty-six, maybe? We had a sitter for little William. Sam and I were out for a night of big-city living. I ended up passed out on Dale's couch. My god, doesn't Rupert look young and handsome." She tossed the photo back to Dusty. "What's your point?"

Dusty lifted the photo. "When did you give up smoking?"

"Early seventies." Ruth Ann cocked her head as though trying to fathom his meaning.

Dusty took a deep breath. "In the picture, Rupert is smoking Lucky Strikes."

Ruth Ann shrugged, but she appeared uncomfortable. "Yes, so? He always smoked Lucky Strikes."

Dusty frowned. "You told me once you liked to get the good stuff fast. You and Rupert opened that site together, didn't you? You rolled the slabs off the witches, and Rupert took the wolf mask. That was your pack of cigarettes and maybe even your beer can stuffed into the wall crypt. What did you do? Screw him in there, too? Right in front of the mask? In front of those skeletons?"

She watched him from the corner of her eye, thinking, calculating what he could know. After a long pause, she said, "What if I did, William? Are you going to run back to Agent Nichols and have him add antiquities violations to my rap sheet?"

"You were the one who put Hawsworth together with Rupert, weren't you?" Maureen asked. "'Carter and his witch,' you said at the Loretto that day. But you'd been doing a little studying on your own. After all, you'd been there."

Ruth Ann smiled coldly. "Finding a witch was a rush. So I tried witchcraft. It didn't work. What was the point of sticking with it?"

"What did you do to Dale? Did you use witchcraft to get him to Casa Rinconada that last time in sixty-nine? We read the journal yesterday. He drove out there to tell you that he never wanted to see you again. That he thought you were killing Sam. Dale even called you a witch in his diary. But the next day, the entry was: '*Dear*

God, what have I done? There she was, standing naked in the firelight. God, forgive me.'"

Ruth Ann lifted her hands in a gesture of innocence. "Is it my fault that he couldn't resist me? But for that night, Yvette wouldn't be here."

"Alas, Mum, I am," Yvette said as she straightened.

Ruth Ann gazed at her, looking bored. "Well, I should be going."

She started to rise.

"'Fraid not, Mum." Yvette raised her voice. "Magpie?"

Dusty was watching Ruth Ann's face as Maggie pushed the little cedar box across the table.

Maggie opened the box and said, "Let's have it, Dr. Sullivan."

"Have what?" Ruth Ann pulled away from the box.

"What you took from the female skeleton in Owl House," Maggie told her.

Dusty crossed his arms and said, "Hand it over."

"Hand what over?"

"The basilisk, Mum." Yvette sat up on the couch and shoved ash-blond hair behind her ears. "The one I saw in Dusty's trailer."

Maggie shoved the box closer, her eyes burning brilliantly, powered by an inner strength Dusty had never seen before. "Lift it off of your neck and drop it into the box."

"I will not!"

"Yes, you will," Dusty said. "That thing is filled with evil. Either the basilisk goes into the box, or you don't leave this place alive. Think about it."

Ruth Ann, for the first time, glanced fearfully around the room. "Oh, do be serious! You'd kill me for a silly pendant?"

Dusty slid off the counter and stood over her with his

fists clenched. "I don't want to rip it off your throat. But I will."

"Are you threatening me?"

"Dusty," Yvette said. "She's not going to cooperate, you may as well just kill her."

Ruth Ann met his eyes, saw the resolve, and wavered. "Oh, what the hell." She reached inside her blouse, lifted out the black stone pendant, and dropped it into the box.

Maggie snapped the box shut and reeled, as though in pain.

"What's the matter?" Dusty asked.

"You should have heard it," Maggie whispered hoarsely. "It screamed when it died."

Ruth Ann Sullivan looked from one person to the next, then shoved to her feet. "Well, if you're satisfied, William, I'm going." She marched for the door.

Maggie and Dusty stood side by side on the rickety porch watching Ruth Ann Sullivan walk to her rental car. When she drove off into the late fall evening, Dusty didn't even wave.

Reentering, Maggie lifted the box from the table and shook it. "Do you think *el basilisco* had any inkling that Ruth Ann would drop him into a mirror-lined box?"

Dusty leaned heavily against the door frame. "Thank God, it's over."

From the couch, Yvette asked, "Is it? What happened to the mask?"

Dusty turned to look at her. He remembered the feel of the wolf mask, warm and tingly, as though it were alive and breathing on his hands. "I threw it in the fire at Casa Rinconada. I'd swear, as it burned, I saw the Shiwana dancing in the shadows it cast on the kiva walls."

Yvette rose to her feet and stretched. "Well, that's enough spooky stuff for me. Good night, all. I'm off to my hotel for a real night's rest. I'll see you in the morning. *Huevos* at eight, right?"

"Right. Good night, Yvette," Dusty said.

"I'm out of here, too." Maggie clutched the cedar box. "I think I might drive by the Rio Grande bridge west of Taos. It's a long way down to the rocks below."

"Take care," Maureen said.

Maggie smiled and walked to her pickup.

As Maggie's truck wound its way up the driveway to Canyon Road, Dusty's stomach muscles suddenly clenched. He bent double and couldn't seem to catch his breath.

"What is it? What's wrong?" Maureen asked as she rushed to his side.

Dusty held up a hand, walked to the table, and eased down. All of the fear and desperation had seeped out of him, leaving a hollow shell. He started trembling for no reason.

"My god," he whispered as he dropped his face in his hands. "Dale is dead, Maureen. Dale is dead."

Maureen inhaled a deep breath. She didn't speak for a time.

Finally, she said, "But we're alive, Dusty. Let's see if we can find the future together."

Bibliography

Acatos, Sylvio. *Pueblos: Prehistoric Indian Cultures of the Southwest.* Translation of 1989 edition of *Die Pueblos.* New York: Facts on File, 1990.

Adams, E. Charles. *The Origin and Development of the Pueblo Katsina Cult.* Tucson: University of Arizona Press, 1991.

Adler, Michael A. *The Prehistoric Pueblo World* A.D. 1150-1350. Tucson: University of Arizona Press, 1996.

Allen, Paula Gunn. *Spider Woman's Granddaughters.* New York: Ballantine Books, 1989.

Arnberger, Leslie P. *Flowers of the Southwest Mountains.* Tucson, Arizona: Southwest Parks and Monuments Association, 1982.

Aufderheide, Arthur C. *The Cambridge Encyclopedia of Human Paleopathology.* Cambridge: Cambridge University Press, 1998.

Baars, Donald L. *Navajo Country: A Geological and Natural History of the Four Corners Region.* Albuquerque: University of New Mexico Press, 1995.

Becket, Patrick H., ed. *Mogollon V.* Report of Fifth Mogollon Conference. Las Cruces, New Mexico: COAS Publishing and Research, 1991.

Boissiere, Robert. *The Return of Pahana: A Hopi Myth.* Santa Fe, New Mexico: Bear & Company Publishing, 1990.

Bowers, Janice Emily. *Shrubs and Trees of the Southwest Deserts.* Tucson, Arizona: Southwest Parks and Monuments Association, 1993.

Brody, J. J. *The Anasazi.* New York: Rizzoli International Publications, 1990.

Brothwell, Don, and A. T. Sandison. *Diseases in Antiquity.* Springfield, Ill.: Charles C. Thomas Publisher, 1967.

Bunzel, Ruth L. *Zuni Katcinas.* Reprint of Forty-seventh Annual Report of the Bureau of American Ethnography, 1929-1930. Glorietta, New Mexico: Rio Grande Press, 1984.

Colton, Harold S. *Black Sand: Prehistory in Northern Arizona.* Albuquerque: University of New Mexico Press, I960.

Cordell, Linda S. "Predicting Site Abandonment at Wetherill Mesa." *The Kiva* (1975) 40(3): 189-202.

---.*Prehistory of the Southwest.* New York: Academic Press, 1984.

---.*Ancient Pueblo Peoples.* Smithsonian Exploring the Ancient World

Series. Montreal: St. Remy Press; and Washington, D.C.: Smithsonian Institution, 1994.

Cordell, Linda S., and George J. Gumerman, eds. *Dynamics of Southwest Prehistory.* Washington, D.C.: Smithsonian Institution Press, 1989.

Crown, Patricia, and W. James Judge, eds. *Chaco and Hohokam: Prehistoric Regional Systems in the American Southwest.* Santa Fe, New Mexico: School of American Research Press, 1991.

Cummings, Linda Scott. "Anasazi Subsistence Activity Areas Reflected in the Pollen Records." Paper presented to the Society for American Archaeology Meetings. New Orleans, 1986.

--."Anasazi Diet: Variety in the Hoy House and Lion House Coprolite Record and Nutritional Analysis," in *Paleonutrition: The Diet and Health of Prehistoric Americans.* Southern-Illinois University at Carbondale, Occasional Paper No. 22, Sobolik, ed., 1994.

Dodge, Natt N. *Flowers of the Southwest Deserts.* Tucson, Arizona: Southwest Parks and Monument Association, 1985.

Dooling, D. M., and Paul Jordan-Smith, eds. *I Become Part of It: Sacred Dimensions in Native American Life.* San Francisco: A Parabola Book, Harper; New York: HarperCollins Publishers, 1989.

Douglas, John E. "Autonomy and Regional Systems in the Late Prehistoric Southern Southwest." *American Antiquity* 60:240-257, 1995.

Downum, Christian E. *Between Desert and River: Hohokam Settlement and Land Use in the Los Robles Community.* Anthropological Papers of the University of Arizona. Tucson: University of Arizona Press, 1993.

Dunmire, William W., and Gail Tierney. *Wild Plants of the Pueblo Province: Exploring Ancient and Enduring Uses.* Santa Fe: Museum of New Mexico Press, 1995.

Ellis, Florence Hawley. "Patterns of Aggression and the War Cult in Southwestern Pueblos." *Southwestern Journal of Anthropology* 7:177-201, 1951.

Elmore, Francis H. *Shrubs and Trees of the Southwest Uplands.* Tucson, Arizona: Southwest Parks and Monuments Association, 1976.

Ericson, Jonathan E., and Timothy G. Baugh, eds. *The American Southwest and Mesoamerica: Systems of Prehistoric Exchange.* New York: Plenum Press, 1991.

Fagan, Brian M. *Ancient North America.* New York: Thames and Hudson, 1991.

Farmer, Malcom F. "A Suggested Typology of Defensive Systems of the Southwest." *Southwestern Journal of Archaeology* 13:249-266, 1957.

Fewkes, J. Walter, and J. J. Brody, eds. *The Mimbres: Art and Archaeology.* Albuquerque, New Mexico: Avanyu Publishing, 1989.

Fish, Suzanne, K., Paul Fish, and John H. Madsen, eds. *The Marana Community in the Hohokam World.* Anthropological Papers of the University of Arizona, No. 56. Tucson: University of Arizona Press, 1992.

Frank, Larry, and Francis H. Harlow. *Historic Pottery of the Pueblo Indians: 1600-1880.* West Chester, Pennsylvania: Schiffler Publishing, 1990.

Frazier, Kendrick. *People of Chaco: A Canyon and Its Culture.* New York: W.W. Norton & Co., 1986.

Gabriel, Kathryn. *Roads to Center Place: A Cultural Atlas of Chaco Canyon and the Anasazi.* Boulder, Colorado: Johnson Books, 1991.

Gumerman, George J., ed. *The Anasazi in a Changing Environment.* New York: School of American Research, Cambridge University Press, 1988.

---.*Exploring the Hohokam: Prehistoric Peoples of the American Southwest.* Albuquerque: Amerind Foundation; University of New Mexico Press, 1991.

---.*Themes in Southwest Prehistory.* Santa Fe, New Mexico: School of American Research Press, 1994.

Haas, Jonathan. "Warfare and the Evolution of Tribal Politics in the Prehistoric Southwest," in *The Anthropology of War,* Jonathan Haas, ed. Cambridge, U.K.: Cambridge University Press, 1990.

Haas, Jonathan, and Winifred Creamer. "A History of Pueblo Warfare." Paper Presented at the 60th Annual Meeting for the Society of American Archaeology. Minneapolis, 1995.

---.*Stress and Warfare Among the Kayenta Anasazi of the Thirteenth Century A.D.* Chicago: Field Museum of Natural History, 1993.

Haury, Emil. *Mogollon Culture in the Forestdale Valley, East-Central Arizona.* Tucson: University of Arizona Press, 1985.

Hayes, Alden C, David M. Burgge, and W. James Judge. *Archaeological Surveys of Chaco Canyon, New Mexico.* Reprint of National Park Service Report. Albuquerque: University of New Mexico Press, 1981.

Hultkrantz, Ake. *Native Religions: The Power of Visions and Fertility.* New York: Harper & Row, 1987.

Jacobs, Sue-Ellen. "Continuity and Change in Gender Roles at San Juan Pueblo," in *Women and Power in Native North America.* Norman, Oklahoma: University of Oklahoma Press, 1995.

Jernigan, E. Wesley. *Jewelry of the Prehistoric Southwest.* Albuquerque: School of American Research; University of New Mexico Press, 1978.

Jett, Stephen C. "Pueblo Indian Migrations: An Evaluation of the Possible Physical and Cultural Determinants." *American Antiquity* 29:281-300, 1964.

Komarek, Susan. *Flora of the San Juans: A Field Guide to the Mountain Plants of Southwestern. Colorado.* Durango, Colorado: Kivaki Press, 1994.

Lange, Frederick, Nancy Mahaney, Joe Ben Wheat, Mark L. Chenault, and John Carter. *Yellow Jacket: A Four Corners Anasazi Ceremonial Center.* Boulder, Colorado: Johnson Books, 1988.

LeBlanc, Steven A. *Prehistoric Warfare in the American Southwest.* University of Utah Press, Salt Lake City, 1999.

Lekson, Stephen H. *Mimbres Archaeology of the Upper Gila, New Mexico.* Anthropological papers of the University of Arizona, No. 53. Tucson: University of Arizona Press, 1990.

Lekson, Stephen, Thomas C. Windes, John R. Stein, and W. James Judge. "The Chaco Canyon Community" *Scientific American* 259(1): 100-109, 1988.

Lewis, Dorothy Otnow. *Guilty by Reason of Insanity. A Psychiatrist Explores the Minds of Killers.* New York: The Ballantine Publishing Group, 1998.

Lipe, W. D., and Michelle Hegemon, eds. *The Architecture of Social Integration in Prehistoric Pueblos.* Occasional Papers of the Crow Canyon Archaeological Center No. 1. Cortez, Colorado: Crow Canyon Archaeological Center, 1989.

Lister, Florence C. *In the Shadow of the Rocks: Archaeology of the Chimney Rock District in Southern Colorado.* Niwot, Colorado: University Press of Colorado, 1993.

Lister, Robert H., and Florence C. Lister. *Chaco Canyon.* Albuquerque: University of New Mexico Press, 1981.

Lomatuway'ma, Michael, Lorena Lomatuway'ma, and Sidney Namingha, Jr. *Hopi Ruin Legends.* Edited by Ekkehart Malotki. Lincoln: Published for Northern Arizona University by University of Nebraska Press, L993.

Malotki, Ekkehart. *Gullible Coyote: Una'ihu: A Bilingual Collection of Hopi Coyote Stories.* Tucson: University of Arizona Press, 1985.

Malotki, Ekkehart, and Michael Lomatuway'ma. *Maasaw: Profile of a Hopi God.* American Tribal Religions, Vol. XI; Lincoln: University of Nebraska Press, 1987.

Malville, J. McKimm, and Claudia Putman. *Prehistoric Astronomy in the Southwest.* Boulder, Colorado: Johnson Books, 1987.

Mann, Coramae Richey. *When Women Kill.* New York: State University of New York Press, 1996.

Martin, Debra L. "Lives Unlived: The Political Economy of Violence

Against Anasazi Women." Paper presented to the Society for American Archaeology 60th Annual Meetings. Minneapolis, 1995.

Martin, Debra L., Alan H. Goodman, George Armelagos, and Ann L. Magennis. *Black Mesa Anasazi Health: Reconstructing Life from Patterns of Death and Disease.* Occasional Paper No. 14. Carbondale, Illinois: Southern Illinois University, 1991.

Mayes, Vernon O., and Barbara Bayless Lacy. *Nanise: A Navajo Herbal.* Tsaile, Arizona: Navajo Community College Press, 1989.

McGuire, Randall H., and Michael Schiffer, eds. *Hohokam and Patayan: Prehistory of Southwestern Arizona.* New York: Academic Press, 1982.

McNitt, Frank. *Richard Wetherill Anasazi.* Albuquerque: University of New Mexico Press, 1996.

Minnis, Paul E., and Charles L. Redman, eds. *Perspectives on Southwestern Prehistory.* Boulder, Colorado: Westview Press, 1990.

Mullet, G. M. *Spider Woman Stories: Legends of the Hopi Indians.* Tucson, Arizona: University of Arizona Press, 1979.

Nabahan, Gary Paul. *Enduring Seeds: Native American Agriculture and Wild Plant Conservation.* San Francisco: North Point Press, 1989.

Noble, David Grant. *Ancient Ruins of the Southwest: An Archaeological Guide.* Flagstaff, Arizona: Northland Publishing, 1991.

Ortiz, Alfonzo, ed., *Handbook of North American Indians.* Washington, D.C.: Smithsonian Institution, 1983.

Palkovich, Ann M. *The Arroyo Hondo Skeletal and Mortuary Remains.* Arroyo Hondo Archaeological Series, Vol. 3. Santa Fe, New Mexico: School of American Research Press, 1980.

Parsons, Elsie Clews. *Tewa Tales,* reprint of 1924 edition. Tucson: University of Arizona Press, 1994.

Pepper, George H. *Pueblo Bonito,* reprint of 1920 edition. Albuquerque: University of New Mexico Press, 1996.

Pike, Donald G., and David Muench. *Anasazi: Ancient People of the Rock.* New York: Crown Publishers, 1974.

Reid, J. Jefferson, and David E. Doyel, eds. *Emil Haury's Prehistory of the American Southwest.* Tucson: University of Arizona Press, 1992.

Riley, Carroll L. *Rio del Norte: People of the Upper Rio Grande from the Earliest Times to the Pueblo Revolt.* Salt Lake City, Utah: University of Utah Press, 1995.

Rocek, Thomas R. "Sedentarization and Agricultural Dependence: Perspectives from the Pithouse-to-Pueblo Transition in the American Southwest." *American Antiquity* 60:218-239, 1995.

Schaafsma, Polly. *Indian Rock Art of the Southwest.* Albuquerque:

School of American Research; University of New Mexico Press, 1980.

Sebastian, Lynne. *The Chaco Anasazi: Sociopolitical Evolution in the Prehistoric Southwest.* Cambridge, U.K.: Cambridge University Press, 1992.

Simmons, MaTc. *Witchcraft in the Southwest.* Bison Books, reprint of 1974 edition. Lincoln: University of Nebraska Press, 1980.

Slifer, Dennis, and James Duffield. *Kokopelli: Flute Player Images in Rock Art.* Santa Fe, New Mexico: Ancient City Press, 1994.

Smith, Watson, with Raymond H. Thompson, ed. *When Is a Kiva: And Other Questions About Southwestern Archaeology.* Tucson: University of Arizona Press, 1990.

Sobolik, Kristin D. *Paleonutrition: The Diet and Health of Prehistoric Americans.* Occasional Paper No. 22. Carbondale: Center for Archaeological Investigations, Southern Illinois University, 1994.

Sullivan, Alan P. "Pinyon Nuts and Other Wild Resources in Western Anasazi Subsistence Economies." *Research in Economic Anthropology* Supplement 6:195-239, 1992.

Tedlock, Barbara. *The Beautiful and the Dangerous: Encounters with the Zuni Indians.* New York: Viking Press, 1992.

Trombold, Charles D., ed. *Ancient Road Networks and Settlement Hierarchies in the New World.* Cambridge, U.K.: Cambridge University Press, 1991.

Turner, Christy G. and Jaqueline A. Turner. *Man Corn: Cannibalism and Violence in the Prehistoric American Southwest.* Salt Lake City, Utah: University of Utah Press, 1999.

Tyler, Hamilton A. *Pueblo Gods and Myths.* Norman, Oklahoma: University of Oklahoma Press, 1964.

Underhill, Ruth. *Life in the Pueblos,* reprint of 1964 Bureau of Indian Affairs Report. Santa Fe, New Mexico: Ancient City Press, 1991.

Upham, Steadman, Kent G. Lightfoot, and Roberta A. Jewett, eds. *The Sociopolitical Structure of Prehistoric Southwestern Societies.* San Francisco: West-view Press, 1989.

Vivian, Gordon, and Tom W. Mathews. *Kin Kletso: A Pueblo III Community in Chaco Canyon, New Mexico,* Vol. 6. Globe, Arizona: Southwest Parks and Monuments Association, 1973.

Vivian, Gordon, and Paul Reiter. *The Great Kivas of Chaco Canyon and Their Relationships.* School of American Research Monograph no. 22, Santa Fe, New Mexico: 1965.

Vivian, R. Gwinn. *The Chacoan Prehistory of the San Juan Basin.* New York: Academic Press, 1990.

Waters, Frank. *Book of the Hopi.* New York: The Viking Press, 1963.

Wetterstrom, Wilma. *Food, Diet, and Population at Prehistoric Arroyo*

Hondo Pueblo, New Mexico. Arroyo Hondo Archaeological Series, Vol. 6. Santa Fe, New Mexico: School of American Research Press, 1986.

White, Tim D. *Prehistoric Cannibalism at Mancos 5MTUMR-2346.* Princeton, New Jersey: Princeton University Press, 1992.

Williamson, Ray A. *Living the Sky: The Cosmos of the American Indian.* Norman, Oklahoma: University of Oklahoma Press, 1984.

Wills, W.H., and Robert D. Leonard, eds. *The Ancient Southwestern Community.* Albuquerque: University of New Mexico Press, 1994.

Woodbury, Richard B. "A Reconsideration of Pueblo Warfare in the Southwestern United States." *Actas del XXXIII Congreso Internacional de Americanistas,* 11:124-133. San Jose, Costa Rica, 1959.

--."Climatic Changes and Prehistoric Agriculture in the Southwestern United States." *New York Academy of Sciences Annals,* Vol. 95, Article 1. New York, 1961.

Wright, Barton. *Kachinas: The Barry Goldwater Collection at the Heard Museum.* Phoenix, Arizona: Heard Museum, 1975.

A look At: The Morning River
By W. Michael Gear

A classic tale of danger and possibility in the American frontier, *The Morning River* is the thrilling first book in Saga of the Mountain Sage series by *New York Times* bestselling author W. Michael Gear.

It's the year 1825 in the untamed vastness of the American frontier. Richard Hamilton, a Harvard philosophy student, arrives in St. Louis on business. Stripped of his possessions and left bruised, he seeks refuge on the *Maria*, a sturdy keelboat destined for the Upper Yellowstone River, helmed by a seasoned fur trader. Thus begins Richard's voyage into the heart of the wild, a journey that will challenge him beyond his wildest dreams.

Simultaneously, a Pawnee warrior named Packrat ensnares Heals Like a Willow, a spirited Shoshone medicine woman. But spiritual slaves possess an uncanny resilience, a will to resist. And in the raw, unforgiving wilderness, the hunter and the hunted lock in a desperate struggle for survival.

As the *Maria* penetrates further into the untouched territory, the lives of Richard and Willow converge. Both are seekers—of knowledge and of spirit—yet divided by time and destiny. When their paths intersect, an improbable love emerges, spawning consequences both palpable and hidden.

"Gear creates believable fiction that transcends and transforms."
—*Kirkus Reviews*

AVAILABLE NOW

About W. Michael Gear

W. Michael Gear is a *New York Times, USA Today,* and international bestselling author of sixty novels. With close to eighteen million copies of his books in print worldwide, his work has been translated into twenty-nine languages.

Gear has been inducted into the Western Writers Hall of Fame and the Colorado Authors' Hall of Fame—as well as won the Owen Wister Award, the Golden Spur Award, and the International Book Award for both Science Fiction and Action Suspense Fiction. He is also the recipient of the Frank Waters Award for lifetime contributions to Western writing.

Gear's work, inspired by anthropology and archaeology, is multilayered and has been called compelling, insidiously realistic, and masterful. Currently, he lives in northwestern Wyoming with his award-winning wife and co-author, Kathleen O'Neal Gear, and a charming sheltie named, Jake.

About Kathleen O'Neal Gear

Kathleen O'Neal Gear is a *New York Times* bestselling author of fifty-seven books and a national award-winning archaeologist. The U.S. Department of the Interior has awarded her two Special Achievement awards for outstanding management of America's cultural resources.

In 2015 the United States Congress honored her with a Certificate of Special Congressional Recognition, and the California State Legislature passed Joint Member Resolution #117 saying, "The contributions of Kathleen O'Neal Gear to the fields of history, archaeology, and writing have been invaluable..."

In 2021 she received the Owen Wister Award for lifetime contributions to western literature, and in 2023 received the Frank Waters Award for "a body of work representing excellence in writing and storytelling that embodies the spirit of the American West."

Made in United States
Troutdale, OR
03/05/2024

18147614R00253